Portrait

of a

PROTÉGÉ

PORTRAITS SERIES
BOOK II

J . B . CHICOINE

Straw
Hill
Publishing

Straw
Hill
Publishing

strawhillpublishing@jbchicoine.com

Cover art: original watercolor painting—*Portrait of a Protégé*—by J.B. Chicoine
Cover and interior design and art by Straw Hill Design

ISBN-13:978-0-615-89195-8
ASIN: 0615891950

Printed in the United States of America

ACKNOWLEDGMENTS

MANY, MANY THANKS TO MY WRITING PARTNER, ROBYNNE Marie Plouff, and my beta readers, Craig A. Chicoine, Carol Newman Cronin, Ryan Skidmore, Marie Skidmore, Liza Carens Salerno, Carol Newman Cronin, Lindsey Hanchett, Laura Martone, and Beth Zygiel. I would also like to thank Lisa Porter for her wise insights.

Most of all, thanks to my Todd

For my beautiful daughter, Heather

Portrait of a PROTÉGÉ

Portraits Series:

BOOK I
PORTRAIT of a GIRL RUNNING

BOOK II
PORTRAIT of a PROTÉGÉ

BOOK III
PORTRAIT of a GIRL ADRIFT

BOOK IV
PORTRAIT of a SOJOURNER

❧CHAPTER 1

Summer 1982, New Hampshire

T HE LAKE'S TRANQUILITY EXPLODED WITH A prelude of July 4th firecrackers and bottle rockets echoing into the cove, drowning out the ringing telephone. As the sulfur smoke dissipated, Leila's nerves settled. The phone rang again, startling her, and she sprung to her feet, praying it would be Clarence calling from Cricenti's Market. The screen door slammed as she picked up on the next ring."Hello," she said, winded.

"Hi—" Clarence's voice trailed with hesitation.

Her heart withered. "You're not coming …."

"I'm so sorry, Leila. I would have called sooner, but I was holding off until Bonnie got word from the specialist. He's willing to fit Peter in early on Monday morning. His next available slot wouldn't be for over three months."

"Oh well …."

"Bonnie really wants me to be there."

"No, you should definitely go with them." She stifled unjustifiable resentment—after all, an only daughter and grandson ranked higher than friend, even if exceptional.

"I could still come this weekend," his words lacked conviction, "but I could stay only one night."

Leila pulled the phone cord out through the back door onto the deck. Birch leaves fluttered, launching a dragonfly. "No, that's crazy. It's an eight-hour drive and on a holiday weekend—that's too much. You have enough stress without cramming all that in."

"It's just that of all weekends ...." Worry laced his voice. She pictured him raking fingers through his thinning salt-and-pepper hair.

"You know me. I'll be fine ...." She sat on the top step of the deck, swatting a mosquito. "I'll go see the fireworks or just hang out at the movies or something."

"Please don't stay holed up in a theater all weekend."

"I won't."

"Promise?"

"Yes. And honestly, don't worry. You can come up when things settle down a little. Maybe in a few weeks or sometime next month, before school starts."

"I will. Let me get through this next week and see what this shrink has to offer. Then we'll put something on the calendar."

"Okay, then. I'll let you go."

"Oh, by the way, Bonnie sends her regards and apologies for detaining me."

Leila's pulse flared. "Tell her it's fine. I just want what's best for Peter, too."

"I will, but she knows it's not easy for you, either."

"It's not easy for any of us."

"Well, I'll let you go."

"We'll talk soon." Leila clicked the receiver and sat for a moment, playing with the end of her long braid like a fine-point sable brush, painting imaginary circles on her knee. An early firefly blinked in the cove, its light diffuse in the humid evening air.

Resigned, she stood and plodded her way to the screen door. Its creak grated her nerves as she stepped back into the kitchen. She hung up the phone beside the butcher-block island and then paced the span of windows overlooking the lake. Standing before her gleaming appliances, she wiped down the granite counters one more time, draped the folded dishtowel over its rack, and returned to the deck. She rocked on the gliding settee until the moon rose and mosquitoes became as unbearable as the bottle rockets and firecrackers splintering the lake's calm. There would be no escaping the stomach-churning sounds of it all. Perhaps the basement cinder block might baffle the noise and provide relief.

From the kitchen, she descended the stairs and landed in her husband's photography studio, imagining Ian might return home at any moment—that she should dust so he wouldn't think she had been idle in his absence. Ian had always been one to spring a surprise on her. Without more than a glance, she slipped on past into her own little studio.

The nearly full moon washed her room in an ethereal blue and dissolved with a flip of the light switch. She stood before the one large window looking out onto the little sandy spot they called 'the beach.' She turned to face her room. Tidy and predictable as always. Her controlled environment. The taut quilt of the bed Clarence was to sleep on beckoned. She dropped to the mattress and lay down.

Within minutes—or hours—of drifting in and out of sleep, she awoke with a start. She wasn't sure if a firecracker, a barking dog, or another intense dream jarred her awake. As always, her first thought was Ian. Then, the peripheral flash —Clarence's cancellation—cut in, deepening the ache. She rose from the bed and smoothed the quilt, each stroke an attempt to quell her disappointment. It would be hours before she could settle down to sleep for the night, and so she headed upstairs.

Standing in front of her piano, she stared out the window, out at the front dooryard, her thoughts returning to Clarence Myles. It had been months since she last saw him. Even if his visits had not been frequent, at least he had followed through on his promise when she left Long Island four years ago.

Back then, while Ian renovated this cottage on Pleasant Lake, she had rented a tiny cabin on nearby Little Lake Sunapee. She had started working at the local art supply store and lent a hand with remodeling what became their honeymoon cottage. The sale of Ian's prime real estate on Long Island's south shore had given them a good start and a nicer home than she had ever known. Just the same, she still remembered her rustic little 'camp' with fondness. She and Ian's relationship had bloomed during that summer of 1978.

That was also the summer she met Bonnie, who accompanied Clarence on his first visit. *Ah, yes. The estranged daughter*, Ian had surmised. *Coming to size up her competition.* Leila had cringed at Ian's astute observation, and she would never forget one detail of that visit four years ago. Her heart pounded now as it had then, as if she could hear Clarence's old Volvo pulling into her dooryard. She closed her eyes, the scene rushing in at her. Bonnie had sat in Clarence's front seat, the sight of his daughter restraining Leila from rushing to his arms.

"Hi," Leila had called out as Clarence shut his door.

Bonnie emerged without acknowledging her. Leila caught only a glimpse of bright green eyes before Bonnie bent to pull her sleeping three-year-old from his car seat. Her designer shorts hid little of her derrière. When she stood, even with her little boy covering much of her front, her snug tank top revealed a figure worth flaunting. Bonnie looked nothing like the rehab waif Leila had expected.

"Hi," Leila said, extending her hand.

Bonnie looked her up and down, both hands keeping hold of her child. "Sorry, he's an armful."

Leila withdrew, wiping her hands on her cutoffs, stalling in the awkward moment, and then turned to Clarence as she led the way. "How was the drive?"

"Not too bad north of Hartford," Clarence said as they stepped inside. He glanced from the yard-sale furniture to the particleboard paneling and chipped linoleum. He winked. "This is certainly adequate if not rustic."

Leila smiled, directing her attention to Bonnie, still carrying the sleeping armful of her tow-headed son.

"The two of you can take my room." She led Bonnie through the skewed bedroom door. "It's closer to the bathroom and not as musty as the basement where the bunk bed is."

Bonnie scanned the room, expressionless. "Thank you."

Leila opened the closet. "There's plenty of space for your clothes. As you can see, I'm a bit of a minimalist."

"Yes. I see."

"Your father says you were a fashion designer. You probably have a lot of nice clothes."

Bonnie stared at Leila as if scrutinizing each feature of her heating face.

"You look a lot like her," Bonnie said, with the first hint of kindness.

Leila's heart jumped.

Bonnie's expression softened more. "Mostly in the eyes. Not just the blue, but the shape … the expressiveness …."

Leila's eyes fogged. "Did you know my mother very well?"

She laid Peter on the bed, smoothing his hair. "How can anyone truly know someone else?"

Bonnie's question took Leila aback. "But you spent time with her in rehab. What was she like?"

Bonnie paused before turning to Leila and looked at her level-eyed. "She was a good person. I'm so sorry about how all that turned out. I wish you could have received her note in an easier way."

"Suicide is never easy, right?"

Bonnie sighed and firmed her chin as if restraining its quiver. "Do you mind if I use your bathroom?"

"Not at all. Just make sure you jiggle the toilet handle." Leila pushed open the door outside the bedroom. She still had so many questions about her mother—questions that vacillated between simple curiosity and a longing ache. Bonnie was the doorkeeper and a reluctant one at that.

Joining Clarence, Leila slipped her arms around his waist and gave him a less reserved greeting, withdrawing as soon as Bonnie reappeared with now wide-awake Peter. He clung to his mother's leg, reaching up for her.

"He's awfully cute," Leila said as Peter buried his face in his mother's shoulder.

"He's playing bashful, but that won't last." Bonnie kissed his tuft of silken hair as she adjusted him on her hip. "Soon he'll be climbing all over Grandpa—won'tcha."

"Supper is nearly ready if anyone's hungry," Leila said, anxious to avoid uncomfortable silence.

"Smells wonderful. Italian?" Clarence said.

Leila smiled, anxious to show off her newfound cooking skills. "Lasagne di Bugialli."

A glint of approval shot from his eyes. "Excellent."

Bonnie quirked a brow, perhaps annoyed by their apparent rapport.

Leila cringed at her own insensitivity but rebounded. "Sorry about the kitchen heat. We can eat at the picnic table on the deck, and swim after dinner, if you'd like."

"Terrific." Bonnie snuggled the boy. "Peter will love that, won'tcha."

Bonnie lightened up, and Leila relaxed, although she sensed Clarence's stifled spontaneity. Leila had hoped he and his daughter had come to enjoy an easier rapport—apparently they hadn't.

"I have a few more preparations in the kitchen," Leila pinched Clarence's sleeve.

"Let me help," he said as Bonnie sat the boy on her lap in the dining nook, adjacent the kitchen.

Clarence followed Leila. She bent to remove the casserole dish from the oven. "Salad makings are in the fridge."

Clarence maneuvered around her, removing lettuce, dressing, and a tomato from the refrigerator. Like synchronized dancing partners, they ducked and wove around each other in tight quarters, one brushing comfortably against the other between the kitchen and the deck. Bonnie watched, her mouth twisting.

Outside at the picnic table as they ate, Bonnie sipped lemonade, more intent on studying Leila's mismatched table setting—the antithesis of all fashion sense—than finishing her lasagne. Peter grinned at Leila between bites, diminishing some of the tense silence. Leila had hoped Clarence might be more conversant with his daughter, but he had little to say as he fidgeted with cutlery, and his foot wiggled beneath the table.

Monitoring Bonnie, Leila formulated a question, weighing the prudence of again bringing up her mother. When Bonnie's gaze met Leila's, she ventured, "So, what was my mother like?"

Bonnie's focus shifted and came back to Leila. "She was quiet."

"That's all?"

Bonnie drew in a breath, bordering on irate. "Marilyn—your mother—was in a bad place when I knew her. I can't imagine how you must feel, but—" she looked away, "—there's nothing I can say—"

"But there must be something—"

"Rehab was hell. You don't want to know."

That was at least partly true—Leila didn't want to know enough to push it. Her mother would remain the big unknown, the vacant space consumed by only vague stirrings of something like emotion. Was Leila so broken she didn't really want to know, or was it still true that she couldn't miss what she never had?

Leila retreated to the kitchen and returned with a bottle of Merlot and a corkscrew.

"Why don't you do the honors," Leila said, plunking them both in front of Clarence.

He glanced at his daughter feeding Peter from her own plate, and then back to Leila. "Why don't we save this for later?"

"Oh, right. I'm sorry, of course." How could she have so quickly forgotten about rehab?

"So, how is Ian's renovation project coming along?" Clarence asked.

"Really well. It's going to be beautiful. It's not too far from here."

"Will we be seeing him?"

"Yes. He's coming by tomorrow. I thought we might grill out here. The weather's supposed to be good." Directing her attention to Bonnie, Leila added, "See, there's a nice little beach area and the water is shallow for several feet out. Peter might like playing in it."

"Sounds wonderful." She smiled. "Who's Ian?"

"He's—" Leila glanced at Clarence, "—he's a friend of ours." Why should she hesitate to call Ian her boyfriend? Clarence had given his blessing—more or less—but would he think they had been sleeping together, that they had been moving too fast?

Bonnie's eyebrow flicked. "Really, Dad? Where do you know him from?" Apparently, Clarence hadn't filled Bonnie in on Leila and Ian. Perhaps their relationship still made him uncomfortable.

"He and I had positions at the same high school on Long Island."

"A teacher?"

His jaw shifted. "A coach."

"Does he just vacation in New Hampshire or does he live up here?"

"He's renovating a house—doing the work himself," Leila said with pride. "He'll be living here year-round."

"How curious."

Leila strained a smile as Clarence intervened. "Dinner is excellent."

"Yes, dinner was lovely," Bonnie's kinder smile returned.

"Thank you. Would Peter like a little cheesecake?"

Bonnie kissed the boy's forehead. "No sugar after six, thank you."

Peter climbed over to his grandpa's lap, brandishing a Band-Aided boo-boo on his finger.

Bonnie rose from the table. "I'm going to change into my swimsuit. Dad, would you occupy him?"

Clarence bounced the little boy on his knee and stroked his hair. "I'd sure like some of that cheesecake."

Leila served him a large slab on another mismatched plate.

"Wedgewood. Nice." Clarence winked.

"It clashes perfectly with everything else in the cabin, don't you think?"

"Not everyone can pull off tacky with this much style, you know."

She grinned. "Indeed! I know how to make a *real* fashion statement."

While Bonnie and Peter waded in the lake, Leila and Clarence kept conversation light as they cleaned up after dinner, reserving their deep discussion for later when they could savor every morsel in private.

As soon as Bonnie turned in for the night with Peter and his bedtime story, Leila grabbed the bottle of wine, which Clarence had already uncorked, allowing it to breathe. She led him out to the sand under the light of the half-moon. He sat on a lawn chair, and she pulled one right next to him as he poured the Merlot into their happily mismatched goblets. Silently, they watched the distorted reflection of the moon stretch and break apart on the placid water. The bluish light accentuated the gray at Clarence's temples. Leila swallowed a mouthful.

Over the past month, Leila had been thinking of—obsessing over—what she had surmised about Ian's past relationships. The number of women had been enough that Ian wouldn't elaborate on how many he had been with—Leila assumed the worst—but he had divulged that he'd been seduced by an older woman when he turned thirteen. At any rate, he was adamant that he and Leila wait until they were in a committed, marital relationship before consummating their love in bed. She was pleased that Ian placed a high value on her virginity, and under the circumstances, she understood why, but all those other women crowded in, echoing her father's warnings about men and their 'nature.'

Now that she had Clarence to herself, she needed to talk and ventured a question without prodding. "Clarence, how much does a person's past weigh in on a new relationship?"

"That is a big question." He crossed his ankle over his knee, raising a brow. "Such a subject requires a little more wine."

He topped off each of their glasses, sipped, swallowed and exhaled, swirling the burgundy liquid in crystal.

Leila waited.

He sipped again. "How much it weighs has much to do with its inherent weight."

"That sounds redundant and mathematical."

"In a way it is. Every past has a weight or value, if you will, placed upon it. Long-term consequences weigh more."

"For instance?"

"Heavies may be things like divorce, death, addiction, pre-existing offspring, financial debt, a prison record."

"What about abandonment, abuse—*promiscuity*?"

"Those, too. But with some things, the value is more subjective and fluctuates based on the scale and whose scale it is. And of course, then there are the counterweights—the other party's baggage."

"What if one side significantly outweighs the other, I mean, *bottoms it out*."

"Hopefully, then, whoever is in control of the scale adjuster is insightful, generous, and forgiving. But remember, the weight values are always shifting. No one is ever in full control all the time."

She reflected on the truth of his statement.

"Leila, we are the sum total of our past. We can only hope that if someone worthwhile comes along, they will see enough good to make us want to reach beyond our past. To be better than who we are right now. Not everyone is that fortunate. But the ones that can't forgive, or can't see potential, risk ending up very lonely. The truth is, before long we all accumulate weight that needs mitigating."

His clear and succinct evaluation settled her heart as she swallowed the last of her wine and yawned. "I think it would be too weird if we shared the bunk bed. I'll take the sofa—you're too tall."

🐉 THE FOLLOWING MORNING, LEILA ROUSED TO the aromas of coffee and bacon and the sound of a wire whisk scraping the inside of a stainless steel bowl.

Bonnie stepped from the bathroom looking as flower-fresh as an advertisement for Midol, a product Leila could have used that early morning as she made a trip to the bathroom, and then collapsed back onto the sofa.

Hovering over Leila in a tight, low-cut halter-top and short shorts, Bonnie said, "Not a morning person?"

Leila massaged her abdomen. "Not *this* morning."

"Poor thing. Can I get you some coffee?"

"Sure."

Bonnie smiled as Leila accepted a cupful, unsure of how to read her sympathy. She gulped coffee, hoping to be showered and dressed in case Ian arrived early.

Breakfast aromas lingered past eleven o'clock when the sound of Ian's Saab rumbled in the dooryard. Her heart pounded with nerves and excitement. As he entered through the front screen door, Bonnie—poised and cross-legged at the table—immediately sat erect with undisguised pleasure.

Looking at Ian objectively—through the eyes with which Bonnie must have been assessing him—Leila had to admit, he was undeniably handsome. He exuded sensuality. From the just snug-enough fit of his clothes, to the way his hair swept back from his face and held its place, perfectly framing his square jaw. He smiled in his affable way. It was no wonder he attracted women.

Under his arm he carried a large wrapped gift and smiled at Leila.

"Good morning," he said. "Sorry I'm a little late—trouble with my table saw."

He approached Clarence with an outstretched hand. "Myles. Good to see you."

Clarence smiled and gave Ian's hand a firm shake. The sight of it warmed Leila—perhaps her two favorite men had progressed beyond merely tolerance and would become friends after all.

The little boy hid behind his grandfather's leg. Ian crouched in front of him.

"This must be Peter." Without moving toward him, Ian held out the gift. "This is from Leila and me. I think you're really going to like it."

Leila had no idea about Ian's thoughtful plan. She wondered why the notion of a gift hadn't occurred to her. Peter glanced at his mother, who nodded. He snatched the wrapped package.

Bonnie stood. "What do you say, Peter?"

"Thank you." The boy grinned, tearing at paper.

Clarence said, "Ian, this is my daughter, Bonnie."

Ian offered his hand. "It's a pleasure."

"Thank you for the gift." Bonnie's eyes sparkled.

"Leila and I thought he might like it."

"It's a boat!" Peter interrupted. "Does it work?"

"It sure does." Ian bent on his knee. "We'll put it in the water later, if you want."

"Can we, Mommy?"

"Of course!" Bonnie smiled broadly. Her dimples rivaled Leila's.

"Can we go now?" The boy's voice quivered with excitement.

"We just have to put our swimsuits on." Bonnie tousled Peter's hair.

As Bonnie exited, Ian moved to Leila's side and grabbed her hand. Giving it a squeeze, he kissed her cheek.

Clarence stepped back into the kitchen. "Why don't the two of you head on down to the water while I work on my marinade."

"Are you sure?" Leila said.

"Indeed! Now go on."

Leila and Ian each carried lawn chairs down to the small patch of pebbled sand.

"You okay?" Ian opened the chairs and they sat.

"Bad time of month. Weird circumstances."

He nodded. "Don't sweat it. Just sit and relax."

"Thanks for thinking of the gift. That was really sweet."

He patted her thigh. "If you weren't so nerved up about this visit, I'm sure you would have thought of it yourself."

Leila breathed deep and grinned. "Is it too early to start drinking?"

He squeezed her knee. "Given the company, you might want to wait till at least noon."

Peter ran down the path with his new boat.

"Slow down, Peter!" his mother called from behind. "You'll break it before you even get it in the water."

Ian withdrew his hand and craned his neck to watch the boy. Out of breath, Peter halted in front of Ian and looked at his mother, "What's his name again?"

"Ian," she whispered.

"Ian, thank you for the boat."

Ian leaned forward in his seat. "You're very welcome."

Peter glanced back at his mother. With her nod, he bolted to the lake, several yards ahead.

"He's one cute kid." Ian extended his legs, clasping his hands behind his head.

"He's a good boy." Bonnie sat beside Leila.

"C'mon, Ian!" Peter called out.

Pushing out of his chair, Ian obeyed. He peeled off his shirt, revealing tanned and well-developed pecs. Bonnie let go of a quiet sigh.

The water was shallow for at least twenty feet out, allowing for plenty of room to play speed sailboat versus sea monster. Ian submerged in the knee-high water as Peter bounced the boat off his head. Leila had never seen him with a child before. She smiled at the way he bobbed and swam, playing with the boy. Peter squealed and splashed when Ian roared.

Bonnie inched her chair closer to Leila. "Last night, you mentioned that he's mutually friends with my dad."

"That's right."

"What is he, about twenty-seven or twenty-eight?"

"Yeah. Twenty-eight."

Bonnie sighed. "You have no idea how hard it is to find men like him." She pulled her shirt over her head, revealing her bikini top but mostly flesh. She adjusted the scant fabric as though her breasts needed any enhancement.

Oh, good grief. "It doesn't seem like you'd have any trouble finding a man."

"You're so sweet." She smiled. "Tell me, is he available?"

"Available?"

"Yeah, I mean, he's not your boyfriend or anything, is he?"

"Actually, he is."

Bonnie suppressed a giggle. "Well, you can't be too serious. I mean, it's pretty obvious you're not sleeping together."

Leila blinked. "Excuse me?"

"I mean, the way the two of you interact—it's pretty obvious that you're not lovers. And a man like him—well— why would he do without?"

Leila exhaled irritation. "You're making an awful lot of assumptions about people you don't even know."

"I don't mean anything by it. I'm just calling it the way I see it."

"Things are not always as they appear."

"So, you're saying you *are* lovers?"

Leila tried to calm her ire. "I don't know you well enough to be having this conversation, Bonnie."

"Don't be so touchy. I only wanted to know if he's available."

"Why don't you ask him?" Leila shot back as she rose. "If you'll excuse me—I need to set up the grill."

As Leila climbed the stairway, Clarence bent, inspecting the propane bottle. She paused beside him.

"How's it going down there?" he said.

"It's going ...." Leila stepped into the kitchen and stood at the old chipped sink. Clarence came in behind her. Through the window, Leila watched as Bonnie waded past Ian and dove into the water beyond him. Leila had never felt particularly insecure about her own body until she compared herself to Bonnie who could have modeled for a centerfold.

"What do you think of her?" Clarence asked.

"I think she's beautiful."

"That's not what I mean and you know it." He grabbed the platter of salmon.

"I'm not sure this is a good time of month for you to be asking me that question."

"Don't be dodgy. Just tell me your first impression."

Leila pushed open the door for him. "She's a good mother—"

"And?" He set the platter beside the grill.

"She's presumptuous and full of herself." She glanced at him. "But then, as I recall, those were my first impressions of you. But that didn't stop us from becoming friends."

"True."

"How is it going with her?"

He lit the grill. "It's slow going. Very slow, but I'm grateful."

As Clarence lowered the lid, Leila moved close to him. From their perch, they watched Bonnie come up out of the shallow water just in front of kneeling Ian.

Leila now wished she hadn't left them alone. "From a man's perspective, what do you suppose Ian thinks of her?"

"I think he's no fool. The bigger question is, what do *you* think he thinks of her?"

"I'm not sure."

"Look at him—" Clarence directed her attention with a nod, "—and his body language."

Without looking at Bonnie, Ian came to his feet with his arms tightly folded. As she moved in, he backed away.

"Now, tell me you aren't sure."

Leila had no doubt. Still, she knew what a weakness Ian had had with women. As she and Clarence set the picnic table, she was constantly aware of the two standing together in the ankle-deep water, while Peter dug in the sand at the lake's edge. She wished she could have overheard their conversation.

Clarence called out, "Dinner is served."

Ian took a seat beside Leila on the bench. Bonnie sat opposite Ian, placing Peter in a chair at the end. The chef placed a tidy slab of perfectly grilled salmon on each plate and spooned the sweet-and-spicy marinade over it. Each one helped themselves to coleslaw with water chestnuts and currants. Sweet corn, still in charred husks, cooled in front of them.

"Oh, my goodness," Leila said between mouthfuls. "This is amazing."

Ian agreed.

Peter's recounting of the sea monster adventures passed the next few minutes before conversation devolved into visual volleying.

"So tell me," Bonnie looked at Leila and then at her father. "How exactly was it that the two of you became such good friends?"

Leila glanced at Clarence. She then settled on Bonnie. "I'm sure he must have told you."

"I know you had a student-teacher relationship, but I'm a little vague about the details."

Clarence wiped his mouth. "Any vagueness on my part was in consideration of Leila's privacy."

Bonnie's lips pressed.

Leila sat erect. "I first met him at the record store where I worked. He was my customer from hell, turned homeroom and math teacher. We just hit it off. What can I say?"

"So, you were his star pupil?"

Leila giggled. "No. I was probably one of his worst."

"And so he took pity and decided to tutor you."

"No. Actually, he refused. He said I wasn't applying myself."

Bonnie rolled her eyes. "I've sure heard that before."

Leila had no intention of divulging the full scope of their friendship—how a year after her own father died, leaving her a burdensome plan to stay out of foster care, Clarence had stepped in and been a real father to her. And Leila certainly would not tell how Clarence had petitioned the court and been awarded legal guardianship after Ian's former lover and phys ed assistant assaulted Leila during a self-defense demonstration. She hadn't thought of that whole episode in quite some time. It now heated her cheeks. "Anyway, one thing led to another. And here we are."

"So, it's been all flowers and blue skies."

"Oh, we've had our ups and downs." Leila smiled at Clarence.

"I'll bet. He must have really wigged out when you got together with your coach." She made it sound so simple and clear-cut.

Leila glanced at Ian. He stopped chewing. Likely, the whole sordid scenario—the assault, accusations, and hearings—flashed through his mind, too. "He had his reservations," Leila continued, "but I think he's used to it now."

"Being *used to it* is much different than having his blessing," Bonnie said.

"He gave me his blessing."

"Oh, how sweet." Her sarcasm seethed as she turned to her father. "I had no idea you were such a liberal, Dad. Tell me, are you really as tolerant as you've led her to believe?"

Clarence drew in a long breath. "Leila has my blessing to choose as she wishes."

"Yes, but that's a far cry from blessing their relationship."

Clarence's deliberate eyes traveled from Bonnie to Ian and Leila and back. "She and Ian have my blessing."

"Oh, please. You could no more bless a student-teacher liaison than you could the birth of—"

"The fact of the matter is," Clarence cut her off, "whether you choose to recognize it or not, given sufficient time and evidence, I *am* capable of looking at the broader scope of things."

Bonnie's glare challenged him.

He continued, "I have had the opportunity to observe Ian Brigham over a period of time and telling circumstances. He has proven himself to be substantial. Leila would be hard-pressed to find another man of his caliber."

Leila's eyes welled.

Clarence swallowed. "As for the circumstances surrounding Peter's birth—of course I would prefer he had a father, in theory. But then, not all fathers are good ones, are they." He reached for her hand. "How ever Peter came to be does not diminish my love and acceptance of either of you, nor my desire to be part of your lives."

Bonnie bit her lip, her eyes shifting.

With perfect timing, Peter interjected, "Grampa, let's play with the boat."

Ian checked his watch and whispered to Leila, "Why look at the time!"

Leila rose from the table, collecting plates and cutlery. "We'll take care of the dishes."

With his own armful of leftovers, Ian pulled the door open and followed Leila in as Bonnie followed Clarence and Peter to the water.

Leila shook her head and moved to the sink. "Is this why it's supposed to be good for families to eat together?"

"That's the theory." Ian scraped plates.

Leila rolled her eyes. "She seemed a tad hostile, don't you think?"

Ian chuckled as warm water filled the sink. "Oh, did you pick up on that, too?"

"Well, at least she's not repressing, right?"

"No. I'd say she's very good at expressing herself."

With her hands in the suds and Ian beside her, Leila gave him a sidelong glance. "Speaking of which, it looked like the two of you were having an interesting conversation earlier."

Ian turned to her as she passed him a dripping plate. "Yes. She was testing the water, so to speak."

"Do tell."

"Well …." He wiped the dish and set it aside. "She implied that you don't consider our relationship serious."

"I can't believe her!" Leila tossed her dishrag into the sink with a splash and an exaggerated eye roll. "And what did *you* say?"

Ian wiped suds from Leila's chin. He grinned but then turned pensive. "I told her you have an endearing way of understating things. I assured her that I am very serious about you, that in fact, I have never been more serious about any woman."

With wet hands grabbing her waist, he pulled her close and kissed her with tenderness, reassurance, and even passion. He was wholly devoted to her, of that Leila was certain. The weight of his past dissolved as they continued washing dishes the way they often had—a domestic ritual performed together, a sampling of conjugality.

🦢 CHAPTER 2

July 1982, New Hampshire

T HERE WAS NO USE SULKING OVER CLARENCE'S cancellation on this July 4th weekend, but Leila couldn't help reminisce about his previous visits to New Hampshire, as if reminiscing might fill the void, perhaps cork the emotions that threatened to gush. Clarence had made the trip numerous times in the past four years, but the memory of his first stay over, and one other pivotal visit, absorbed Leila's idle time. She recalled with clarity that February evening when he pulled into the driveway in the bitter cold, back in 1980.

After eight hours in his Volvo, his eyes lacked luster, and his expression appeared as weary as his slack posture. He and Ian had carried his luggage down to Leila's studio and spare bedroom as she followed. Clarence had yawned repeatedly as he trudged back up the stairs and into the living room.

"I think the trip took more out of me than I expected," he said, settling into the Windsor rocker across from Ian and Leila on the sofa. Their surroundings were markedly more tasteful than Leila's little old cabin. Mitered crown moldings and hardwood floors boasted Ian's craftsmanship. Natural wood finishes and neutral shades lent an airy yet warm atmosphere.

"We won't keep you up too late," Leila said, rising from her seat. "But I have just the thing to help you sleep."

She returned with the bottle of cognac he had sent them as a one-year wedding anniversary present.

"I need you well rested for tomorrow." She poured him a healthy dose. "The temperatures have been hovering around zero for the past week, so the lake is good and solid. Tomorrow, it's supposed to be near thirty—perfect for skating. Ian's already cleared the ice."

"I have not skated in over twenty years." Clarence sipped and exhaled.

Leila grinned. "You can't be any worse than me."

"And I have no skates. You'll have to skate without me."

"What size do you wear?"

"Ten."

"Perfect! Same as Ian. He has an old pair of hockey skates."

Clarence grimaced. "Can't you let an old man rest?"

Ian smirked. He seemed to take delight in Leila cajoling Clarence.

"Old man?" Leila laughed. "Look at you. You're practically as fit as Ian."

Ian let out an incredulous snort. "Doubt it."

Clarence chuckled. He patted his firm abdomen. "Don't worry. I have no intention of making you look bad in front of your girl."

The following morning, after a full breakfast, Clarence lagged behind with Leila as Ian skated circles around them. As he came near her, Leila grabbed hold of Ian's gloved hand, and her skates kicked out from beneath her. As she landed on her back, Ian fell to his knees beside her. Clarence skated from behind, pale, his brow pinched.

Ian assisted Leila to her feet. He cast Clarence a quick glance. "You okay, old man?"

"Who are you calling old?" Clarence barked and glided on past.

Now stabilized on her skates, Leila slid in closer to her husband and playfully kissed him.

He pushed her away. "Get off me, spaz. You're going to bring me down!"

Leila thought she had a grip on his hand, but she pulled away, leaving her with merely a glove. She was about to come after him with flailing arms when Clarence caught her eye, about thirty feet beyond them. He came to a complete standstill and then dropped to his knees. His arms crossed his chest, and he rolled onto the ice.

Leila froze. In an instant, Ian was at Clarence's side. Pulling at his buttons and loosening his scarf, Ian put his ear to his chest. He shouted to Leila, "Call 911," and tipped his friend's head back. Pinching his nose and bringing his mouth to Clarence's, he puffed.

Leila could not breathe, let alone move.

"*Now*, Leila!" Ian placed the heel of his palm upon Clarence's chest and compressed, finally sending Leila back toward the shoreline. Her heart pounded as she slogged on the skate's toe picks through knee-deep snow, glancing back at Ian, kneeling beside her Clarence.

In the kitchen, she dialed the phone. As she watched Ian through the French door, it felt as if it were her own chest being compressed. Choking out her name and address to the emergency dispatch, she stifled tears until she hung up the phone. All at once, she realized the full import of the words she had just spoken. *I think he's had a heart attack.* Terror surged through her like an electric shock, stealing her air.

Leila could make the three-mile trip to town in less than ten minutes. She hoped the emergency vehicle could do it in less despite the icy back roads. On the deck, she changed from skates to sneakers, watching Ian tear off his own coat and continuing CPR. Plowing through the snow, she ran back onto the ice.

"Go back up and wait for them!" he shouted.

Leila hesitated. Ian shouted at her again. She slogged back up the slippery incline, tears burning like fire down her cheeks.

The rest of that afternoon was a blur, but she never shook the sight of Ian trying to resuscitate Clarence. Even from a distance, his torment crushed her as the emergency squad transferred unconscious Clarence from the ice onto the stretcher. Her husband bent, breathless, exhausted, and defeated.

Defibrillation revived Clarence, yet he was still unconscious and in precarious condition. The next morning, after Clarence's surgery, Bonnie arrived at Dartmouth Hitchcock Medical Center.

Leila sat at Clarence's bedside as he slipped in and out of consciousness. Tubes and wires connected him to all sorts of whirring and pulsing devices. She had sat in so many hospital rooms with her own father, where the certainty of death encroached upon her hopes, becoming almost as constant as the drone of machines around him. Sitting with Clarence—realizing he had been on the brink of leaving her—she could not imagine her life without him.

She turned at the sound of the nurse's voice. "Only one at a time."

Bonnie stood in the doorway, her mouth agape. Their eyes locked. For having driven straight through from Philadelphia, Bonnie appeared composed and carefully pulled together, not a hair out of place.

She approached her father's bed, offering Leila a quick nod as they sidled past each other. Pushing through the waiting room door, Leila found Peter and Ian on the couch. She overheard the five-year-old. "I still have the boat. I take good care of it so I can play with it in the lake again."

Ian tucked the boy under his arm. "Good on ya, mate."

A few minutes later, Bonnie came through the door, more composed than Leila expected. She approached Ian.

"Thanks for looking after Peter," she said.

"It was no problem. He's a good boy."

Peter sniffled and wiped his nose.

"Use your tissue, Peter." Bonnie glanced back up at Ian. "It's not a cold. He has allergies."

"Well, if you're okay with it, and if Peter would like, we could take him back to our place. Leila needs to rest up a bit. We'll be back later on, and then you can take a break."

Peter perked up, "Can I, Mommy?"

Bonnie tousled her little man's hair and lightly touched Ian's sleeve. "Yes. That would be wonderful."

Over the next forty-eight hours, they all took turns at the hospital. Peter spent a good deal of time with Ian, and Leila monitored Bonnie's attentiveness every time Ian stepped into the room. It didn't take a lot of intuition to see that Bonnie still had a thing for Leila's husband. In fact, Ian and Bonnie had been in each other's company for long periods of time while Leila sat with Clarence. It wasn't until Ian first went in to sit with Clarence that Bonnie and Leila spoke more than a greeting.

As Ian headed for the nurses' station beyond the heavy doors, Bonnie said, "Ian has a wonderful way with Peter. He's such a natural father."

Leila offered a tight-lipped near-smile.

Bonnie sighed. "I'll bet you can't wait to have children with him."

"Actually, I'm in no hurry for motherhood."

"Oh." Bonnie's brow rose. "My misunderstanding."

Leila didn't consider Bonnie's statement an overt dig, but what had Ian and Bonnie discussed in her absence? Leila returned to thumbing through a magazine, trying not to dwell on it.

When Ian finally came through the waiting-room door, he squared his shoulders and sighed, swallowing uneasily. Reading her husband's state, Leila rushed to his arms. His embrace pushed oxygen from her lungs, nearly crushing her ribcage. She reciprocated with all her might as he broke down and cried on her shoulder. When he withdrew, he threw back his head.

"Oh, God," he exhaled. He took her by the hand, leading her out of the waiting room. "Walk with me."

They left Bonnie without a word.

Ian shook his head, unable to speak. As far as Leila was concerned, he didn't need to say a word. She could imagine what his exchange with Clarence had been, and when he got around to divulging it, she would be his confidant—not Bonnie.

They didn't speak much until their drive home. Ian would likely not talk about Clarence, but he might be inclined to divulge something else of concern to Leila.

"Does being around Peter make you want to have kids?" she asked.

His eyes shifted to the rearview mirror and then to Leila. He seemed to be weighing his words. "I guess someday it might be nice."

"By *someday*, you mean—?"

"Whenever you're ready."

"What if I'm never ready?"

"Lei," he said, looking at her sideways and smiling. "If having kids was all that important to me, we would have already discussed it. In fact, I would have brought it up before I married you."

"Really?"

"I think having a family is a nice notion, but I also think the reality of it is far more difficult than it looks."

"I'm not saying that I won't ever want children—but I just can't picture it."

"Just let it rest, Lei. I'm very content, just me and you."

"But what if—" she caught herself as Ian cast her another look. "I know—*what ifs* are a slippery slope. I really am trying not to obsess."

With Ian's assurance, Leila was able to let go of the 'what ifs' regarding motherhood, but as hard as she tried, she couldn't stop obsessing over Clarence and his heart attack.

For the next two weeks after Clarence returned to Philadelphia, her agitation escalated. She wasn't sleeping, and her appetite waned, as did her interest in activities that normally brought her pleasure—painting, running, music, and lovemaking. At work, she couldn't concentrate and made stupid mistakes. Her mind kept returning to Clarence, to wondering what he was doing at the moment—replaying the vision of him collapsed on the ice. She started calling him several times a day, but he limited her to calling only every evening, and he seemed barely tolerant of that. But if she could just hear his voice—it was as if she'd had her ear to his chest, listening to his heart's continuous beat. Only then could she sleep but never soundly.

One evening, the third week after Clarence's heart attack, Ian came into their bedroom after stoking the woodstove. She turned toward the bedside and tugged the down comforter up to her ears.

He sat at the edge of their mattress, pulling off his shirt. "You still awake?"

"Yeah," she whispered, though she felt like saying no.

He slipped under the blankets and spooned her body but made no further advances. "Lei ... we need to talk about this."

She recoiled. "What—you can't go a week without it?"

"First of all, it's been well over a week. And I'm not talking about just that."

"Some men go months, you know."

"Lei, I'm not accusing you." He stroked her arm. "I'm concerned. We both know this isn't like you. It's not like *us*."

He had every right to feel concern. She rolled to her back and slipped her hand beneath his on her tummy. "I know. I'm sorry. I don't mean to be defensive. I honestly just don't—*feel*—like it. I think it's just stress or something. I've heard that affects libido."

Ian caressed her hand but was as quiet as the snow falling outside.

She turned to look at his face in the dark. "You don't want me to do it if I'm not in the mood, do you?"

"Of course not."

"I'm sorry, Ian. I think I just need a little more time."

He moved closer and kissed her cheek. "You know I love you, don't you?"

"Of course. And I love you."

Every day for the next week, Ian planned activities—things designed to distract her. She went through the motions of running at the indoor track at the college in town, snowshoed, and went to the movies, but she wasn't in the mood for any of it.

Nights passed before he again nudged her to make love. Leila blew up. She accused him of pressuring her and making things worse, triggering a flood of tears. Every time she even thought of making love, fear of losing Clarence choked her desire. She climbed from bed and spent the night on the sofa. The following morning, she could scarcely look at Ian's pained expression, let alone speak to him before he left for work. She dreaded noon, when he always came home for lunch between classes. If only it were a workday, she could escape to the art store and avoid the whole situation for a few more hours. Why couldn't she get her fear under control? Why must she make her loving husband pay?

A burst of cold air hit her tear-stained face when Ian came through the front door. As he hung his Colby-Sawyer assistant coach's jacket on the hook, she hid behind the book she had been trying to read, and sank deeper into the cushions. Her insides knotted. Her heart throbbed.

Sitting beside her on the edge of the sofa, he stared ahead and then glanced at her. "How are you doing?"

Short of breath, she lowered the book. "Aside from feeling like the worst wife ever—just great."

"I didn't mean to make you feel like a bad wife." He faced her. "I'm sorry if I did."

Her chest constricted. "I don't know what's wrong with me."

"Tell me what I can do to help." He took her hand.

"I don't know …. Make me stop worrying about Clarence."

"I don't know how, Lei. *You* have to make *yourself* stop."

"It's not that simple." She pulled her hand from his and folded her arms.

Ian sank back into the sofa, moving closer. He rubbed his face and exhaled. "Do you think it would help if you saw him?"

It was as if her airways suddenly opened. "What, like go visit him?"

"Yeah."

"Really?" She drew in a long, easy breath.

"If he's agreeable. And you really think it would help."

Leila disregarded the resignation in his voice. "I'm going to call him right now."

In an instant, she headed to the phone. She expected Clarence to be excited as she explained her plan.

"Absolutely not, Leila. It's ridiculous for you to come all the way down here just to check on me. How many times do I need to tell you that I'm doing fine? Even better than expected."

"But please, Clarence. I *need* to see you—*please* say I can come."

"Leila," he continued in a kinder tone, "I am not going to play into these unhealthy compulsions of yours."

His words jolted her. "But Clarence—"

"*No*, Leila. That's enough. You are behaving like a manipulative child."

"Fine!" She hung up the phone, her heart pounding.

Leila ran downstairs to her studio. She slammed her door. Images of Clarence fell into the shadows, as if they had slipped into some vortex—still there but more of an echo than a shout. A minute later, Ian entered and sat on the bed beside her. She tucked her hands beneath her thighs and stared off at nothing. How could she possibly explain what she was feeling?

She would not look at Ian. "He said no."

"I'm sorry, Lei. I thought it might be a good idea."

"No—it's fine—I'm fine," she said, even-toned. "I'm just going to hang out down here for a little while, okay?"

"Okay."

At dinnertime, she cooked and was unemotional. Afterward, she washed dishes with Ian in tense silence and then returned to her studio, where she spent the night. The following morning, her apathy had not lifted. Just before she left for work, Ian detained her. He took her by the hand, forcing her to look into his eyes. Feeling for her husband, Leila absorbed Ian's own fear and turmoil, drawing them into the undercurrent of pain that churned and choked the words she wished she could speak. He didn't try to kiss her lips—he simply grazed her forehead. She remained stiff and unresponsive. Without a word, she left for the art store, leaving Ian alone.

That afternoon at work, she received a phone call from her husband. "Tell Ben you need a few days off, then come home and pack your bags. Clarence is expecting you tomorrow."

🌿CHAPTER 3

March 1980, Philadelphia

L EILA HAILED A CAB FROM THE AIRPORT DESPITE Clarence's offer to pick her up. She insisted he not exert himself. With her carry-on luggage in hand, she walked up the short concrete path to his front porch. She steadied her nerves, not just because of her anxiety over his recent surgery, but because Ian had had to persuade Clarence to let her come. Ian wouldn't elaborate on just what he had said, but she feared Clarence might consider her a manipulative child who had stomped her feet.

It was past dusk. A quick burst of light shot through two slats of the window blinds as he peeked out. Her heart leapt. Within seconds, the door opened wide.

He smiled as though the visit had been his idea. "How was your flight?"

"Uneventful." She hesitated to approach, although he didn't look as gaunt as she had expected.

"What? No hug?"

Leila dropped her bag and slipped her arms around him. At once mindful of his surgical scar, she withdrew.

"I won't break," he said.

"I don't want to hurt your incision."

"It doesn't hurt." He closed the door and went to lift her bag.

She moved to reclaim it. "You're not supposed to be lifting things, are you?"

"I dare say your bag weighs less than fifteen pounds. I think I can handle it." He grabbed it from her.

Gesturing toward the living area, he asked, "Well, what do you think?"

Leila stepped forward, running her hand along his familiar Mission oak furnishings as she strode to his leather chair, which sat in front of the centerpiece fieldstone fireplace facing the front door.

She turned to him. "Where's the kitchen?"

He pointed toward the back, opposite corner of an open dining area.

"And the bedrooms are upstairs," he said, waving a hand at an open staircase on the far wall opposite the dining area.

"It sort of reminds me of your old place—it has the same feel. I'm glad."

"It's the same era. Same bungalow style."

She grinned. "It smells like you."

"Come on," he winked and led her upstairs. "The bathroom adjoins both bedrooms, so be sure you knock if the door is closed, or you're liable to get an unpleasant surprise."

She peeked into the first bedroom as they passed by. He pushed open the door beyond that.

"Here you go. Peter usually sleeps in here when he stays over, so don't mind the toys."

"Will we be seeing Bonnie and Peter?"

"No, but I do have a special activity planned for tomorrow morning."

"Really?"

"Yes. I have a follow-up appointment with my cardiologist. I thought it would be good for you to come along."

"Okay." She agreed, but with reservation. Doctors' offices turned her stomach.

After Leila situated herself, Clarence gave her a complete tour of the house, including his study. It was dim, as expected, with a large, centered desk, leather-covered chairs, and lined with built-in shelves full of books and a complete stereo system. In the corner sat his saxophone on a stand. Approaching it, she queried, "Why don't you ever play your sax for me?"

"Why don't you ever play your piano for me?"

"You've never asked."

"And neither have you."

"I guess we both know better."

🐾QUELLING HER STOMACH, LEILA THUMBED through a *Good Housekeeping* magazine she could have sworn she had read in her shrink's waiting room two years earlier. Sometimes she wished she had kept in touch with Valerie Jennings—not for therapy, but because she liked the woman.

"Clarence Myles—" the nurse called out.

He stood and gestured at Leila. "Come along."

"Oh—" she gasped. "I didn't know I was coming *in* with you."

"Of course you are. That's why I've brought you along."

Leila obeyed.

After recording Clarence's blood pressure and informing him that only the shirt need come off, the nurse gave Leila a look. On her way out of the small cubicle-of-an-examining-room, she said, "Dr. Wilson will be in shortly."

Leila averted her eyes as Clarence unbuttoned. She looked out the small window, asking, "Will he be hooking you up to wires today?"

"I doubt it. This is a follow-up to the tests they did last week."

As she turned to face him, he was pulling off his T-shirt. She caught a glimpse of his bare back. He had broad, strong-looking shoulders. Her gaze returned to the parking lot below.

With two taps, the door cracked open, and the doctor poked his head in. He was a silver-haired man about Clarence's age.

"Good to see you, Myles." The doctor smiled, his delicate hand enveloped by Clarence's.

After introductions, Leila finally looked at the incision. Speckled gray hair had grown back in across his chest. The scar extended from below his collarbone down to his diaphragm. She cringed. The doctor listened to his heart. Clarence's chest expanded as he breathed in and exhaled deeply several times.

Consulting the medical papers and test results, Dr. Wilson nodded with satisfaction. "Excellent."

Clarence gave Leila a gloating stare. "Dr. Wilson, would you please, in a nutshell, explain to my friend Leila, the results of my tests?"

The doctor directed his comments to Leila. "In short, Clarence Myles is the poster child for mitral valve repair. He has actually exceeded the standard for recovery—a credit to his surgeon, no doubt, but even more to the patient."

She nodded, still dubious. The glowing report sounded almost too good to be true—almost like a setup. Doctor and patient exchanged glances as if sensing Leila's skepticism.

Clarence elaborated, "Leila is afraid that with any exertion, I run the risk of another heart attack."

With a raised brow, the doctor looked at Clarence, then at Leila, and back at Clarence. "Is there a *specific* exertion about which she might be concerned?"

Clarence glared at him. "I'm talking exertion in general."

Dr. Wilson said to Leila, "His heart is more sound now than it was before the surgery. He'll probably outlive us both —well, perhaps not you."

Leila sipped her Pinot noir as she eyed Clarence across the butcher-block island.

"Mmmm …." It swirled around her tongue. "No wine for you?"

"I'm not allowed any alcohol yet."

"Too bad." She grinned with excitement, taking inventory of the ingredients set out before her: eggplant, zucchinis, onions, green peppers, garlic, tomato pulp, and a few sprigs of parsley. "What are we making?"

"Come now, can't you guess?"

"Ratatouille?"

"Good girl."

He passed her the eggplant. "Now, peel and quarter this and cut it into bite-sized pieces."

Leila focused on her slicing.

"So. Are you going to start talking?" he said, likewise processing the zucchini. "Or am I going to have to drag it out of you?"

"Talking about what?"

Turning on the burner beneath a skillet, he looked at her sideways. "You don't think Ian sent you down here just to go to my doctor's appointment and cook, do you?"

Leila rolled her eyes, assuming her two men had spoken in depth. "I suppose then he's told you all about it."

"He told me very little," Clarence said, passing her an onion. "Peel and slice."

"What did he tell you?"

"I believe his exact words were, 'I'm afraid I'm losing her.'"

The shock of hearing Ian's words filled her with remorse. Had she really frightened him that much? She hacked at the onion, saying nothing.

"Are you going to tell me what's going on between the two of you?" He smashed a bulb of garlic.

"Nothing's going on."

"Nothing?"

"That's right, absolutely nothing."

He glanced over his shoulder as he added a layer of eggplant to the heated pan. "And by *nothing* you mean—?"

Leila whacked at a pepper and then set the knife down. "I mean, we're not—we're not being intimate. No sex."

Clarence shot her a glance, his spatula at the ready. "How long has it been?"

Leila knotted her arms around her middle, resigning herself to the fact that this issue was going to be talked out, whether she wanted it or not. "About a month."

"Since my heart attack."

She watched him flip the contents of the pan. "Yes."

"And this is unusual for the two of you?"

"From almost every day, to nothing …." She rolled her eyes. "Yeah, I'd say so."

He raised a brow. "Why do you think that is?"

"Because I couldn't stop worrying about you," she blurted.

"So, then, now that you can see for yourself that I'm fit as a fiddle, things should go back to normal as soon as you get home?" He transferred the eggplant into a dish and started on the zucchini. "Those peppers won't slice themselves."

Leila stared off and then refocused on her cutting as the zucchini joined the eggplant. She wasn't sure why she couldn't agree with him.

Clarence then scraped the onion, garlic, and pepper into the skillet. "You're ignoring my question."

"I'm not. I'm thinking."

He adjusted the burner, added tomatoes to the skillet, and covered it. "Leila, let me tell you a story."

She sighed and pursed her lips.

"Hear me out. It's about a little girl who always dreamed of getting a car and her driver's license—"

"That's not what little girls dream about."

"For the sake of the illustration, this little girl does."

"Fine."

"Unfortunately, just after she gets her license, but before she has a car of her own, someone she loves very much is tragically killed in an automobile wreck. She becomes nervous about driving, but someone comes along and gives her a sweet Jaguar coup. Her most favorite car in the world, in her favorite color, with leather interior and an incredible sound system. Even though she is nervous, she cannot resist taking it out on a safe stretch of road. Before long, she is having the time of her life in her new car.

"Sadly, someone else that she cares for very much is hurt in a car accident, which reminds her of just how dangerous driving a car can be. So she takes her Jaguar to a high cliff, gets out of the car, and pushes it over the edge. It crashes far below." He gave her a penetrating look. "Why does she do that?"

Begrudgingly, Leila answered, "So that she can never be in a car wreck of her own, or hurt anyone else with her car."

"Yes, but the result to her car is the same—it's wrecked."

"Yes, but she got out. *She* didn't get hurt."

"That's right. And she'll probably never drive again, just to be safe."

As Myles lifted the lid, Leila breathed in the aroma of stewing vegetables and said nothing as she correlated the narrative to her own situation.

He added the eggplant and zucchini and again covered the pan. "Do you get the point of my little story?"

"You think I'm pushing my relationship with Ian over the edge so I can't get hurt if anything ever happens to *him*."

He smiled with satisfaction. "Let me offer you an alternate ending. The girl's friend has an accident, which understandably makes her nervous. So she parks her car in the garage, reminds herself of how important it is to be careful with her car. Maybe she washes it. Maybe she even gets a tune-up and does some precautionary maintenance.

Probably she'll miss driving it so much that finally, after a month or so, she takes it out for a spin. Why is that a better ending?"

"Because she knows that there's always the risk of an accident, but it would be stupid not to drive the car while she has it."

"See? You do get it."

"Yeah. I get it."

Myles checked under the lid as Leila considered his parable. She loved Ian so much and missed their intimacies —physical and emotional. He must have been feeling so alienated. Why did it take Clarence Myles to reveal it to her so effectively, when she should have allowed her husband that satisfaction?

Standing across from her good friend, talking about the most intimate issues, spiked her curiosity regarding him, about aspects of Clarence's life that were almost entirely unknown to her. She thought about how he had probably not made love to anyone in a very long time.

As he reduced the flame, Leila ventured, "Is that why you don't own a car?"

He gave her a twisted look. "Let's just say I've grown quite accustomed to walking."

Leila squinted. "So, how old were you when you got married?"

Clarence lifted a couple of plates from the cabinet and faced her. "Twenty-three. And so was my wife."

"How old were you when Bonnie was born?"

"Twenty-four."

Looking straight at him, she nudged his boundaries. "What happened? I mean, why did you divorce?"

Without looking at her, he finally said, "Essentially, because she decided that I was not what she wanted." He now met her stare. "Sufficient for now?"

"You really hate talking about all that."

His gaze did not deviate. "Let's just say it's my least-favorite subject."

She pushed one more time, certain she could pull one last admission. "Did you still love her when you divorced?"

He flicked the burner knob, extinguishing the flame. "Yes. And *that* is all I have to say about *her*."

Clarence topped the two plates with cloth napkins and deposited cutlery atop them with finality, like a garnishing sprig of parsley—*fini*—as if that phase of their conversation was also complete. But Leila was by no means done. "Have you been in love with anyone since?"

His brow narrowed as he held open the door to the dining room. She stepped through.

"Well? Have you?" she persisted.

"Why is this a matter of curiosity?"

She set the table. "Why wouldn't it be? I mean, why must you always be the one to get inside my head, and when I try to get in yours, I'm left feeling like I've violated some unspoken boundary."

Clarence remained silent as he took two goblets from a built-in cabinet. "Just a moment while I get water."

Leila followed, holding the door open as he stood at the tap. She continued her rant, "For instance, I'm expected to spill my guts about my most intimate marital problems, and then I ask a simple question regarding if you've been in love since your ex-wife, and you look at me as if I were an impertinent twelfth-grader."

He returned, passing her in the doorway. "I'm sorry. That may not seem fair of me, but you forget that I am of a generation of men that do not talk about those things—" he set the filled goblets on the table "—least of all with a girl nearly young enough to be my granddaughter."

Leila exhaled annoyance as he returned to the kitchen. He grabbed a couple of hot pads and carried the ratatouille casserole.

"My mistake," she said. "I was under the impression our relationship transcended all that nonsense."

"Perhaps there are aspects of our relationship that are transcendent, but that doesn't change the fact that you are, compared to me, very young." They took their seats. "Even though you have experienced things many young women your age have not, I suppose I view your grasp of certain things as limited." He scooped the vegetables, placing a portion on each plate. "For instance, you have never known, to any consequential degree, the pain of rejection. How can you know what that is to a grown man?"

Leila stabbed eggplant. "Why do I have to experience it firsthand for you to confide in me? If that was some requirement for friendship, who would have any friends at all?"

"Alright," he conceded. He drew a deep breath. "Yes, I have been in love since my ex-wife—twice."

Leila's brows arched and her steadfast eye would not allow him to stop there, even while he chewed a bit of zucchini. He swallowed, keeping his eyes on hers, acknowledging that he was not off the hook.

"The first, decided she liked the—" he cleared his throat, "liked me in the bedroom—more than she actually liked *me*. And the second was married. It never went beyond friendship."

Leila said nothing, but the shift of her eyes away from the pain in his assured him she would not press further. She took a bite of her own dinner, and so ended that particular conversation.

The next day, she returned to her husband.

Two-and-a-half years later, Leila's mind frequently drifted back to that conversation, but mostly to the night when she arrived back home and reunited with Ian. She still remembered their passion like no other time in their marriage. They had made love from nearly the moment they stepped back into their cottage and on through the night—vulnerable yet equally sensual intimacies that wove through and wound around the hours until morning. She replayed the images often, though the pleasure of it now mingled with pain.

🐚CHAPTER 4

July 1982, Philadelphia

P ETER'S APPOINTMENT WAS THE FIRST OF THE day. Clarence Myles shook Dr. Flanders' hand, assessing him as average, though his dossier indicated the opposite in spite of his youth and casual attire. Peter sat with the doctor's assistant, Trish, at a child's table in the center of the large playroom.

Flanders directed Myles and Bonnie to a pair of small adjacent sofas in the corner.

"Please have a seat." Flanders joined them. He opened Peter's file on his lap, covering his threadbare jeans. He peered at the papers through a mop of loose blond curls, raking them back.

"I've reviewed the neurological reports," Flanders said, "and I'd like to interview the two of you privately after I've had a chance to examine Peter myself. Please make yourselves comfortable over here while I play with him for a bit. This will take more than a few minutes."

The psychiatric team sat with Peter between them, endeavoring to engage the seven-year-old using various toys and changes of posture, attempting to manipulate his focus. Trish cupped his chin to turn his head toward her, drawing his attention with word and object. Flanders jotted notes. The doctor also spent a fair amount of time simply talking to Peter, who never once responded verbally, if at all. Finally, Flanders turned Peter's face toward him. The boy allowed it. The doctor's natural rapport with Peter impressed Myles.

"Peter, I'm going to leave now and talk to Mom and Grandpa alone for a few minutes. Trish is going to stay and play with you for a little while—unless you'd like Mom to stay over there on the sofa." Peter's shifting eyes registered awareness, but he remained expressionless and disengaged. "Alright then, I'm going into that room over there, beside the big mirror. If you want your mother at any time, just come over and knock on the door, okay?"

Flanders stood and motioned for Myles and Bonnie to follow. Once inside the observation room, the three sat in close quarters. Flanders set the file on his lap.

"Well, there's no doubt Peter is intelligent and above average for a seven-year-old. He is interactive, albeit borderline, but there is distinct cognizance. He seems to be a perfect candidate." Louis Flanders had been working in close association with a professor of Psychiatry at the University of Pennsylvania. They had been expounding upon an emerging approach to psychoanalytic concepts.

Flanders divided his words between Myles and Bonnie. "A cognitive approach to therapy, if you will. As far as its efficacy with Peter, well, there are, of course, no guarantees. This is a relatively new therapy, although it is in the process of being scientifically tested. We're finding it effective in many clinical trials for a number of different disorders. Any questions?"

Myles asked, "Would you explain what you mean by a 'cognitive' approach?"

"Simply put, we focus—that is, we help the patient to focus—on identifying and evaluating distorted thoughts. From there, we can modify his perceptions of events and situations and thus change unhealthy behaviors."

Myles found it a logical methodology and nodded.

Flanders continued, "As you're probably already aware, Peter's symptomology is not entirely consistent with elective mutism, inasmuch as he does not speak to *anyone* at *any* time—as far as you're aware. Additionally, he did not seem to display increased anxiety during our examination and only minimal separation anxiety. Rather, his symptoms are consistent with Post Traumatic Stress Disorder, although his mutism is a relatively rare manifestation of it."

"So, it's post-traumatic Mutism. We already know that," Myles interjected. Bonnie glared at her father as if he had meant to be contrary. He had not.

"Yes," Flanders elaborated, "but fortunately, we can pinpoint the traumatic incident. From there, we can work on his perceptions of it, his cognitions, if you will."

"How do we do that?" Bonnie asked. "He won't tell us his perceptions."

"There is a lot that we can presume, but it's imperative that we reconstruct the events just prior to the incident and immediately afterward. There may be seemingly small details that might be important in understanding how he interpreted the whole event."

Bonnie looked at her father as he stiffened. Myles shifted his gaze from Bonnie to Flanders and then closed his eyes. He hadn't anticipated this approach.

"I'm afraid I can't offer anything," Bonnie said. "I wasn't there—against my better judgment."

So quickly, the blame had surfaced. Myles drew in a breath of restraint. "It's true. Bonnie was not there. She had an urgent last-minute situation arise at work. Peter had been looking forward to this trip for months, and so Bonnie, who did not *express* her concerns about me taking my grandson to New Hampshire for the weekend, remained here."

Flanders leaned forward on his knees, looking at one and then the other. "I understand this is a difficult revisitation—

for both of you. Is it going to be a problem for either of you talking about this in front of the other?"

Bonnie's foot tapped erratically as Myles' jaw tensed.

Flanders sat back, glancing from one to the other. "We can talk separately if you prefer, but I think more is to be gained if you're both present."

Myles responded, "I'm sorry—no, this is fine, it's just that—"

Bonnie interrupted, "—it's just that he has scarcely told *me* any of the details of what took place before I arrived at the lake to bring Peter home."

"Then, Bonnie," the doctor placed his hand on hers, "perhaps it would be best if you just allowed him to speak and not interject any commentary quite yet."

Myles stared off into mid-space, summoning any bit of mettle to stay his nerves.

"What day of the week did you head up?" Flanders asked.

"Friday morning of the Fourth-of-July weekend. A year ago. Peter was happy and excited all the way up. He dozed a little. We stopped for lunch—he was with me the entire time. He was really looking forward to seeing Ian and Leila, but especially Ian. He had brought along the boat Ian gave him. It was one of his prized possessions, and he couldn't wait to show Ian what good care he had taken of it—and to take it out in the water.

"He called his mother before bedtime and slept downstairs with me, on his own cot. No problems. No accidents. No indications of anxiety."

"How did he seem to you on the phone, Bonnie?" Flanders asked.

"He sounded wonderful. Excited. I didn't think he would be able to sleep that night." She wiped a tear. "It was the last time I heard my little boy's voice."

Myles inhaled a constricted breath. "The next morning, July fourth, Peter couldn't wait to get in the water. There was someone with him at *all* times. Ian had promised to take him out on the boat—his sailboat."

"What size boat?"

"A daysailer, about a fourteen-footer, not big enough for more than three or four people. He had it rigged up with a little two-horsepower motor, enough to get it out of the cove."

"Was he an experienced sailor?"

"Yes, I would say so." In fact, Myles had sailed with Ian the evening he arrived. "But Ian and Peter weren't going to sail. They were going fishing, out beyond the cove. It was just out of sight of the cottage, but away from all the other boaters and water skiers. He said he planned to drop anchor there and see if anything would bite. He even tied Peter's boat to the stern, so they couldn't have been going *too* fast. When I gave them a shove-off, Peter was wearing his life jacket. I put it on him myself. Ian's jacket was beside him—" Myles rubbed his brow and coughed. He had been standing in the waist-high water beside the sailboat, steadying it as Ian climbed in from its mooring dock. Myles had lifted Peter into the vessel so it wouldn't tip, and then double-checked the boy's vest. The weather was perfect. The water was perfect. It should have been the perfect day.

It was the very last time he would see his friend. The profundity of it struck him, wringing his insides. He had trouble finding words to continue.

Flanders prodded, "How did Peter seem then?"

Myles returned with difficulty. "Excited. Talking a mile a minute. He was sitting at the stern beside Ian—and they both waved goodbye."

Myles was silent again. He should have gone with them.

"What happened next?"

Myles inhaled.

"Take your time," Flanders said.

"I went to town for a few groceries—they wanted me to barbecue something special in case they didn't catch fish. Leila was going to clean up while they were out. I was gone for maybe forty-five minutes ...." Myles again sat as mute as Peter, organizing his thoughts and the sequence of events. How could he describe what had next transpired? A whirl of images cut through him like shrapnel.

"On my way back to the cottage, a police cruiser had been following me. When he pulled into the driveway behind me, I was irritated. I thought maybe I hadn't signaled or come to a full stop or something, or that I was being singled out because of my out-of-state plates." The first thing Myles had noticed was the officer's shock of red hair—and his youth. He had climbed out of the cruiser immediately, without the usual delay. "As I approached the officer, he asked if it was Ian Brigham's place."

Myles cleared his throat. "And then I saw Peter in the front seat of the cruiser ...."

"How did he look?"

"Lost. Distant."

"Anything else?"

"He didn't look like he'd been crying or anything. I told the officer he was my grandson, and when he opened the car door, Peter just sat there." With a deep and fast breath for composure, he recounted in quick succession, "I asked where Ian was—the officer hesitated—Peter wouldn't look at me— I pulled him out of the car and picked him up—he had his boat in his arms—the officer was about to speak and Leila came out of the house—" Myles' heart wrenched in his chest as if someone squeezed the blood into his throat. He choked back the swelling sensation. "I'm sorry—I need a moment."

"Take your time," Flanders said.

Images of Leila flashed. She had stepped out onto the porch with a smile. *"They're not back yet,"* she said, apparently before she noticed Peter in his arms or spotted the officer and the cruiser. As soon as she stepped off the porch, her countenance changed. The officer appeared almost as traumatized as Peter. Leila's eyes widened as she approached. *"Where's Ian?"* The officer hesitated. *"I'm Officer Strand—are you Ian Brigham's—are you a family member?"* *"I'm his wife. Where is he?"* Leila hadn't raised her voice, but it felt like a shriek in Myles' ears. All the emotion came flooding back as Myles sat before Flanders and Bonnie as though he were in that moment when the officer told her, *"I'm sorry ma'am ... he's ...."*

Myles finally looked at Flanders and continued, "Leila came out of the house—she looked at Peter and me and then at the officer who told her that Ian had drowned."

Tears flowed from Bonnie's eyes as she covered her mouth as if hearing the news for the first time.

Flanders sighed. "How did Leila react?"

"She didn't react at first, like slow motion ... I watched it come over her ...." He grimaced. "I cannot describe the look on her face ... or the sound that came out of her. It was utter and unrestrained horror." He swallowed again. His eyes and nose burned. "I wanted to go to her, but I had Peter in my arms. Then she looked at Peter. He was staring straight at her the whole time as she approached him. Just then, she covered her mouth, and Peter turned away. She didn't say another word. She wasn't crying, but she was heaving with pain. I was so torn. I wanted to console Peter ... I wanted to comfort her—" tears gathered, but he restrained them. Bonnie wiped her face.

Myles continued, "Then the officer said that Leila needed to go to the morgue with him and identify Ian's body—" he paused, reliving his conflict. "I wanted to go with her—I couldn't let her go alone, but I couldn't leave Peter, and I couldn't bring him there ... so, I took him in the house as Leila left—alone—" he choked, "—without me." Myles covered his mouth and stared at the floor, remembering the image of Leila turning, and the tortured way she looked at him just before she climbed in the cruiser, all by herself.

"I asked Peter what happened and couldn't even get him

to make eye contact, let alone speak. He was completely unresponsive. We just sat together on the sofa—I had him in my arms, and he fell asleep. That's when I called Bonnie. She wanted me to bring him home immediately, but I would not leave Leila. So she drove up that afternoon and arrived around midnight. Peter slept almost continuously. He wet the bed that night. First thing in the morning, she took Peter home, and I stayed behind."

Flanders rubbed his chin, his brow furrowed with empathy. "That's very tragic—it must have been very difficult for you both, and a very long year." He allowed them a few moments before continuing. "Everything you've told me is very helpful. It would be even more helpful if we knew what transpired between the time that Ian and Peter set out and when the officer arrived with him. You didn't happen to see the police report, did you?"

"Actually, yes. Apparently, there was a gentleman who was out sailing. He was quite a distance away, but he saw Ian go over and found Peter alone in the boat. Apparently, Ian's foot tangled in the anchor line, which tangled in some branches deep below the surface. Ian sustained some sort of head injury. The man couldn't get to him soon enough. He brought Ian ashore and called for the police. That's all I know."

"Well, whatever happened, Peter saw it." Flanders sat pensively and jotted in his notes. "Tell me, do you have any pictures of Ian?"

"Oddly, No. Though he was a photographer."

"When was the last time Peter saw Ian's wife, Leila?"

"That day, when the cruiser drove her away."

"Not afterward?" He directed his question to Bonnie. "Not before you took him home?"

"No," she said. "I didn't want him traumatized further."

Flanders made note of it.

🐉CHAPTER 5

Pleasant Lake, New Hampshire

ON MONDAY, LEILA AWOKE AT DAYBREAK TO THE melancholy call of the loon. The July 4th weekend— the one-year anniversary of Ian's death—was behind her. She hadn't slept well the entire weekend, and this morning she blamed it on menstrual cramps. She headed upstairs to the bathroom, paused at her and Ian's bedroom door, staring in at the stillness of the bed she had shared with him for only two-and-a-half short years. The sun was just starting to make its appearance. It flickered up over the swaying treetops and drew her to the window. The loon skimmed the lake's surface, cutting through a thin blanket of fog and came to rest. By the time she had to leave for work at ten, the mist would slowly dissipate into the sun-warmed atmosphere.

Leila's life had been on hold for the past twelve months. Although a modest sum of life insurance cushioned her finances, she continued to put in full-time hours, working the same job at the art store. The brochures for Colby-Sawyer College art curriculum still lay undisturbed on her nightstand along with everything else in the room. She had not swum in the lake. Her running was perfunctory and joyless and so was her painting. She had not undertaken any serious art project or even finished a simple one. She had not been out of state or out of a thirty-mile radius in over a year. The Saab had not been tuned-up—and neither had her beautiful piano; it had received no attention since the prior spring. The fallboard remained locked since just before Peter came.

"This is ridiculous. Just when *do* you plan on getting back into life? You are so pathetic," she said aloud, as if hearing her own words might move her to action.

She headed to the bathroom. Popping a couple of Midol, she looked at her reflection in the mirror. The eyes of someone much older, someone sadly jaded, stared back. She dragged her fingers through her waist-long hair. It was tangled, stringy, and needed a wash.

"Could you possibly have more boring hair?" she spoke to her reflection, a scowl carving unhappy dimples and a crease between her brows. "Well, at least you don't have to worry about being pregnant."

In fact, she and Ian had only one scare when her period had been four weeks late—about a week before Clarence came with Peter last year. It occurred to Leila that had she been pregnant, she would now have a three-month-old baby to care for. As scary as that thought was, it paled with the sad realization that she would never have Ian's baby. Just the same, she couldn't imagine herself as a mother under any circumstances.

She turned on the faucets and stepped into the shower.

Hot water ran down her back, though it could have been cold for all she noticed. Numb and in a daze, minutes passed —minutes of no consequence in a day of no consequence in a string of days that blurred into months and now an entire year. Each minute of each day slipping, as if beads on the unknotted strand of time, never accumulating to anything. She stood in the stream of water, watching it swirl down the drain just like her life. When she stepped out of the tub and caught sight of her naked body, she felt like a corpse.

She pulled at her tangled tresses. *And this hair* ....

She tried to drag a comb through its tangles and forced back a tear as she grabbed the scissors in the vanity. She began sawing through a thick lock, all the way up close to her chin. Splitting the mass of it at the back of her head and drawing it to the front, she lopped off one side and then the other. She made no attempt to trim its unevenness; she just stared at the long, severed ends on the floor. She looked at her altered appearance in the mirror and back at the floor. Now she felt something. Agonizing sadness.

"Go ahead! Cry over your stupid hair when you can't even cry for your husband—go ahead, cry—" she said aloud, but the tears receded like waters waning from the ocean's shore, retracting and mounting for the next wave, predictable only in the knowledge that they would indeed come. But who knew when? With disdain, she glanced again at her frowning reflection and then walked out without sweeping up the mess she had made.

An hour before work, she walked into a salon in town and approached the hairdresser at the front desk.

Leila said, "I had an accident with a pair of scissors."

"Oh my," the woman exclaimed. "I guess so!"

Later on that evening, she sat in front of her drawing table, staring at an unfinished painting. Every day, she pushed herself to work on it for at least a few minutes, which had become evident in the discordant product before her. She didn't feel like painting, but she wouldn't sleep unless she had followed through on her self-imposed ritual.

Pigment from an earlier attempt had pooled, gathered, and dried at a hard edge of an ill-attempted wash. Without swabbing any color, she applied the brush loaded with clean water and scrubbed the offensive areas. Her paper towel pulled up the too-brash flesh tone. Time to switch to some vibrant color and work on an area that was not glaring back so much. In five minutes, she met her obligation. As she pushed away from the table, the phone upstairs rang. *Clarence.*

"Tell me you didn't stay in all weekend," he said as soon as she picked up.

"No. I didn't." She pulled up a stool at the butcher block. "I went and saw *ET The Extraterrestrial*, four times."

"*Four* times?"

"I would have stayed for a fifth if there'd been one."

"Leila—"

"Oh, yeah, and I almost went for a swim on Saturday."

"Did you?" he sounded pleased.

"I put my suit on and everything."

"How far did you get this time?"

"My big toe got wet."

"Well, that was quite a feat—no pun intended."

She pulled her bobbed hair from her face and tucked it behind her ear. It wouldn't stay. "I was actually planning on going in the water when you came up, so I'm just going to postpone it till you get here."

"Promise you'll go in then?"

"I promise." She glanced at an envelope in front of her. "By the way, I received another note from my grandmother."

"Did you?"

Leila pictured Clarence's brow, arched with intrigue. "Yes. Another invitation to visit."

"Are you considering it?"

She tapped the envelope's edge on the hardwood maple. "Yeah—maybe this winter."

"I think that would be a fine idea."

"Maybe you'd like to come along. Angela always asks that I send you her kindest regards."

"Yes, and you're always so diligent about passing them along."

She stood, moving to the French door and stared at her reflection overlaying cove lights. "You should call Angela sometime."

"Are you trying to set me up with your grandmother?"

Leila chuckled. "I know the idea doesn't repulse you."

"Never mind that, young lady."

"Fine." She turned, tangled in the cord. "So, when are you coming up?"

"Tomorrow."

CHAPTER 6

TRAFFIC NORTH OF SPRINGFIELD, MASSACHUSETTS, thinned. Myles let up on his grip of the steering wheel and turned up the volume on Mozart's Symphony No. 25, the music he had shared with Leila upon her graduation. In his quiet moments, it still amazed him that he, a fifty-six-year-old man, should have a twenty-two-year-young woman as his closest confidant. Not that he confided everything in her, but there was not another friend—since Ian—that had any interest in what he thought or felt. Aside from his ex-wife and daughter, no other individual had so altered the course of his life. In fact, where would his relationship with Bonnie be if not for Leila and her own tumultuous past? As much as he looked forward to seeing her, he did not look forward to the dual purpose of his visit.

Driving secondary State Route 11, he rolled down his window, allowing the early afternoon air to cool his brow. A high-pressure system forecasted blue skies and strong breezes over the Lakes Region for the next several days. Perhaps good weather would elevate both their moods.

Myles had no sooner pulled into her dooryard when Leila sprinted from the cottage to his door side. She hadn't mentioned her new bobbed hairstyle, and he almost didn't recognize her. Even though he had been to visit several times since Ian died, this time she appeared more mature than the young woman she was a year ago.

He pulled himself out of his car as she squealed and threw her arms around his neck. After a quick squeeze, he held her at a distance. Moving her chin one way and then the other, he inspected her new look.

He flicked a lock near her jaw. "I like it."

"Really? You don't think it makes me look too boyish?"

"You couldn't look boyish if you tried."

She smiled at his endorsement. "What did you bring for dinner?"

"You'll see. You grab the groceries, and I'll get my luggage."

When they entered the cottage, he forced himself to think only of the happy times he'd had there. Yet, the corresponding season, the sounds and heat of summer—compared to autumn and winter—made it difficult not to remember Ian last July. The controversial young coach turned comrade had always made him feel so welcome in spite of their rocky past. He was grateful to have had his Leila in solid, caring hands.

Myles scanned the living room—the imprint of Ian's taste. Leila cared little about decorating unless Ian solicited her opinion—even then, it didn't matter to her. In fact, Myles always liked Ian's preferences better than Leila's. She would have happily kept all her mismatched dishes and furnishings.

Myles made for the basement where he always slept, as Leila poked her head from the kitchen.

"Why don't you take the room upstairs?" she said.

"Don't be ridiculous. I'll sleep in your studio."

She came to his side, reaching for his bag. "No, I insist."

Myles flashed one of his incisive squints. "You haven't been sleeping upstairs."

Leila shrugged. "I did once … for a few minutes."

"And when I last visited?"

"Sofa."

"Well, it's time you start." He headed downstairs.

Leila followed. She hugged her studio doorjamb as he laid his bag on the bed.

"What do you want to do this afternoon?" she asked.

"I would love to take a swim and just relax."

"Ah yes—" she sighed. "A swim."

"So, you *do* remember your promise."

"I guess so."

"Go on then. Get your swimsuit on."

LEILA took her time changing. She didn't feel like swimming, but Clarence Myles had given her a directive, and part of her still had difficulty disobeying him. She stood at her bedroom window overlooking the cove. Clarence stepped into sight as he walked from the basement exit below her to the patch of sandy beach. When he reached the shore, he shrugged off his shirt, exposing his broad back. He turned and looked up toward her window as if wondering what had detained her. The sight of his physique surprised her. Although she had seen a glimpse of it in his doctor's examining room a few years ago, she didn't remember him looking so—so fit.

Without further delay, she headed out onto the back deck and down the stairs toward the beach. He had walked out onto the long, narrow dock, where Ian used to moor his sailboat, and motioned for her to join him. She met him at the end.

He nudged her. "On the count of three, then?"

Leila's lungs constricted and her mouth dried at the sight of all that water. It wasn't even the same water as a year ago —not the same molecules—not Ian's last gulp …. Leila rubbed her eyes, already short on breath, and nodded. When Clarence counted off and dove, her feet remained securely anchored to the safety of the dock. He emerged and gave her his censuring glare.

"I was going to," she said. "But my feet wouldn't cooperate."

He treaded water. "You are getting wet, or I will come and pull you in myself."

"I will, I will." She plunked herself onto the edge of the dock, her knees to her chest.

He waited a moment and then squinted. "Feet in."

She slipped her toes and then ankles beneath the surface and then up to her mid-calves. He moved toward her.

"Do I have to come over there?" He inched his way closer and grabbed her ankle.

She retracted her leg as if his touch stung. "Please don't, Clarence ... I can't. I mean, I just realized that I need to do it all by myself, when I'm alone .... But I'll do it before you leave, I promise."

"Alright. But you're missing out," he said and mercifully swam away. She kept her eyes on him, not allowing her gaze to wander out over the foreboding lake. After several minutes, he approached again, but this time, hoisted himself back up onto the dock and sat beside her.

She smiled. "I guess all of your early morning swims at the pool have paid off."

"Yep." He thumped his chest. "The old ticker is better than ever. Nothing like a heart attack to motivate a man to get in shape."

Leila turned and looked at his chest. She touched the scar, parting the hairs that covered it. "Is there any sensation?"

His eyes widened with a quizzical glint. She withdrew.

"A little bit," he said. "You're not still worried about my heart, are you?"

"Not really. No. You take better care of yourself than practically anyone I know, with all your vegetable juicing and vitamins. I mean, look at you, you're in great shape." His quizzical expression returned and she quickly added, "—

for an old guy, I mean."

He chuckled and slipped back into the water. He swam around the cove, his strokes strong and precise as he moved toward the mouth of the lake. It had never occurred to her that a man his age could look athletic. The word virile came to mind and she blushed.

He swam a wide circle back and dove deep, disappearing and then emerging a short distance from the dock. "I'm starving. Let's start cooking."

MYLES WATCHED WITH AMUSEMENT AS LEILA cracked a couple of eggs over a mound of flour, and began squishing it through her fingers. The tip of her tongue pressed between her lips like a child. He added a pinch of salt.

"Oh, I forgot." She held up her sticky fingers. "Music. Go turn on the stereo. There's a tape already in there."

Myles hit play. As the symphony began, Rachmaninoff's piano joined the strings.

"Ah," he said as he reentered the kitchen, "the Rach three."

Leila's wrist nudged a stray hair from her forehead. "I've always wondered why you gave me that particular music selection."

He winked. "Reminds me of you."

"Really. How so?"

"It has such a sweet melody as it begins, and then plays contrapuntal with intense and agitated undercurrents."

"Hmm …." She looked at him askance. "Actually, it has always reminded me of you for the very same reason."

"Imagine that."

They listened without a word as the music continued. Leila kneaded the pasta dough with all Rachmaninoff's fervor, as Myles affixed the pasta machine to the countertop. "I'll crank. You feed."

Leila flattened her dough and began the process. "So, tell me about Peter's meeting with the doctor. Did he have him sticking square pegs into round holes?"

"No. Motor skills are more the neurologist's job. The psychiatrist ran a similar gamut of responsiveness tests but seemed more interested in the actual incident that precipitated the mutism."

"I see. So I suppose you had to recount the whole thing."

Myles peered at Leila as if he were wearing his readers. "Which is a secondary reason why I've come to visit."

Leila did not react. He continued, "You see, the doctor believes that knowing any additional details regarding that interval while Peter and Ian were out in the boat could be crucial in helping him to deal with the trauma. I was hoping that through the police report we might locate the man who retrieved Peter."

"We don't need the police report for that. I know who it was. Raymond—something. He stopped by—I think it was last August—still summer, anyway."

"You never told me about that."

"Didn't I?"

"No, you didn't. What did he want?"

"To see if there was anything I needed. You know, help putting the boat away, which of course you had already done before you left. He brought the float in, though, and covered it for winter, and—" she gestured toward the window with her flour-covered hand "—there it sits. He gave me his number in case I needed anything. I still have it somewhere."

"Well, if you could find it, that would be great."

"Sure. I'll look after we eat, and I'll give him a call."

Leila draped the pasta atop a cotton cloth over at the table. Myles sliced shallots and chanterelle mushrooms as the olive oil heated in the pan.

"The important thing," he said, blotting sea scallops as the oil began to smoke, "is that once the scallops hit the pan you don't disturb them until they're crisp and golden brown, otherwise they will exude their liquid and steam or poach. Cook them two or three minutes at the most. Flip them only once. Are we ready with the pasta?"

Myles poured Sauvignon Blanc as they sat to eat. Although the sun was only just dipping below the tree line of the shady little cove, he lit candles. One could never have too much ambiance.

"This is really nice," she said.

Myles gestured at some flour on her nose and she dusted it.

She continued, "I wish we could eat together every night."

"I'd question the prudence of that. We'd both end up the size of a mammoth. Besides, I don't cook this way every night."

"It's not a matter of the food. It's the company."

Myles smirked, "One week and I would bore you."

"I doubt it."

Myles chuckled at the notion, appealing as the idea was. If only life were that simple.

"So," he changed the subject, "where shall we go tomorrow?"

Myles had hoped to visit the White Mountains, but Leila opted for Portsmouth—she and Ian had not been there as a couple, and she wanted new memories. In fact, all three had hiked parts of Mount Washington together. He agreed, someplace new would be best.

"Portsmouth is very historical," she said as she brought their plates to the sink. "You'll love the old architecture, and we can hang out at the water for a little bit."

"Sounds perfect." Myles rose. "Let me help with dishes."

"No, I'll take care of it."

"Don't be ridiculous. We both made the mess. We'll both clean up."

"I said no!" she snapped, catching him off guard. "I'm sorry. It's just that it was mine and Ian's little ritual. It would feel weird if *you* were washing dishes beside me."

"Alright then, let me do the dishes, and you find the phone number."

"Okay." In a few minutes, she returned. "That's so weird, I don't even remember writing it in my phone book, but here it is. Paul Raymond." She dialed the phone.

Myles was amazed that she had no qualms about placing the call. She sounded almost businesslike when she said, "I wonder if Paul is available."

A moment later, she responded, "Hi, this is Leila Brigham, I don't know if you remember me—I'm fine, thank you. A friend of mine, Clarence Myles, is in town—the grandfather of the little boy, Peter. If it wasn't too much of an imposition, he was wondering if he might have a word with you in person, sometime—Whenever it's convenient for you, although, I guess the sooner the better."

She was downright charming as she concluded the call. "That would be perfect. Thank you so much—we'll see you tomorrow morning, then."

She hung up the phone and glanced at Myles. "All set."

Myles wiped his hand on the dish towel. "Leila, you don't have to come along. It may be very unpleasant ... and—"

"And what? It might upset me and I might cry?"

Myles' brow narrowed at her aloofness.

She shrugged. "I haven't cried yet. Not really. So even if I did, that's supposed to be good, isn't it?"

He ached at her remark. "You haven't cried for Ian?"

She moved toward the living room. "I did ... a little, I guess, at the morgue ... but then, time was up, and I had to get back home."

In fact, Myles had not actually observed her crying in all those days before he left. Not even at the funeral home during visiting hours. He ascribed her composure to distraction, since there was a continuous trickle of people. There had been no preacher or eulogy—nothing that might have evoked tears. She had chosen a simple memorial, not unlike her grandfather's—old Artie Sparks, legendary Delta-blues musician—where only a few gathered afterward.

Setting the towel aside, Myles followed Leila to where she sat on the sofa. "You've been holding it in all this time?"

"Not really on purpose. It just doesn't come." She shrugged. "I know that's not normal."

Myles beheld her with alarm. "What about when your father died? You cried then, didn't you?"

"I cried a lot the afternoon he died, but then I had to get on with life—with the plan. I guess there were other times when I cried—but it took a long time."

Myles' concern spiked. "Have you considered—?"

"Considered what?" She slumped deeper into the cushion. "Sitting around in a bereavement group, spilling my guts in front of a bunch of strangers?"

"I'm not a huge proponent of psychotherapy, as you know." He sat on the edge of the sofa beside her. "Yet, there are times when I think it has some value."

Leila looked on the verge of rolling her eyes.

He continued, "Perhaps you might consider it. You could always call Doctor Jennings. At least you're familiar with Valerie."

"Clarence, I know you're just trying to be helpful, but you know that I deal with things in my own way—" She gave him a sharp look that said *back off.*

Myles ignored it. "I'm not altogether convinced that you are dealing with it."

"This is just what I do." She pushed herself up to stand. "So why don't we go for a walk and work off some of that pasta so your arteries don't clog up."

He was up against the immovable Leilian wall.

CHAPTER 7

I N THE DARK, MYLES STARED AT THE CEILING AS HE folded his hands upon his chest, acutely aware of his pulse. The thought of Leila repressing so much emotion quickened his heartbeat. This would be her first full night in her and Ian's bed. The ache she must be feeling made his eyes burn.

Upstairs, he heard shuffling and then the creak of the screen door. Leila must have decided to postpone her bedtime. Answering his intuition, he rose and stepped over to the window beside her drawing table.

By the light of the full moon, Leila walked to the end of the dock, where she stood for a minute. Then, in a blink and with one quick, simultaneous movement, her robe dropped to her feet as she dove into the placid lake. She caused barely a ripple as she cut through the water and disappeared. An eerie tranquility glazed the surface as seconds passed—long seconds. Myles waited. His heart raced, eyes darting over the moon's reflection until she resurfaced only feet from shore. Stunned at the sight of her naked body, he averted his eyes and returned to the edge of his bed.

Soon, the screen door creaked and he heard her footfall all the way to her room above his. He rubbed his eyes as he sat hunched, resisting flashbacks of Ian and that terrible day—

and the look on Leila's face as she left with the police officer. He dreaded his conversation with Paul Raymond, some poor soul who was likely traumatized in his own way.

Myles flipped on the light. As he opened the door, his long shadow fell across the floor of Ian's studio. Moonlight beamed from the front of the room, lighting his way to the worktable. He switched on the retractable lamp.

Sitting on Ian's stool, he examined the photographs that lay undisturbed for a year. A black and white panoramic view of the cove from the end of the dock. A thin and dense layer of mist hovered over the water like carded wool. Beside it, another black and white of Leila, coming up out of the water. How Ian had shot it, to capture each illuminated droplet falling from her body with her sunlit face tipped skyward, was a technical mystery to Myles.

Here he sat with this man's work of a short lifetime surrounding him, and to what end? To what did it amount? To what would Myles' own life amount? Heaviness settled on him as he thought again of his own mortality and whom he would leave behind. Bonnie, Peter—and his Leila.

The stairs groaned as Leila descended, tightly wrapped in her robe, her hair still damp.

"Restless, too?" Myles said.

"Yeah." She approached him in the spotlight.

"I'm sorry, I hope you don't mind …."

"It's alright. I know you miss him, too."

They fell silent as he looked around the room. "What will you do with all this?"

"I don't know. Leave it as it is, I suppose. It's not in the way of anything."

"Hmm." He repositioned the photos in front of him. "Just the same, letting these get buried in dust is probably not the best thing for them."

"I suppose. I just like the way they looked there, as though he were going to return and finish the layout." She glanced at them. "But of course, he's not coming back."

"No. He's not."

Leila picked up the two photos and blew dust from them as she stepped toward the filing cabinet beside Myles. She pulled the middle drawer. Selecting the lake scene, she isolated a folder and tucked it inside. She looked at the photo of herself. "And I belong in the *Girl Running* file."

"Girl running?"

"Yes." She pulled a folder from the top drawer. "Named after the girl running on the beach, who later turned out to be the girl whose tire he changed—"

"—who turned out to be you." Myles nodded with recollection.

Leila removed the proof sheet of that summer day and handed it to him. "See." She also gave him the enlargement of the one she liked best. "Seems like such a long time ago."

It did indeed seem like a very long time ago. She looked so much younger, making him feel that much older.

"Yes," he finally responded.

She handed him another proof sheet.

"What's this?" He didn't quite know what to think of the sensual images.

"Me—from that infamous day when I went to his house to see his photography."

He raised his brow as he glanced at her and back at the sheet. "You never mentioned that he photographed you that day."

"No, I didn't. You would have freaked. Besides, it was just far too intimate to share."

"So I see." He handed it back, not feeling awkward that she had shared them but curious about why she chose to do so.

She then tucked it away, saying, "Of course, there are plenty of other far less provocative ones of me."

"Actually, I wouldn't mind having one of them—the less provocative, I mean."

"I'll leave the file out. You can look through it when you want—I just wouldn't open the brown envelope—not the sort of picture of me you want."

"Thank you for the warning." He had already seen far more of her tonight than his comfort allowed. "You wouldn't happen to have one of Ian you could spare, also?"

Leila opened the middle drawer again and pulled another file. She handed it to Myles. "Take whatever you'd like. I have most of the negatives."

"I want you to pick one for me."

"Seriously. Thumb through it." She shoved the folder at him. "Just choose what you like."

He would not take it from her. "No. *You* pick for me."

"Fine." She sighed. "Let me sit at the table."

Myles moved from the stool, and she took his place in front of the lamp. She opened the file and quickly lifted the first one from on top and handed it to Myles. "Here, this is a very good one. I took it of him out on the lake." Just as quickly, she folded the file closed and rose.

Myles sat back down. "Tell me about it."

Leila faced the window. "It was autumn, before we were married. He had just showed me how to use his camera, and we went out sailing for the afternoon. I tucked myself down in the hull toward the bow and started shooting. He was so cute, all self-conscious at first. He was even blushing. But when the breeze picked up and he focused on sailing, he almost forgot I had the camera. I shot picture after picture. He said they were really good."

"Do you have anything more recent? Something from just before—you know when his hair was shorter?"

She turned to him. "Probably. But you'll have to dig for it yourself."

"What were the last pictures he took, do you know?"

"I guess they're still in his camera. He took it out with him that day, I guess to shoot pictures of the 'big catch.'" She nodded at his camera on top of the file cabinet.

Myles reached for it. "Do you mind if I have them developed? Dr. Flanders might find them of interest."

"That's fine, go ahead. I wish I could offer more."

"Actually, there is something you could do."

"What is it?"

Myles inhaled. "Flanders is hoping that you'll come down and see Peter."

"And what does Bonnie think of that?"

"She's willing to do anything that might help Peter, you know that."

Leila folded her arms. "So, what is this? Some part of his therapy?"

"Dr. Flanders believes that Peter needs to see you. He needs to have you talk to him about that day."

"Oh, I see." She sounded almost blasé. "I guess then it's a good thing that I'm not a big crybaby—wouldn't want to traumatize him all over again."

"The idea doesn't … upset you?"

"Why should it?"

Her nonchalance twisted his brow with distress. He said nothing.

"I know. You think I'm completely stifled, and there's no doubt that I am. So, we may as well strike while the iron's hot, right?"

Myles ached for the pain Leila had not yet come to terms with. The burning behind his eyes returned as he searched her face.

"Oh, Clarence," she said, bringing her hand to his peppered cheek.

He moved her palm to his lips and kissed it tenderly. He whispered, "I worry about you, Leila."

"I'll be fine, Clarence. I promise." She kissed his forehead. "Goodnight."

CHAPTER 8

MYLES COLLECTED HIS THOUGHTS AS LEILA drove Ian's Saab to the tiny village of Elkins at the southeast end of the lake. He would have enjoyed the unpretentious quaintness of its old houses, post office, and tiny beach, had it not been for the task before him. He glanced at Leila, who remained as stoic as she had all during breakfast and for the ten-minute drive that should have taken five.

She slowed on a short stretch of road.

"This is the place. That's Paul Raymond," she said, pointing to a corner house with green shutters. On the side lawn, a man stood by a Sunfish sailboat, hosing it down. She drove past. "I'm just going to sit at the water and wait."

Not three hundred yards down the road, she pulled into a small parking area adjacent the dam. Putting the car in park, she tensed.

"You'll be okay?" Myles asked.

"Of course."

He left her sitting on the bulwark dam, staring out over the water—facing the end of the lake where her cottage tucked deep beyond the narrow mouth of the cove.

Myles hated to leave her there alone with her thoughts, but it was the lesser anxiety. He drove back beyond the second road and pulled up in front of the curbless yard. The athletic-looking man in his mid-forties waved. Myles climbed out, eyeing the old clapboard house with a wraparound porch.

"Nice place," Myles said.

The man dropped the sponge in a bucket and extended his wiped hand. "Paul Raymond."

"Clarence Myles." He gave him a quick shake. "Thank you for meeting with me."

"No problem. If it were my grandson, you can bet *I'd* have some questions." He tipped back his cap's visor and rubbed his forehead.

"Do you have children?"

"Yes, three. Eight years old, eighteen, and twenty. I understand you're from out of town?"

"Yes. Philadelphia."

The man nodded, scratching his jaw.

Myles gestured toward the small sailboat. "What is she, about twelve foot?"

"Yeah." He tilted his visor level again. "Do you sail?"

"A few times. With a friend …."

"So … Brigham was a friend of yours?"

"Yes."

Raymond shook his head. "I'm so sorry. I wish I could have gotten to him sooner."

"I appreciate that," Myles said, drawing in a deep breath. "I know this is very unpleasant for you."

Raymond swallowed, as if trying to keep his stomach down. "What would you like to know?"

"Anything you can tell me. Especially about what Peter might have seen."

Raymond turned back toward his small fiberglass boat as Myles stepped closer. Stroking her hull with a rag, Raymond exhaled with faraway eyes. "I was out tooling around the lake early, you know, before a lot of the motor boats and water skiers came out. I had tacked down to this end, was going to call it quits, but the wind picked up, and I decided to jibe back up to the northwest tip one more time.

"I had just fixed my sights on a boat at the far end, up around where it starts getting shallow again. It's an odd spot, just past the mouth of the cove—crazy wind effects—can produce sudden gusts. It's about a mile away. I wasn't sure what I saw at that moment. The boat rocked. I thought maybe the boom swung, but wasn't sure, though it looked as if someone went overboard. People swim from their boats all the time, so normally I wouldn't have thought anything of it, but what I saw gave me a bad feeling. I cut the jibe to get up there quickly, watching for someone swimming. The closer I got—" he wagged his head and tugged at his visor "—I recognized the sailboat. I'd seen him out there lots of times … sometimes the only one brave enough to be out. Kind of a unique-looking boat. A lot of mast for its length."

He glanced at Myles. "The closer I got … well … there was no one in the water. Just the boy sitting very still. When I got close enough, I yelled. The kid didn't respond … he was just staring at the water."

"Where was he sitting?"

"At the stern. Port side, facing starboard … just staring at the water. I hollered again, and he didn't respond. I don't know when it struck me … I guess I was about five to ten yards away, and I went in—" he paused to grip his boat "—it's real deep at that spot, but I thought I saw something as I approached. I dove and made out his body … he wasn't struggling …." He drew in another long, tight breath. "As I got closer, I saw the anchor line around his chest and ankle, all tangled in the branches of an old submerged tree. I cut him loose with a pocket knife."

Myles' sight blurred and, he folded his arms, trying to keep a grip on his emotions.

Raymond wiped his mouth. "I brought him to the surface. We were less than a hundred yards from shore. I swam ashore with him to a small sand bank—he had a good-size knot and a gash on his head—and—he was blue and—" he choked. "I went ahead and tried CPR anyway, but his chest wouldn't rise. His lungs were full. By then his boat had drifted close to shore several yards away."

A wave of nausea overcame Myles. "And Peter?"

Raymond responded with a grimace and a nod. "The boy saw it all."

Myles looked away, trying desperately to maintain composure.

Raymond continued, "By then, a woman came out of a nearby house. I shouted at her to call 911."

"In all that time, did Peter say anything?"

"Not a word. We couldn't even get a name out of him. I felt just terrible about leaving him there on the boat when I pulled Brigham to shore. I didn't know what else to do. It all happened so fast. Then the police came, via the northwest. Since he had no ID, they ran the boat registration and came up with Brigham's name and address. Then they took the boy, but not before he saw them take Brigham away. I remember the officer trying to get him to talk, but it was pretty obvious that he was in shock." His eyes welled with tears and he swallowed. "I am so sorry."

Myles nodded as tension shifted his jaw. "I really appreciate your talking with me."

"There's one other thing. The boy was holding a toy boat, about yay big—" he gestured about a foot or two long. "He was holding onto it tight the whole time."

Myles nodded again, "That's very helpful, thank you."

"How is he doing?"

"Hasn't talked since then."

"Not a word?"

"No."

Raymond winced. "Jeez. Poor little guy."

"By the way, thanks for looking in on Leila."

"No problem. How's she doing?"

Myles offered a vague shrug.

🐟 THE MOON WAS AGAIN BRIGHT, THOUGH HAZY, over the lake as Leila and Clarence stepped onto the deck. Leila wiped humidity from the back of her neck. Grateful for any warm weather, she never complained about the heat.

"Did you at least have an okay day, in spite of our morning?" Clarence asked, sitting beside her on the gliding settee.

She looked out over the water. "I did. Portsmouth was fun. We'll have to do that again sometime."

"We will," he said, pouring Hennessy's into two snifters.

Leila sipped, feeling that wonderful and familiar weakness in her knees. "While I was sitting at the dam today, I was thinking about my dad and Artie and Joe."

"Oh?"

"It's still kind of weird to think that Joe is my biological father, and that he's black—well, half black. Only lately has it really begun to sink in—just how peculiar my whole upbringing was. I mean, I don't know anyone who was raised by two fathers—unless they were—you know, homosexual. And I've never even heard of anyone in that situation. Probably that's what people thought about my dad and Joe—I mean, to anyone outside looking in, why else would they have stayed together all those years, right?"

"Don't you think traveling around with the band—a child hanging out almost exclusively with a bunch of pot-smoking blues musicians and moving so many times—was just as strange as two straight guys raising a little girl?"

"Yeah—I guess that's what I was thinking about. How weird all that really was. What if I'm even more screwed up than I realize? I get scared that some day I'll just be walking down the street or standing in the produce aisle at Cricenti's and completely melt down."

Clarence stared at her, saying nothing. His silence made her uneasy, as if her fear seemed plausible to him. She veered back to something a little safer.

"Sometimes I wonder how much different my life would have been if I'd been born looking more like Joe—if I had nappy hair and all."

"I'm sure it would have been significantly different."

"I don't like that. How appearance—and race—make so much difference to people."

"Well, there's nothing you can do about that, and no point in speculating."

He was right. Thinking about racism only made her angry.

"Have you heard from Joe at all?" he asked.

"He sent a mix tape a few months back, but we haven't talked since right after Ian—" she sighed. "I think Joe likes the insulation that distance provides. Sometimes I just don't know what to think of him. I try not to worry about his lifestyle. I miss him—I mean, I miss the old Joe. Now, I don't know. He's kind of out of sight, out of mind."

Clarence's brow fixed with irritation.

"But I don't want to talk about him." She was more interested in Clarence's insights on her grandmother. "I'm curious—do you really think Angela and I are alike?"

Now his brow quirked.

"I mean, I know there's a physical resemblance," she said, "but what about personality-wise?"

"I can't say I know her well enough, but from what brief interactions we've had, I'd say there are similarities."

"You like that about her. I can tell."

He chuckled, swirling the liquid in his glass. "What? This again?"

"What do you mean, *again*?"

"You have a propensity for bringing up your grandmother and any interest I may or may not have in her."

"I just think the two of you would be a good match. I mean, we get along great, so why wouldn't you two? I don't remember a whole lot about Ian's memorial, but I do recall that you and Angela spent a good deal of time talking. Seemed like if you weren't with me, you were with her."

"I suppose that's true." He sipped.

"Well, I was just thinking how cool it would be if we both went down to visit her this winter."

He flashed a sideways glance. "Is that right?"

"It would be fun." Leila smiled. "Have you ever called her?"

Clarence rolled his eyes for the first time. "Of course not."

"Why not?"

Now, he looked directly at her. "Have you considered how awkward it would be for all of us if I pursued her and it didn't work out? Besides, Angela is a lovely and refined woman. I dare say she has a high standard when it comes to men with whom she keeps company."

"Well, I know she holds you in high esteem."

"And I think this conversation has exhausted itself."

Leila grimaced. "You can't change the subject just like that."

"I certainly can."

"Not without a trade-off."

"Fine. You pick the subject—other than your grandmother."

"Okay." Leila pondered her main curiosities regarding her tight-lipped, of-a-more-reserved-generation friend. "I want to know about *your* father."

"What about him?"

"What was he like?"

Clarence splashed a little more liquid amber in his glass. "From what I remember, he was quite unpleasant."

"How so?"

"He abused my mother." He offered Leila another splash, and she held up her snifter. "She tolerated it until he turned on me."

He added just a swallow more to her cognac as she recalled what he had told her in his classroom one morning, back in high school. "She divorced him, right?"

"Yes."

"That was a pretty big deal back then—what was that, like back in the thirties or forties?"

"Yes. The thirties. I was around eight. We lived with my grandparents through most of the Depression years, and then she moved us out on our own."

"That must have been hard. Did your mother ever remarry?"

"Yes, but not until after I was out of the house. I'm afraid that for years I thwarted her prospects, since I was—"

Leila finished, "Difficult?"

"Yes. I was difficult, but perhaps we could start using a kinder term, such as *complex*."

"Alright. But I bet you didn't start out complex—that's what difficult people turn into when they get older and mellower. Just the same, I guess it's no wonder—poor little kid."

"Okay." Clarence inspected his drink and took a gulp. "My turn to ask a question."

Leila frowned. "No, I'm not done."

"Well, that's hardly fair."

"Sure it is. You're always the one probing my mind. Now it's my turn."

"Alright. One more question." His brow arched with reluctance.

"When Ian died, did you cry?"

His penetrating eyes fixed. "Yes. Several times."

"I don't mean like sniffling or getting choked up." She cocked her head. "I mean like bawling your eyes out."

Clarence's stare did not waver. His jaw squared and tendons in his neck strained. "Yes. I've bawled my eyes out over Ian."

Leila's own emotions rose, though not for Ian, but at Clarence's watering eyes. "When?"

"When I got home. In fact, as soon as I was all alone."

Leila's chin quivered, and her eyes welled. "You loved him."

"Like a son."

"He loved you too, you know."

"Yes. I know. He told me."

"Really?"

"At the hospital, after my surgery."

Leila placed her ring-laden hand atop Clarence's. Chirping crickets amplified the stillness of the moment and the gravity of his loss.

"Oh, Clarence, I'm so sorry you lost your good friend," she whispered.

He positioned her hand so that her engagement ring sparkled in the moonlight. She centered the alexandrite above her wedding band.

"I don't know why I still wear it." She twisted the gold band. "I mean, I know why I wear the alexandrite. It's the most beautiful stone I've ever seen. But the wedding band … I don't know …." She spread her fingers. "I don't know when I'm supposed to take it off."

"You'll know when it's time." Aligning their hands palm-to-palm and slipping his fingers between hers, he wrapped her hand in his. For the first time in a long time, she felt a glimmer of security.

CHAPTER 9

Philadelphia

T HE OBSERVATION ROOM. LEILA DIDN'T LIKE the sound of it, and liked its implication even less. As for Dr. Flanders, he didn't fit the stereotype. No horn-rimmed glasses, no receding hairline, nor pocket protector, and she expected someone more officious. But there he stood, in his faded jeans and madras shirt, making her feel overdressed in her cotton skirt. He wasn't her doctor, so why should any of that matter?

She braced herself as he ushered her and Clarence inside. A thread of illumination from beneath the opposite door disappeared when Flanders flipped on the light. As he furled the blinds, she caught their reflection in the large, one-way viewing window. She quickly turned away from the image beyond them. The low-tiled ceiling clipped the room to within an inch of claustrophobia.

Dr. Flanders directed her attention to the little boy and his mother sitting at the low table in the adjoining room. "Peter's been playing long enough to relax. I bet he's grown quite a lot since you saw him last."

Their nearness wrung heat from her core. The tips of her ears burned. "I suppose he has grown."

Her eyes darted to the doctor, to the folder on a chair, and then to the exit. The room felt stuffy and too warm, yet she wrapped her arms around her middle as if warding off a chill.

"Would you care to sit?" Flanders' eyes followed her, even as he took a seat. He appeared young for his PhD, but perhaps only in his demeanor. He wasn't as handsome as Ian, but he had an attractive way that felt familiar—a modesty akin to her husband's.

"I'd rather stand," Leila said as Clarence claimed a seat.

The bulk of the folder now lay on Flanders' lap. As soon as his eyes landed on her wringing hands, she slipped them into her deep pockets.

"And how are *you* doing, Leila?" The way he spoke her name—not as if he had just met her two minutes ago, but as if he had known her for years and had a file on her as thick as Peter's—made her want to lash out at him. She squared her shoulders as though better posture might smooth the anxiety from her face.

"Me? I'm very well, thank you," she said, surprised and impressed at how chipper she sounded.

Clarence and Flanders exchanged a skeptical look.

"Any questions?" Flanders asked.

"No," she said, her stare slipping from his, unsteady in its return. "I just wish it didn't have to be *me* going in there."

Flanders folded his hands on the file. "You do understand why it needs to be you."

"Yes. But how can you be sure I'm not gonna go off on him?"

"From what I've heard about you, that seems quite unlikely."

"I see." Her eyes darted to Clarence. They had likely spoken about her at length.

Flanders continued, "It's perfectly alright to show emotion in there. In fact, it would be beneficial for Peter to see a natural display of sadness."

"I'll see if I can muster something," she said, her voice bland but for the snatch of sarcasm.

"Just try to avoid hysteria." He raised a wry brow and smiled. With no response from Leila, he pulled a large white packet from the folder. "Also, I'd like for you to share these with him, keeping them in sequence." He removed several eight-by-ten photographs. "Do you think you can do that?"

The photos—the 35mm roll of black and whites Leila had given Clarence permission to develop.

"I suppose I could." She reached for the bundle, yet he handed her only one. She finally sat across from Flanders. Their knees touched. He waited for a response to the first photo before feeding her the next. As if they were someone else's vacation mementos, she gave each a cursory glance.

"He might or might not look at them, but if he should, don't hurry on to the next until he averts his eyes."

Flanders paused, holding back the last one until he had her full attention, and then handed it to her. It took a moment to realize that the photo, not her own vision, was out of focus. "Alright."

The thought of what came next, of sitting with the little guy—passing him each picture, forcing the memories—made her wish she hadn't come. Back in New Hampshire, she had practically boasted her lack of feeling, but now she feared what might happen next. Perhaps she was not ready to move on.

Flanders stretched back in his seat and crossed his ankle over his knee. His sneaker nudged her thigh. How could he sit there so relaxed and comfortable in his own skin, while every fiber of her body bristled with dread? He said nothing. He simply watched, massaging his chin. He finally spoke. "You don't have to do this."

It was not as if she needed him to introduce the notion, but his words made the idea conceivable—a viable option, as if she had never considered it before that moment. It sounded like an offering of cool water for her parched psyche but for its cowardice-laced aftertaste. She inhaled a labored breath and exhaled her worst reservations. "I just want it over with."

"Okay then, wait here till I signal you," he said, turning a knob beside the window. A low hum came through the loudspeaker as he exited into the playroom.

Peter sat beside his mother, pushing a toy car in figure eights on the table, accompanied by none of the usual engine-revving boy sounds. He only sniffled. Apparently, his allergies still bothered him. He didn't acknowledge Dr. Flanders' approach.

Clarence grabbed Leila's hand. "Are you okay?"

"Sure I am."

Bonnie rose from the table and headed for the observation room. As she stepped in, their eyes met. Bonnie nodded. "Leila."

Leila forced a smile, and they all turned to the window. Clarence stood between his daughter and his friend.

Flanders' voice came through the sound system as he sat beside the child. "Peter, someone has come to see you today —someone very special."

Peter bore down on the car as it rocked back and forth. Flanders turned the boy's face toward his. Peter allowed it.

"You remember Leila, don't you?"

The car halted. Peter covered it with his palm as his concentration shifted.

"She's very excited about seeing you. Would it be okay if she came in for just a minute to say hello?"

Peter's eyes widened and then narrowed.

"You don't have to see her if you don't want. All you have to do is get up and walk out of the room at any time. Okay?"

The boy's attention flashed toward the door. Leila could have sworn he looked right at her. They both shivered at the very same moment. She thought for sure he would head for the exit. He remained at the table, but his car tapped the surface in an irregular pattern as if in Morse code, sending a distress signal.

"Well, then, I'm going to invite her in."

Rubbing the boy's shoulder, Flanders turned to the mirrored window and nodded.

Leila entered the room and paused. Perhaps now the child would flee, and then so could she, but Peter continued to fixate on his car, tapping erratically. Flanders motioned for her to sit on the floor beside the boy. He didn't smell of fresh air and soil the way she remembered, but of stagnant air and closed-in spaces.

She touched his shoulder as cautiously as she whispered, "Hi, Peter."

He recoiled. Flanders' hand moved from the boy's back, guiding Leila's hand beneath his. When her caress replaced Flanders', Peter began trembling, which devolved into deep inhalations that slowed as she continued to stroke his back.

"I'll tell you what, Peter," Flanders said, his voice low and strong, "I'm going to get some cookies and juice for us, okay?"

As Flanders stood, both Leila and Peter remained, one as mute as the other. Leila stared at the side of the youngster's head, at his cherub's profile and pallid complexion.

"I suppose we're both a bit nervous," she said. "Grandpa told me you're not talking much these days—but to tell you the truth, I'm not much of a talker either, especially when I'm sad, so I guess we have something in common."

She touched his short-sleeved arm without rebuff. Indeed, he did appear bigger—more height than girth, but he still had the same Dutch-boy haircut and gnawed fingernails.

"Grandpa says I should talk about ... well, you know ... that day—" she said and he stiffened. "But I don't like to." She sighed. "It was sort of that way when my dad died." She folded her arms on the table, resting her chin on her forearm.

"I guess you probably didn't know about that—that I don't have a daddy either. He was very sick for a long time ... and then he died."

She gazed off, making no attempt to engage him. Then Peter looked at her.

"Can I tell you a secret?" she asked, as if expecting consent.

He rubbed his nose. The familiar gesture indicated *Okay.*

"I've never told anyone this, but—do you know what made me feel really weird after my dad died? I thought he might be watching me from somewhere else. I wasn't sure where he was, but it made me feel uncomfortable that he might still be able to see me. I guess that sounds pretty silly, huh?"

She laid her head on her arm, looking up at him. His eyes flinched.

"The thing is, I was there when he died, and just before it happened, I made him tell me something he didn't want to talk about." She paused, repressing a strong twinge. "Anyway, I begged and begged, and he finally talked about it. It made him so tired. And then he fell asleep. And he never woke up. He died right there in front of me. I was all by myself with him, and it was really scary.

"When they finally came and took him away, I kept getting those bad feelings that he was watching me, that he was ... that he was mad at me ... even though I didn't mean for it to happen." Leila snagged quick eye contact and sat up a little. "I had that feeling for a long time, but then it finally went away."

Peter tipped his head back and breathed through his mouth the way he used to when contemplating something Ian had explained to him. She hoped he might utter a word, perhaps just a syllable, or at least move his lips as though forming a word, and she could just be done with it and forget about the pictures on the floor beside her. He only scratched his nose.

"Anyway, I just wanted to tell you that," she said, giving him another opportunity to spare them both. He didn't. Instead, he peeked over and snuffled at the sound of her finger inattentively tapping paper.

"Oh, I almost forgot," she lied. "I brought something."

Leila placed the photographs on the table. She inched toward him and nudged the photos closer. Slowly his line of sight rested upon the top one. She nudged it again.

"This is of the lake. Remember?"

Now her own memory resurfaced—a breeze so light that it felt more like a whisper. The water in the cove, so placid that it mirrored the sky, unbroken. And then that all-too-familiar sensation of being sucked under, the pressure inside her chest and head.

Peter closed his eyes. His lids twitched. Perhaps he felt it, too. When his eyes flashed open, they fixed on the photo. He considered it for a long minute, his breath uneven. Finally, his gaze returned to the pile.

She placed the next photograph in front of him. A shot of the sailboat tied at the dock. She looked away, nearly forgetting to note Peter's reaction. He drifted off and then eventually moved back to the pile.

She placed the next one before him. Peter. They both tensed with acute focus. Peter might have been ready to move on, but she remarked, "I love this one. It's the perfect shot. Look at the way the sunlight is in your hair and on the water. Ian really would have liked this one."

Leila smiled. Peter glanced at her, then back at the photo, and then at the pile. Another one of him, inside the sailboat, lay on top. It joined those in front of Peter. For the first time, Leila noticed the anchor line coiled, there in black and white, on the floorboards—the oversized anchor Ian had found at a yard sale. She envisioned its rope strangling his ankle, like the memory squeezing air from her lungs.

Next. Peter's toy boat.

His eyes widened as he fingered the two-dimensional object. He stared without blinking, tracing the line that tied his boat to the stern. Back and forth, he rubbed as if trying to erase it. Finally, without moving his head, he glanced over at the blurry last photo.

Ian.

Leila placed it before him. Peter backed away just a bit, and his eyes darted as his body rocked. She stroked his arm and moved close enough to feel his skin radiating heat.

"It's just a picture, Peter. It's actually a very good picture. I guess you must have taken it—he used to let me try his camera too."

His eyes fixed on the photo again. His body continued rocking. Leila drew the photo back toward her, luring his gaze.

"Look," she pointed at the picture, "you caught the sunlight in Ian's hair."

He squinted and sniffed. Leila moved in closer, her own head grazing the sweating bangs across his forehead. He grabbed the picture. The rocking ceased, but he drew in quick breaths as his forehead pressed against hers with increasing force. Leila's chest tightened. She had difficulty breathing, as if Peter's rhythm had thrown hers off.

His pale face reddened, and the tiny veins in his temples swelled as he pressed hard into Leila's forehead, as if pushing his thoughts into her skull, pushing through the thick of bone, through a vast, impenetrable silence. His dry lips quivered and parted as he panted, trying to drive the words out.

In a breath quieter than a whisper, he said, "I didn't mean to."

Leila let out a long sigh and placed her hand on Peter's. A gentle squeeze coaxed his next words, an exhalation. "I just wanted my boat."

"It was an accident," she whispered as the burning behind her eyes gave way. A tear trickled onto the photograph. She beheld it with puzzlement. An orphan tear, surely not her own.

When his head no longer pressed hers, she pulled away and held his hand. She whispered, "It was an accident, Peter…. No one is mad at you. Ian's not mad at you, and *I'm* not mad at you."

Peter nodded with his mouth open. He breathed, "I want Mommy."

Leila glanced toward the mirrored wall. Flanders opened the door as Bonnie rushed to Peter's side. Before Leila could escape, Flanders grabbed her arm but directed his comment to Peter.

"Your grandpa and Leila and I are just going to sit over there in the corner for a few minutes, Okay?"

In his mother's embrace, Peter glanced at Leila.

"Actually," Leila whispered to Flanders, as tears streamed down her expressionless face, "I'd rather get out of here."

"Actually, it's best if you don't just disappear again." He directed her to the set of corner couches. "Let's sit for a few minutes, where he can keep an eye on you."

Clarence sat beside Leila as Flanders took a seat across from her. He handed her a box of tissue. "You're leaking."

Leila did not smile. "Am I? What do you make of that?"

"I think that it means—"

"It was rhetorical," she shot back. "Besides—look—it stopped."

Flanders studied her. "Leila, you did very well with Peter. I honestly did not expect those results so soon."

Leila stared ahead, much the way Peter had.

"Unfortunately, our mic didn't pick up on what he said. Perhaps you would fill us in on that."

The anxiety Leila had subdued returned with intensity. Without flinching, she stated, "He said that he didn't mean to. He just wanted his boat."

Clarence closed his eyes and pinched the bridge of his nose.

Flanders placed his hand on hers. "That must have been very difficult for you to hear. Would you like to talk about it?"

Leila clenched her jaw. "I was under the impression that this was about Peter, not me."

"I understand that this is very difficult for you."

Ignoring his statement, the next wave of emotion mounted. "How long must we sit here?"

"Just long enough for him to look for you one more time." As soon as those words left the doctor's mouth, Peter glanced over at Leila, looking her in the eyes. She held back her tears.

"Well, then, if you'll excuse me. I'll just wait in the little room." She rose from the sofa, trying to catch one last breath. On her way, she crouched beside Peter and forced a smile. "I'm so glad I got to talk to you, Peter, and I'm sorry but I really have to go right now. Maybe we could talk again, sometime soon, alright?"

He nodded, quick and subtle.

Leila rushed into the observation room. In a continuous stream, unaccompanied by any other sensation, tears slid down her face unhindered as she watched Clarence join Bonnie and Peter at the low table. Dr. Flanders approached the small room. Her chest constricted as he entered and stood beside her.

He touched her arm. "Leila—"

She looked at him through blurred eyes.

He guided her to a chair. "Sit down."

Without resistance, she sat. He handed her a tissue and she looked at it, unsure of what to do with it.

He cocked his head. "You do know that you're crying, don't you?"

"It doesn't feel like it."

"Perhaps because you haven't consciously given yourself permission, have you?"

She shrugged.

"What do you think would happen if you did?"

"I would start crying and never stop."

"Do you think that's really true? That you would *never* stop?"

"That's what it feels like."

"But really, have you ever known anyone that started crying and *never* stopped?"

She shrugged again.

"In my profession, I have seen literally hundreds of sad people. I've never seen one who didn't stop crying at some point."

"I'm afraid I would completely lose control."

"If you completely lost control, what would happen then?"

"I'd end up in the mental ward."

"Again, I've known many people in mental wards, but not because they cried very long and hard over something very sad. In fact, I'm more likely to see someone in a mental ward because they wouldn't let themselves cry, when crying would have been a very normal and healthy reaction to their sadness."

He seemed to be waiting for a response. She said nothing.

He added, "You seem like an intelligent young woman, Leila. The way you handled Peter indicates that you're also intuitive. The fact that you were willing to participate in Peter's recovery indicates that you perceive the importance of getting out in the open and dealing with very frightening and traumatic events. Intellectually, I know you understand that. But perhaps your fear holds you back, just as Peter's fear has been hindering him. What do you think?"

"Perhaps."

"You were able to convince Peter that he could safely express himself. Perhaps you could think of some safe place or some safe person to be with and at least start talking about Ian and the things that happened that day."

Her chin quivered. "Perhaps."

Flanders nodded. He waited a moment before rising. "I'll get Clarence."

CHAPTER 10

WRAPPED IN AN EGYPTIAN COTTON ROBE, Leila drew bathwater. As she adjusted the hot and cold, Clarence tapped the door.

"You decent?" he asked.

She tightened her robe's belt and cracked open the door. "Yeah."

He stepped inside with a snifter of cognac. "How's the head?"

"About the same." She pulled at her neck and shoulder.

"Sip this." He passed her the glass. "Turn around."

Leila faced the fogged mirror and sipped as he loosened the collar of her robe, just enough to expose her neck. His cool hands worked her tight muscles, his palm slipping to her shoulders as she kept her robe secure. While his thumbs massaged between her shoulder blades a sensation traveled along her spine. She set down the glass and let out a soft groan as her hands fell to her side. At that moment, she caught their hazy outline in the mirror; their bodies melded, one form indistinguishable from the other.

"Clarence …." She turned to face him. Their eyes met in a flurry of tenderness. She yearned to bury herself in the security of his embrace, that he might swallow up her fears.

"Water's ready," he said.

"Clarence ...."

He searched her eyes. "What is it?"

So many feelings churned inside her, but none would form words. "I ... I just ...."

He stroked her cheek. "Just have your bath—and we'll talk downstairs."

He left before she could respond.

Aromas from the kitchen wafted up as she slipped into the tub, submerging herself up to her chin. The cognac and almost-too-hot water drew her raw emotion to the surface like a poultice, though the tears that merged with bathwater still seemed foreign. She couldn't quite own up to them. Before the water cooled, images began trickling back—details she hadn't thought of for a year. She couldn't stop them, but she didn't dare remember—not alone. Staving off what had begun that afternoon, she climbed from the tub, dried herself, and slipped into white cotton lounge pants and robe.

⛄THE AIR CONDITIONER STRUGGLED WITH THE humidity as much as Myles' breathing did. He would have blamed it on his mitral valve, yet he couldn't discount the emotional stress of the past weeks. His heart was breaking with Leila's. Strengthening his own composure, he focused on the broccoli crown in front of him, cutting it into bite-sized pieces to the serenade of light classical music. Without a sound, Leila appeared in the doorway with vacant eyes. She tucked hair behind her ear and folded her arms.

"Better?" Myles asked.

She said nothing. She simply moved to a stool at the end of his butcher block and sat. He continued processing his vegetable but kept an eye on her.

She looked at him long enough for his gaze to penetrate. What he saw was anything but vacuous. Though her expression did not contort with emotion, did his?

Without preamble, she began, "The room wasn't as big as

what you might expect. It's just a small hospital after all, and they don't handle a whole lot of dead bodies I guess. I mean, not all at once."

Myles stopped chopping.

"All the way over there, sitting in the cruiser, I tried to imagine what it was going to be like. I tried to prepare myself, to reassure myself that it might not be him—that there was some terrible mistake. I remember the elevator ride down and the narrow corridor—one of the fluorescent lights was flickering and buzzing—like some bad movie. The hospital person was leading. The police officer was following me. We pushed through a wide door. I waited with the officer near the door as the hospital guy flipped on the light switch over a metal table.

"There was a sheet over him—I thought they were going to pull him out of a drawer or something, like you see on television—" She glanced at Myles, and then her focus again drifted. "It smelled of antiseptic, or something. Everything looked grayish—just shades of gray. The man that brought us pulled the sheet back just enough to show his head. It had a deep gash, but no blood."

Now her face twisted with anguish as she paused long enough for Myles to envision himself right alongside her, looking down at Ian.

"The second I saw his hair—" she covered her mouth as tears streamed down her cheek. Her face and voice distorted. "—I knew it was true."

Myles laid down his knife and moved toward her, his own emotion rising as she continued.

"He was sort of pale grayish-blue, like the sheet. I wanted to touch him but I was afraid. I was afraid he would be as cold as he looked, so I didn't." Her words mingled with tears, making it difficult to decipher. "—and then I had to throw up, and he gave me a pan, and I cried … I cried really hard. I didn't want to leave him … how could I leave him there in the cold gray room alone … all alone. But they made me leave." She sobbed into her hands.

Myles stood before her, listening and aching, restraining tears. He reached for her as she grabbed him and cried into his shirt. "The officer said we had to go … and I just shut off the tears."

Her body heaved as Myles kept his arms tight around her. He no longer resisted all he had been holding back for Leila's protection. They cried together.

Myles never finished preparing dinner that evening. Instead, he sat with her into the night as she cried continuously for hours. When she finally dozed on the sofa, he covered her with a spread and spent the night in his chair.

Leila slept until almost noon. Myles remained close by, reading and then preparing a light breakfast. He was in the kitchen when she appeared in the doorway, wrapped in the sofa throw.

He tilted his head with inquiry.

"I don't feel too good," she said as tears leaked from the corner of each eye.

"Sit." He positioned a chair at the table, facing him. "You need to eat."

She held her stomach as the blanket slipped from her arms. "I don't think I can—"

"I made a fresh fruit salad, and you're going to at least sample it." He scooped a few berries into a small bowl. "If you can keep that down, we'll get some protein in you after an hour or so."

He placed the bowl before her. He handed her a spoon for the fruit and a paper towel for the tears.

She took a bite, swallowed, wiped her face, and then repeated the sequence. "I knew this was going to happen. I just can't seem to control it. I don't even feel like crying, but they're like a leaky faucet that I can't shut off."

"So, then, let them come. We're not going anywhere or doing anything today, and your flight isn't till the day after tomorrow. So you may as well let it work itself out while you're here."

Leila grabbed his hand as he stood over her. "I love you, Clarence. Thank you."

He squeezed her hand, his heart swelling with a mixture of emotion that defied description. As difficult as revisiting the event had been, he felt gratified that he had finally been there for Leila—that in some small way, he consoled her now when he couldn't a year ago. As she leaned into him, he drew her to his waist, and she nestled her cheek in his shirt.

"I love you, too, sweetheart."

CHAPTER 11

New Hampshire

TRAFFIC IN THE STORE HAD BEEN BUSIER than usual for most of Monday morning. So far, Leila had managed to keep up with customers while her boss, Ben, attended the New Hampshire League of Craftsmen fair this August week. Normally, any elderly woman insisting on help finding gesso would not have annoyed her, but Leila also had a customer waiting to be rung up.

"Go ahead and help her," said the clean-cut man clutching several brushes. "I'm not in a hurry."

"Thanks." She came from behind the counter as another patron asked a question. She offered a quick response and led the gesso-seeking woman to a middle aisle. Trying not to hurry the indecisive matron, Leila glanced back at the young man. His hair was so black it appeared almost blue under the fluorescent lights. He seemed familiar.

"Pretty busy, huh?" he remarked when she finally returned.

"Sorry about that. It's been crazy all morning." She met his gaze and squinted at his bright eyes, trying to place him. "I know you from somewhere—I just can't remember."

He smiled. One eyebrow rose independently of the other.

"We were both in that watercolor workshop that the store sponsored last spring."

"Oh yes. That's right." She grinned. "Wearing out brushes, are we?"

"I wish." He tugged his diamond-studded earlobe. "Actually, just hoping that a good brush might improve my work."

As he examined the Kolinsky sable round and flat brushes, she took note of his hands—broad and meaty but not huge, and his fingers, long and more sculpted than tapering. No rings. His downcast eyes accentuated thick lashes that batted when he brought his intense blue—almost cerulean—gaze back to her.

Leila squinted again. "I'm sorry, could you remind me of your name?"

"It's Jared."

She extended her hand. "Leila."

"Yeah, I know." He gestured at her lapel card, his lone brow again arched.

"Right." She half-rolled her eyes. "Did you find everything okay?"

"Yeah. Thanks."

They exchanged cash for goods. The older woman came up behind Jared as he stepped aside.

"Jared, if you'll wait just a second, Ben has a new schedule for upcoming workshops. I can get one for you, if you'd like."

He nodded.

Leila rang up her gesso customer, completing that transaction. "Thanks, come again," she said, sending the woman off, and returned to him. "Hold on a second. I know it's back here somewhere." She leafed through several paper stacks, looked in a drawer, and then disappeared into the back room, only to emerge with nothing. "This is so embarrassing. I just saw it yesterday—the one in November is on The Human Form."

"Oh yeah?"

"Yup."

"Nude?"

"That's right," she said, looking under a couple of other piles. Jared waited with a quizzical single-brow arc and a grin. Between misplacing the form and the idea of a naked model, Leila's face heated. Fortunately, the poser would be female, and she wouldn't squirm as much.

"I'm not usually this disorganized …." Leila sighed. "Oh well. I'm sorry. I thought I could lay my hands on it."

"It's okay." He smiled broadly. He had the slightest gap between his two front teeth. "I'll stop in for it sometime later."

"Bye," she said, as he exited the store, leaving the door jingling.

After Jared left, traffic quieted. Leila pulled her lunch from a brown paper bag. Swallowing the last of her sandwich, she stared at her left hand. How much longer would she wear her wedding ring? More to the point, how long did she intend to remain unavailable? Would she consider dating someone? What if an attractive man, like Jared, ever asked her out? She did not feel married, yet she did not feel unmarried. Was the ring simply another device that kept her from moving forward with her life?

Later on that evening, in the upstairs bedroom, as she lay between her sheets, she twisted the gold band round and around. She switched on the lamp and pulled the ring off. The concave inscription read—*keeper of my heart*. She pulled the drawer of Ian's nightstand, revealing his matching wedding band—with the same inscription. Laying her ring to nest in his, she closed the drawer. The next morning, she opened the drawer and replaced the ring on her finger, atop the alexandrite stone.

LEILA STOOD AT THE END OF THE DOCK AS sunlight beamed through the tips of trees around her little cove. She punched numbers on her new cordless telephone. Clarence picked up.

"Guess where I am!" she said

"Wherever it is, you sound far away."

"I'm talking on my new cordless phone that Ben gave me. I'm standing on the dock."

"I can hear you well enough. So what's up?"

"Not much." A dragonfly skimmed the water's surface. "It is so tranquil. The sun is getting ready to set and it's so beautiful. So I thought I'd call and share it with you."

"Sounds wonderful." His voice conveyed a smile. "So what's the real reason for the call?"

She loved the way he always knew when she had something on her mind.

"Okay, there was this guy that came into the store last week. I guess he made me think about the possibility of dating. It's not like he asked me out or anything. I was wearing my wedding band, after all." She held her hand out, gazing at the set. "But it made me wonder ... if my wedding band weren't there ...."

"So, you're still wearing it."

"Yeah. I guess the thought of dating really freaks me out. I mean, I never really dated in high school—not the way everyone else did. And with Ian—we didn't actually date, we just came together."

"It's true that as an adult it's not like dating in high school."

"So, when's the last time you went on a date?" She lowered herself to sit, dangling her feet off the end of the dock.

"Let's see. That would be Valerie Jennings—the spring after you and Ian married."

"What! You actually dated her? My shrink? Why didn't you ever tell me?"

"Why would I? It never went beyond one date."

"Was it the doctor-patient ethics thing?"

"No. Actually, we mutually agreed that although I sat in on a couple of your sessions, she never viewed me as a patient any more than I viewed her as *my* therapist—*you* were the primary focus of all that."

She flung water with her big toe. "So, what happened?"

"I wanted to move closer to Bonnie, so I had to choose which relationship to pursue."

"Wow. So what other dates have you been on that you haven't told me about?"

"Why all this interest in my social life?"

"Because it's what friends talk about."

He sighed loudly.

"Come on, I'm serious," she said. "Who else?"

"No one else."

"Why not?"

"As you well know, I've grown accustomed to my own company."

"Yes but, with all the women out there looking for a good man, you could have your pick. In fact, I bet I could name at least *one* that would be agreeable to dating you."

"It's quite obvious that you do not have a realistic view of what's available out there, a certain grandmother notwithstanding. And have you forgotten about my *complex* personality?"

"You've toned down so much that's not even an issue. I know that if I was thirty years older—or twenty—or even ten, I would definitely go out with you." Leila's admission caught her by surprise. "Okay, that sounded really weird. What I meant was that—"

"You're just trying to make an old man feel better. That's very sweet, but my life is working just fine without any romantic attachments. And I'd rather keep it that way."

"Alright. Well then, back to me!" She thrust both feet in the lake, making a splash. "It's not as if *I* necessarily want to date anyone right now, but dating brings up the whole sex thing. You know, like my daddy said, 'all men are pigs.'"

"Well, as much as I hate to admit it, it's good that you understand that."

"But it's not *always* true, in *every* case."

"I think the point is that men have a particular *nature*. True, some manage to keep themselves more closely reined in. But essentially, my gender tends to have that capacity."

"Well, *you're* not that way."

"Admittedly, I do keep myself tightly reined. Then again, you have not been exposed to that particular aspect of my personality."

"It's not *all that* hard to imagine."

"Yes, well—"

"I know. These are girly things you don't want to talk about. But who else do I have?"

"Well, have you ever thought about cultivating a friendship with someone of your own gender? Perhaps *you* are the one who ought to be pursuing a relationship with your grandmother."

"I'm not ashamed to admit that women in general bore me." She raised her feet to the dock and hugged her knees.

"Well, if you didn't limit your association in general, perhaps you would find that women of substance *do* exist, and your grandmother may be one of them."

Leila chuckled. "Is that right, Clarence? And may I quote you on that?"

"I'd rather you didn't .... Not to change the subject, but Peter was asking about you."

"How is he?"

"He's doing quite well. In fact, he wants to know when you're coming for a visit."

"I guess it would have more to do with *your* schedule, and when you feel like having me. Although I guess I wouldn't necessarily have to stay at your place. I don't want to be presumptuous—"

Clarence hesitated. "Are you uncomfortable staying here, Leila?"

"Why would I be?"

"You tell me."

"*I'm* not uncomfortable with it. I *love* being there. I just wouldn't want you to—I don't know—I mean, has it ever occurred to you that we have sort of an unusual relationship?"

"I suppose we do. I'm just wondering where this is coming from—has something happened to make you uncomfortable with it?"

"No. It's just that—do you think people assume things about us?"

"Probably they assume you're my daughter."

"You're right—" She exhaled.

"What is it?"

"Am I a daughter to you?"

"Hmm …. I can't say that is the most apt description, given my view of daughterhood has long been skewed. Perhaps initially I viewed you more as a protégé."

"A protégé? That sounds so archaic—and detached."

"Well, in the strictest sense of the word, I was interested in seeing to your protection and welfare, interested in securing your future, but I'll admit, I've had a longstanding affection for you—you know that."

"It's odd, but you never really felt like a father to me, given my skewed view of fatherhood. You've always been far better than that."

"Given that neither of us have a true handle on how the father-daughter relationship is supposed to work, perhaps it's safer to say we are exceptional friends."

"Yes. Exceptional," she said with resolution.

"So, you're comfortable staying at my house?"

"Of course. When can I come?

"How about we plan on Thanksgiving weekend."

After her conversation with Clarence, Leila stretched out on the dock, processing their conversation. She wasn't certain if she was more intrigued with the idea of Clarence Myles dating—courting—a woman, or her own future prospects. Given Valerie Jennings' grace and intelligence, Leila could see why he found her attractive. She wondered about the other women he had confessed falling in love with, but what about now? What sort of female attracted him? Was he the type of man who needed emotional intimacy before climbing in bed with a woman? Oh, what was she thinking, even he as much as admitted he was a potential pig, but still, that didn't fit the profile of the man she knew.

And what about all the other men out there—potential suitors. How many of them were more interested in a roll between the sheets than something long term? Leila had difficulty imagining herself with anyone but Ian. As she dozed, she again replayed their lovemaking.

🐛✣CHAPTER 12

HAVING TAKEN FRIDAY AFTERNOON OFF FROM work, Leila tidied the living area while she waited for the piano tuner. At the sound of each leaf-peeper that drove past, she glanced out her window. Outside, gold and red rustled in the breeze. Autumn had always been her favorite time of year, and even more so after she and Ian had fallen in love on brisk runs through fallen leaves and passionate kisses under sugar maples. Ever since then, autumn always made her feel amorous.

In preparation for the tuning, she cleared the piano top of framed photos, and gave it a thorough dusting.

"Gross," she muttered, carrying her dust cloth to the back door and shook it over the edge of the deck. She had never met the piano tuner, but Leila recalled how much he had impressed Ian. When she heard rapping at the front door, even though she still shuddered at the idea of inviting a stranger into her house, she fortified herself with Ian's impression of "The Tuner."

Bracing herself, she opened the front door.

Jared stood before her.

She glanced at what looked like a small black suitcase in his hand, and back at his face, and smiled. "You're the tuner?"

This time, both brows rose. "You're Mrs. Brigham?"

She returned his shock. "You've been here before?"

"You're Ian's wife?"

Leila blushed. "Ian is …."

"Yes, I know—I just didn't make the connection. I'm so sorry. I feel so stupid."

"No. Don't worry. Come on in."

Leila moved aside and he stepped in. His eyes moved around the room as if calculating. "You're his wife—the *watercolorist*. He talked about you all the time. But he always called you Lei."

"He talked about you too." She half chuckled. "Oh my goodness—we were even going to invite you to dinner."

"I would have enjoyed that." His brow jumped as he placed his tuning kit on the bench and began rolling up the sleeves of his white Oxford shirt, exposing substantial forearms.

"It was on our To Do list, but then …."

Both shifted their gaze.

"Yeah, I tuned last spring … just before …."

"I got the card you sent. That was really nice of you." Her eyes returned to his. "What a coincidence, huh?"

His expression turned wistful. "No kidding."

After lingering in each other's gaze for a moment short of discomfort, Jared lifted the strobe and placed it on the bench, then returned his attention to her. He slapped the tuning hammer against his palm. Leila took that as her cue.

"Okay, well, I'll leave you to it. If you need anything, I'll be downstairs."

From her studio, she listened to the repetitive strike of single and then double notes of each octave interval. For nearly two hours, she tried to recall just what Ian had said about 'the tuner,' as he often referred to him. Ian probably did mention Jared by name at times, but without any context, she never would have made the connection. Ian had found him very interesting—a person like himself who dabbled in many things, knowledgeable, but not quick to let on. That was true, for if Jared had told Ian he was also a watercolorist, Ian would surely have mentioned it. Leila's regard for Jared lay not so much in what her husband had said, but in Ian's desire to invite Jared into their life.

When she heard him playing scales, she deduced the tuning was complete and she ascended the stairs.

She approached the piano. "It sounds wonderful."

He stood. "Would you like to try it out?"

"I'd be too self-conscious—I haven't played in over a year. If truth be told, I really don't deserve a piano this nice."

"I don't get to tune too many Chickerings of this vintage," he stroked its hand-rubbed rosewood. "Ian said you play blues."

"Yes. What about you?"

"I actually only just started taking lessons. Tuning is more of a mechanical thing for me, something that I learned first."

"Ian said you fix clocks and watches, too."

He shrugged. "A little."

She glanced at his hands with wide eyes.

"What?"

"I guess I just assumed someone who works on something so delicate would have more delicate-looking fingers."

"What can I say—these sausages are nimble."

"And you paint."

He smirked. "Not very well."

"What else do you do?"

"I don't know that I do a whole lot. I just try out a lot of things. I'm probably not exceptional at any of them." He packed up his tuning hammer and strobe.

Leila smiled at his diffidence. "How much do I owe you?"

He passed her an invoice. "Forty dollars."

"Will you take a check?"

"Of course."

As Leila handed him payment, their eyes met. He folded and tucked the check into his breast pocket. "Don't let it go a whole year this time—it was really flat. I could call and remind you in the spring, if you like."

"Okay." She followed him to the door. As he stepped outside, she said, "Would you be available for dinner sometime?"

His expression went blank but for his one arched brow. "You mean, like a date?"

Leila hesitated. "I suppose."

"Leila ... I'm married."

"I'm sorry. Ian had given me the impression you were single, and I didn't see a ring."

"I don't wear one." He tugged on his earlobe. "We exchanged diamond studs, instead. We've only been married about a year and a half."

"No rings—how unconventional." A smile twitched her lips. "Just the same, you might want to consider wearing a wedding band when you're tuning ladies' pianos."

He glanced at her hand. "And if you're available, you might want to consider putting yours away."

🎵 THE OVERHEAD BELL JINGLED AS LEILA OPENED the shop door and swept wayward leaves out into the parking lot. As soon as she stepped back inside, Jared's Toyota pulled up to the storefront. As awkward and disappointing as it had been to find out he was married, knowing he wasn't available put her even more at ease in anticipation of seeing him again.

From behind the counter, she watched as he climbed from his front seat and then opened the back passenger door. Reaching inside, he emerged with a pink bundle, situating it upon his hip. When he stepped inside, Leila's chin dropped.

"You have a baby—" she said.

Jared smiled, bouncing the infant. "Yes. This is Emily."

Two small teeth showed between her rosebud lips. Jared pulled her fleece cap from her head, revealing curly strawberry wisps.

"Oh my goodness. She's adorable. How old is she?"

"Thirteen months." He wiped a bit of drool smeared across her rosy cheeks and kissed her forehead.

"Then you've sure got your hands full," she said, trying to subtract thirteen from eighteen and add nine—or would that be subtract nine. Either way, it didn't matter to her.

He chuckled and glanced at her hand, brow raised. "I see you've decided to go ringless."

"Yeah. I'm just trying it out. It's kind of crazy, but I still wear it to bed."

"That's not crazy. Not at all."

She fished around in her pocket and pulled out the gold band. "I keep it with me, just in case."

"You really aren't ready to start dating, are you?"

"No. Not really. I don't think so." She laughed. "I don't know."

"Then why'd you ask me over for dinner?" It didn't seem like a vain question, rather, one intended to make Leila analyze her reasons.

She shrugged. "Ian liked you. You made me comfortable."

"Well, I read someplace that after a death or divorce, you should give yourself at least two years."

"Really?"

He grinned. "I don't know. I might have just made that up."

Leila sighed. "Actually, two years sounds about right."

"Hey listen, I have my registration slip for next month's workshop." He tried to juggle the baby while fumbling inside his tweed blazer.

"Great."

"Would you mind holding her a second?" he said, passing the baby to her over the counter.

Before she had a chance to resist, she accepted the little creature named Emily, holding the child as if she were a potted plant—a poisonous one.

Jared removed the slip from his breast pocket and glanced at Leila. He chuckled. "You look as if you've never held a baby."

"I haven't."

"Seriously?"

"Yes." Her eyes widened. "Could you please take her back so I don't break her?"

He laughed and traded Emily for the registration form. "Well, not that I'm partial or anything, but babies are awesome."

"Is that because you only have to babysit on rare occasions?"

Emily wrapped her pudgy hand around Jared's finger as he jostled her. "Actually, I probably have her more than her mother does."

Leila folded her arms and looked at Jared with amazement. "If Ian and I had reproduced, I think he'd be stuck with the kid most of the time, too."

Emily started to fuss and the two adults took that as their cue.

On his way out, Jared stopped at the door. "Will you be attending the workshop?"

"Yeah. It's mandatory. Ben thinks people like to see his help struggling alongside them."

"He's right."

Leila hadn't even picked up a paintbrush since before she went to Philadelphia for Peter's doctor appointment. She did not look forward to this upcoming Saturday's workshop, not just because she hated the classroom setting, but Ben always presented her to customers as if she were some kind of watercolor expert. Which she wasn't. It was true, her technique had improved and her style had developed, but she cringed at the thought of anyone looking at her work as an example.

CHAPTER 13

THE STOREFRONT ADJOINING BEN'S ART SHOP made the perfect classroom—as if 'perfect' and 'classroom' were reconcilable terms. As Leila pulled her supplies from her Saab and surveyed the parking lot, Ben arranged tilting tables and stools inside. He waved at her through the large plate-glass window. She waved back, shuddering in the November wind.

"It's hot enough to breed sheep in here," she said as the door closed behind her.

"We've got a model coming, in case you've forgotten." Ben continued arranging stations in a two-tiered semi-circle.

Leila refrained from rolling her eyes. She did not envy the woman who would be modeling nude. Leila could manage her own uneasiness with naked without adding to the model's physical discomfort.

"We will adjust the temperature to her comfort," he stated. "Now, put on your name tag."

"You know how kindergarten these things are?"

"It may surprise you to know that people appreciate them."

Leila shook off Ian's old peacoat as she headed into the shop through an adjoining door. She returned wearing a button-down shirt over jeans—her typical attire. Having peeled away the backing of her nameplate, she pressed it to her chest with a thud. "There. Are you happy?"

Ben smiled and checked his watch. "Please make sure each station has a filled water cup and paper towels—I've got to make a phone call."

Leila stocked all the stations and straightened tables, making sure each participant would have an unhindered view of the instructor's large easel and the model's platform. She reserved her own place at the far corner and another one beside her. Mel, the instructor, arrived next, and then attendees began trickling in. Leila kept an eye out for Jared. Not until after most of the seats had filled did his car pull into the parking lot. It came to an abrupt halt a couple of rows back. He was not alone.

From her stool, Leila glanced at Ben, who looked at his watch and then back at her. He seemed perturbed, but she was too preoccupied with Jared's delay to wonder why. Finally, both the driver's side and front passenger doors flung open. Both occupants climbed out. A dark-haired beauty slammed her door and rounded the front of the car. Jared opened the back door and tucked his head inside. Leila thought she saw a familiar pink bundle. In a moment, he emerged with his zip-up portfolio as the woman climbed behind the wheel and slammed the door. As soon as he stepped away from the car, it was in gear and peeling away. His shoulders dropped and then squared. *Yikes! Could that be his wife?*

When Jared stepped in, Leila waved him over. She was glad she had saved him a seat. He and Ben made their way toward Leila at the same time. As Jared sat, Ben approached her.

"I just got a call," Ben whispered. "An emergency came up. The model isn't coming. The class is supposed to start in five minutes."

"Oh no."

"I need you up there."

"What?"

"I need an impromptu model—and you're it." He may have been whispering, but his voice carried all the force of a drill sergeant.

She shook her head, trying to keep her voice down. "You expect me to model nude?"

"Don't be ridiculous—I just need a body up there, clothed or not."

She sighed, "Seriously?"

"Leila. People have paid good money for this workshop. They are expecting a live model."

"Ben, I am no model."

"Don't tell me you never modeled for Ian. And don't make me pull the I'm-the-most-lenient-and-accommodating-boss-you-could-ever-hope-for card. Do I need to mention the whole month I'm letting you take off in February—the days off I've given you on short notice?"

Leila sat, stunned. "I'm going to be sick."

"And lose the blouse—I know you're wearing one of your tank tops underneath there."

"What?"

"Don't be a prude. We are studying the human form—not fashion design." Ben walked away. There would be no further debate.

She looked at Jared, who apparently had overheard the entire exchange.

"Wow—that trumps my crappy morning," he said.

She rolled her eyes and began unbuttoning her blouse, revealing her tank top.

Jared leaned over and whispered, "Just pick a focal point at the back of the room. Everyone else will disappear."

She inhaled a deep, uneven breath.

As she stood, he added with a wink, "And think sexy thoughts."

She couldn't help smirking at the irony of it all. She hadn't wanted to paint, and now she didn't have to.

Mel gave a five-minute introductory speech, including apologies for the not-so-nude model, while Leila stepped into the shop. In the dim light, she removed her shirt, sneakers, and socks, then securely tucked her tank top into her waistband, relieved she had opted for the bra that morning.

Ben stepped in beside her. "I owe you one."

"No, Ben," she said, her voice tinged with annoyance and gratitude. "I owe you."

As Mel gave her the signal to take her place on the stool, she shoved her clothes at Ben.

"And for Pete's sake, try not to look so angry," Ben said under his breath as she walked away.

Without looking at the class, she sat, trying to come up with a comfortable pose. How had Ian positioned her when she sat for him? Where was the light coming from? What should she do with her hands, and what angles had she always found interesting to paint? She straightened her back as Mel continued talking. She anchored one foot on the floor and the other beneath her thigh. She twisted her torso slightly, laying one arm across her lap, and with the other, she braced herself from behind. As she lifted her chin toward the back of the room, Jared cocked his brow. She focused on him. Ten minutes later, her entire body ached and then numbed.

Leila had no idea how much time passed. Jared had come in and gone out of focus so many times she felt cross-eyed. Her neck strained and her ribcage throbbed, and that was to say nothing of her derrière.

"Alright," Mel finally said to the class. "Let's have a look at your results."

Ben came to Leila's side and handed her a cup of water. Her shoulders slumped as she rested her elbow on her knee and sipped.

"You were great," he said, offering his hand to help her up.

"Yeah, yeah, yeah." She shook feeling back into her legs and arms. "Just give me my shirt."

The class milled around in the workshop and store for about a half hour longer. Leila manned the cash register, while Ben and Mel made artsy small talk with the attendees. By seven o'clock, almost everyone had left, except Jared. He stood waiting at the storefront with his artist portfolio resting against his leg. She closed out the register and came up beside him.

"Where's your ride?" she asked.

He looked as strained as she felt a couple hours ago. "Late."

"You want to use the phone?"

"She won't be home."

"How long are you going to wait?"

He shrugged.

"If she doesn't show up by the time Ben locks up, I'll give you a lift."

He stared ahead, biting the inside of his lip and nodded with resignation. Slowly, he came around and looked at her. "You did really well up there."

"I'm just glad it's over."

Eyebrow up, he asked, "Did it work?"

"What—focusing to make everyone disappear, or thinking sexy thoughts?"

"Either one."

"Well, I can assure you—not one sexy thought crossed my mind. Focusing on you helped."

"Okay, I'm having trouble not taking that as an insult."

Leila smacked his arm. "You know what I mean."

Ben walked up behind them and handed Leila an envelope. "I'm kicking you out. Thanks again, kiddo."

Jared followed Leila to her Saab and climbed in through the passenger door, wedging his portfolio behind his seat. She started the engine and pulled a check from the envelope.

"Wow. Three hundred bucks! Gee, maybe I ought to do this for a living."

"You could. You've got the—poise."

She shifted into first. "Well, I sure hope Ben doesn't want me to do it again. It's no fun."

They drove for a few minutes in silence, aside from the directions he gave her to Sunapee's lower village.

"So," Leila asked, "that woman who dropped you off was your wife?"

"Yeah. Sarah."

"She's beautiful. Though I guess I was expecting a redhead."

"Yeah." His response cut and then amplified the tension.

Leila shifted to something she considered neutral. "So, you support a family on piano tuning?"

"That and a bunch of other stuff."

"Like what?"

"I manage properties."

"What does that entail?"

"Opening and closing rich peoples' homes seasonally. Plumbing, heating, renovating, general handyman stuff. Plus, I refinish and rebuild pianos on the side."

"Wow. I guess that must keep you busy."

"Well, I can work on a flexible schedule. It gives me time with Emily."

"She's a real doll."

"Yeah. I've gotten pretty attached to her."

The far away sound to his voice struck her as odd. "Why wouldn't you be? You're her daddy."

"Yeah." He sighed and his brow twitched. "It's complicated."

He looked as if he wanted to say more, but didn't. He just shook his head.

"Sorry. It's none of my business."

"No. I'm sorry. I didn't mean to give the impression that things aren't fine. Everything's good."

Leila turned down his road.

"Pull over here," he said.

"This is your house?"

"No. It's up the road a bit. It's just better if you drop me here."

Leila turned to him. Their gaze met but she couldn't bear the anguish behind his eyes; she quickly looked away.

"Thanks for the lift." He climbed out, shut the door, and didn't look back.

TRAFFIC IN THE STORE SLOWED TO A POST-AUTUMN pre-holiday trickle. Leila had waited on only one customer all morning. She had straightened and organized shelves and inventory, tidied the register counter, swept the entryway, washed the front window, and now eyed Jared's black portfolio.

She didn't expect him for another hour, when he would collect his belongings between tunings. She looked forward to seeing him again. As she sat, staring at his portfolio, a notion struck her—he had painted her, and that the very painting lay only inches away, albeit out of sight. Her heart raced. She chewed her lip. How had he perceived her? Had his rendition come close to the way she pictured herself?

She lifted the case. Only a thin layer of polypropylene separated her from the object of her curiosity—and an invasion of Jared's privacy. Fiddling with the zipper, she imagined how she would feel if someone took the liberty of helping themselves to her personal and private work. Though likely he had shown it to Mel. Perhaps even other members of the class had seen it. Why shouldn't she? Still, it didn't seem right. As she flicked the zipper pull, the door jingled.

Jared approached the counter. "Sorry about leaving my stuff in your car. I guess I was distracted the other night."

"It was no inconvenience to me." She continued to stroke the case, disinclined to hand it over.

His eyes darted from her face to her lap and back. "Did you have a look at it?"

"No, but I sure was toying with the idea." She perched it upright, hoping for permission. "Do you mind?"

He tucked his hands in his jeans pockets and bit his lip. "Okay ... but bear in mind that it was a study on the human form."

From his portfolio, Leila pulled the paper block and flipped back the cover. Her face bloomed with a neck-to-cheek blush. "Oh, my ...."

Her clothing appeared as more of a vapor than of any substance, and he certainly had an eye for anatomical detail.

He drew a nervous breath. "I hope I didn't offend you."

Leila's brow twitched as their eyes locked. "You have quite an imagination."

Something in his eyes sparked and his cheeks colored as one brow arched. "It didn't take much imagination."

In her core, Leila knew she should look away, that she shouldn't wish that he would imagine anything about her. She repressed a shiver and closed the cover.

He shook his head and now averted his own eyes. "I'm sorry. That was a really inappropriate thing for me to say."

As soon as the words left his mouth, their eyes again locked. Simultaneously, they both struggled for the same breath of air—for the same will to look away.

"I've really got to go," he finally said, taking the painting and his portfolio, one in each hand. He turned and left without another word.

CHAPTER 14

Philadelphia

L EILA WOVE HER WAY THROUGH THE HORDES of holiday travelers and stood on her tiptoes, keeping an eye out for Clarence. He stood at the end of the gate. Their eyes met. At that moment, nothing could look as good as her Clarence Myles, clean-shaven in a trench coat.

"You shaved. That's nice," she said as she stroked his smooth face and gave him a hug.

"I'm glad you appreciate it. How was your flight?"

"A little turbulent, but we made it. Thanks for picking me up. I could have taken a cab."

"You'd be hard pressed to hail one tonight."

She snuggled into his side. "What's for dinner?"

"Honestly, you should be immense, given how much you think about food."

"I'm not like this until I'm around you," she grinned. "So, are we eating in or out?"

"In. Soup and sandwiches."

"Yay."

As they drove, with the ever-shifting shadows and light from street lamps and traffic, Leila glanced at Clarence. She scrutinized his profile as he maneuvered through the metropolitan area, and into the suburbs. Feature for feature, his pale blue eyes, straight nose, high cheeks, square jaw and cleft chin were the same as when they first met. But something about him was different.

He caught her staring. "What?"

"Nothing. You just look—you look good."

"Well then, dim lights, a clean shave, and tired eyes make for a good combination. I'll have to remember that if I ever get up the courage to ask someone out again."

"No, I'm serious. You're not dying your hair or something are you?"

"Don't be absurd."

"Hmm." She squinted and passed it off.

"Not to change the subject from absurd to even more absurd," he said, "but guess who's coming to dinner tomorrow night?"

"Well, I assume Bonnie and Peter."

"And Dr. Flanders."

"Really?" Leila exclaimed, connecting the dots. "I guess it's a little unexpected, but how is it absurd?"

"Think about it. A psychiatrist—dating my daughter. How insane is that?"

"So, is he no longer treating Peter?"

"Apparently not. Not formally, anyway."

"Wow. Well, I hope for Peter's sake they aren't just playing around."

"That is, of course, my only concern. As challenging as it is for me, I'm keeping my mouth shut. I'm assuming they are both fully aware of the ramifications of their relationship, especially if it should end in disaster."

MYLES PUSHED OPEN THE FRONT DOOR, allowing Leila in ahead of him. George the cat scurried into the kitchen. Myles couldn't help comparing the ease of inviting Leila into his domain with the edge of anxiety he experienced on the rare occasion when Bonnie came to visit. If not for Peter's overnight stays, his daughter would likely have no clue about Myles' personal life. As it was, she had no idea what he did at home alone or in his spare time. Perhaps it was her subconscious payback for his years of non-involvement.

Bonnie certainly had the capacity to show kindness; he had even observed surprising sensitivity and intuition. Her mothering attested to that. Yet, even as a youngster, she had shown little comprehension of life outside of her personal sphere unless there was something to be gained. He supposed that was typical of many children, though Bonnie seemed not to have progressed beyond self-absorption, or perhaps she chose not to extend herself in his case. Either way, what did she hope to gain from their always-at-arms-length relationship? On some level, Myles was looking for redemption, but what need or want, if any, did he fill for his daughter? That was another thing he couldn't help comparing—how he never had to wonder about Leila and what she expected or wanted.

Leila stepped inside with a predictable smile. She breathed in. "Mmmm … smells like you."

"Well, who did you expect it would smell like?"

She rolled her eyes. "I'm only saying that it smells good to me—like home."

"You're getting sentimental in your old age," he said as he headed toward the stairs.

"And you love that I notice the ambiance of your house. Don't tell me it's not all carefully designed to evoke a particular feeling."

Her assumption was a case in point—Leila knew him that well. She cared to notice things important to him, to indulge him with appreciation.

"And you are also getting wise …." Myles said, not suppressing his pleasure as he glanced back. She followed as they ascended the stairs and entered her room. "You've packed heavier than usual."

"You noticed."

Yes. He liked to think he also noticed subtleties. Hanging her garment bag in the closet, he cast her an inquisitive look. "I presume you brought something nice to wear for dinner tomorrow?"

"Yes, as per your request." Leila's eyes glimmered as she laid her suitcase on the bed. "Actually, I bought something special. Something I thought you would particularly like."

Knowing how little she cared for shopping, he was surprised and delighted she had gone to such efforts. "Did you?"

"Yes."

"And you think you know me well enough to know what I like?"

"Yes, I do. I think you'll be pleased."

"This should be interesting." His brow arched with curiosity, not only because she had shopped, but also because she had shopped with him in mind. "You get organized up here, and I'll start supper."

Myles was slicing fresh mozzarella when Leila appeared in the kitchen doorway wearing her usual attire and stocking feet.

She smiled. "Smells like roasted garlic. What's it going in?"

"I'm spreading it on half the ciabatta for the sandwiches, and I've already added a pureed dollop to the barley soup, with leeks and celery."

Two ripe plum tomatoes sat on the counter. "Shall I slice?"

"Yes, and remove the seeds. And then smear the other half of the sandwich with the pesto."

"We're grilling it open-faced, are we?"

He smiled at her assumption. "I've brought you up right."

"Indeed," she said, mimicking his favorite exclamation,

and then sipped the wine he had poured for her. "So, what are you preparing for Thanksgiving dinner? Something exotic and completely nontraditional, I hope."

"So sorry to disappoint. Bonnie requested turkey, stuffing, mashed potatoes, gravy, cranberry sauce, corn, and to finish it off, pumpkin pie with whipped cream."

"I see," she said, arranging a tidy layer of tomato atop pungent basil. "One does what one can."

"Yes, exactly."

"Well, I know for sure it will be the best turkey dinner *I've* ever had."

"Of course it will. And that's because you will be doing just as much of the preparation." He passed her the mozzarella.

She nudged his arm. "I'm glad you let me work with you in your kitchen."

"I enjoy having you in my kitchen." He glanced at her as she laid cheese over the tomato.

"Yes. In your kitchen. In your house. You're so accommodating. But just the same, you must be glad when you have it back all to yourself again."

"Not so glad as you might think." She always left a void. His house smelled different after she had been there, but her scent always dissipated, leaving him more than a little let down.

As he placed their sandwiches, open-faced under the broiler, she carried their bowls of soup to the dining room table, already set for dinner, and returned for their wine.

With their dinner before them, Myles sat at the head and Leila to his right. They ate as Tchaikovsky played in the background.

Leila stopped chewing and looked at him. "Clarence, why don't you ever play blues when I'm around? I know you have an exhaustive collection."

"Because I don't know what sort of memories they might stir. And I'd like to think I'm creating some new ones for you."

"Is *everything* you do calculated?"

His impulse was to say *yes,* but he needed to calculate his reply. He chuckled. "I suppose it is."

"Haven't you ever done a spontaneous thing without thinking about every possible outcome?"

He pushed back in his armchair as the grandfather clock at the far end of the room chimed the first time. Folding his hands upon his stomach, he combed his past for a spontaneous action. By the time the clock struck nine, he had come up with nothing and shrugged. "No. I don't think I have."

"That's impossible."

"Is it?"

"Come on—not even something like kissing a girl?"

He shook his head gravely. "Very risky business. Always calculated."

She rolled her eyes. "Okay, at the grocery store. You are planning on filet mignon, but lobster is unexpectedly on sale, and you just switch your menu on the spot."

"Doesn't count. I always plan on an unexpected sale— leave an opening in my menu for that very possibility." He chuckled again. "Besides, you're one to talk—always with plan A, B, and C."

She sat up straight as if that might give credibility to her words, "*I* can be spontaneous."

He stared her down. "Name something."

"After your heart attack I called to visit on the spur of the moment."

"Calculated."

"How so?" she squinted with irritation.

"I'm not saying you were being overtly manipulative, but on some level—even if subconsciously—you knew what sort of behavior would get a result."

She winced. "You make it sound so ugly."

"And calculated."

Her fingers tapped the table and her foot jiggled his trouser leg. "Okay, well, last month, on a whim, I invited my piano tuner over for dinner—just the two of us at my house. A date."

His brow rose with surprise. "You met this tuner before?"

"No, but Ian did. He liked him a lot."

"Aha! Calculated!"

"What?"

"Husband's approval equals safe. Comes into people's homes equals trustworthy. And I'll bet he's *hunky* to boot. All calculated."

She matched his folded-arm repose and frowned.

"Well?" His brow remained arched. "Did he say yes?"

"*No*," she said stretching the syllable like a twelfth-grader. "He's married."

"Ouch. Sloppy calculation there, Leila."

"Well, you of all people know I was never any good at math." She pushed away from the table. "Just the same, I'll have you know there are things you don't know about me, Mr. Myles. Things that would surprise and even shock you."

Now he laughed, carrying his own dishes and following Leila into the kitchen. "Is that right, Mrs. Brigham, or shall I say Miss Sanders."

As they stood at the sink, he said. "Just leave the dishes. I'll take care of the cleanup."

"No. We'll do them together."

He found her insistence odd, given her stern refusal when he had offered as much at her house. *Different setting*, he presumed.

He tossed her a towel. "Alright. I'll wash—you dry."

AS EXHAUSTED AS SHE WAS FROM ALL THE anticipation, the flight, and now the late hour, Leila tossed and turned, unable to sleep. She listened to Clarence go through his nightly checklist: lock the doors, turn off the music, feed George, lights out. The stairs creaked and she heard him in the bathroom, and then in his bedroom. She still lay awake as he began lightly snoring on the other side of the wall. Soon, sounds of the house receded and peaceful sleep overtook her—until those early, in-between hours, when the dreams invaded, stirring her pain and longing. She woke in a cold sweat, with every nerve ending electrified. *Shake it off. Breathe.*

Enticed by the smell of strong coffee, she donned her robe and padded downstairs to the kitchen. She hesitated in the doorway.

"Sleep well?" Clarence asked.

"Yes."

He approached with a hot mug and a smile. "Good. I thought we'd eat light this morning, given our big dinner."

"Wonderful." She remained in the doorway, watching him—the way he moved.

He glanced at her sideways. "You okay?"

"I'm great." She smiled and proceeded to the small breakfast nook at the back of the kitchen. "I guess I just forget how nice it is to wake up to someone in the morning."

"Oddly enough, I agree."

He set a bowl of fruit salad in front of her. "There's plenty more."

By midmorning, she stood opposite him at the butcher block with dinner preparations well underway. As much as she loved consuming whatever food they made, this was what she truly enjoyed. The preparation. Even though Clarence had been busily chopping, mixing, or sautéing, Leila always felt as if she were the exclusive object of his attention. Anything could be revealed as easily as peeling the layers off an onion. He tenderized her with a smirk, sometimes like a piece of meat beneath his mallet, but often like a gentle marinade, permeating the tough sinews of her reluctance.

Before extracting the giblets, Clarence gave his long sleeves several quick, neat folds. She had never noticed his forearms before—they reminded her of Jared's. Her knife slipped at the distracting sight of the hair on his muscular arms.

"Ouch!" She gasped at the sight of blood.

"What have you done?" he scolded. "And on our shallots, no less—"

She pinched her finger.

He grabbed her hand. "Is it bad?"

She grimaced. "I don't know—I can't look—I don't think so."

"Let me see."

He pulled her over to the sink and ran cold water over it, inspecting the slice. "Nice. It doesn't need a stitch, but it's close."

"Oh great … and now I'm getting woozy."

He grabbed a paper towel and led her to a stool. "Sit. I'll get a Band-Aid."

She rested her head on her knees as vague patterns of light behind her eyelids intensified. When he returned, she held up her index finger and breathed erratically.

"Don't you pass out on me," he said.

She sat back, panting.

He gingerly applied the Band-Aid. "There."

She looked at the repair and then pointed it back at him with a twisted little smile. "Aren't you going to kiss it?"

He chuckled, gathering her fingertips and planted a quick kiss on her knuckle. "There. And no more cutlery for you, young lady! Now, go set the table."

CHAPTER 15

MYLES SHOWERED, SHAVED, AND DRESSED FOR dinner. Standing before his mirror, he snugged the knot of his narrow tie. Too formal. Allowing for a finger's breadth, he undid his top button and readjusted the knot. Better.

Downstairs, he lit a match to paper and kindling in the fireplace, and, having allowed himself spare time, he sat in his armchair. As he reached for his book, Leila's door upstairs clicked open and closed. Ah, yes, her grand entrance. How well did she know his taste?

He turned around in his chair, catching a glimpse of black. Pointed toes and slender heels. Seams running up her ankles disappeared into a flared hemline, skimming her upper calves. Her fingers, peaking out from long, tapered sleeves, slid down the handrail. Holding his breath, Myles stood and faced her. Black velvet floated from her hips and then settled where she stood on the midway landing. She turned toward him. Her neckline scooped out a wide swath of black cashmere, allowing ample view of her shoulders and a hint of cleavage. She had even gone to the trouble of applying makeup and fluffing her hair.

He squinted with feigned nonchalance and cocked a brow. "Very nice. Hmm … but something's missing."

Leila's shoulders slacked and she bit her lip. "But you do like it, don't you?"

"Oh yes, it's perfectly lovely," he stated matter-of-factly. "But ...." He folded his arms and tilted his head as if dissecting each element of her attire—in fact, he was. He had to admit, he could not have chosen a more flattering silhouette. She did indeed know his taste, which for some reason astounded him.

Waiting for his verdict, she puffed a strand of hair.

"I know what it needs ...," he said, approaching her and whisking past. "Follow me."

LEILA stepped into his bedroom doorway behind him as he switched on the overhead light. She inhaled his scent and held her breath.

Clarence stood before his large mirrored dresser and opened a dovetailed box. "Come over here. We haven't much time."

She approached as he lifted a worn, black velvet pouch. Grasping her shoulders, he positioned her to face the mirror. His firm clutch sent a shiver up her spine.

He emptied the contents into her palm and drew out a double-stranded, pearl choker, leaving a pair of drop earrings in her hand. Now behind her, he draped it across her chest, holding it there for a moment.

Her eyes met his reflection. She could hardly breathe. "Oh, Clarence."

Bringing both ends together, he fastened it at the nape of her neck.

His cool hands rested upon her shoulders. "That makes all the difference, don't you think?"

She touched the necklace and then glanced at the two remaining earrings.

"They're beautiful .... Are they—?"

"Yes, they're the real thing—my mother's. A gift from her second husband. She remarried, shall we say, advantageously. They do me no good, so you may as well have them."

"Clarence, I couldn't. Bonnie should have these."

"Honestly, Leila, can you picture Bonnie wearing pearls? In fact, I myself have heard her say that the only time she'd be caught wearing pearls is—well, when she's laid out in a casket. Strictly a diamond girl." He grasped her shoulders and gave them a gentle squeeze. "Besides, as far as I know, she's not even aware of their existence. Mother didn't pass away until after I divorced. And so now they're yours."

Leila stared at his handsome reflection and then at the pearls. She felt beautiful in a way that she hadn't felt for a very long time.

"Now the earrings. Perfect for you since they're not pierced and neither are you."

With her bandaged finger, Leila fumbled with the screw back of the drop earring. Clarence took them from her, drawing her hair away from her lobe as he twisted the gold rod. She watched in the mirror, his cool hands now on her neck, and caught the scent of him. Glancing up to inspect the one earring, he smiled with satisfaction and moved to the other. She held her breath.

Stepping back, he smiled again and whispered, "Perfection."

"I don't know what to say."

"Thank you is sufficient." He turned toward the door, allowing Leila to exit ahead of him. She glanced back into his bedroom before he closed the door, the cool beads against her flushed body.

As they descended the stairs, the door knocker indicated their guests had arrived, but Clarence did not quicken his pace. Leila smoothed her skirt as he opened the door.

Peter sandwiched himself between Louis Flanders and his mother, hiding behind more thigh than skirt. Bonnie's stilettos gave her an inch of height over her date, but mostly,

Leila noticed the snug red angora turtleneck. As Louis shook Clarence's hand, they looked like bookends in their matching black dress pants, white shirts, and narrow dark ties.

"Sir," Louis said, handing Clarence a bottle of cognac.

Bonnie glanced her father's cheek with a kiss and then gave Leila the head-to-toe, offering little more than a smile and brief hello.

Leila reciprocated, quickly turned her attention to Peter, and squatted in front of him. He retreated behind Louis' leg.

Taking Peter's hand, Louis crouched beside the boy. "What are you thinking, Peter?"

"She might not like me."

"Does she look as if she doesn't like you?"

Leila grinned and touched his sleeve. "Hi, Peter. I'm so glad to see you. I can't believe how much you've grown."

Offering a shy smile, he moved toward her and accepted a hug.

Since dinner was ready to come out of the oven, Clarence invited all to sit at the table. Leila followed him into the kitchen. When she returned to the dining room with a dish of stuffing, she noted her place. Naturally, Clarence's seat was at the head. Peter sat to his grandfather's right (the place Leila preferred) as Bonnie claimed her father's left, and Louis beside her. Leila would sit beside Peter and across from Louis. She again retreated to the kitchen. When she returned with another dish, she caught Bonnie staring. Clarence followed with the platter of turkey.

He began passing dishes of food. "Please, help yourselves."

As she forked turkey from the platter, Bonnie remarked, "Leila, I don't think I've ever seen you dress up. You look as if you stepped right out of a *Talbots* catalog—only—more retro. It works on you."

There was nothing demeaning in her tone, but Leila was, as always, unsure of Bonnie's motive.

"Tell me," Bonnie continued, "how do you manage to maintain that virginal demureness, yet pull off sultry at the same time?"

Uncertain of what *Talbots* was, or how to interpret Bonnie's comment, Leila said, "I can assure you it was completely *un*calculated." She flicked a brow for Clarence's benefit.

Bonnie's own brow rose with skepticism.

"But, thank you," Leila said. The truth of the matter was, she had chosen the outfit because she hoped to come across as demure and feminine. She hadn't thought of it as sultry until that moment. Did Clarence also infer sultry? It warmed her to think so.

Bonnie stared at her neck. "And, I think those pearls are the perfect embellishment."

From the choker up, Leila blushed. Her eyes involuntarily darted from Bonnie to Clarence and back.

Bonnie shot her father a curious glance and returned her attention to Leila. "They're stunning. I'm no expert, but they look positively authentic. An heirloom, no doubt?"

"Yes," Leila stroked the beads. "I suppose they are."

"Well, they're lovely. I'm impressed that you've actually developed your own distinct style."

Leila pursed her lips. "Thank you." *I think.*

To Leila's relief, Bonnie took a bite of food and now focused on Peter.

Louis Flanders had remained silent, yet Leila sensed his careful observation of her. He struck her as a student of human nature even in his off-hours. What conclusions might he have drawn regarding Leila's relationship with Clarence Myles? His face lit with a question.

"How is everything going in New Hampshire?" he asked.

She translated that as *How are you coping in your grieving process?*

"To be honest, it's a lot of up and down. I never would have imagined the gamut of emotions involved in grief." She snagged Bonnie and Clarence's attention. What had possessed her to be so open?

"I think it's difficult for anyone who has never experienced it to fully comprehend the changes we go through—how unique it is to each person, and the intense mixture of emotions it stirs."

"You've been through it?"

"Yes. Having loving support can make a big difference." He glanced at Bonnie. Leila glanced at Clarence.

Peter spoke up, directing his quiet words to his grandfather. "Can I sleep over tonight?"

Peter's assertiveness took all aback.

"I'm sorry, Peter," Clarence said, "Leila is sleeping in your room. Perhaps next weekend."

Peter's eyes shifted to Leila. He frowned. "Can't she sleep in your bed with you?"

Leila blushed as Clarence replied, "No, son, Leila needs her own room."

"But why? Mommy always lets Louis sleep with her."

Bonnie squirmed. "This just isn't a good weekend, sweetie—"

Leila interrupted. "I'd really like for Peter to stay overnight. Couldn't I just sleep on the sofa? I've slept on it before. It's comfortable. That way he could have his own bed."

"I wouldn't dream of putting you out," Bonnie said.

"I'd be happy to. Really."

Father looked at daughter and then at the boy. "Peter, there would be no going home in the middle of the night."

"I know, Grandpa. Please?"

Clarence looked at Bonnie. She nodded.

"Alright then," he said.

"Yay." Leila grinned, hoping to diffuse the tension as Peter smiled, leaning in her direction. She nudged him back and then pushed away from the table, gathering up a couple of dishes. "Is it time for pie?"

"I think so." Clarence rose at the same time as Leila. They both headed to the kitchen, leaving their guests.

Leila stood across the butcher block, facing Clarence as he sliced pumpkin pie. Caressing her pearls, she gazed at him, full of affection.

He glanced at her. "Whipped cream won't dollop itself."

Leila whispered, "She knows."

"Regardless—" he sipped a glass of ice water, "—it's of no consequence."

"Yes, but why do I feel like the *other* woman, afraid that your *wife* will find out?"

"That's ridiculous."

"Perhaps, but I feel like the mistress without the benefits." She could have choked on her own words as soon as they slipped from her lips.

Clarence coughed, nearly losing his mouthful of water as Bonnie stepped into the kitchen. She looked at one and then the other before placing dishes in the sink.

For the rest of the evening, Bonnie had her constant eye upon her father and Leila. It was as if every time Leila touched him with an innocent gesture, or lingered in his gaze as he spoke, it snagged Bonnie's attention; she didn't glare or grimace, she simply watched. Leila thought she even saw her nudge Louis' attention toward them as Leila laughed at some silly joke Clarence told. Admittedly, it hadn't been all that funny, except for the fact that he had told it. Perhaps she did giggle a little too long.

Leila never thought to stifle the esteem that had become so much a part of their interactions and surely beamed from her eyes. And then there was that moment when she looked at him afresh, as if for the first time, and saw what other women might notice in him.

When Bonnie and Louis finally left, both Leila and Clarence

exhaled relief. They washed and dried dishes, side by side.

"I think that went off pretty well, don't you?" Leila said.

"I couldn't have done it without you."

"Yes you could."

"But not with such thorough enjoyment. Thank you for being my hostess."

Peter tugged Leila's hand. "I need to put on my pajamas."

Leila smiled. "Me too."

"I'll finish up the dishes," Clarence said. "Peter, don't forget to brush your teeth, and then I'll read you a story."

Before long, Clarence had Peter tucked in bed while Leila waited on the sofa, wearing her pajamas. The last of the fire flickered. Clarence descended the stairs in his robe. She pulled her knees to her chest.

At the fireplace, he stoked embers with the poker. "Would you like me to add another log to the fire?"

"No, let it go out." He looked so handsome and distinguished, standing there like Cary Grant. All he needed was a pipe.

"It was nice of you to let Peter have the room. You sure you're okay on the sofa?"

Leila grinned. "Yes, but if I get scared in the middle of the night, I might show up in your bed."

"Don't be absurd. That is *not* funny."

"Of course it's absurd. That's why it *is* funny."

He scowled.

"Oh, Clarence, lighten up—I was just joking."

"Sorry." He paced to his chair and back. "I guess it irks me about Bonnie and Louis—that they aren't more discreet around Peter."

Leila giggled.

He folded his arms. "What?"

"Can you imagine Bonnie's reaction if Peter came home with tales of me in your bed as he suggested?"

Clarence chuckled and then caught himself. "That's

enough of you and your twisted humor." As he walked past his chair to the stairway, he said, "Goodnight, Leila."

"Goodnight, Clarence."

He turned one last time at the landing and gave her a perplexed look before heading up.

Clarence Myles may have dismissed Leila's joke, but was he now wondering if there was some truth in her jest? The thought of him thinking she might want to share his bed flooded Leila with embarrassment. Why on earth had she pushed his sensibilities? Worse yet, as she closed her eyes, she envisioned the comfort of lying beside Clarence.

CHAPTER 16

M YLES PREPARED A FULL BREAKFAST. BELGIAN waffles with maple syrup, sausage, eggs, toast, juice, and more coffee. The three enjoyed a leisurely meal as Peter divided his attention between the two adults. Myles loved having his Leila and Peter under the same roof, enjoying his hospitality. In ways that he had not yet experienced with Bonnie, this felt like family—even better than family.

After breakfast, Peter grabbed Leila's sleeve, intent on showing her one of his games.

"Do you mind?" Leila asked Myles as Peter pulled her by the hand, toward the living room. "I hate to leave you with all the cleanup."

"Go ahead," he smiled and proceeded to put his kitchen back in order.

At eleven-thirty, he entered the living room, wiping his hands. The two lay on their bellies in front of the fireplace, finishing up a game designed for ages six through ten.

He tousled his grandson's hair. "Peter, go pick up your toys in your room and brush your teeth before your mother arrives."

The boy rose and headed upstairs.

Leila gathered up the board game. "Can I help finish up in the kitchen?"

"All done."

She stood and slipped her arms around him. "It's wonderful being here, Clarence. I'm having such a good time."

Indeed, Leila was better than family.

He gave her a quick, affectionate squeeze and she pulled away. A knock at the door startled them.

When Bonnie stepped inside, she asked, "So, how did both of you sleep?"

Myles now found Leila's late-night joking amusing as they responded in unison. "Perfectly."

"I'll go get Peter," Leila added and headed upstairs.

Bonnie and Myles stood in silence, though he read puzzlement in her expression. As soon as Leila was out of sight, Bonnie spoke her mind.

"What are you doing, Dad?" Her brow narrowed.

Myles matched her puzzlement. "What are you talking about?"

"I'm talking about you and Leila. What are you playing at with her?"

"If you're talking about the pearls—"

"I couldn't care less about Grandmother's pearls."

Her knowledge of the jewelry did not shock him as much as what she implied, and it must have shown on his face.

"Oh, *please* Daddy. I know it's been a long time, but you can't honestly be this naive."

His ire rose. "What exactly are you insinuating?"

"I'm insinuating nothing. I'm simply stating the obvious fact that Leila is—in love with you. Even Louis could see it." Bonnie huffed. "Tell me this is not news to you."

Clarence Myles was speechless. Peter came running down the stairs, breaking the exchange, but not before Bonnie gave her father one last glare and huffed again with displeasure.

Leila joined the three as Bonnie switched her attention to Peter, her voice transforming from grave to lyrical. "You ready, Bud?"

Peter nodded.

"Now, tell Leila goodbye," Bonnie said, and, after offering cordial thanks, she departed with the boy, leaving Leila standing alone with Myles.

For a moment, he stood in shock until the cat rubbed against his leg.

"I forgot to feed George." He brushed past Leila.

In rapid thought, he calculated his daughter's words, weighing them out and comparing them with what he believed. Leila could never have those feelings for him. What he did believe and felt he could substantiate was that his daughter was jealous by nature. She was not above attempting to sabotage his relationship with Leila. The poorly calculated gift had been a sufficient trigger for Bonnie's envy, envy not of pearls, but of the intimacy and exclusiveness of his relationship with Leila. Even to court the idea that Leila could possibly have amorous feelings for him seemed the epitome of arrogance and conceit. He would not entertain the idea of it any more than he would confront Leila with Bonnie's accusation.

After a moment, Leila joined Myles in the kitchen as he placed George's dish on the floor.

Leila stood opposite him. "She knows about the pearls."

Myles hated the idea that she might believe there was remorse attached to the gift. He nodded.

"She's upset?"

"Not that I gave them to you instead of her. I think she's just miffed that I was not forthright about it—that it seemed to be *our* little secret. Honestly, I wish she would just get over herself."

"You can't really blame her. I don't think there are too many people who would easily understand our *exceptional* friendship."

"You're too kind and forgiving of her."

"Perhaps. But she seems to be putting forth effort to be nice to me."

"And you believe she's being genuine?"

"Well, I know she had an audience, but at least she was playing nice. Besides, I've seen her softer side."

"It's true that she does have the capacity to be kind. Just the same, Leila—and I hate to say this about my own daughter, but —please don't let your guard down around her. She does not possess your guilelessness." Bonnie would not hesitate to accuse Leila to her face if it served some selfish purpose.

After an early dinner of leftover turkey sandwiches, they passed the afternoon happily absorbed in their reading. The fireplace flickered while each turned pages. As Leila sat snuggled into the corner of the sofa, stroking George on her lap, Myles caught her staring a time or two before abashedly looking away. When the flames died down, Leila yawned, drawing his attention once again.

"Clarence?" she said.

He laid his book on his lap.

She scratched behind George's ear. "Do you think Bonnie and Louis will marry?"

"I honestly don't know. I certainly hope that's the direction they're moving in."

"So, you like Louis?"

"I do. I just have a hard time imagining what he sees in my daughter."

"Oh, that's not really so hard to imagine, is it? I mean, just because he's some bigwig professional in the mind industry doesn't mean he can't be swayed by his *nature*."

"True. But there's no doubt his profession is an asset to their relationship. Perhaps he's able to see her potential. Perhaps he's a rescuer by nature."

George purred loudly.

She smirked. "Perhaps they're just having hot sex."

"That is not something I care to think about."

"You mean in general, or regarding her specifically?"

"Both." He gave her a quizzical look and folded his hands over the book. "Why the interest in Bonnie's love life?"

"I don't know. If they did marry, I was just wondering if you would stay in the Philadelphia area."

"Even if they did marry, why would I move? There is still Peter. Besides, where would I move to?"

"I don't know. You might move to New Hampshire. Newlyweds love time alone. Peter would probably visit frequently, even if you were farther away."

He cocked his head. "And how do you suppose that would affect my relationship with my daughter?"

"Frankly, if it didn't put an end to it, I think it would improve it significantly. The less she knows about your, life the better she seems to like you. And vice versa. I mean, the way you talk about her, she's not above phasing you out if she feels she has a viable father figure for Peter in the person of Louis—the potential step-father."

"I can't say the notion hasn't occurred to me also." After a moment, he added, "And just where in New Hampshire would you suggest I move to?"

"Somewhere very close to me, of course."

"You're not turning into a schemer, are you?"

She drew her hand from the cat's head all the way to her tail. "No. I just—I love being around you. I wish we didn't live so far apart."

"And what about my job?"

"Well, the pay up there probably wouldn't be as good, but it's not like you've got tenure where you're at. Besides, I've never gotten the impression that money is an issue for you."

"Is that right?"

"Yes," she said, looking squarely at him. "Move to New Hampshire, Clarence."

He stared at her in wonder. "Why do you want me in New Hampshire?"

Leila looked at him with bafflement. "Because I love you —that's why."

There was no heat of passion or lust in her words. It was not as if she hadn't expressed as much on a number of other occasions, but now her words impressed upon him with more truth and earnestness. He could not comprehend how someone like Leila, so young and capable, with all of her future ahead of her, would desire, in any form, his companionship. In that instant, he was utterly overwhelmed with a feeling of unworthiness. In that same instant, his view of her transformed. Sitting before him was a beautiful woman, desirable, and with desires. Could there be any basis to Bonnie's observations?

Myles set his book aside and stood. Facing the hearth, he wondered at his own perceptions of Leila.

"It's getting late," he said. "I'm going to bed."

"I'll be up after a while."

He barely looked at her and made for the stairs. "Goodnight, then."

"Clarence," she said.

He turned to her. "What is it?"

"I do love you."

He studied her face, unsure of what he saw. "I love you too, Leila."

🐉 AFTER DINNER, ON THE EVENING BEFORE Leila's flight home, she packed her bags and thought of Clarence. Her visits with him were such a combination of relaxation, stimulation, and intensity. Her conversation with him the night before left her exhausted and wove its way into her dreams that night. Even in the morning, she had trouble dismissing all the churning emotions. Yet by the time they had prepared a meal and gone for a leisurely walk, most of it spent in silent contemplation, she was ready for more discussion. About what, she wasn't sure until she sat staring at him in his big leather chair. This evening, George sat on his lap.

She simply couldn't resist a verbal poke. "Clarence?"

"Yes?" He did not lower his book.

"How do you think marriage would alter our relationship?"

Now the book nearly dropped from his hand. George cringed. "What?"

"Marriage—how do you think it would alter our relationship?"

He squinted, as if computing. "Would you care to rephrase that question?"

She then realized the ambiguity of her inquiry. In a split second, she thought of all the ways marriage would simplify and complicate their relationship.

She blushed. "I meant, if you *or* I got remarried—not to *each other*. I was just wondering. How do you think that would affect what we have?"

He peered at her over his readers. "Well, you were married and that didn't seem to interfere with us."

"Yes, but that was Ian. He was part of our shared history. And you and I weren't as close then as we are now. All of this would change, wouldn't it?"

"You're probably right about that. A marriage mate should come first in a person's life. Ian certainly did in your life, as well he should have."

"I don't want things to change. But I don't want you to be alone."

"Do you assume it would be me that remarries?"

"It's possible."

"But not as likely as you remarrying. You're young and—I'm, well—old."

"You're not old."

"Yes, well, I'm much older than you."

"What difference does thirty-five years make?"

"It's actually thirty-four years, and it makes a great deal of difference. You and I are a generation apart."

Suddenly, Leila was unsure if they were still speaking about each other's prospects for remarriage in general, or just what?

Clarence removed his glasses and studied her face. "It seems you've been giving this a great deal of thought."

"I guess I have." She pondered her scant prospects. "Last month, when I asked the tuner over for dinner, I guess it got me thinking."

He stroked George. "Were you disappointed that he was married?"

"A little. But mostly relieved. It sort of took the pressure off. It's easier to be just friends."

He stared off for a moment, and then his gaze returned. "Just be careful. Inappropriate feelings can ignite without warning."

Leila recalled a past conversation. "That's right. You were involved with a married woman—"

"We weren't actually *involved*, per se."

"But you were in love with her. Was it mutual?"

"She never expressed as much, but yes, I believe it was."

"What ever happened to her?"

"I moved away. We didn't keep in touch."

"You must have missed her."

"Yes." He rubbed George's jowls. "But it was for the best. It was a very frustrating situation for us both."

Leila's eyes widened with curiosity. "Did you ever—you know …?"

"I can't believe you even need to ask." He frowned. "You know me better than that."

She half-rolled her eyes. "Of course you didn't …. You are all propriety and boundaries."

"Indeed."

They kept their eyes on each other.

Leila ventured, "Don't you ever get tempted to push boundaries?"

He gave her one of his most incisive stares. "In case you hadn't noticed, Leila, I have pushed many boundaries. But there are some boundaries not even I would cross."

CHAPTER 17

New Hampshire

IT WAS NOT UNTIL LEILA STEPPED THROUGH HER front door that it struck her with all the force of a tsunami. She was alone. Ian would never be on the other side of the threshold waiting for her. And neither would Clarence Myles; she could not fathom the emotions he stirred. When with him, she reveled in his attention; and when away, she yearned for his company. She had always thought he had handsome features, but how could she feel even a glimmer of physical attraction for him, to desire his touch? Her stomach churned with shame at even the notion. He had been better than a father, and now, her closest and most intimate friend. As much as she missed him, it was for the best that she had time away—and plenty of distractions. That would surely cure her peculiar feelings. She couldn't wait to return to a busier work schedule.

With holiday shopping in full force, she took on extra hours. After several weeks of a more hectic pace, she found it easier to pass off feelings for Clarence as loneliness, missing intimacy, and nothing more. Monthly hormones were the culprit, or simply the lack of male companionship. Besides, she didn't *need* a man in her life, did she?

As Leila rung up a customer, Ben placed a schedule beside her.

"When you get a minute, mark the days you want off next month," he said.

Leila hadn't had time to give much thought to her upcoming visit with her grandmother. Other than a mental picture of three weeks blocked off at the end of January and into February, she hadn't any idea of what day she planned to leave. She still needed to double-check dates with Angela and book her flight. When she arrived home that evening, she found an envelope from Miss Angela Phillips in her mailbox. A Christmas card, she presumed.

Leila tossed her jacket on the chair and tore the seal. Inside, she found a one-way airline ticket and a note.

> *Happy Holidays, my dear Leila!*
>
> *I hope you don't mind the liberty I have taken. Once you have arrived, you may decide upon a departure date at your leisure.*
>
> *During your visit, I hope to introduce you to my long-time friend and business partner, François Goulet. In addition to our New Orleans gallery, we have a pending venture in Boston. May I impose upon you to bring along a portfolio of your late husband's work to show Fran? And by all means, include a sample of your own watercolors.*
>
> *I am so looking forward to finally getting to know my granddaughter—I think we shall get on very well!*
>
> *My very best regards,*
> *Angela*

Leila didn't know if she ought to feel grateful or manipulated. She saw no benefit in allowing herself to feel corralled. After all, she had promised she would visit, and there was merit to keeping busy, but now she had no choice. Placing the note and ticket on her kitchen counter, she sighed.

"I guess it's a done deal."

As she filled her teakettle at the sink, her phone rang.

"Clarence. Hello," she said at the sound of his voice. Her insides fluttered.

"You'll never guess what just came in my mail."

Leila glanced at her parcel on the counter. "An airline ticket from Angela?"

"Funny you should guess that. It actually is something from your grandmother."

Leila's heart kicked in. "Really? What is it?"

"An invitation—a rather formal one."

"Read it to me."

"Alright." He paused for a moment. "It states, Miss Angela Phillips requests the pleasure of your company at a formal dinner party to be held on the fifth of February, nineteen hundred and eighty three at seven o'clock in the evening at Grand Oaks, Natchez, Mississippi."

The heart that had been fluttering a moment ago, caught in Leila's throat. "Are you planning to go?"

"Would you like me to?"

"Well, it would present you with an opportunity to get to know Angela better."

"More likely, it may be hoped that my attendance will ensure that you actually show up."

"She's already ensured that. She sent me an airline ticket today."

"You still haven't said if you'd like to have me attend."

"Well, seeing as this dinner party is probably so Miss Angela Phillips can parade me in front of her friends—it would be nice to have you as my chaperone."

"Then I shall accept with pleasure."

IT WAS A TOSS-UP BETWEEN GANDHI AND THE *Man from Snowy River*. The adventure flick won out. If only Clarence would simply show up in the theater, the way he had on the one-year anniversary of her father's death. The fact that he had been the sort to spend the Christmas holiday at the theater should have been a strong indication that they would be exceptional friends—kindred spirits, dare she say, soul mates?

When Leila entered the dim theater, she quickly scanned the auditorium. So few moviegoers occupied seats that she gave little consideration to anyone nearby—not until she had chosen a seat, centered and halfway back. When she looked up, Jared sat two rows behind.

"Hi," he said, his brow mirroring her surprise.

She smiled. "I thought I was the only weirdo who spends Christmas at the movies."

"Apparently, you're not."

Leila looked for any indication that Jared's wife might join him at any moment. "No wife or kid?"

He blinked. "They're out of town for the holidays."

"Oh. So you're here alone?"

"Kind of looks that way."

"Me too. I've spent a lot of holidays in the theater."

"Really? Why?"

"Oh, it's a long, boring story."

"Long—maybe." His brow shot up, "Boring? I doubt it."

"Okay. Well, it's going to feel very awkward to me if you're sitting behind me, staring at the back of my head. Do you mind if I sit in your row? You know, with a few seats between, so it doesn't look like we're actually together."

"Be comfortable—that's my motto."

Leila moved up to his row and sat, picking at her popcorn. "So, why not *Gandhi*?"

"I already spend too much time thinking about heavy subjects. I need a light diversion. I suspect that's true of you, too?"

"Yep. It sure would be nice to switch my brain off when I need a break from all my big thoughts."

The lights lowered, and music began playing. Leila quickly found herself immersed in another world—a world of wonder and no consequence, of victory against all odds. When the movie ended too soon, Jared stayed in his seat, and so did Leila.

"Good movie," she said. "Maybe I'll move to Australia."

"Sure wish I could. I was actually considering it at one point."

"For real?"

"Half for real. I'm always open to options, but some aren't necessarily realistic." His focus transformed to a faraway look—one she had seen before. It made her scramble for a change of subject.

"Um, I was wondering if I could give you a call," she said.

He raised a perplexed brow.

"I mean, I'm going to be away for a while this winter, and I was wondering if you could come over and winterize my house—you know, so the pipes won't freeze."

"Oh. Yeah. Sure." He reached for his wallet. "Let me give you my card."

She took it from him and neither moved.

"You plan to stay for the next showing?" she asked.

"Yeah."

"Me too. I've been known to stay all day."

"Well, I hadn't planned on *that*. I think once more will do it for me."

"Me too."

CHAPTER 18

THE DAY AFTER CHRISTMAS, MYLES WOKE, feeling more than the usual post-holiday letdown. He felt old and dispossessed. He studied his face in the mirror. He could trace none of the lines back to his youth. Even when he'd had his heart attack, when he first contemplated his own mortality, he felt younger than he did in this moment. He yearned to hear Leila's voice.

As he sipped his coffee, he checked his wristwatch. Leila had probably spent her day at the theater, but she likely didn't stay out too late. Would seven be too early to call?

He dialed. On the other end of the line, she sounded hoarse.

"Are you okay?" he asked, now feeling bad that he had woken her.

"It's kind of early."

"Sorry, I should have waited till eight."

"It's okay. What's so urgent?"

"It's not necessarily urgent. But, I do have news." In fact, the urgency was not in the news but in his need for her reassurance.

"Yeah?" she yawned. "What is it?"

"Bonnie and Louis are engaged to be married."

"Really? When?"

"May."

"Wow." They were both silent until Leila said, groggily, "That's good, right?"

"Yes. But Louis is also accepting a job in Pittsburgh."

"How far away is that?"

"Three hundred miles. About a five-hour drive."

"Oh. Wow. That stinks."

"Yeah."

"Well, how do you feel about that?"

Myles retorted, "How do you think I feel about it?"

"You tell me."

He exhaled with emotion. "I feel like I'm being phased out of their lives ... out of Peter's life. It's foolishness on my part—I know. Peter should have a father, not just a grandfather."

"You'll still see him, won't you?"

"Of course. But with that distance, it may as well be six hundred miles away."

"Will you stay in Philadelphia, or move with them?"

"For one thing, I have not been invited to move with them, and I'm not certain that would be prudent. For all I know, they could move every year. Would I automatically follow, hoping that I'd fit into their life somehow? I've been relegated to such a marginal part of Bonnie's life as it is. If it wasn't for Peter, I doubt our relationship would have amounted to anything of consequence. She is so much like her mother." There, he'd said it. *So much like her mother.* No qualms about up and leaving once she was through with him —after she had made him believe he was lovable.

"I'm so sorry, Clarence."

He heaved a long sigh filled with more pain than he had allowed himself to acknowledge until this moment. "I've been thinking about what you said ... about distance perhaps being good for my relationship with Bonnie. You may be right."

Leila remained silent.

It didn't take much imagination to know what thought he had planted and now germinated in Leila's mind, but he hesitated to ask.

"You're awfully quiet," he said.

"Yes, well, you already know what I think." Indeed, he did know, but in the most poignant way, he needed to hear her say that *she* wanted him, that she would be the constant in his life. He needed to hear the words without her being prompted.

"Clarence," she said with such tenderness that it brought tears to his eyes. "… move up here with me."

He rallied his composure. "That is an option, I suppose."

"I just get so lonely for you sometimes. I feel as if I'll never have the closeness I want with someone like Ian … or with you …."

Could she actually be making a correlation between Ian and him, in the way Bonnie had implied? Dare he even consider the notion seriously, let alone the practicality—or *im*practicality of it? To be with Leila, enfolded in her youth, beside her every night? For a certainty, she would be loyal, even in his old age, even when his flesh withered. When his own child could abandon him—and she surely would if he took up with her younger rival—Leila would never leave him. But, in his heart, as much as it pained him, it defied logic. In fact, it defied the life Leila should have. He could never push that boundary. Although their relationship had evolved into something exceptional, in too many ways he was still and would always be her teacher—her superior. He could not betray the fiduciary aspect of that equation. And he would not indulge the fantasy of it a moment longer.

He stifled his frustration. "Well, you likely wouldn't be so lonely if you didn't stay holed up in theaters or in your house. The best way to meet someone is to go out to places you enjoy. That's where you'll find other like-minded individuals. It wouldn't kill you to go to a museum or even eat out once in a while."

"You don't know—it *could* kill me."

"Don't be ridiculous. Has it ever occurred to you that your soul mate could be right down the road? You'll never know if you don't get out—and not just to the movies with all the other heliophobics." As soon as he said it, he realized he needed to apply his own counsel.

It TOOK MOST OF THE DAY FOR LEILA TO mobilize. She not only washed her hair, but she brushed on a smidge of mascara and a swipe of blush. No point in looking like a zombie.

At Clarence's suggestion, she decided to get out of the house. She had no intention of speaking to another human being except to order a glass of wine and perhaps a bowl of French onion soup. She particularly liked the ambiance of Peter Christian's Tavern, the local English-style eatery that served 'Victuals & Strong Waters.' It would be easy to disappear into a dimly lit corner and simply be.

"Table for one. A booth would be nice." Leila said to the hostess.

Tucked around the corner from the entrance, and in sight of the bar, the young woman laid a menu on a small, lacquered wood-slab table. "Is this alright?"

Leila smiled with a nod and sat.

"May I start you off with a drink?"

"A glass of Pinot noir."

"I'll need to see some I.D."

She fished out her wallet. As the waitress checked dates, Leila glanced at the bar. Her eyes met Jared's and then flashed away. How could he be here? She couldn't keep her lips from curling. He must have taken that as an invitation, because in three heartbeats, he stood beside her table, his beer mug in hand.

"Mind if I join you?" he asked, brow cocked.

"Not at all."

He placed his dark beer on her table with its thick, frothy head.

"What are you drinking?" she asked.

"Guinness. Ever had it?"

"No."

He pushed it toward her. "Have a sip."

She brought the mug to her lips and her eyes to his. "Mmmm. Good. How come everywhere I go, you're there?"

"How come everywhere *I* go, *you* show up? I didn't take you for a stalker."

She licked the foam from her lip.

"Missed some." He moved as if he might wipe it, but stopped.

She used her own finger. "How would I possibly know where you'd be?"

"Perhaps we just like the same places."

"I've never seen you in here before—not that I come here a lot."

"I don't usually hang out at the bar."

"Special occasion?"

He sipped his stout with his eyes still on her—his brow resolutely level—but said nothing, even after he set the beer down. The waitress placed Leila's wine in front of her as he slouched into his seat.

"So, when's your wife coming home?" Leila said.

"Don't know yet." He glanced at her hand. "I see the ring is still off. Still carrying it around in your pocket?"

"No. Does she leave you alone often?"

"*Often* is a subjective word. So anyway, not wearing your ring, that's progress, but I'm telling you—two years. You need to give yourself more time before you can get serious about anyone."

"And what makes you such an expert on relationships?"

"I'm no expert. But I do read, and I'm an astute observer of human nature. I talk to people. I'm not sure why, but people tell me things."

"Is that right?"

"Maybe it's because I go into their homes. They entrust me with all their valuables. I mean, I'm bonded and everything, but people just seem to feel like I'm trustworthy, and so they open up to me as if I were their therapist or something."

"Well, you do have a way about you. And you come across as if you know what you're talking about."

"To be honest, I don't say much. I just listen and ask questions about what they tell me."

"For instance?"

"Okay. I tune for an older woman. Her husband died ten years ago. She told me that for two whole years, she still expected her husband to walk through the door at any time. It's like her brain couldn't begin to process the loss for two years. So, I store the information. Next time I meet a widow or widower, and they start opening up, I ask them about the two-year thing, and they more or less confirm it, though it is different for everyone. People need to share their experience. Even if the one they're sharing it with can't relate, they just want to know that someone is interested in their journey."

"Why do you even care?"

"I don't know. I guess I just want to leave people feeling good. I want to understand why people do what they do."

"Why?"

"Because I learn something from everyone I interact with."

"You should go into psychology."

"Yeah, or arbitration, or mining, or biological research—or maybe I could be an Australian jackaroo."

"Your wife is fortunate to have someone so interested."

He drew in a long breath and exhaled slowly, "Yeah ...."

Leila wished she could come up with the right question to get him talking about his personal experience rather than someone else's.

"So where're you headed this winter?" he asked.

"Down to Mississippi."

"Friend or family?"

"Grandmother, though I hope to see an old friend, too."

"Do you still keep in touch with Ian's old friend? What was his name—Mills or something?"

"Clarence Myles. You know about him?"

"Ian told me about his heart attack. The first time I tuned was less than a month afterward. Ian was still pretty shook up. In fact, I think I came while you were down visiting him."

"Wow. You have a really good memory."

He shrugged. "Ian really impressed me …."

"So, what information did you extract from *him*?"

He winked. "Can't tell you—I'd have to kill you."

"Did he talk about me?"

"Maybe."

"We were having a bad time then."

"I know. I admired how he handled all that."

"All that?"

"I'm sorry. I said too much."

Leila folded her arms across her chest. She felt naked. "Okay, now you really need to tell me what he told you, or I'm going to assume the worst."

He squinted. "Okay, but prepare to die."

Leila rolled her eyes as he grinned and then turned serious.

"He only told me that Myles' heart attack brought out a lot of your fears. That as much as he wanted to be the one to help you through it, he knew you needed to see your friend. I've always been struck by his love for you. His willingness to sacrifice his own pride for what was best for you. He set a standard I've never forgotten."

Tears filled Leila's eyes.

He glanced away. "I'm sorry. I didn't mean to stir up stuff."

"No. It's okay. It actually makes me happy to hear you say those things. Sometimes it feels like he was just some fantasy man. Could he have really been *that* wonderful?"

"He was a good man. Your friend Myles also sounded like a good man. I wish I could meet him someday."

"That would be interesting …."

COPPER PIPES TRAVELED ALONG THE FLOOR joists overhead, weaving in and out and up and around like a Dr. Seuss illustration. Valves and levers jutted from fittings and juxtaposed joints. Leila knew which tank heated the water, and she had been there when Ian installed the water pump, but she didn't trust her memory well enough to gamble on frozen pipes. Jared was willing to come and take care of it, but she had hoped she could handle it on her own. After an indecisive minute, she left the utility room, walked through Ian's darkroom, headed upstairs, and dialed Jared's number. An hour later, he arrived.

"I apologize again for not calling sooner." She hung his coat on the door-side hook. "I thought I could handle it myself."

"I told you—it's not a problem."

"No tools?"

"I won't shut things down tonight. You'll want water until you leave. I just need to know where stuff is, and then I'll come back tomorrow after you've gone and do what needs doing."

Leila led Jared downstairs. As they walked through Ian's lit studio, he slowed, looking at the displayed photography.

She showed him the layout of the utility room, and a minute later, they made their way back through Ian's work area.

"Wow," Jared said, "Ian did some real nice work. I haven't seen these."

"Yeah. I was just compiling some to bring down to my grandmother's. She's part owner of a gallery in New Orleans and one that's due to open in Boston this spring. I'm having a little trouble choosing."

"I've got an objective eye." He exaggerated the arc of his one objective eye.

"You wouldn't mind? You've got the time?"

"Sure. I have a few minutes."

"Okay." Leila opened the black portfolio on the worktable and fanned out at least a dozen samples. "I have no idea how many to include."

"Better to bring too many than not enough," he said, leafing through them. He paused a little longer at some than others. "These are all great. Striking compositions. None of you?"

"No. No one wants to look at me."

"I wouldn't be so sure. If Ian was this good with these subjects, I bet there are at least a couple of you that might complement his portfolio. When you have an intimate rapport with your subject, that spark can't help but come across. You can't hide chemistry."

"I suppose. I mean, I know that's true. I would just feel weird having the general public looking at me."

"They wouldn't be looking at you. Just a facsimile."

"I don't know …."

"Why don't you let me have a look at a couple? I'll evaluate them based on composition and stuff."

Jared's disarming way made her want to show him what she considered some of Ian's best work. "I guess I just don't want you to think I'm a narcissist or something."

"Too late. Step aside."

"Okay," she moved to the file cabinet and removed the master folder labeled *Leila*. Furtively, she peered inside and slipped out one of her favorites. One she had shown Clarence last summer, of her coming out of the water. She laid it on the table.

Jared adjusted the retractable lamp. "Nice—Now, something for comparison?"

"Okay, here's a couple more."

"Your hair was long."

"And how does that affect the composition?"

"It doesn't. I'm just sayin'." He divided his attention between the three on the table and then glanced at the folder, snug to her chest. He gave the file a tap. "You're holding out. Are there shots in there I *shouldn't* see—you know, nudes or something?"

"No. Those are in a special folder."

"Then how 'bout it?" His brow cocked. "Don't worry, I won't think you're conceited."

"Fine." She surrendered the file, which contained several subfolders.

"*Girl Running*." He glanced at her. "That's right. You run."

"He took those the day we met, though he didn't know it was me till he developed them."

"So, how exactly did you meet?"

"I had a flat. He changed my tire."

"Romantic. I like this one, where your feet aren't touching the ground."

"One of our favorites, too."

After a moment, he moved back to the file, "Hmm …," he said, thumbing the tab, "*Negotiations* …." Both brows arched. "Sounds interesting. May I?"

She nodded. Even after five years, she still blushed at the memory of posing for Ian in his studio, but now her blush was at the idea of sharing these with Jared. Why did she want him to see her? Did she simply want him to comprehend her loss?

"You look so young. Downright virginal."

"I was only seventeen."

He pulled out one in particular. A full-body shot—three-quarter, over-the-shoulder view. "Wow. This one is amazing. He placed it on top of the other portfolio designates."

"It is a pretty good composition."

"It's not just that. Whatever it was you two were *negotiating*—" he tapped the photo as his brow flicked, "—high stakes beam from your face."

Jared was right. Something about him made her want to open up to him. Was it simply his nonjudgmental attitude? "He was a coach. I was a student."

"I thought it was likely something unconventional."

"That doesn't creep you out?"

"Knowing what I do of the two of you, there were probably some extenuating circumstances."

"Well, you sure know a whole lot more about Ian and me than most people do. We're—I mean we *were*—that is, I am —pretty private."

Jared swiveled the stool to face her. "Listen, I hope I didn't make you uncomfortable the other night, telling you that Ian and I had talked about you."

"I just feel a little bit at a disadvantage." She wanted to step closer but didn't. "You seem to already know me, but I don't really know much about you."

"Yeah, that's true."

"Why don't you ever talk about your wife?"

"I guess that's kind of a sore subject for me right now. She and I are working through a few problems of our own. I guess it would be like if Ian had confided his marital issues to a pretty young piano tuner—that would have bothered you a whole lot more than talking to some dopey schlep like me."

"Yeah. For sure."

"So don't worry about it." He winked. "I'm confidential. And as for Sarah and me, I'm sure we'll work things out just like the two of you did."

"Well, I hope so—for Emily's sake."

"Yeah. She's a pretty big motivator for such a little package."

Chapter 19

Natchez, Mississippi

I N A FULL OUT RUN, LEILA COUNTED OFF EACH gnarly live oak on the long stretch of red soil. Spanish moss clung to outstretched branches, each reaching for their partner across the driveway. The warm Mississippi breeze swayed tresses of wispy green as shafts of sunlight sliced through the hazy morning. Leila's mind charged with pleasure.

Rounding a bend, she left her grandmother's Greek revival, antebellum plantation house in the distance. Had Angela referred to it as such during their chauffeured drive from the airport, rather than simply calling it 'home,' Leila would have been better prepared for the sight of it. Even that morning while she stretched under the front balcony, surveying the span of six massive columns, her senses reeled as she peered down the tree-lined drive.

New Hampshire and everyone in it seemed a million miles away. Here on the far outskirts of historic Natchez, a sleepy town on the high fertile banks overlooking the Mississippi River, Leila's imagination soared. She couldn't wait to capture it on paper.

And her grandmother! Miss Angela Phillips managed to pull off fiercely independent and Southern belle in one graceful swoop. Leila had squirmed at the stereotypical black butler. He hadn't appeared frail, yet she respected the gray that wove its way through his hair. He shouldn't have had to carry her luggage when she was able. When Leila had made to grab her garment bag, Garrison's crinkled eyes smiled as he reclaimed it.

"I have it, Miss." His voice resonated like a beautiful bass cello.

"If you think you are going to reform him, think again," Angela chuckled. "And don't worry—he makes far better than minimum wage."

Garrison winked at Leila. She didn't know quite what to think of Garrison, but she liked him. Leila thought she also liked her grandmother but found Angela increasingly presumptuous.

"So little luggage for a month," Angela had remarked, as if Leila actually planned to stay a full month. They followed Garrison up the sweeping half-circle staircase, which split left and right at the first landing. They veered left.

Leila had given her usual response. "I'm a minimalist."

"Well, we'll see what we can do about that while you're here." Perhaps Angela had only been testing Leila's willingness to be doted on, but again, it seemed presumptuous.

Leila established her first boundary. "I don't need you to buy me clothes I'll never wear."

Garrison hung her bag in the cherry armoire and placed her suitcase on the blanket chest at the foot of the canopied double bed.

"Thank you, Garrison," Angela said. "Please, let Jenny know we'll have dinner at five."

"Yes, Miss. Will Miss Leila need help unpacking?"

"No, thank you," Leila shot back. "I don't need to be waited on."

Garrison chuckled, giving Leila a final long stare. He shook his head and cast Angela a smile.

"That will be *all*, Garrison," Angela frowned good-naturedly and then turned her attention to Leila. "I'll leave you to freshen up a bit, then."

The wood floors creaked as Leila walked the perimeter of the worn carpet, like so many others who had paced before her. A span of floor-to-ceiling windows—a set of French doors—accessed a balcony. She stepped out, overlooking the vast side and back gardens. Statues and dormant fountains protruded like tombstones from the thick ground cover of latent rosebushes, magnolias, and other yet-to-bloom shrubberies, all gilt in late afternoon light.

With an hour before dinner, Leila showered and lay down. The sun cast long shadows across the bed. Unable to rest, she scanned the large room, formally appointed with antiques of an era she could not name. Ornate carvings of rosettes and pineapples embellished the deep reddish wood furniture, all polished to a luster like her piano. The aroma of what she imagined was tobacco clung to the dusky atmosphere; the room felt full yet open.

The surroundings sparked her creativity. To capture in watercolor on paper everything that inundated her senses would be the epitome of artistic achievement. She was glad to have packed a few art supplies. She also wished she had brought along something more ladylike to wear for dinner.

She laid her jeans on the bed, and slipped into her white linen shirt. Standing pantless in front of the full-length mirror, Leila felt plain and completely unadorned compared to her elegant surroundings. *Oh well.* She stepped into denim and pulled its snugness up over her hips. *These will have to do.*

Checking her watch, Leila left her room. She paused outside her door and visually traced the balcony that wrapped around the entire second story, except for just above the front foyer. On the opposite side of the wide-open space, corresponding doors ran the length of the railing. More bedrooms, no doubt. She wondered which room might be Angela's, and which room Clarence might occupy once he arrived—perhaps one of the three remaining rooms on Leila's side of the balcony.

Running her hand along the rail, she followed it to the top landing at the back corner of the house and wound her way down to the polished marble-floored foyer. Massive raised-panel doors with beveled glass sidelights stood before her. Garrison appeared from behind the staircase.

"Miss Angela is this way, Miss." He directed Leila, leading her to the rear corner.

He opened the large door to the dining room. Angela sat at the head of an elongated table formally set with more chairs than Leila was inclined to count.

"And prompt, too," Angela remarked. "Tell me, how do you like my house?"

Leila perused the room and exhaled. "It's more beautiful than any house I've ever seen."

"No doubt. But how do you *like* it?"

"What's not to like? Unless you have to clean it."

"Hmm," Angela hummed in an almost wistful way. She did that a lot.

"How old is it?"

"Built in 1820, by my great-great-grandfather, Virgil Phillips. That makes me fifth generation," she stated, as though the admission were tedious.

"Wow." Leila exhaled as Garrison served clear consommé.

"Yes. Quite astonishing. And to assure that it remains the lofty Phillips Estate, my father placed half of his fortune in trust for the maintenance of his ancestral domain, into—" she drawled with exaggerated Southern inflection, "—per-pe-*tuity*."

Leila raised a curious brow. "But you haven't always lived here, have you?"

"Hmm .... No, I haven't. Not from the age twenty and until I was past forty." Angela did not need to elaborate on the reason why—on that much Joe, Angela's illegitimate and black son, had informed Leila. "Having conceived me later in life, my parents were both quite elderly by that time. So when the opportunity came for me to do the right thing and care for them in their old age, I was permitted to come home."

Leila nodded, not judging whether altruism or desire for reinstatement as the sole benefactor of her father's fortune had spurred Angela's daughterly attentiveness.

"Thank you, Garrison," Angela said as he removed bowls and set dinner plates before them. "I travel frequently, and so live here only part of the year. Mostly during winter. It makes a lovely place to come home to. And even lovelier for throwing dinner parties."

Leila knew what was coming next.

"How would you feel about a dinner party, dear, so I can show you off to my friends?"

Leila rolled her eyes sideways. "From what I understand, plans are already underway, and invitations have already been sent."

Angela winked. "Indeed. Then you've spoken with Clarence. You'll be happy to know he plans to attend."

"I know. I understand you're also providing accommodations here."

She smiled demurely. "And why wouldn't I, with all this spare room? It's simply good manners."

Leila smiled at the idea of Clarence staying there, though it stirred the slightest apprehension. Perhaps Leila hadn't sufficiently sorted through her own feelings for him. Or was it the idea of sharing him with her grandmother?

Angela rested her hand on Leila's. "Have you something elegant to wear?"

"To be honest, I'm not sure what constitutes elegant. I doubt I have anything you'd want me seen in."

"That's easily cared for. What style do you like?"

"Simple."

"Perhaps vintage?"

"Perhaps."

"Hmm ...." She rubbed her hands with glee. "I have a whole closet of designer vintage. You'll have to give it a look. Surely there'll be something to your liking."

The two chatted about Natchez history during the remainder of dinner. Angela exuded disparagement toward her Southern heritage, yet in her Southernly proper demeanor, she belied her disdain.

"Shall we retire to the drawing room?" Angela rose from the table and pushed open a large adjoining door.

The drawing room overlooked the front yard and smelled of leather and old books, like generations of gentlemen smoking long cigars and breathing bourbon and Southern politics. Garrison had already lit a small ambient fire and switched on several floor lamps. Invited to sit, Leila chose one of three leather armchairs. She pictured those plantation owners who could never have imagined the likes of these two women brazenly sitting in their gender-restricted sanctuary, where they discussed manly things while women retired to the parlor, fanning away the midday heat and sipping ice tea from sweating glasses.

Broken in and smoothly patinated, the chair creaked as Leila sat and breathed in. The ambiance reminded her of Clarence, and even more so as Angela stood before varying shades of amber liquid in cut glass decanters.

"It's cognac, isn't it?" Angela pulled the stopper from one, and poured.

"Yes."

Angela sat opposite her granddaughter, staring. "You really have no idea, do you—just how much you resemble me when I was your age? All but the hair color." Angela seemed beyond pleased. "If anyone doubted your lineage, they need only compare us, side by side. Or better yet, with a photo of me way back when."

"I'd like to see them sometime."

"Would you? But of course you would. We'll do that tomorrow." She flicked a gesture. "Oh, wait. That probably won't work. Fran is coming by tomorrow morning on his way down to the gallery in New Orleans. Who knows how long he'll be here. Much of the day I suppose."

"Fran?"

"François Goulet. I mentioned him in my correspondence. He and his son are my business partners in the gallery."

Leila sipped and pursed her lips.

"Don't worry," her grandmother continued. "He's no bother. In fact, he's quite entertaining. You won't be bored. How could you be? So many new things to see and new people to meet."

Leila flashed alarm.

"Darling, you mustn't act like a coon in the headlights every time I mention meeting people. A little growth in that direction would do you good. A woman can never have too many connections."

"I'm not afraid of meeting people. I just … I don't like hordes of them."

"Nonsense, dear. What you do not seem to realize is that you are quite up to it. You're articulate, well mannered—you know the proper fork and spoon to use at dinner—and look at you. Your beauty and poise give you the advantage in any situation if you use it judiciously."

Leila recoiled.

Angela chuckled softly. "Surely you realize this world is ruled by money and beauty. If you don't have one, by God you'd better have the other and know how to use it."

Leila's eyes darted at her grandmother's flagrant conviction.

Angela sipped her glass and inhaled a higher tilt of her chin. "At twenty, I may have been pregnant, but I was *never* barefoot."

"You don't really believe that do you? That you need money or beauty to be happy?"

"I didn't say you need it to be *happy*, did I?"

"No, but you implied it."

"Leila, money and beauty won't provide you with happiness—that's true. But being self-sufficient—knowing you can provide for yourself under any circumstance—having money or beauty can help you to that end. Beauty is a natural resource that is at your disposal. And money, that is a protection. If you have one or the other—better yet, both—use it to safeguard your independence."

Leila's bemusement must have shown on her face.

With a quick turn, Angela inquired, "Tell me dear, how much money *do* you have?"

Leila's eyes came squarely back to her grandmother. "Excuse me?"

"I asked, how much money do you have?"

"I have enough that I can visit you for several weeks without setting me back, or worrying if I have a job when I get home." Reclaiming her boundary, she glared. "And if you'll pardon me for saying so, that question—in any circle —is just rude."

Angela Phillips smiled with apparent satisfaction. "You answered well, my dear. A woman should never—ever— divulge how much money she has or has not. Better that you disclose the deepest secrets of your heart than your financial assets—or lack thereof."

Later that night as she lay in bed, Leila distracted herself from thoughts of Clarence, pondering her grandmother's philosophies on womanhood and life. Now, as she continued her morning run, Angela's words came back to Leila. She wondered about the world into which she had just stepped. From Leila's standpoint, it seemed surreal, completely out of sync with her life. Although her grandmother seemed eager to have her participate, Leila could not imagine herself as a part of it. Just the same, it would be an interesting adventure. The thought of meeting new people was strangely appealing, like a game of no consequence. After all, what did Leila have at stake but a little time?

Sweat gathered at her hairline as she sprinted in the sixty-degree humidity. Moisture trickled down her neck and the sides of her face as she continued to run at full speed back toward the house. From behind, an engine and tires crunching gravel approached. She maintained her forward focus and did not slacken her pace as the late-model Mercedes-Benz decelerated, passed, and progressed around the bend and down the long driveway toward the circular front dooryard.

Soon navigating the bend herself, Leila slowed to a jog and then a cool-down walk. Two people emerged from the car. After a moment, Angela stepped out onto the front porch. Leila's grandmother embraced one visitor. Her cooing voice carried, conveying surprise and pleasure as she hugged the other. With a gesture from Angela, the two men turned in Leila's direction, putting her on edge. What did it matter if Miss Angela Phillips wished to display her like a new toy? Neither their curiosity nor their approval was of any consequence to Leila. It should be easy enough to play along nicely, like a good guest.

Mopping her face with her sweatshirt sleeve, Leila approached the three on the front steps. She wiped her hands on her shorts and smiled with her grandmother's demureness.

"François Goulet, I present my granddaughter, Leila Brigham."

Leila extended her hand to meet his.

"It's truly a pleasure." He had an accent as thick as his wavy white hair and looked to be in his sixties, near Angela's age.

Angela continued, "And this is his son, André."

He bent to look her in the eye, and brought her hand to his lips. He seemed so pretentious that Leila had a hard time suppressing her usual eye roll.

She played along with a head tilt. "It's a pleasure to meet you."

"The pleasure is all mine." His accent was only vaguely Southern, if at all. His curly brown hair grazed his upturned collar, and the sleeves of his sport coat rolled up his forearms. She caught a whiff of what she assumed was expensive aftershave.

"I apologize for my appearance," she said, for her grandmother's benefit. "If you'll excuse me."

"Not at all," François said as Leila stepped past them and in through the opened door. She overheard him say, "Uncanny. I could fall in love all over again."

🌿CHAPTER 20

H URRYING SO AS NOT TO KEEP THEM FROM breakfast, Leila quickly showered. She made no attempt at make-up, and, in twenty minutes, loped her way downstairs. She ran fingers through damp hair as she stepped into the dining room, wearing jeans and a plain T-shirt.

Again, Angela sat at the head of the table with François at her right and André to her left. As Leila entered the room, both men politely rose and sat as she took her seat at her grandmother's right.

"I'm sorry to keep you waiting." Leila expected Angela might be annoyed with her cavalier deportment, yet the amused curl of the woman's lip said otherwise.

Garrison served omelets and croissants with a side dish of grits and gravy. Leila ate quietly as the three speculated on the success of their Boston venture. In fact, François had just purchased a townhouse on Beacon Hill to be near their Newbury Street gallery. André intended to take up full-time residence there. As the three friends chatted, Leila hypothesized on the relationship between Angela and François. Their interaction seemed familiar—flirtatious yet nonsexual. With little more to be learned during breakfast, she switched her surmising to André. She caught him looking at her, brazenly waiting to be acknowledged. Leila offered a polite smile and then refocused on devouring her grits.

"I understand you're an artist," André said, recapturing her attention.

Licking gravy from her fork, she looked up from her empty dish. "That's an opinion, I suppose."

"I hope you brought along a sampling so that we might see for ourselves."

She tried to smooth her smirk to a smile. "Unfortunately, I seem to have left them in New Hampshire. Perhaps some other time?"

Angela flashed her a look that could have passed for one of Clarence's censures. "I can attest to her skill, although I believe she could benefit from some formal instruction."

"No doubt I could if I were actually inclined."

"I happen to know an accomplished artist who could be persuaded to give you a few pointers."

"You assume that I hope to accomplish something with my watercoloring—beyond self-gratification." Without smiling, Leila looked squarely at her grandmother. "I don't."

At the wide eyes of her audience, she reclaimed her polite smile. "But thanks so much for your interest, Angela ... really."

Angela squinted in the most ladylike and forceful way. "Leila, it would serve every young lady to be accomplished in as many endeavors as possible. Especially ones for which she has an aptitude."

André grinned at the clash of strong wills, as did François. The elder cut in, "Well, I think her most obvious assets are serving her quite well."

Unsure of what he implied, Leila was grateful that Angela now backed off.

"At any rate," François continued, "we look forward to seeing your late husband's work."

FLOORS CREAKED AND A DRAFT COOLED THE afternoon air as Leila followed her grandmother from room to room. Miss Phillips' visitors had departed for New Orleans by early afternoon, and so the ladies of the house spent the better part of remaining daylight touring the grounds of the old plantation and then the house. Leila lost count of the bedrooms—not to mention the billiard parlor, conservatory, ladies parlor, and modest ballroom with a Steinway grand, in addition to the kitchen and servant quarters.

Angela explained, "Garrison and Jenny, the cook, are the only full-time, live-in help. Winnie, the housekeeper, comes a couple times a week. The gardener is more or less seasonal. Then, there is the occasional carpenter and maintenance man, but Garrison sees to all that."

"The two of you seem to have a comfortable rapport."

"Yes, well we've known each other practically all our lives. You see, my father employed his father. Garrison and I were childhood playmates, until ... well, until Father felt it was, hmm ... unseemly ...." She gazed off and then lightened her expression. "Now then, shall we have a look at something for you to wear to the dinner party?"

Angela led her upstairs to the master quarters, centered at the back of the house and overlooking more gardens.

"I don't sleep in here. It was my parents' room and I never cared for it." Angela scanned the room with a shiver. "I had Garrison bring out some of my nicer party dresses from my younger days. If you can't find anything you like, we'll shop tomorrow."

Angela left her alone. Leila tried on dress after dress, evening attire and daywear. They could have all been tailored to fit Leila. She'd never given fashion much thought, but Angela's vintage wardrobe felt like long lost friends, bolstering and clarifying her self-image. She wasn't sure why she should feel surprised, but she liked her grandmother's taste. Very much. After an hour or so, she slipped back into her own clothes and joined Angela for dinner.

"Did you find anything that suits you?" Angela asked.

"Yes, several—" she minimized, "—but one I especially like."

"Don't tell me which. Surprise me. And did you find the shoes?"

"Yes."

"And they fit?"

"Yes."

"And tell me, what did you think of André Goulet?"

Leila hesitated. "Uh … he's handsome."

"Yes, just like his father—in appearance."

"Are they alike in other ways?"

"Hardly. Although not to André's discredit, mind you. He has a very good business sense. And I can tell he has an eye for you."

Leila glanced at Angela, wide-eyed. "Why would you assume that? We spent only a couple hours together."

"For one thing, he likes a pretty face. In fact, he rarely arrives here without some lovely on his arm. And I'm certain he will arrive on Saturday without a date in hopes of your attention."

Leila's countenance fell with apprehension.

"Don't look so panicked dear. He's harmless enough as long as you don't fall for him. In fact, you should be quite flattered. He's a desirable catch by anyone's standard."

"Wonderful," Leila said, though it did occur to her that André might be just the distraction she needed. If only he weren't so *not* her type.

Over the course of dinner, Angela divulged that she expected nearly forty guests, some closer to Leila's age, but mostly older.

"My dear old friend, Marvelle, is looking forward to meeting you." Angela chuckled. "I can't wait to see how you get on with her."

Leila looked up from her plate. "Why? What's the matter with her?"

Angela smiled. "You'll love her. She's a dear old soul."

Leila mimicked her grandmother's *hmm* …. "Will there be music?"

"Of course."

"Blues?"

"No, dear. Nothing quite so gauche. A jazz quartet. But I'm certain you'll enjoy them just the same."

"That'll be something to look forward to."

"Speaking of which—your guardian shall be arriving on Friday afternoon."

Leila made no attempt to hide her excitement. "I haven't seen him since Thanksgiving—I can't wait."

"I'm so pleased he accepted my invitation. And such a nice note he sent along …. His attendance will certainly make things more *interesting* for me." She smiled wistfully. "Hmm …."

"I hope you don't mind my saying, but it seems you could have all the *interesting* you want, without Clarence Myles."

"It would appear that way, wouldn't it? And yet here I am, still unmarried." She looked off longingly. "Silly … sometimes I'm actually hopeful that the perfect man might still come along—even at my age—just like a schoolgirl."

"Well, surely you've had opportunity, haven't you?"

"Of course. And many advantageous matches to be sure. But I guess I'm too much of a romantic … I actually wanted to marry for love."

"You *have* been in love, haven't you?"

"Oh yes. Many times. Unfortunately, the first man I loved was a Negro. The second turned out to be married. The third had just come out of divorce and decided his true preference was not female." She sighed. "The next was interested only in my inheritance. And the last ended up in prison for embezzlement. For the most part, a rather pathetic run of men."

Angela gave Leila an embarrassed look and then collected herself. "To be sure, I'm better off without a man. To be independent has always been more important than anything... but still...." She paused and brought her eyes back to Leila. "And look at you—so young with your whole life ahead of you." She smiled, placing her hand on Leila's. "Well, enough of that mush. I'm going to retire early this evening, so you may have free rein of the house. Help yourself to the liquor, if you like."

❧CHAPTER 21

BIDING TIME UNTIL CLARENCE'S ARRIVAL ON Friday, Leila ran each morning, shot photographs at daybreak and late afternoon, read, walked, and shared meals with her grandmother. She also painted in the yard and gardens, which was how she occupied herself on Friday morning.

Leila hunched over her work, sitting before the garden's centerpiece, a Grecian maiden perched in a dried-up fountain. Spanish moss grazed the greenish patina of the statue's shoulders, glowing in the gradient light of late afternoon. She loomed as guardian over Leila. Her watchful eye alerted the artist to unwanted attention approaching from behind.

Sensing an intrusion, Leila arched her aching back and quit with her paintbrush. She pulled the paper block to her chest. Cocking her head, she met an old woman's piercing eyes.

The woman frowned, folding her arms and taking an abrupt suck from her cigarette. Standing less than five foot, the well-into-her-eighties matron swept a strand of white hair up and poked it into the knot crowning her head. She drew a long drag from the cigarette that doubled as a gesturing baton, leaving a thin trail of smoke.

"Well?" the woman said.

Might this be Marvelle? Leila clutched her work even tighter.

The old woman flicked ash to the grass. Grinding it under foot, she thrust out her hand with all the authority of God.

"Don't be ridiculous, child! Let me see!" Her smoker's voice chopped with a Bostonian inflection.

Taken aback, Leila glowered at the encroachment while sizing up her opponent. A long, loose-fitting tunic hung from a buttoned neckline and square shoulders, covering most of her shapeless trousers. She looked well on her way to the grave, and yet Leila hesitated to disobey.

Crooked fingers snatched the tablet, held it at a distance, and then brought it closer to her spectacles. "You're overworking it, child."

"Yeah?" No news there.

"And you're including too much detail."

"I like detail."

"That's fine, da'ling, but until you can make your point with a few strokes, you have no business with detail. You haven't earned the right."

Leila's attention darted from fierce wrinkles to her own disappointing efforts. Was this feisty and officious bit-of-a-woman the 'dear old soul' of whom her grandmother had spoken?

"However, your perspective and proportions are impeccable. Perhaps you ought to stick with sketching and not waste your time with paint."

"I like to paint."

"Could have fooled me. You look as uncomfortable as a cat in a cage, and your work is as passionless as a peck on the cheek." She wielded the pad as though swatting mosquitoes and then shoved it back at Leila. "You can't tell me you're happy with this."

"I wasn't expecting a great work of art. It's just a pastime."

"Rubbish! What prevents you from greatness?"

"What?" Wide-eyed and then with a squint, Leila sat erect.

"Fear—that's what! When you're ready to own up to it, come and see me, da'ling." With that, the old woman spun on her heel and headed jauntily back toward the house, belying any readiness for the grave.

MYLES LEFT PHILADELPHIA IN BLUSTERING WIND and snow flurries. What a difference a thousand miles and a few hours made. Even inside the chauffeured and air-conditioned ride, he soaked in the sun's heat as they wound around back roads through gauzy veils of moss. Angela Phillips' invitation could not have come at a better time. Not only would he see his Leila, but also he harbored a glint of hope that Miss Phillips might bear some potential as a female of interest. In all honesty, he hadn't been able to define that interest as romantic, but in his loneliness he wished for something more intimate than Leila could provide.

Dusk had settled on the Delta and shaded the front porch where Leila sprung to her feet. Even before Myles emerged from the back seat, Leila stood ready to throw her arms around him.

He pressed his lips to her forehead and then held her at arm's distance. "You're letting your hair grow."

She beamed. "Why is my hair the first thing you always mention?"

"I suppose it's a man thing," he said. "You look wonderful."

"You look better than wonderful."

Myles retrieved his suitcase from the trunk, allowing Garrison to carry his garment bag. Leila looped her arm in his, leading him to the steps.

At that moment, Angela stepped out on the porch. His heart skipped as dimples graced her cheeks. Her loose outfit fluttered in the light breeze, skimming her svelte curves.

"Welcome," she said, extending her hand.

As soon as Myles lowered his suitcase to accept her hand, Garrison scooped up his bag.

"Angela." His lips grazed her fingers. "Always a pleasure."

"I do hope you have an appetite." Her eyes flickered. "But of course you'll want to freshen before dinner. Garrison will show you to your room."

She parted with them in the foyer, glancing back at him as she stepped into a doorway to the right. "Perhaps you'd care for a drink before dinner?"

"I would."

"Then join Leila, Marvelle, and me in the drawing room at six." She turned and disappeared behind the closing door.

He turned to Leila. "Who's Marvelle?"

Leila shook her head. "She is—well, let's just say she's a real piece of work."

As they ascended the stairs together, she whispered, "Isn't this amazing?"

Myles scanned the vast open space as their footfall echoed. He had to admit, it was impressive.

Garrison had already carted the luggage upstairs; he had veered right at the top landing and now emerged from one of the rooms.

"Mine's on the other side," Leila said. "Opposite yours."

Myles nodded.

Garrison stood in the open doorway as they approached. "May I assist you with anything further?"

"Thank you." Myles extended his hand. "That won't be necessary."

Garrison gripped his hand cordially and met Myles, level-eyed. "Very well, then."

"And thank you for meeting my plane." Neither man had loosened his grip.

Garrison smiled, releasing Myles. "Miss Angela wouldn't have it any other way."

Leila followed Myles into his room. She approached the open armoire. "Wow—a tux."

"It is a black-tie affair." Myles noticed not only his suitcase lying on the valet, but his hanging garments had been relieved of their cramped bag.

"You're going to look so handsome." She patted his Oxford collar. "Not that you don't always look handsome." She backed off, averting her eyes. "I guess I should let you— you know, do whatever you do to 'freshen up.'"

She turned to leave and he grabbed her hand. He studied her face a moment, awash with gratitude. "It's so good to see you, Leila."

Her cheeks colored. She swallowed, stood on her toes, and kissed his cheek. "I've missed you, Clarence."

ANGELA LEANED AGAINST THE LIQUOR CABINET and faced Marvelle. Scotch and water swirled in her glass before she sipped. Even as she swallowed, she could not suppress a smile.

Marvelle sat on leather, sampling her gin. "Well, you're in a rare mood."

"Oh, you know me, Marvelle—I can't help but get my hopes up."

"Well, da'ling, I haven't seen your hopes up since Al Capone, or whatever his name was."

Angela flashed disparagement and paced the drawing room.

Marvelle kicked one knee over the other. "He must really be something if he's caught your fancy."

"Hmm ...."

Clarence Myles looked even better than Angela remembered, though the circumstances surrounding their last two encounters had been anything but ideal. Funerals rarely brought out the best in anyone. Just the same, a man's most tender side—if he had one—was more likely to emerge at such a time, and what she observed of Leila's guardian impressed her. So principled and controlled and yet so compassionate and supportive. A true gentleman. He made her insides spin so fast they unraveled.

Marvelle raised her empty glass for a splash more. "And what is his connection to the girl?"

"He is—was—her guardian." Angela fetched the decanter and poured a quick shot. "She's quite attached to him."

"Attached?"

Angela considered using Leila's term, 'exceptional friends' but refrained. "He's like a father to her."

At that moment, the door opened and Leila stepped inside. She smoothed taupe linen that flared from her cinched waist. "I hope you don't mind. I helped myself to one of your vintage outfits."

Angela gasped, covering her mouth. "My Christian Dior... oh my...."

"I'm sorry—if I shouldn't have, I can go change."

"Oh, heavens no ... you are stunning. I dare say I'll never have my twenty-six-inch waist again. Please help yourself to any of them. They are all as good as yours." Seeing her granddaughter wearing the clothes she had once flaunted—and wearing them well ... Angela's heart ached for her lost youth. "A drink before dinner, my dear?"

"No, thanks." Leila cut a wide berth toward the front window, as if avoiding Marvelle. Angela would have made more of an attempt to facilitate a relationship between the two artists, but at that moment, the drawing room door opened. Garrison stepped aside allowing Clarence entry. He had dressed up for dinner, trim in his tweed and slacks, yet casually tieless. His clear blue eyes first fell upon Leila.

"This is a nice change," he said as Leila approached him.

She blushed. "It's Angela's."

"You wear it well." His eyes shifted to Angela's with a raised brow and flirtatious glint. "Stunning."

Many suitors had flattered Angela in the past, but she couldn't remember ever feeling so solicitous of any one man's attention.

She gestured toward the sitting dowager. "May I introduce my dear friend, Marvelle Harding—Marvelle, Clarence Myles."

Clarence approached and took her hand. "A pleasure, Ms. Harding."

Marvelle squinted hard, looking him over. "Indeed," she said. "So, you're a teacher."

"Yes."

"What subject?"

"Math."

She rejoined as if cross-examining him. "How many years?"

"Thirty-five."

"Do you like teaching or is it just a thirty-five year rut?"

"Please pardon my friend—she gets a little testy on her second gin." Angela secretly admired Marvelle's brash tactics.

"No pardon necessary—" Clarence came back. "I do enjoy teaching."

Marvelle threw her head and shoulders back. "Oh—the molding of young minds—breaking down walls—setting spirits free. It is truly a calling."

Angela hoped Clarence found Marvelle's dramatics as droll as she did. His eyes flashed back to Angela with amusement.

"May I offer you a drink?" she said. "It's cognac, isn't it?"

She had his full attention. "I'll drink whatever you're having."

🐦 LEILA'S SPOON CLANKED BONE CHINA AS THE four began their five-course dinner. Angela spoke something to Garrison while Marvelle tore a bit of bread and dipped it in her bowl. Leila looked up from her soup and successfully caught Clarence's eye. She kept her gaze fixed on him. Neither of them smiled and neither spoke. Perhaps it was just the lighting, the ambiance, or simply missing him, but the way he looked at her from across the table sent a frisson through her body and would not allow her to look away. His eyes danced with inquiry.

Her gaze fell back to her soup, wide and embarrassed that he might have caught a glimpse of something she herself couldn't quite understand, let alone admit.

"Is everything to your liking?" Angela asked, with some concern.

Leila quickly sipped a spoonful of soup. "Oh yes. French Onion is one of my favorites."

"And how about you, Clarence? How are you finding everything?"

He looked directly at her. "Very much to my liking."

Leila nearly choked at what likely would have brought her pleasure only months ago—her "guardian" and her grandmother obviously smitten and perhaps on the brink of a substantial relationship. Clarence had the right to it and so did Miss Angela Phillips, but why did it spark jealousy?

Marvelle shifted at Clarence's side. Leila caught the matron's blatant stare. Was the ancient woman making an estimation of the chemistry between Leila and her older friend? Had Leila's own disconcertion become obvious to onlookers? Rallying her poker face, Leila ignored her.

"So, what time will François and André be arriving tomorrow?" Leila said.

"François and André?" Clarence asked.

Angela replied, "François is an old friend and business partner. And André—I believe he is Leila's new suitor."

"Is that right?" Clarence again studied Leila with questioning eyes.

Angela's presumptuousness and Clarence's curiosity warranted only an eye roll and a huff but not as loud as the huff Marvelle let out.

"Oh! What fun!" The old woman threw her head back and clutched her flat chest.

🙚 MARVELLE WAS THE LAST OF THE GUESTS TO turn in. Not drowsy enough for sleep, Angela retired to the drawing room. She poured just enough bourbon to wet her tongue, and sat in front of fireplace ashes. A few embers still smoldered.

Behind her, the door opened and then closed. The ground glass stopper slipped from its neck and then liquid glugged. She waited.

Garrison took his usual seat beside her with his usual scotch.

Angela sighed. "Thank you so much for playing butler for me, yet again."

"Oh, I rather enjoy it," he chuckled. "You know I don't care for socializing with your company, but I do like being in the mix."

"You are too good to me, Garrison," she said, staring straight ahead. "You always have been."

They sipped quietly in the dim light. Garrison's sonorous voice peeled back the silence. "Are you looking forward to your dinner party?"

"Hmm …. Yes, though I feel a little out of sorts."

"It's not just another dinner party, is it."

"No. I'm afraid it feels more bittersweet than I expected." She sighed, "—so many memories."

"Can't change any of it, Angela."

"I know. God, I do know that." She shook her head. "I thought I had come to terms with Joseph, and how things turned out. In fact, I have. Hmm … but Leila … I'm seeing myself, way back then …."

"You mustn't ...."

Her weak smile blossomed into one of genuine affection. She placed her hand on his. "You have been my constant. Even when ...."

He interrupted, "Can't change it. No point in thinking of it."

Again, they sat in silence, but she couldn't stop thinking of it.

"Garrison," she said, looking at him and hoping to catch his truest emotion. "In your heart of hearts, will you be disappointed if things progress between Clarence Myles and me?"

He squeezed her hand. "All I've ever wanted was for you to be happy, Angel."

CHAPTER 22

L EILA PUSHED THE REMAINS OF A POACHED EGG
around in its cup and glanced at Clarence across from
her. She hadn't rested well, knowing Clarence slept in a
room across the balcony. If they had been at his house, they
would have talked late into the night, exhausted or not, but as
it was, he retired early with nothing more than a quick
goodnight. It wasn't as if he had stayed up talking to her
grandmother instead of her, so she couldn't label her 'off'
mood as jealousy, but as she lay alone in her bed last night,
she wished for his company—for his nearness—to fall asleep
to the rhythm of his breath as she had done with Ian.

Leila set her fork down as Miss Phillips pushed away
from the breakfast table.

"If you'll excuse me, I have a few details to go over with
Garrison." Angela lingered in Clarence's gaze. "I hope the
two of you will make yourselves at home."

"Thank you." He patted his mouth with the starched linen
as Angela stepped out of the room. With a smile, Clarence
turned his attention to Leila. "I do believe I'll go for a walk."

She had already been for her early morning run, but she
chimed in, "How about some company?"

He stood. "If you don't mind, sweetheart, I think I'd like

some time alone with my thoughts."

"Oh. Okay," she rose with him, feeling put out and then embarrassed at her possessiveness.

He stroked her arm and grinned. "Don't worry, I'll be back."

"I know. I just …."

"What?" he stepped closer, his head tipped. The inquisitive eyes she had seen at dinner stared down upon her.

He looked different to her—perhaps more relaxed, maybe younger. *Something* was different.

"It's nothing." Leila blushed. When he shot her his incisive squint, she turned away. "I have stuff to see to, anyhow."

He followed her out of the dining room. "You're sure?"

Sure that it's nothing? No. Sure that I have stuff to see to? "Of course." She was not accustomed to withholding thoughts or feelings from Clarence, but if she tried to put her anomalous emotion into words, it would have come out as *I want you!* Those words did not set well with her, and they would have freaked him out, for sure.

"Alright, then." He exited through the front door as she paused near the ballroom; familiar sounds of piano tuning lured her to its entrance. Perhaps she would spend a little time out on the back patio alone with her own thoughts. She needed to smooth her angst or agitation or whatever it was that coursed through her every time she looked into Clarence's eyes. As she stepped into the ballroom and walked past the Steinway on her way to the rear French doors, she smiled, thinking of Jared for the first time in days. She wondered how things were working out between him and Sarah.

Sitting under the trellis, where dormant planters and pillared railings bespoke antebellum grandeur, Leila tugged at a pair of her grandmother's vintage capris. She thought about Marvelle Harding. Leila had to admit, she was stagnating—maybe that was part of her angst. Was it fear that stood in her way as Marvelle asserted? Fear of unleashing her deepest desires? Fear of falling flat? Of rejection? Fear cut such a wide swath through so many aspects of her being. Fear. And boredom. And grief. Putting a name to her angst made no difference. It all left her in turmoil. And now, on top of all that, she had to contend with an uncomfortable yearning she could not define, yet somehow, fear also encroached upon it.

As the piano tuner tweaked the last few notes of the treble register, Leila rose and stood in the wide French doors. Large round, linen-clothed tables adorned the perimeter of the ballroom—seven in all, each seating six, still leaving sufficient space for a little dancing. Winnie, the housekeeper, along with an additional eight helpers—of varying age and race, male and female—wearing pressed black and starched white, set the tables and folded napkins.

Leila ambled over to the piano as the tuner left. She took the bench and stared out at the patio. Impulsively, she struck middle-C. Clean and crisp. Without a thought, she played a few chords, and then hammered out a long string of bluesy notes, surprised at how easily they came. Perhaps Mississippi—home of the Delta Blues—was in her blood.

Several of the staff girls giggled. Rather than bashfully backing off, Leila continued playing a few seconds longer. The notes came with amazing fluidity. If only her painting flowed so well. Tapering off with some vibrato, she pushed away from the piano. A figure in the entrance caught her eye. Clarence.

Standing in the doorway as she rose, he crossed his arms and kept his eyes on her. She grinned in return as she strolled toward him.

"I had no idea," he said, bemused but smiling.

"You've always known that I play."

"Knowing and hearing for myself are quite different." His eyes flashed, as if taken aback. "I must say, I'm pleasantly surprised."

"Then you approve?"

"Of course."

Tentatively, she met his gaze. It wasn't as if he stepped back, but some shift in his stance put distance between them —even if slightly. At that moment, a tall, very dark-skinned man came up behind them in the doorway, and sidled past with a guitar case. Clarence and Leila stepped into the foyer.

"Perhaps later on they'll let you play." Clarence winked as another musician lugged a sax case past them and the bassist followed. The percussionist set one of his drums inside the doorway.

Leila smirked. "And you could accompany me on the saxophone?"

Clarence chuckled. They both understood the absurdity of the notion.

"There you are, Leila!" Miss Phillips called from the stairway, in her genteel way. "You should be upstairs getting dressed, dear."

🌊 BLACK SILK TAFFETA SLID OVER LEILA'S ARMS, beyond her bust, down her hips and just barely skimmed her knees. She liked the illusion of modesty the high front neckline provided—no one would be hoping for a glimpse of her unimpressive cleavage tonight. But oh! the view from behind. She had no idea what Miss Angela Phillips had worn for underpinnings back in the day, but there was no way the back, plunging to within a hair of her waist, would accommodate a bra. At least Leila was perky enough to pull it off—one of the blessings of small breasts. A matching wrap would provide coverage of her bare arms, but she didn't want to mess with accessories.

Three raps at Leila's door announced Angela's curiosity.

"Oh good. Just in time," Leila said. "Fasten my hook and tell me what I should do with my hair."

Angela's iridescent sapphire silk turned burgundy as she brought her hand to her lips. "Oh, Leila. I so hoped you'd choose that one. I was afraid you might find the back a little risqué for your taste, but I see you appreciate the drama of an exit."

And Clarence would appreciate Angela's plunge neckline. The long tapered sleeves and flared, mid-calf skirt provided an illusion of demureness. The silhouette reminded Leila of the outfit she had worn for Thanksgiving.

Leila stood at the full-length mirror brushing out her shoulder-length hair. Angela came up behind and connected the hook and eye at her waist.

"Sit at the dressing table," Angela said, taking the brush from her granddaughter. "A French twist—and a pearl choker."

"I already have one." Leila pulled open the drawer, revealing the gift from Clarence. "And earrings."

"Perfect." She swept her hair up and pinned it securely. "Come to my room and we'll spray it in place."

Leila followed Angela to her bedroom—the door beside Clarence's. It was about the size of Leila's room and smelled of her grandmother's jasmine perfume.

"Not too much spray. Men don't like that. They don't mind if a little wisp lets go. Makes you look far more accessible."

Leila frowned. "I don't want to look accessible."

"Looking accessible and being such are two entirely different things, my dear. Though it is my impression that this is a concept you inherently know. You are such a natural flirt."

"I am not a flirt."

"Wrong word choice. You simply possess that *je ne sais quoi* that men can't resist." She breathed in excitement. "Now go and put on some make-up, and I'll fetch you for a quick drink before guests arrive."

In her own room, Leila applied a little eye shadow and mascara, wondering about her grandmother's words. Did Leila possess a quality that inherently attracted men? It seemed conceited to think so. Just the same, had Clarence ever thought of her in those terms—as attractive? She stroked her pearls. What would he think of her dress? He seemed to like sultry. And this Dior was that and more. It made her look older, more sophisticated. Could her best friend ever view her as more than simply a *young* woman, but as a woman in her own right—a desirable woman? Again, she blushed for even entertaining the notion.

Angela cracked open the door, interrupting her application of rouge. "They've arrived dear. And, André—without a date. Hmm."

As they came out of her room, Leila glanced at the father and son in tuxedos and bow ties, chatting with Garrison beside the drawing room door. Leila wondered when Clarence might make his appearance—until he stepped out of the drawing room. Her heart jumped as he looked up at them and smiled. She wished the pleasure beaming from his eyes was meant exclusively for her.

Angela whispered, "Whenever possible, use the staircase to make your entrance—so dramatic—and nicely displays our feminine curves."

Leila tried not to rudely stare at only Clarence. After all, François also cut a nice figure. And then there was André. His hair no longer grazed his collar—it looked as if he had been to the barber. When she met his eyes, he held her gaze uncomfortably long, not that his stare was altogether unpleasant. Perhaps he would indeed make a fine distraction.

Clarence stepped forward and kissed Leila's cheek, though his attention was clearly divided. "You are both lovely."

Angela gestured at Leila. "Just like Audrey Hepburn, don't you think, Fran?"

"I'd say more like Miss Angela Phillips." François took Leila's hand and presented it to André.

As he accepted her hand, he only smiled, though his eyes sparked with approval as they moved up and down her body and back to her eyes.

Garrison escorted the small party into the drawing room. For several minutes, they chatted about the gallery before Marvelle stepped in.

"Ah! My two most favorite men in the world." She said, accepting polite kisses on each cheek. "I assume we shall all be seated together?"

"Of course," Angela said as Garrison entered the room, announcing that guests had begun to arrive.

In the foyer, Leila took her place between Angela and Clarence. When all guests had been greeted and introduced to the newcomers, they joined everyone in the ballroom. François and André mingled freely with Angela's friends. Leila assumed they were all well acquainted. The quartet had begun playing.

Angela ushered Leila and Clarence over to where Marvelle, François, and André gathered in front of the quartet.

"I think I'll get myself a drink," Leila said, glancing at the open bar.

"Allow me," Myles said.

"No, that's okay, you stay and visit."

Clarence did not balk. She half wished he had, but at the same time she was relieved he didn't insist.

Leila maneuvered her way to the bar. She wanted a stiff drink but opted for sparkling water with a wedge of lime instead—fizzy and refreshing, offering the illusion of worldliness. She took a long sip. Suppressing a belch, she strode back over to the group where they were discussing several pieces of Marvelle's artwork and which ones they planned to exhibit for the Boston grand opening. Leila feigned interest, sipping her drink with her back to the band.

"I'm contemplating a special piece for the big day." Marvelle waved her hand, swirling air as if fluffing the atmosphere might evoke inspiration. "I just don't know *what*, yet."

A few staccato notes introduced a lively number, diverting Leila's attention. She cast her view over her shoulder. The pianist caught her eye as he played solo for a minute, returning her glance with a smile.

"You find the musicians very distracting—" Marvelle rattled her amber liquid on rocks as though irritated. Everyone in their little group looked at Leila.

Angela interjected, "You'll have to forgive Leila. She was raised by *musicians*—"

"Not to be confused with being raised by wolves," Leila rejoined. "Although I'm sure Angela views it as all the same."

Marvelle eyed Leila with a dire squint. "And you play an instrument, da'ling?"

"Piano." Leila returned the old woman's penetrating stare. "But as uncomfortably as a cat in a cage and as dispassionately as a peck on the cheek."

Marvelle's eyes flickered. "And are you as uncomfortable and dispassionate about life in general?"

The four onlookers—particularly André—smiled with amusement.

Leila straightened her posture. "I'm contentedly uncomfortable, and vehemently dispassionate."

"Cagey girl! Tell me—are you ready to confront your fears?" she said as a server with a platter paused beside them.

"I'll tell you what I'm ready for—" Leila speared a shrimp. "An hors d'oeuvre to poke in my mouth before I divulge too much to people I barely know." Devouring the bit of seafood, she smiled obligingly. "If you'll excuse me for a minute—"

Leila turned, and, as she walked away, feeling all five pairs of eyes upon her bare back, she overheard Marvelle say, "The dress suits her. Up front, she's all tightly concealed. But walking away, she leaves one wondering."

Leila had to admit, she did like the drama of a memorable retreat.

As she moved across the room, the crowd closed in around her. So many faces—so much activity. Garrison stood at attention in the doorway. She approached, hoping for some light, non-taxing conversation.

"Do you mind if I stand here for a minute?" Leila asked sheepishly.

"Not at all, Miss."

"Perhaps we could look like we're chatting, like I'm not being antisocial."

He smiled. "Yes, Miss, whatever you like."

"Tell me, do you know most of these people?"

"I know who they are, if that's what you're asking."

"Does my grandmother throw a lot of these parties?"

"Few times a year."

Leila scanned the room. "Always these people?"

"Most of them."

"What do *you* think of them?"

"I think they're just people. Just people who are here to have a good time."

Leila nodded. That was the truth of the matter. Although some of her grandmother's guests might have been curious about Leila, all they were really interested in was having a pleasant evening—enjoying good food, music, and conversation. Perhaps socializing wasn't as bad as all that. Even Clarence chatted, smiling freely as he mingled, but perhaps that had to do with Angela's arm locked in his.

At dinner, Leila sat between André and Clarence. Marvelle eyed her from across the table, chewing a forkful of Cornish hen as she squinted at Leila. Trying to ignore the old woman, Leila hoped to strike up conversation with Clarence, but Angela kept him occupied in a lame conversation about some anti-industrial movement and some guy named William Morris—it seemed to have something to do with architecture, decorating, and socialism, as far as she could tell. They both basked in each other's smiles, obviously enthralled with the other's opinions. Leila found it uninteresting enough to turn her attention to André, who spoke before she had the chance.

"Bored, are we?"

"Not at all," she lied. "Just not up on my economic and social reforms as they pertain to aesthetics." She couldn't repress a half-eye roll.

André chuckled. "More hands-on than philosophical, are we?"

One brow nudged upward. "That depends."

"On what?"

"On how much I've had to drink." She tossed her head back, gulping the last of her ice water as if it were hard liquor.

"Looks as if you could use a refill," he said as a waiter placed dessert in front of them.

Before either had a chance to flirt any further, Marvelle cut in.

"Tell me child—what *do* you do?"

Marvelle's audience all stopped chewing and tuned in.

Leila swallowed a mouthful of mousse and cocked her head. "Pardon me?"

"What do you *do*?" Marvelle restated, with impatience. "How do you spend your time?"

Leila sat back in her seat, blotted her lips, and then folded her arms across her chest. She did not tilt her head. "Exactly what portion of my time are you interested in?"

"Don't be impudent," Marvelle scolded.

Angela's eyes widened.

The interrogator continued, "I mean, what is your livelihood? How do you support yourself?"

"I'm a store clerk."

"And that supports you?"

"I know I'm thin, but I do eat regularly and keep a roof over head." Leila glared at her. "—just the way I've been doing since I was sixteen."

Marvelle jabbed her dessert fork at Leila. "With your artistic potential, you would do well to set your sights a little higher."

Leila smiled with feigned politeness. "And you would do well not to make presumptions regarding someone you know very little about."

Marvelle snorted. "Indeed! A very cagey girl, you are!"

The old woman lit a cigarette, turning her attention to François. André chuckled under his breath. As waiters cleared the tables, several couples moved to the dance floor. André draped his arm over the back of Leila's chair.

"Would you care to dance?" he asked.

Leila was grateful for the distraction as André followed her onto the dance floor, joining the other couples.

Taking her hand, he pulled her close enough for conversation. He smelled of spicy lime.

"Don't let Marvelle get under your skin—she means well. She's a very successful and marketable artist. In fact, you should be flattered that she seems to have taken an interest in you."

"You mean in Angela Phillips *granddaughter*."

His smile burst with a quick laugh. "And *that* shows how little you know of *her*. There are dozens of young artists—

and old—who would give anything to be under her tutelage. You might actually want to consider a few lessons."

Leila gave his admonition a second thought. "Well, even if I did, I'm sure I've ruined any chance of that with my *impudence*."

"To the contrary. If there's one thing she cannot abide, it's a young woman without a mind or a voice. But I must warn you, she'll continue to provoke you—to the point of tears if she has her way. She loves drama and the passion of all that."

Leila gazed off, carefully considering his words.

Drawing her eyes back to his, André continued. "You see, you've only just whetted her appetite—and not only hers."

Leila could not mask her candid surprise, nor think of a reply.

"Tell me, do you run *every* morning?" he asked.

"Most mornings."

"So, you're a serious runner?"

"Define serious."

"Are you competitive?"

Leila chuckled. "You tell me—since my grandmother's friends seem to presume they know me—do *you* think I'm competitive?"

"I would suspect not."

Leila nodded.

André pulled her closer. "At any rate, do you object to running *with* someone?"

"Depends on who that someone is."

"Well, me of course. I also run every morning, and, since my father and I are staying the night, I hoped we might run together."

Leila could think of no good reason to decline. In fact, he was growing on her. "Alright."

"I must warn you though, *I'm* very competitive."

"Then you'll find *me* a very dull running companion."

"I doubt it."

The song ended and Leila turned to the band, applauding and offering the pianist an approving smile.

"They're very good," she said as they returned to the table. Leila directed her further comment to Angela. "Are they local musicians?"

"Yes. I always hire local—although the pianist is new. I believe he's from Hattiesburg."

"They are quite good," Clarence chimed in and then turned his attention to Leila. He moved a stray hair from her brow. "Leila, how about a dance?"

Her stomach fluttered. "Okay."

Clarence pulled her chair from the table and took her hand, escorting her to the floor. Although he moved seamlessly, his every shift, every motion heightened her awareness of his proximity, of his hands—one clutching her fingertips and the other against her bare back. He maintained a comfortable distance, but when he spun her, she returned close enough to pause her breath. If this dance had taken place six months ago, she would have met his gaze and giggled and conversed, amused at how good a dancer he was. She would have stroked his lapel and complimented him on how dashing he looked—for an old guy. She would revel in the idea of having such an exceptional friend who didn't care how they appeared to others. She might have even given him an affectionate hug and said, *I love you*, the way she had a hundred times before. But now, she fixed her sight over his shoulder—three-inch heels made it difficult to avoid looking him level in the eye. His thumb stroked hers.

"The pearls are lovely," he said.

"Yes …." She flashed back to the afternoon he had given them to her, to him standing behind her, to his hands on her, fastening the strand.

"You are a bit distant," he said.

Her eyes reflexively met his and returned to the French doors behind him. She couldn't form a rebuttal.

He cocked his head. "I'm sorry I didn't invite you on my walk this morning. I wasn't trying to exclude you."

"No, that's fine," she forced nonchalance, keeping her sights fixed. "We're all entitled to private time."

He pulled her closer. "Is everything okay?"

His voice drew her focus to his mouth. She was near enough to detect scotch mingling with his scent. His lips formed a soft, inviting smile, daring her to imagine ... she caught herself. "Of course, everything's fine ...." In a heated panic, her discomposure shifted to his searching eyes.

As he seized her gaze like a hypnotist, his expression changed, as if he had easily read her the way he always did. "Are you sure?"

She withdrew, now absorbed in the stitching on his collar. "Yes, I'm fine. It's just these shoes are killing me. I think I need to sit."

"Very well."

The song wound down just in time. Clarence followed Leila off the dance floor and eased her chair from the table as André accompanied Marvelle to the new group forming for the next dance.

"Thanks," she said without looking at Clarence.

"My pleasure."

Before he had a chance to sit, Angela stood and placed her hand on his. "Perhaps you'd care for another dance?"

Clarence's smile reciprocated her coyness. "Indeed, I would."

Angela had been overtly flirting with him all through dinner, and as they danced, it didn't take Clarence long to close the distance between them until there was no distance at all. He brought her palm to his lapel; she stroked it affectionately.

Leila wished she could overhear their conversation—it seemed to come easily, with the naturalness Leila and Clarence had always enjoyed. Was it so wrong that she longed to be the one snuggled into his chest, comfortable in his embrace, hoping it might lead to something more? Alone at the table, Leila shivered, her cheeks heating with embarrassment that such a thought could plant itself so brazenly. She looked away with shame, but mostly disappointment, hoping no onlooker could detect her angst.

I need a drink.

Leila made her way to the bar, keeping her sights upon Clarence and Angela; when the song ended, he did not immediately release her. They spoke a few words and then Angela departed. When Clarence turned toward the bar, Leila grabbed the attention of the bartender.

"Hennessy, straight up, please."

Clarence came up beside her, close enough to give her a nudge and a smile.

She looked at him askance. "You're enjoying yourself?"

"I am. Two scotch on ice, please," Clarence said as the bartender placed Leila's drink before her. Clarence now moved so he could look directly at her. "You are having a good time, aren't you?"

Her eyes darted. "Of course."

"Is it somehow—" he was choosing his words carefully, she knew the look, "—is it unexpectedly strange for you to see me enjoying myself with Angela?"

She folded her arms across her middle and met his stare. "Enjoying yourself? It looked as if the two of you should have traded the dance floor for a bedroom."

Clarence's deportment faltered. What had possessed her to say something so stupid—so accusatory? In another wave of embarrassment, she snatched her drink from the bar and walked away before he could react. Her eyes burned from cigarette smoke and her rising emotion. She strode to the patio door. Cool night air refreshed her lungs and brought goosebumps to her torso as she slipped out. She fanned her moist eyes, hoping to keep her mascara from smudging, and swallowed a gulp of cognac.

This is crazy.

A spotlight beamed down onto the garden beyond the patio. Another light behind the patio rail illuminated it from the ground up. Situated in the dark, close to the house, some cast-iron furniture provided a place to sit in the shadows. She breathed in the night air, trying not to think of Clarence and Angela. Wasn't this what she had wanted? To see Clarence happy, to see them together? She didn't begrudge her grandmother, but why did Leila wish it were she in Clarence's arms? *Oh, stop it already!*

Leila bent over, fighting the image, the thought of him so close to her. What kind of twisted feelings were these? She slumped back into the chair and took another gulp as the door beside her cracked open. A guest slipped out. Stepping beyond the shadows, he moved to the backlit rail and turned toward the house.

"There you are," André said, his face shadowed. "You're not hiding are you?"

"Just getting some air."

"I think you *are* hiding, otherwise you'd be standing here —" He gestured beside him. "—where you could better display your silhouette with the light behind you."

"*If* I were interested in displaying my silhouette."

"Did you want to be alone?"

Her first impulse was to say *yes*; but no, she did not want to be *alone*. "Not necessarily. I just don't like crowds. I'm afraid that Angela's idea of a *small* dinner party differs from mine."

"And how many would be at *your* small dinner party?"

"Two. Although I can't really complain about my grandmother's guests. Most have been very pleasant." She sighed and stood. "Well, I'd hate to appear impolite as though wolves did raise me. Besides, it's too cold out here anyway."

"Then perhaps you would indulge me with another dance?"

Back on the floor, André's hand warmed her back as he held her closer than last time—the way she wished Clarence had held her. She did not resist as André brought his cheek to her ear and slowly swayed her body to the music. No one had held her like that in such a long time. She yearned for Clarence, but perhaps André would do.

CHAPTER 23

LEILA MUST HAVE SLEPT IN SOME UNNATURAL contortion all night long, because her neck pinched and her back ached. Her dreams blurred images of Clarence and André. Perhaps all the upheaval was just the excitement. Or the fact that she hadn't made love to anyone in a very long time. Maybe her hormones were screwed up from traveling. There had to be some reason, some excuse to explain it away. She shook her head—how could she even think of kissing Clarence ... yet the image returned.

Stop it! She shot out of bed. *You do not want him that way!*

The rising sun eked up over the treetops, flickering in the wavy glass as she dressed in running shorts and a sweatshirt. She then stretched in front of the French doors, flexing her hamstrings. And why had she promised to run with André? She did not want a running partner. She needed to run and run hard—to run Clarence and her jealousy out of her mind and body. She had no desire to entertain some guy who was probably more intent on impressing her with his athletic prowess than actually running.

Exiting her room, Leila prepared herself for what little socializing she could get away with. She glanced across the balcony at the two bedrooms. Whose beds—or bed—had

Angela and Clarence slept in? Why did she care? The thought stung.

André and François—the only other early risers—stood below in the foyer. Leila breathed deep. As she descended the stairs, André smiled, "Good morning."

She forced a half smile and a polite nod at François. "Are you the only ones up?"

"Us and Garrison." François gestured toward the dining room. "There's coffee if you need it."

"No coffee for me." Leila headed for the door and then turned briefly, double-checking. "You're ready, then?"

André followed. "I couldn't be readier."

Leila loped down the front steps, preparing to take off with or without him. He stepped through the front door and bent at the waist. *Great.* Now she had to wait for him to do his stretches.

He looked at her quizzically. "You're going to warm up, aren't you?"

"I already did. In my room." Her feet moved in place.

"Listen," André straightened. "If you don't want me to run with you, just say so."

"I'm sorry. I *do* want you to." Leila sighed. She did not want to be rude. "I'm just a little wound up, that's all. I'll stretch with you."

Joining him on the steps, she went through the motions of warming up, performing much the way she had with Ian. André had legs like Ian's only a little longer. And yes, he was attractive—probably near Ian's age if he were still alive. But very different hair; his was so curly, it looked almost springy to touch, which she was not the least inclined to do. He caught her inspecting gaze and smiled.

"Do you always wake up on the wrong side of the bed?" he asked with a wink.

"What's it to you which side of the bed I wake up on?"

"Only that it would be a shame if you were to wake up this tense every morning."

"I'm not tense," she snapped.

He smiled. "I see."

Leila ignored him and started out slowly on the driveway.

He jogged at her side. "You know, there are ways to relieve that tension."

"Yes—and that's why I run." She picked up her pace. "—and run hard."

"Is that right?" He matched her increasing speed. "So, what sort of running have you actually done?"

"Long distance. Boston Marathon."

Leila detected a tinge of smug. She had no desire to outrun him for the sake of proving anything except for the fact that he would not easily catch her. And so, at her own ever-increasing pace, running faster and pushing herself harder than she had in years, she ran the way she did in high school—putting distance between her and all the things catching up to her.

André kept apace—at least for a sprint. Soon, he was faltering.

About three miles from the house, Leila cast him a glance. "Shall I cut my pace?"

He huffed, red in the face. "You said you weren't competitive—"

"I'm not." She dropped her speed a little and kept her eyes to the ground ahead of her. "I just really needed that."

"What you need—" he panted, "—is not nearly so painful —and—would be far more enjoyable—for us both—"

Astonished at his proposition, she cast her eyes toward him. In one tangled gawky movement, she stumbled over her own feet, sending her to the ground, knees first.

Throwing her head back and grabbing her skinned knee, she laughed in pain. "I am such a spaz!"

André crouched at her side. "Are you alright?"

"*Oouuch—*" she gasped, rocking her leg.

"Let me see."

"No! I'm fine." She closed her eyes, wincing. "It's just a little scrape."

"Let me see." André pried her hand from her knee. "You're a bloody mess."

Leila looked at it. Something sharp had given her a gash and the sight of it made her woozy. She covered her knee again and flashed a look at André. "This is all your fault."

"My fault?"

"Yes."

"How is it my fault if you spaz-out at the mention of sex?"

"So that *is* what you were implying."

"Good Lord, girl. Has it been *that* long?"

Feeling lightheaded, she replied weakly, "It's none of your business how long it's been."

"Let me help you up," André grabbed her hand and began pulling her to her feet.

"I don't think I can." Her full weight bore down on his arm and her good knee gave out.

He lowered her back to the ground. "You're not going to pass out, are you?"

"No. I just need a minute," she said, tucking her head between her knees and breathing evenly. Why did she have to be so squeamish at the sight of blood, and now of all times?

"Let me go back and get the car."

She threw her head back. "No! I'm fine. Just give me a second."

"This is ridiculous. You're bleeding down your leg. Now, stay here. I'm going to get the car." He took off in a run, leaving Leila without an option.

In frustration, tears welled up and streamed down her face. She wiped them away with her dirt-covered cuff.

Unable to inspect her wound, she hoped she would not need stitches. Her other knee was also scraped in addition to her burning palms. She cursed, feeling like an uncoordinated ten-year-old. At least her lightheadedness had subsided.

André returned in a few minutes. He wiped her face with his handkerchief.

"I'm sorry. Had I realized you were so easily thrown off balance, I would have waited for a more opportune time to make such a *suggestive* remark." He wrapped his handkerchief around her knee, laid his jacket on the passenger seat, and assisted her into the car.

"It's just that it's been so long since anyone's said anything like that to me."

André stood beside her open door. In all seriousness, he said, "I can't imagine that."

"Well, I don't exactly leave myself open to it. I'm not the sort who would take a man up on such a proposition. I guess most guys pick up on that."

"Well, I hadn't picked up on that, and I'm usually right on target when reading what a woman is up for." He looked her in the eyes. "Are you sure I misread you?"

"Very sure!" Feeling her resolve slipping, she quickly looked away. Why did he have to be so attractive!

When they pulled up in front of the house, Angela and Clarence stepped off the porch. Clarence opened Leila's door. She swung one leg out and lifted the other.

"Let me see." Clarence tried to unwrap her knee.

Restraining tears, she pushed his hand aside. "It's just a scrape."

"Come on," he said, assisting her. Clarence's strong arm supported her up the steps, through the front door, and to the kitchen, where he personally saw to her injury. She remembered how he had attended her sliced finger on Thanksgiving, back when she'd had him all to herself.

Angela stood by his side. "Will it need stitches?"

"I don't think so. Just a bandage and time off it."

Angela handed Clarence gauze and tape. "It's a good thing André was with you."

Leila rolled her eyes as she looked at André. "Yeah. Good thing."

"Come on," André said, helping her up, "Let's get some nourishment in you. Time for brunch."

As she hobbled along with André's assistance, Leila's empty stomach gurgled at the thought of food. They joined other guests in the dining room where Garrison and Jenny served brunch. As André helped Leila into her seat, Clarence and Angela lagged behind. They remained out of sight for long seconds before they entered the dining room. Miss Phillips wore a full blush as she smoothed her hair. Clarence adjusted his collar. What *had* happened last night? Leila lost her appetite.

When Marvelle finally joined the group at the dining table, she singled out Leila and her extended leg.

"Was *this* all the commotion that woke me?" She looked at Leila with irritation. "What have you done?"

Leila poked at her eggs Benedict. "It's just a scrape."

"Good heavens, child. That's a poor bit of drama! I was hoping for a broken limb or at least a sprain."

"Well, perhaps André and I could arrange that on our next jaunt."

"Humph—"

André winked at Leila. "I'm allowed another jaunt, am I?"

"Not unless you're planning to stick around till I'm healed."

"*Actually*, I've decided to stay on for a few days—the least I can do is entertain you while you're convalescing."

"Actually, I thought I might read, and then when I have nothing better to do," she cast a sarcastic eye at Marvelle, "I might climb back into my cage and paint."

"You are an impertinent child." Marvelle stabbed a bit of egg and jabbed it in André's direction. "As for you, young man, you'll have to wait your turn. Miss Leila should not be wasting time reading, or dallying with you for that matter." Biting the egg from her fork, she turned her implement on Leila. "You should be *living* rather than reading! No! Your paints shall *wet* your paper with passion."

Leila slouched, abandoning her own fork. "I will only frustrate you with my apathy."

"Rubbish! You take me for a fool, do you? You think I cannot see the passion bubbling up within you? I will have no part in your so-called apathy—and neither will you!"

Leila's blood ran hot and cold at the same time.

"There it is—in your face—" Marvelle glared. "I am no fool when judging the heart of a young woman."

MONDAY MORNING, MYLES STARED AT HIS reflection in the airplane window. The glass obscured many of his creases and wrinkles. His heart felt younger than it had in a very long time. Could he have fallen in love? All he knew was that he couldn't wait to hear Angela's voice, even if he didn't know when he might feel her lips on his again. He replayed the night they danced, how she felt so natural in his arms. But not only that—the confidences they had shared. Still, Myles had uncertainties about how her butler fit in. Myles had observed Garrison and Angela's familiarity in their most ordinary interactions, in the way Garrison had grazed her arm as he asked, "May I see to anything else, Miss?" when all but Myles and Angela had left the drawing room after the party ended.

"No, Garrison. Thank you, dearest," she had replied. "Goodnight."

Myles and he had exchanged curious, if not wary looks as Angela's 'butler' shut the door behind him.

She kicked off her heels and collapsed into her chair. The front of her evening dress gaped pleasingly. "Every year, I'm less and less inclined to throw dinner parties."

Although he would have liked to sit, Myles remained standing between her and the fireplace. He was enjoying the view. "Then why do it?"

"I suppose old habits die hard." She met his eyes. The sparks he had seen earlier flickered, now more like the twinkle of a far away star as her gaze drifted. "It's crazy—I keep very busy. I have people when I want them around. And I very much enjoy my own company. Still … I get lonely."

"You should never be lonely."

She slowly brought her eyes back to his. "Loneliness is just a part of life, don't you think?"

"I think perhaps. I also think at our age it's a shame—it doesn't need to be that way."

She sat up in her chair, now very focused. "Clarence. Let's not talk in circles."

He beheld her for a moment, impressed that she wished to be direct. Searching her eyes, he asked, "What is it you want, Angela?"

"Hmm …." She smiled. "You first—I'm not nearly as confident as I present myself."

"Very well." He had given his wants and needs considerable thought lately. "I want a loving relationship with a woman I respect and admire—someone who is my equal intellectually and challenges my perceptions." He allowed a moment for his words to settle and then added, "What I don't want is a one-night stand."

She chuckled. "Is that what you think I'm looking for?"

"I'll admit, you have had me wondering—you are a bit of a flirt, after all."

"And I'll admit that's true. I am a flirt. And I won't deny I enjoy the attention of men, but I learned early on how foolish it is to sleep with anyone on mere impulse. I've had my heart broken too many times to be careless at my age—though at my age, I'm not looking to needlessly postpone falling in love with all its *benefits*."

"Angela, please understand, it's not a matter of wishing to unnecessarily postpone anything on my part ...." He did not care to have this discussion while looming over her. He pulled a footstool in front of her and sat. Leaning forward, he took her hand. "There is much more at stake here than just you and me, Angela. For Leila's sake, I think we need to exercise restraint in the timing of things."

"I don't understand. I've been under the impression she'd be quite happy to see us together."

"I believe initially that was true." Myles weighed out how much he felt at liberty to divulge. If Angela were a woman he ever intended to be intimate with, he needed to be honest and open with her. Still, he felt uncomfortable revealing his suspicions. "Normally, I would not divulge something so ... so sensitive as this ...."

"What is it?"

"I believe that Leila may have developed romantic feelings for me. I also believe it's just a phase—something that will pass."

"Perhaps you are misreading simple jealousy. She's not accustomed to sharing you."

"I know how egotistical it must sound that I think she could be attracted to someone like me."

"To the contrary. I can easily see any woman being attracted to you. But, you are far older than twice her age."

"That's true, but Leila is a very complex young woman, and I know her well."

"And you believe she's in love with you?"

"I think she's wrestling with feelings she doesn't understand."

"Oh that poor dear. It can be so difficult to sort out such intense feelings at that age …. Do you think she's simply looking to fill the loss of Ian?"

"Likely that's a key component. I'm no psychological guru, but I think it may be some variation of 'transference,' so to speak. It's not uncommon in a therapy setting, but it's conceivable in the nature of our relationship."

Angela cocked a brow. "And how do you know so much about psychology?"

"I dated a therapist once."

"Well, I wish I were in a better position to console her. If it weren't for the fact that she and I are so alike, I'd scarcely know her. She's a bit of a closed book—and I'll admit that we've already been at odds."

"If it's any consolation, when she and I first met, we were also 'at odds.' Like I said, she's complex—as I imagine you are."

"Complex, indeed." Angela squeezed his hand. Her lips pursed the way Leila's often did when she mulled over a thought. "Clarence, perhaps you should confront her."

"No—she's not ready. When she is, she'll talk, as always."

Angela stared into his eyes and inched forward in her chair. She continued to mull until their lips were only a breath apart. "You are no ordinary man, Clarence."

"And you are an extraordinary woman."

Slipping his fingers into her hair, he drew her mouth to his, lingering in the sort of softness that made him question his own self-discipline.

"I can tell you one thing," he said, when she withdrew. "This pacing ourselves is not going to be easy."

"Have I tested your self-control, Clarence?"

He leaned forward and nibbled at her earlobe. "More than you know."

🝿🝾CHAPTER 24

A NDRÉ STOOD BESIDE LEILA AS THE TINTED, back passenger window rose. She folded her arms and sighed. Leila could not have imagined that the old biddy who had harassed her on the lawn less than a week ago, now solicited sadness at her departure. As the Mercedes pulled away from the front yard, made its way down the drive, and turned the bend, Leila waved goodbye to Marvelle even though the old woman was not the sort to look back. The feisty old dowager's last words rang in Leila's ears. "You will come see me in Boston. Call first. I am a very busy woman."

At first, Leila had bucked at Marvelle's attempts to loosen her up. Having the old woman hover like a schoolmarm didn't help. She had slapped Leila's hand. "You hold your pencil like a petit point needle. Your poor paper! How would you like to be poked and prodded? Imagine you're holding a butterfly wing, not squishing an ant between your fingers! Move your wrists! You're an artist, not a dabber! You control your colors as if you were trying to separate them like vegetables on your plate. Let your colors mingle and breathe —allow them to *bleed*!"

The old woman fanned the pages of a tablet, ranting, "Paper that has been wet with paint, no matter the subject or the artist's displeasure, is happy, fruitful paper, set free! Only blank paper is wasted!" Leila cringed at the notion, but if nothing else, Marvelle gave her permission to 'waste' paper —to experiment, to be messy on purpose. Marvelle had ripped a small tear in the thinning weave of Leila's resistance, and each time the student laid paint on paper, more fibers gave way.

Watching Marvelle drive away left Leila bereft, restless, and churning.

"She's quite something, isn't she?" André said.

"She's something, alright."

"Grows on you. I know."

Leila nodded. Answering her restlessness, she turned to André. "Take me downtown tonight. I want to listen to some blues."

"Is your knee up for that?"

"I suspect a shot of something hard will take care of it."

He winked. "That's right up my alley."

CIGARETTE HAZE FILLED THE SMALL NIGHTCLUB, which under any other circumstance Leila found offensive, but in these surroundings, it flooded her senses with the familiarity of a father's embrace.

Leila hoped for a table near the bandstand, but it was a full house. André maneuvered her through the crowd to a pair of stools at the bar.

"Vodka and tonic," he said to the bartender and glanced at Leila. "Hennessy?"

"No. Um … Guinness stout." She leaned back against the rail, watching the band play. Sweeping hair up off her moist neck, she wished she had worn it up or hadn't worn her black cashmere sweater.

André straddled his tall barstool and faced her. "Your father played blues, didn't he?"

To how much of her past had Angela and or François made him privy? At any rate, she could honestly answer, "Yes" regarding both her dads—Marcus *and* Joe—and the blues.

"So, you were on the road a lot?"

"Not exactly on the road, except during vacations. Mostly we just moved. A lot. Places like this feel like home."

André passed her a sweating mug. "That must have been quite an environment for a young lady."

She sipped and then licked her foam mustache. "At the time I didn't think much about it, but yes, I suppose it was."

"It makes it all the more surprising that you're so virtuous."

Leila chuckled at his impression of her. "Yes, well, believe it or not, my father managed to shelter me from a lot. Actually, my husband probably had much more to do with my continuing *virtue*."

"Really? How so?"

The guitarist began strumming a classic number, drawing her attention.

"Shush. He's playing Artie Sparks."

"Who?"

"You've never heard of old Black and Bluesy, Artie Sparks?"

"I'm not up on blues as much as jazz."

"But still, you've never heard of Artie Sparks? Natchez native—blues legend?"

"Sorry, no."

"Humph." It was then Leila realized that whatever knowledge André had of Miss Angela Phillips' past, it was limited by Angela, François, or perhaps the fact that André was more of a Northerner than a Southerner.

During the song, André ordered Leila a second stout. She eyed it with suspicion. When the song ended, she indulged a polite sip, which felt so good going down that it turned into a gulp.

André emptied half his glass. "Tell me about your husband, Ian."

Leila gave him a sidelong look. "Why the interest in him?"

"I'm curious about him as an artist. But I'm more curious about the sort of man who won your heart and kept you virtuous."

In a torrent, images of Ian flooded back. Their first encounter. Their passionate courtship. Their wedding night —and all the love they made for two-and-a-half years.

"He was …." She drew in a deep, aching breath. Struggling to formulate a concise description, she shrugged, shaking her head and staring at nothing in front of her. Ian could never be summed up in casual bar conversation with a man she barely knew.

"Will you ever get over him?" André asked.

"I don't know."

"You don't need to before you give yourself to someone new, you know."

"I know that I could never give myself to someone else unless I could match the intensity of love I felt for him."

"Do you have it in you? To love that way again?"

She felt intensely for only one other man. Clarence Myles. "Yes," she said, surprising herself. She took another big gulp of beer to cool off. Did she love Clarence Myles that way? She hoped André would drop the subject. As she continued to look straight ahead, she sensed his stare as if trying to lure her eyes to his. She would not appease him.

Drawing strands of hair from her neckline, his fingertips caressed her shoulder. Leila's resolve wavered and she glanced at him and then quickly looked away. Which was more unnerving—the "notion" of Clarence Myles or that André seemed to be trying to seduce her?

"I know what you're doing," she said. "And you may as well know, it's not going to work."

He chuckled, his fingers now at the nape of her neck. "What exactly am I trying to do?"

She looked at him and met his chuckle with a laugh. "Okay, you do understand that I'm *not* a virgin, that I was a very happy and *satisfied* married woman …."

"Yes." He kept his eyes on hers.

"I know how this works, and …." As his caress moved to her earlobe, she lost her train of thought.

"And?"

She drew in a long, flustered breath. "I'm simply letting you know up front that it's not working."

He withdrew his hand. "So I see."

They stayed for an hour longer, mostly listening to the music and keeping conversation light, but he readily reciprocated any attention she spared. It would have been so much easier to ignore him if he hadn't been so easy on the eyes. She occasionally gratified him with a glance, but she was afraid he might interpret any lingering as encouragement. In fact, she enjoyed his interest but felt too conflicted to allow any follow-through. When her knee began a painless throb, she suggested they leave.

It was near one in the morning when they came in. The entire house was still, except for the ticking of the grandfather clock in the foyer. As he assisted her up the stairs, the heat and tension of André's body spiked her own as she anticipated his next move.

He escorted her to her bedroom door and blocked her entrance. She didn't care to meet his gaze, but when he drew her close, she couldn't resist his stare, although she would not melt into him as he likely expected.

"Please don't," she pulled away.

He did not loose his hold. "Leila, you can't tell me you haven't thought of this moment."

She shook her head. She couldn't say she hadn't thought of his kiss and more. "You don't understand. I can't."

He nuzzled her neck. "And why not?"

"My heart's tied up with someone else ...." There! She had said it.

He met her eyes. "You're in love with someone?"

"I don't know."

"Either way, I don't care," his breath caressed her ear. "I just want to make love to you. I'm not asking for your heart."

"For me, the two are inseparable. I just can't—" she drew back from his embrace.

Providing no further opportunity, she slipped past him and into her bedroom, closing him out. Leaning against the door, she listened to him walking away as she bent at the waist, trying to catch her breath. What had she just admitted?

AFTER A RESTLESS NIGHT OF UNSATISFIED desires and missing Clarence, Leila sat in silence at the breakfast table. Angela and François chatted, casting her an occasional glance. They likely speculated on the outcome of her evening with André who had not yet returned from his early morning run. Leila's attention piqued as the front door opened and closed. She'd had several minutes to prepare herself for the sight of him, yet when he finally entered the room after his shower, her cheeks reddened. She fidgeted with her fork.

From the moment he stepped into the room, Leila felt his eyes. With the same hesitation of the night before, she met his gaze. The intensity of their exchange silenced François and Angela.

François then continued, " ... and so, we need to be out of here within a half hour."

Without taking his eyes away from Leila's, André barely acknowledged the itinerary.

"Excuse me." Leila backed away from the table. "I think I'll say my goodbyes now, since you seem to have a tight schedule."

Leila directed her remarks to father and son. "It was a pleasure to meet both of you. I hope our paths cross again."

François rose. "Well, we hope you'll come for the grand opening of *Chez* Goulet. Either way, given what we've seen of your late-husband's work, I have the feeling this won't be the last we see of you."

Leila rounded the table and gave him a peck on the cheek. "I look forward to it." She glanced at André. "Goodbye."

As she hobbled out, André followed her out into the foyer. "Leila …."

He looked at her the same way he had the night before but kept his distance. He pulled a business card from his wallet. With his pen, he scribbled on the back.

"If you're ever in Boston, call me … we'll have lunch."

She accepted the card. "Perhaps."

CHAPTER 25

L EILA WALKED, SWIFT THOUGH LIMPING, DOWN the road about mid-afternoon and had been gone nearly an hour. When she returned, stepping through the front door, Angela came from the drawing room.

"You just missed Clarence's call," Angela said. "He hoped you might be around."

He had already phoned to let them know when he arrived home, and Leila suspected that the ringing phone at eleven last night might have been him, though Angela had said nothing about it.

Leila returned a dismissive, "Oh, well."

"Feel free to call him back, if you'd like. You haven't spoken since he left. I'm sure he'd love to talk to you."

Was she actually trying to mediate Leila's relationship with him?

"Maybe later," Leila said as Garrison stepped into the foyer from the back service entrance. He carried a platter with a sweating pitcher and two glasses. "I thought Miss Leila might be joining you for some lemonade on the porch."

Angela took Leila by the arm. "Oh, please do."

Although Leila would have preferred a shower, the idea of a cold beverage was appealing. And Garrison had been so kind as to consider her. In fact, she had been thinking a lot on her walk. She had questions.

The two sat on large, white wicker chairs angled toward each other with a small service table between them. A gentle breeze swept Angela's hair from her face as she leaned back and closed her eyes. Leila was not a good judge of age, especially when it came to older women, but her grandmother's smooth complexion and lack of a double chin, not to mention her trim figure, lent her a considerably younger countenance than a woman in her mid sixties.

Miss Angela Phillips had effectively encroached upon her granddaughter's life, and yet Leila still knew so little about her. She wiped lemonade from her lip. "How much does François know about my grandfather?"

Angela froze and then slowly turned to face Leila. "Why do you ask?"

"I just get the feeling that André doesn't know anything about Artie."

"It's quite likely he does not. Fran is very careful with my personal and private information."

"So François knows?"

"Yes."

"But most of your friends don't realize that the child you had out of wedlock was with a black man."

"Few—and I mean very few—have firsthand knowledge of your grandfather. I'm sure if some had heard rumors to that effect, they might assume, upon seeing you in person, that the rumors were exaggerated."

Leila looked squarely at her. "And is that why you threw a dinner party in my honor? To dispel rumors?"

Angela sat erect and tilted her head. She stared at Leila for a moment. "I threw a dinner party for you, dear, because I'm proud of the fact that you're my granddaughter. You are the one good thing that came of all that mess."

"Yet if I was your *black* granddaughter, I would not have even been invited down here."

Angela stiffened. "My dear, the ugly truth of the matter is that just as a parent may favor one child over another due to appearance and similar disposition, I was drawn to you from the moment I met you. It may be true that if you more closely resembled your grandfather—if you were black—I probably would not have felt so akin. Just the same, I hope you would attribute me with sufficient fairness not to reject you on the basis of skin color. When I first learned of your existence and then laid eyes upon you—I was overcome with ... how shall I put it? I was overcome with pride and gratitude."

Leila looked at her with revulsion. "Pride and gratitude that I was not black!"

"No, dear. As conceited as it may sound, pride and gratitude that you were so like *me*, not only in appearance but also in disposition. It filled me with hope for your future and an undeserved and selfish hope to be included in it. Admittedly, in some small way, I hoped it might diminish some of my regret and shame."

"Regret and shame for making love to a *Negro*?"

At that moment, Garrison stepped onto the porch with a small plate of triangular sandwiches and placed it between them. Angela looked directly at him. Their eyes met.

"No, dear. Regret and shame for making love to the *wrong* Negro."

Garrison said nothing, though Leila thought she detected a faint smile as he walked back into the house. Leila beheld her grandmother with bewilderment, but before she could say anything more, Angela stood. Color had left her cheeks. She looked her granddaughter in the eye. "Pin racism on me if you wish, but I am merely a woman who hopes to finally have some peace. Perhaps you are still too young to understand that."

Angela left Leila on the porch with even more questions.

THAT EVENING, AS LEILA STEPPED OUT ONTO her balcony, she overheard the tail end of an exchange between Angela and Garrison below on the patio.

"Oh Garrison, I hope you're right, dear," her grandmother said with resignation.

His low voice resounded, "Time, Angela. She's still young...."

"I think I'll turn in early tonight," her voice trailed into the house.

As soon as Angela's bedroom door closed, Leila loped downstairs. The first place she thought to look for Garrison was the drawing room. When she stepped inside, he looked up from one of the leather chairs, a glass of liquor in his hand.

"May I get something for you, Miss?"

"No." She paced from window to window.

"Is everything alright?" His voice was as mellow as the room's ambiance.

"Yes. Everything's fine."

"Why don't you sit? You make me nervous."

"Okay." Leila took the seat beside him.

He looked at her sideways.

Leila exhaled. "I've been wondering about something."

"Have you?"

"Did you know Artie Sparks?"

His eyes shifted. "Yes."

"How did you know him? Wasn't he older than you?"

"I used to run with him back when the Rhythm Night Club opened, till a year before it burned up. He was older than me and used to get me in the club."

Leila had not only read about the infamous black club, but Artie had talked about it when she used to jam with him on Saturday nights, back when she lived in the apartment above him on Long Island. "You used to hang at the Rhythm?"

"Yep."

"Hundreds of people died in that fire."

"I know it. I knew some of them."

"How horrible."

"Could have been Artie." He wagged his head. "But right around that time, the Klan was about ready to set a fire under *him*—" he cut off.

"Did you know Artie when my grandmother knew him?"

Garrison rubbed his whiskered chin, and nodded. "Yep."

"What happened back then? How did all that take place?"

"That's something you best be asking your grandma. I don't wanna be telling tales out of school."

"She won't talk about it."

"Have you asked her?"

"Not specifically, but I know she won't."

"Well, you'll not hear it from me. It's not my place. And Angel—I mean *Miss Phillips*—would be hurt if I did."

Leila looked directly at him. "The two of you have been close friends since you were little, haven't you?"

"Yes, Miss."

"Did your family continue to work for her parents when she was—you know—disowned?"

Garrison hesitated. "No."

"But her moving away didn't have anything to do with *you*, did it?"

"Oh Miss—you're opening a whole can of worms."

"What's the harm in telling me? It's all in the past."

Garrison shook his head. "And that's where Miss Angela wants it. Your grandmother has lots of regrets, but she's a good woman, and she loves you."

~CHAPTER 26

New Hampshire

IT HAD SNOWED OVER EIGHT INCHES THE NIGHT before, and, although plow trucks had already made one pass, the roads glistened white just like the overhanging trees. Ben, Leila's ever-loyal employer, nearly swerved off the road as he gripped his steering wheel and shot Leila a look of disbelief. "Did you just say *Marvelle Harding*?"

"Yeah, why?"

"You do know who she is, don't you?"

"An artist friend of my grandmother." As the words slipped past her lips, she realized from Ben's astonished wide eyes that her answer was far too nonchalant.

He shook his head with disdain. "I cannot believe I hired someone so out of step with the artistic community. Shame on you. For your information, Marvelle Harding is a nationally renowned—no—*revered* artist."

Leila shrugged. "Oh."

Still shaking his head, Ben steered his way around the lake. "When do you start?"

"In a few weeks, weather permitting."

"I suppose now you'll want a raise in order to fund your lessons. Or perhaps you'll hock that alexandrite solitaire, like any self-respecting, starving artist."

"Actually, no."

"Then how will you pay for her?"

"I can't." When Leila had asked what compensation Marvelle required, the old woman burst with irritation. *You can't afford me! Besides, it's not your money I'm after, it's your soul!* Feeling scant on soul, Leila figured she didn't have much to lose.

"I'll be receiving lessons *en gratis.*"

Ben pulled into her already plowed driveway.

"Did you plow for me?" she asked.

"Not me. Looks like you have guardian angels in every state."

Not only had someone cleared the dooryard but also the path and porch. When she stepped into a warm house, she knew Jared must have received her message.

She dragged her old suitcase, and one new bag loaded with Angela Phillips' vintage wardrobe, into her bedroom and then headed to the kitchen. A note lay on the butcher-block island beside a bottle of red wine and a crusty baguette.

> *Leila,*
> *Welcome home! Something to warm and unwind you after your long journey. Picked up a few groceries, too, so you don't have to rush out again.*
> *Jared.*

Leila opened the refrigerator. In addition to eggs, juice, milk, butter, and a wedge of Brie cheese, she found a six-pack of Guinness. Beside the refrigerator, a loaf of whole wheat bread and pint of maple syrup happily awaited their French-toast destiny.

Jared.

How could he have known how much she dreaded coming home to an empty cottage? She immediately dialed his number.

He picked up on the second ring. "This is Jared."

Her breath caught in her chest. "Hi—it's Leila. I just got home."

"How was your trip?"

"It was fine. You are amazing."

"Um—not really. Remember, I open up houses for a living."

"You can't tell me Pinot noir, cheese, and French bread are standard."

He chuckled. "No. And neither is Guinness."

"You didn't leave a bill."

"Didn't I?"

"No."

"I guess I'll have to talk to my book keeper about that."

"Jared ...."

"Never mind that—Listen, I'm missing my tool belt. Would you mind checking your utility room in the basement?"

🐉 EVERY TIME LEILA TORE A PIECE OF CRUSTY bread and smeared it with Brie cheese, she thought of breaking bread with Ian, and how Clarence had always known how to break down her walls of resistance. Her old friend had a way of extracting the truth from her even when she didn't know what the truth was. She took a long sip of her wine. She must never allow Clarence to know the truth of her feelings for him, but she didn't know how to keep it from him. She hadn't spoken to him since just before he left Natchez, and although she yearned for him, she didn't dare contact him. He could always read her, and while she had always taken comfort in that, now it left her vulnerable. Perhaps she would call him in a week, after her meeting with Marvelle in Boston, when she would have something neutral to discuss. She would keep it brief.

Yes, she resolved as she chewed her bread and cheese, *That's what I'll do ....*

A tap at the door interrupted her pondering.

She carried her glass of wine across the room, swishing a mouthful to wash the bread from her teeth.

She opened the door to Jared and swallowed, wiping her mouth. "Hi. Come on in."

"Hi. Sorry about leaving my stuff."

"If I didn't know better, I might think you left it here on purpose."

His brow jumped. "Now why would I do that?"

"So you could come over and help me with this bread and cheese."

He laughed.

"Seriously, though. I ate so much in Natchez that I don't fit into my clothes. I'm afraid I'm going to have to obligate you to stay. Do you have a few minutes?"

"I don't want to impose."

"Don't be ridiculous! You bought all this," she said, grabbing another wine glass from the cabinet. "Or would you prefer the Guinness?"

He stomped snow from his Sorels and then removed them. "The wine's fine."

"How's Emily?" she asked, pouring a glass.

Jared pulled a stool up to the island. "She's good. Tell me about your trip."

"It was like nothing I've ever experienced."

"Did you see your friend Myles?"

She sipped her wine and twisted her lips before swallowing. The whole time, she kept her eyes upon his. "Yeah."

Jared had a way of studying her whole face, the way Ian used to, but he said nothing until apparently done with his assessment. "How is he?"

"I think he's falling in love with my grandmother."

"Is that a bad thing?"

"No ...." Her eyes shifted. "I just ...." She sighed and looked away.

"You're used to having him all to yourself."

"It's not just that." She drew a long sip from her goblet and swallowed. "Jared. What do you think of older men falling in love with young women?"

Now his brow rose with purpose. "Don't you mean, what do I think of a young woman falling in love with an older man?"

His intuition astounded her. "I'm *thirty-five* years younger than him."

"How long have you been wrestling with this?"

"I don't know ... it just sort of crept up on me. I still can't believe I feel this way. Maybe I'm blowing it out of proportion. Maybe it'll just go away."

"Maybe. Then again, maybe it's the real deal."

"It's crazy because I love him—I do. He's been my confidant and friend for so long ... we're actually perfect for each other. But making it romantic, I mean, you know— sexual—it would freak him out. Besides, it couldn't possibly work."

"I guess I'm a romantic. I want to believe that if two people are right for each other they can overcome any obstacle. And then my pragmatic side kicks in. I mean, yeah, when you're at your sexual prime, he'll be *way* past his."

"Why do men always think in terms of sex?"

"Because we're all pigs," he chuckled. "Seriously though, it is a real concern. Not that there aren't other considerations like compatibility and loyalty, and I'll bet there are some rare exceptions where it has worked long term. But here's the issue for you. And don't get me wrong, I'm not trying to play down what you feel for him—"

"But—"

"From what I've read and heard and observed about grief, it stirs a lot of emotions that can't be taken at face value.

Grief is really complex and can get emotions all twisted and tangled, like it short circuits the brain. Try to wait it out. Don't act on it just yet."

"But what if it doesn't go away. My relationship with him is on the line. I can't bear to lose him."

"Don't worry about the what-ifs—that's a slippery slope."

"Now you sound like Ian."

"He was a very smart man."

"I miss him so much." She stared off. "Sometimes I get so lonely."

"Those are really strong emotions."

"Yeah, I know," she rolled her eyes, "it's all part of the *grieving* process."

"It may sound cliché, but it's true."

"Well, I'm sick of blaming everything on grief."

"Hey, at least you've got something to blame wacky feelings on."

"You know, you really should be a therapist." She smiled. "You'd probably make a better hourly wage, too."

"Yeah, well, then I'd be obsessed with checking the clock." With that, he glanced at his wristwatch. "Speaking of which, I've really overstayed. I gotta get going."

🐦CHAPTER 27

Boston

B Y EARLY MAY, LEILA HAD BEEN TO MARVELLE Harding's townhouse on Beacon Hill six times since she arrived home from Natchez. Today she drove the long monotonous stretch of interstate 93 where it droned on in a blur of cars and exits. The first time she drove it, she had lost her way on Boston's ever-changing one-way streets. Fortunately, Ben had prepared her for Boston's inexplicable traffic flow, and so she had factored in the likelihood of getting turned around. She showed up at Marvelle's with one minute to spare.

Marvelle Harding had asserted she wanted Leila's soul. Interactions with the old woman, before and after lessons, had been as uncomfortable as the artistic paces she had been putting her student through, but rather than paying out on a deficit of soul, Leila's inner framework had increased exponentially.

In spite of her discomfort, Leila looked forward to each session, and during her two-hour return drive home, she would revel in the disturbed afterglow of achievement. Marvelle hurled many startling and agitating concepts at her, always trying to jolt her student out of inhibitions and fears. The nature of her art lessons seemed designed more to broaden and extend Leila as a human being, than as a proficient watercolor technician.

The housemaid directed Leila to Marvelle's studio for her next lesson. She ascended the hairpin staircase, raking fingers through rain-dampened tresses while clutching her portfolio. Reverberated fragments of conversation greeted her almost as if Marvelle meant her to overhear.

"… promising … yes … terribly pent … you'll see …."

Leila braced herself before entering the third-floor studio of Marvelle's townhouse. Rain pelted the row of skylights.

"Right on time, as usual." Marvelle grabbed Leila by the arm, ushering her toward the guest. "This is Jenette."

The woman smiled while pulling her mass of jet-black curls away from her face and nodded.

"Jenette, you may disrobe while Leila sets up her workstation. Let me know if it's not warm enough, and we'll tweak the thermostat."

Leila dared not react, yet one glance at Marvelle and her instructor read her discomfiture.

"Surely you're not ill at ease with the human form."

"Of course not." Leila forced herself to look at the model. "I just wasn't expecting it, that's all."

Jenette exhibited no discomfort with her nudity, although the pose must have been awkward to maintain. She sat on an upholstered divan. Her legs curled beneath wide hips and buttocks, with a rounded, almost bulging tummy. Her upper torso twisted toward Leila. One shoulder dipped low and her neck extended. Leila could not help comparing the model's breasts to her own—much larger and lower set.

Leila had grown accustomed to Marvelle's hovering but never entirely at ease with it. She stopped and started several times while sketching out the model's curves, which intensified and faded with changing light cast by the brewing storm outside. Leila waited for the critique that never came.

With each distant flash of lightning, she expected Marvelle would thunder rebuke.

Halfway through the exercise, the old woman meandered away to the rain-streaked window, showing no apparent interest in her student's progress. Leila relaxed, immersed in her painting and soothed by the patter of rain against glass. By the time she gave her brush a final rinse, she scarcely noticed the model's nakedness and even made casual conversation while Jenette dressed.

As Jenette slipped into her shoes, the door cracked open with three raps.

"Oh good, right on time." Marvelle called out. "Enter!"

As if choreographed, and upon Marvelle's cue, thunder announced the arrival of the young man.

"Karl—wonderful! And thank you so much Jenette, da'ling. You were perfect!"

The visitor acknowledged the model with a nod as Jenette exited. Marvelle clutched Karl's arm as he grazed her cheek with a kiss but kept his eyes upon Leila. Raindrops spotted his Oxford shirt and jeans. He stepped barefooted out of his Italian loafers.

"Wet out there, da'ling? So good of you to be prompt."

"I wouldn't dream of keeping you waiting, my dear," he said with affection but still focused upon Marvelle's student.

Leila stepped out of arm's reach, hoping to cool a warm flash, yet she wrapped one arm over the other as if chilled.

"Leila, meet Karl. Karl—Leila. Karl will be modeling for you this afternoon."

"Hi," he said with a wink and offered his hand.

Leila stepped forward and shook his hand. Her cheeks burned at the idea of what her instructor had in mind.

Apparently, Marvelle preferred dark, curly haired models, but it could not have been easy to find one with such intense emerald eyes. Looking for some distraction, Leila turned her attention to the overhead window and then down to the paned glass overlooking Louisburg Square. Wind had picked up, creating a convenient diversion. Leila cared little if she came off as distant or rude.

Marvelle beckoned. "Leila, come sit upon the divan."

With her usual reluctance, she obeyed.

"I thought we'd have tea first." Marvelle smirked. "Karl, won't you join us?"

He took his place beside Leila as the maid brought tea right on time.

The matron remained standing and sipped from delicate porcelain, keeping her eyes upon the pair. She then directed her attention to Karl.

"And how is school going, da'ling."

"Good, Mrs. Harding. Taking my bar exam next week."

"Karl just graduated Harvard. I dare say I'll miss him when he's moved away—or perhaps some law firm on Fleet Street has been courting you?"

"Actually, yes, but they'd probably prefer their associates don't model nude," he said, his gaze still upon Leila, intent on catching her eye. He succeeded.

"I swear, I'll never breathe a word, da'ling." Marvelle nudged an out-of-place curl at his temple, drawing it behind his ear in a not-quite-grandmotherly way.

Leila could not help finding their unspoken exchange curious—affectionate, yet detached in that Karl's sight never shifted from Leila.

"Marvelle has told me a lot about you." He snagged Leila's attention and held it with another coaxing smile. "Her talented and promising protégé."

The blush, which had just receded, flashed from her neck up, yet she couldn't look away. She had never seen eyes more beautiful on any man, woman, or child.

"Oh Karl, some discretion, please. I can't teach an inflated ego." Marvelle looked at her student and began speaking to Karl, "That's the beauty of her, she's so innocent and naive, unaware of her own potential. But what an awful wall of fear I've had to chip away at—look at her—all pinched and tight. Yet, so ready for the plucking."

"Excuse me," Leila cut in. "I'm sitting right here."

"Of course you are, da'ling. You don't think I'm reciting all this for Karl's benefit, do you? I'm sure your inhibitions are all quite evident to him, if not now, then when he takes his clothes off." As if the old woman controlled the elements, thunder and lightening simultaneously collided at her command, charging Leila's entire body.

"Oh, honestly! I'm trying to make inroads on *you*, child! I'm trying to entice your desire—and make you want to reach out and grab what you want!" Marvelle now turned to Karl and spoke of him as if he were invisible. "Look at him. Gorgeous, young and vital. Undeniably manly in his youth. He pursued something that required intense desire—and he's on the brink of it—can't you just *feel* his passion?"

Karl's beaming eyes danced at Marvelle's description as another flash lit the side of his face.

Marvelle continued. "Stand up, let her have a good look at you."

He stood before them both, keeping his bright eyes on Leila's, as hers traveled all over his body. Her emotions rumbled like distant thunder.

Marvelle waved him over to the draped backdrop. "Look at him."

Each item of clothing came off in a manner that any person might undress, as if disrobing in a doctor's examining room, unobserved and without exhibition. He folded consecutive items of clothing and laid them, one atop the other, on a nearby stool. Yet, to Leila it was more sensual than anything she had seen since the last time she made love to her husband.

"Is he not perfect in every way?"

Leila's stomach rolled with excitement as she looked at his naked body, fighting her apprehension, looking away, coming back to his beautiful form, and then withdrawing to behind her station. With her tabletop tilted to obscure his lower body, she swiveled away from them both, trying to steady her breath.

Marvelle yanked Leila's sleeve. "Now *sketch*!"

"I don't think I can," she said, struggling to breathe.

"Rubbish—of course you can—what's the difference between painting Jenette or painting Karl?"

Rebounding, Leila came to her feet and stared down at Marvelle's fierce eyes. "You know very well what the difference is. And you're doing this just to embarrass me."

Marvelle smiled and yet did not come back with her usual ardor. She simply stated, "You tell me what the difference is, and I'll send him away."

Leila wagered her options, staving off tears.

Marvelle added, "And don't tell me it's because he's a man."

Leila's pounding heart begged reprieve. She could scarcely form words without blurring her vision. Hoping Karl couldn't hear, she confessed, "You know that I find him attractive."

Marvelle's brow rose. "Because you feel passion for him?"

Leila nodded, quick and begrudging.

"Good!" She cut a halting gesture at the model. "Karl, stay where you are."

"But you said—"

"Rubbish!" she shot back. "I'm the teacher and I can say whatever I want! You are the student and you are at *my* whim."

Leila recoiled, breathing fury. "You—"

"Oh, you're quite primed now. Passion and anger—so akin." Her eyes flickered with a passion that matched her student's. "Now sketch!"

"I won't!"

Incensed, the old tyrant's face contorted. "*You will.*"

She shoved Leila to her stool and yanked her from behind her station. "*Look* at him, and *sketch!*"

Leila looked. She studied. She held her breath as Karl remained expressionless, staring back, his eyes always on hers. Perfection. She wrestled another pang of desire as she scrutinized the form of the only naked adult male body she had ever seen, aside from her late husband. In fact, in form, they were so similar that she could not restrain tears. As she sketched, anger streamed from her eyes, and frustration and passion and all she had pent up for months, churning within her and steadily escaping. Marvelle looked on, arms folded with satisfaction.

At her subsequent lesson, given a week to regain her composure, Leila was ready to confront Marvelle's harassment. Instead, Leila was confronted with results of her last session. She stared, mouth agape. Asked to critique her own work, especially in comparison with her careful rendition of Jenette, Leila thought for sure Marvelle had switched her portrait. She did not recognize voluptuous Karl. Not only were her loosely drawn lines distinctly accurate by comparison, but also the watercolors were so much more intense and vivid—more lively. Leila looked at the figure and fell in love with him.

"This isn't mine," Leila said.

"Rubbish. Of course it is. You were in such a state, you don't even recognize your own passion when confronted with it. You are a frightful child."

"Oh my."

"Do you see what I have been trying to teach you? Do you see the point of the lesson?"

"I think so."

Marvelle rolled her eyes as if she were about to faint. "You are a stubborn nut to crack. You may be young, but you've already wasted so much time—time you can never get back. I am old, and every minute is precious. Do not irritate me with '*I think so.*' Either you *do*, or you *do not.*"

In fact, Leila now saw how years of constraint had exploded on paper, that allowing an outlet for deep and intense feelings had not left a wake of disappointment but blazed a trail of artistic expression. She had created a true work of art—*she* had created it! Whereas giving expression to her passion had once frightened her, it now excited—yes gratified her. She finally *felt* like an artist.

"Yes, Marvelle, I do see it," she said with gratitude. "Thank you. I'm ready for my next lesson."

LEILA GRABBED THE PHONE AS SOON AS SHE stepped into her house at past nine o'clock, anxious to call Clarence. She usually called him by seven on Friday evenings. Her art instruction provided them with something safe to talk about. As long as she didn't have to look Clarence in the eye and could talk about neutral subjects, she felt she could keep her feelings concealed. Her longings hadn't diminished, but she would not indulge any fantasies about how wonderful it would be to live with him, to share his everyday life, to have him as her ready confidant and companion. Even more so, she forbade herself the pleasure of imagining him in a carnal way.

As the weeks passed and Bonnie's wedding date approached, Leila wondered if Clarence appreciated the weekly diversion even more than she did. She never assumed she would receive an invitation directly from Bonnie or as Clarence's guest, but his lack of discussion over the matter made her speculate on what might have been transpiring behind the scenes. She could only imagine Bonnie's reluctance to provide him with an 'and guest' invitation. Leila might be a tolerable companion for a private dinner, but what would people say if Leila arrived as the father-of-the-bride's date? Scandalous, for sure. Then again, had Clarence told Bonnie about Angela? Might he have invited her if the invitation were extended? Leila wished she had the nerve to ask, but that would leave her far too vulnerable to long awkward silences that might give away her feelings.

Tonight, a week before the wedding, she would keep her phone call brief and neutral, as always. Just the same, her heart raced as she dialed his number.

"Sorry I'm calling so late," she said. "I had a really intense lesson this week and didn't get out of there early enough, and 93 was a zoo—bumper to bumper."

"I almost thought you'd forgotten to call. You caught me in bed, getting ready to turn out the lights."

"I'm sorry, I won't keep you up." Leila pictured him in his pajamas, stretched out, one hand behind his head and the other pressing the receiver to his ear. She wished she were there alongside him, not talking through three hundred miles of telephone wire.

"No, sweetheart, you're fine. I just might not be much of a conversationalist tonight. It's been a day ... and then there was the rehearsal dinner."

"Isn't that usually closer to the wedding?"

"They have scheduling challenges."

"So, I would have missed you if I called earlier, anyway."

"Perhaps, but I cut out early. It's not as if I played any particular role. I'm not actually a part of the wedding. I think my invitation was more of a formality."

"You're not giving away the bride?"

He paused. Now she read his silence—his pain. "No ... it's not a traditional sort of ceremony."

Leila was miffed. She and Ian had eloped, so she hadn't had a traditional wedding either, but if she had, she wouldn't have gone through the motions of inviting her father (either one) and then not include him in the ceremony. She spoke in anger, "Why go at all?"

He sighed. "Because, my dear, there are so few pivotal events in the lives of those we love that no matter what discomfort it may stir, we attend. The regrets of doing otherwise far outlast the alleviation of discomfort or injured pride."

"I love that you're so principled, Clarence, but honestly, she just makes me so mad."

Another silence.

"I'm sorry," she recanted. "I'm not making it any easier."

"It doesn't matter. It will all be over next week. They've decided to forgo a honeymoon until a later date in order to move to Pittsburgh immediately after the wedding. The hardest part will be saying my goodbyes to Peter at the reception."

She ached for him. "Don't worry, you won't lose track of him. He loves you."

Another hesitation. Of course, Clarence knew the dangers of losing track of someone. His heart was breaking and she knew it. She wanted so bad to be there with him, to hold and console him.

"Clarence?"

"What?"

"Do you remember that day you and I walked the beach at Robert Moses State Park, right after you found out that Bonnie was still alive and you might have a second chance with her?"

Another silence—but she knew it was not born of forgetfulness. "Yes. I remember." The pitch of his voice wavered. "I asked you what it was you liked about me."

"Yes. And if you were to ask the same thing right now, I'd have a list one hundred times longer and I'd entitle it—What I *love* about you."

He breathed hard. She knew his eyes were blurring, that she had choked him up.

"Clarence, I told you something else that day. Do you remember?" He exhaled into the receiver. Tears filled her eyes, knowing he was crying right along with her. Her own voice wavered as she whispered, "You'll always have me."

🌾CHAPTER 28

O H NUTS! LEILA SWUNG INTO THE RIGHT LANE, cutting off another vehicle that blared its horn as she steered onto the off ramp toward Storrow Drive. After a few memorized turns, she landed on Beacon Street, south of Marvelle's posh neighborhood.

Sparse parking didn't matter—Leila loved meandering through the Streets of Beacon Hill with its neat rows of brick homes, Georgian, Federal, and Greek revival amidst blooming pear and cherry trees. Parking close to the Boston Common afforded inspiration and creative opportunities. She ambled up the hill, picturesque in every way, weaving in and out of narrow one-way streets.

Toting her large portfolio case up cobble-stoned Acorn Street, Leila breathed in the pungency of spring, eyeing the old gas lamps that Ian had liked so well. Up a bit farther, she approached the stately front door beside the black shuttered window donning the curvature of the brick facade. Bracing herself for her next lesson, she rapped the brass knocker and checked her watch—twenty before noon—near her usual time of arrival. Leila always preferred waiting on Marvelle than to launch her clock-militant tutor into a lecture on promptness.

No answer. Leila then rang the buzzer and it took a long time before Marvelle's housekeeper Gretta arrived. She gave a quick peek from behind the sidelights and straightened her white starched apron.

"Oh, dear," Gretta said. "Come in, dear." Her eyes were red, and her cheeks flushed. She smoothed her face and skirt as she led Leila to the parlor.

"I'm sorry, dear. You've made the trip for nothing. Mrs. Harding wasn't feeling well this morning—it came over her so quickly, and …," Gretta's voice squeaked, "just twenty minutes ago the ambulance took her away—"

"What's wrong with her?" Leila's heart sped.

André appeared in the doorway behind Gretta. Leila backed up at the sight of him, imagining the worst. She felt behind her for a nearby chair.

"Leila, I'm afraid we have bad news." He approached, easing Leila to sit. "I'm sorry—Marvelle passed away this morning."

Leila's chest caved in around her heart. She pressed her palms to her eyes, hearing only snatches of André's words—something about not being able to get in touch with his father, about heading over to the gallery.

"Why don't you come with me, Leila? I don't want you getting lost in Boston in this frame of mind."

She didn't have the wherewithal to resist or come up with a plan of her own. "We should call Angela—she'll want to know."

"We'll do that from the shop. Hopefully Dad will be there by then."

In silence, they drove toward Newbury Street in his Porsche, parking in the public alley behind the gallery. Entering the back storage area, Leila took scant note of her surroundings as André moved aside a few parcels and inspected several envelopes atop the desk.

"Well, Dad's been here and gone—he planned to be in and out of the gallery all morning." He picked up a note. "Says he'll be back in at three."

Leila moved through a short and narrow passage to the large front rooms. Long sheets of white paper veiled the tall, nearly floor-to-ceiling windows, soon to reveal the culmination of months-long planning.

Leila wandered around the room without concentration, passing in front of artwork. Framed work lined up on padding upon the polished floor. Some leaned against the walls around the perimeter of the room, and others against partitions, each beneath what she assumed was their designated space.

Three of Ian's black-and-white photographs caught her off guard, looking as worthy as any work she had ever seen. Pride surged through her and then sudden sadness. It was too much—she broke down.

André approached. Without a word, he took her in his arms and they stood for minutes in their mutual grief. She had not been held so close by anyone since the time they danced together. Oh how she missed the physicality and comfort of a man's arms. Finally she withdrew, leaving his polo shirt damp with tears.

He stroked her face. "I hope you don't mind, I took the liberty of calling your grandmother."

"That's fine. I *hate* making those calls."

"As soon as we know what the arrangements will be, she'll fly up and stay with us. We've got a couple hours, so we may as well get some lunch next door."

"I'm not hungry."

"Well, you should eat anyway. At least have a drink."

"But I look awful."

He directed her to their restroom—more like an elegant sitting room with a separate stall—where she splashed cold water on her face, trying not to look herself in the eye. When she stepped out to where André waited, he brushed a few strands from her face. She hadn't even thought to check her hair and combed her fingers through the tangles.

"You look fine," he said, escorting her by the elbow. Something in his firm direction calmed her nerves as they walked next door to the dimly lit bistro. Within minutes, the maître d' seated them in a remote corner booth at André's request.

"A Manhattan and a Hennessy—strait up," he glanced at Leila. "Or would you prefer Guinness?"

"Cognac, I guess. I need something stiff."

He nodded at the barmaid and then turned his attention to Leila. "What are you in the mood to eat?"

"I don't care. I'll have whatever you're getting."

While nibbling bruschetta, they barely spoke, sharing silence that was far more comfortable than she would have imagined after their encounter in Natchez. He seemed different. Less full of himself. Perhaps it was simply the strain of the day.

At three, they returned to *Chez* Goulet, meeting François at the rear entrance.

"Did Marvelle let you out early today?" François speculated as they all three stepped in together. He added, "You're looking glum, Leila."

André spoke up. "Dad—Marvelle passed away this morning."

"Oh, dear God—" François leaned back against the wall. Leila moved past, to the wide-open front floor. The intensity of it all was too much, and she refused to give in to another wave of tears. In a few minutes, father and son emerged from the storage room.

"Close it up," François directed as he came into view, his face drawn. He shut down the lights and rubbed his forehead. "Let's go home."

"I guess you should bring me back to my car." Leila's second drink and all the emotion left her wilted, inside and out. She dreaded the drive home.

"We'll not have you driving tonight," François said. "You'd end up in full-blown rush-hour traffic. I doubt you're in any condition to drive with all the strain."

"Dad is right." André took her by the arm. "Besides, your grandmother would never forgive us."

Leila acquiesced. When they arrived back at Louisburg Square, she was surprised to find that the two lived only a few townhouses away from Marvelle—no wonder André had been first at the scene.

They all sat in the handsome parlor on traditional yet comfortable upholstered chairs.

François perched forward. "We've been keeping up with your progress, like neighborhood gossip. We've even had a peek at your work. In particular, your painting of Karl is, well, it's as good—if not more provocative—than any I've seen."

Leila blushed. "You saw that?"

"To be honest, we've seen most of the work you've done with Marvelle. It's just that particular piece is most worthy of remembrance." François paused, as if reading her. "In fact, we've discussed the possibility of having something of yours at the gallery, right between your late husband and your mentor."

Under the circumstances, and unsure if he was being sentimental and patronizing, Leila did not know how to respond. For fear of sounding ungrateful, she remained silent, offering only a nervous nod.

André chimed in. "He's quite serious, Leila. We've been talking about it for several weeks. We realize you're reserved about showing your work, however, we hope that a little of Marvelle's boldness might have rubbed off on you. At the very least, we hope we've gained just a little of your trust."

"I don't know what to say."

François leaned back into his chair. "No need to say anything today, and nothing would be cast in stone until after we've seen more samplings of your future work."

Leila gazed about the room at the paintings and sculptures on display all around her. Were they renowned or even famous works of art? She thought she recognized some, but had no idea who the artists were, except a couple that looked distinctly Marvellian. Leila was completely out of her element. Now that her mentor and friend was gone, Leila's insecurities encroached upon her, trying to make inroads on the progress of the past few months. She refused to allow them headway. "Alright. That would be fine."

They ordered take-out from an eatery around the corner. Shortly after dinner, François again slumped back in his seat, loosened his tie halfway down his chest, and rubbed his eyes. "I'm turning in for the night." With a grunt, he pushed himself up and out of the chair.

André gave Leila a brief tour of the downstairs, highlighting his favorite works of art, based more on their relative worth compared to what they paid, rather than aesthetics. It was past the time she normally called Clarence —he would probably be up, waiting. She asked to use the phone.

"That's fine," André said, raking his fingers through curls that sprung back into place. "I'm going to get ready for bed, too."

Leila rose with him.

He winked. "You know, if circumstances were different, I'd be inviting you to join me."

"And my heart is still with someone else."

"Pity," he said and left the room.

Leila followed him into the hall. She waited until he had ascended the stairs and out of hearing range before she sat on the bottom stair tread. She pressed the phone to her ear.

She had merely greeted Clarence before he said, "What's wrong?"

"Marvelle died this morning, just before I got here."

"Oh Leila … I'm so sorry. Where are you now?"

"I'm at François and André's, a few doors down from Marvelle's place ... I'm spending the night."

"Sweetheart ... I'm so sorry. I know you really valued her."

Each phrase of their exchange drew out, extending their conversation without words.

"Oh, Clarence ... I'm just so tired of death."

"I know ...." His voice conveyed such earnestness. "I wish I could be there with you."

"You have no idea how much I wish you were." Leila's emotions stirred, not just those of grief, but she craved his touch—his embrace. Her breath labored. "I just wish ... I wish that ...."

He breathed her name, "Leila ...."

The sound of it consumed her like fire, sending a surge through her entire body.

"I love you," she whispered as tears slipped down her face. "I have to go."

She gave him no chance to respond before she clicked the receiver. She stood and wiped her eyes, replacing the phone in its cradle.

André stood at the top of the stairs, looking at her with curiosity as he descended. "Was that him? Your *love*?"

Leila could not bring her eyes to his. "I wish."

"Didn't I just hear you tell him that you love him?"

Leila shot him a petulant look.

"Sorry. I didn't mean to eavesdrop—I simply overheard."

Like an escaped prisoner, finally caught, Leila confessed. "Yes, I said it. But he'll take it platonically, as he always does."

"Are you saying he doesn't know how you feel?"

Leila shook her head.

"Well, good God, girl, *why not*?"

"It's complicated."

"Did Marvelle teach you *nothing*? What are you waiting for?"

CHAPTER 29

THE TAXI PULLED UP IN FRONT OF THE GOULET'S townhouse. Myles tipped the cabby and removed his luggage from the back seat, setting it on the brick sidewalk. Angela emerged onto the front steps, grasping the wrought-iron handrail. Her black silken suit contrasted stunningly with her white hair. At first glance, she appeared anything but grief-stricken, though she couldn't hide the strain of her lips as she smiled.

"Clarence. I'm so glad your flight arrived on schedule." She came up beside him as the cab drove away from the curb. Slipping her hand through his arm, she gave him a brief kiss on the lips. He would have responded more eagerly, but he didn't know where Leila might be. And, he had been up since three that morning; his neck ached, and his ears buzzed with exhaustion. He had trouble focusing his eyes.

"You look beautiful, Angela."

"I'm so grateful that you've come. And not just for me. This means so much to Leila, too."

He glanced at the townhouse. He couldn't help being impressed, but that was not his main concern. "Where is she?"

"Getting dressed—or André may be occupying her." She led him up the steps. "I have to say, he rarely leaves her side. I've never seen him so attentive to any one girl."

François came into the doorway. "Myles. So good to see you, ol' chap."

Myles chuckled at the Southern gentleman's attempt at sounding British. "Thank you so much for your offer to stay the night, François, but I've decided to head north, instead."

"Oh," Angela cooed. "That is disappointing."

Myles stepped inside, onto the hallway's polished hardwood, glancing at the modest overhead chandelier. He refocused his eyes down the hall and up the staircase in expectation.

"She doesn't know it yet," Myles said to Angela in an undertone, "but I'm spending tomorrow with Leila. Time to get some things straightened out."

At that moment, Leila appeared at the top of the stairway, just in front of them. Her black heels drew his gaze to her black nylons, disappearing at the knee, up under a black pencil skirt. She snugged her arms across a matching cardigan sweater set. The sight of his mother's double strand of pearls and two teardrop earrings warmed him. Although she smiled, it was tense. Tucking her unfettered, past-shoulder-length hair behind her ears, she descended the stairs.

"Hi Clarence," she said, halfway down.

He took her hand, since that was all she offered, and gave her an awkward hug.

"I'm so sorry," he whispered in her ear. "You look lovely, just the same."

She withdrew as André came down the stairs behind her. She replied weakly, "Thanks."

This was not the reception he was used to or hoped for. Perhaps it was simply the sad occasion, but he knew better.

"Good to see you." André shook Myles' hand. "So glad you could come."

"Shall we head over to the church?" François said, opening the front door. "Parking will be the devil, so we may as well all drive over together. It will be tight. I hope you don't mind."

Funerals had a way of imposing the worst discomforts.

Leila scooted across beige leather to the middle of the back seat, between Myles and André. She clutched a small black purse in her lap and crossed one leg over the other, revealing quite a bit more than her knee and a seam running up the back of her calf and under her thigh. Was her display for his benefit or André's? Or was she completely oblivious to her own wiles?

When they drove up to the front of the cathedral, already buzzing and streaming with people, Angela gasped. "Marvelle would have hated all this pomp. It's her children's doing."

"Now, now," François said, as Myles climbed out and opened Angela's door. "Funerals are more for the living than the dead. Don't begrudge the mourners, *da'ling*—it's tacky."

"Oh," she grimaced, "I *hate* funerals."

André offered Leila his hand. She accepted his arm as he said, "Father and I are pallbearers, so we won't be able to sit with you. Do you think you can manage these two lovelies, Myles?" André placed Leila's hand on Myles' arm. For the first time, she gripped him tightly.

"Indeed."

As he began to move forward, Leila remained rigid.

"I don't know if I can do this." She pressed her fingertips to her lips. At his other side, Angela's complexion flushed as her hanky blotted tears from the corners of her eyes.

Angela sniffed. "Oh, I'm afraid we're both coming undone."

During the two-hour ceremony, Myles couldn't help but recall the conversation he'd had with Leila four years ago, almost to the day, as they walked the beach. *What do you think happens to a person when they die?* she had asked, *where do you think they go?* Although he had reluctantly shared his own cynical view of eternal reward or punishment, had Leila found a satisfying answer to her question? The furrow and spike of her brow, and the annoyed twist of her lips indicated that the priest's rhetoric offered no comfort or resolution. On the other hand, Angela's gaze, fixed on the pew in front of them, gave away no indication of how she felt about the hereafter. For the most part, Myles tuned out the oratory and pondered how he planned to approach Leila with the least amount of damage to their relationship. Drawing her out would alter their rapport—he simply didn't know to what extent. His stomach tightened at the thought.

Fortunately, the sheer length of the ceremony had the effect of sucking emotion from the occasion rather than intensifying it, and so the grieving wrecks he had walked in with appeared more relaxed now that the ceremony had ended. They followed the procession back out into sunlight.

"At least it's a beautiful spring day," Leila said as she paused on the grand steps, inhaling the light breeze.

Myles let go of Angela's arm, whispering to her, "Give me a moment, would you?"

Angela stepped away and mingled with other acquaintances.

Leila turned and smiled at him—her first genuine smile since he had arrived.

"You look much better now that that's out of the way," he said.

She tipped her face toward the sun and into the draft. "I feel so much better, though I have a hard time believing that

God has called Marvelle home because he needs another angel. I mean, really?" she rolled her eyes.

Myles shrugged noncommittally, and although he agreed, he would not allow a philosophical discussion to sidetrack him. He nudged a hair that crossed her forehead. "I have a favor to ask."

"What is it?"

"My flight doesn't leave until tomorrow afternoon—from Lebanon. Would you mind giving me a lift to the airport?"

"Lebanon? Not Logan?"

"The connecting flights were better."

She squinted. "Is that so?"

"And I was hoping to spend tomorrow with you. Just the two of us. Angela said you weren't planning to spend the night here in Boston. I'll simply ride back with you. If that's okay."

"Why wouldn't it be?"

"I don't know," he said. "You've been distant these last months."

"We've talked."

Indeed, they had. In fact, he hadn't forgotten anything she had said and the comfort she provided. Still, that was the only time she had let down her guard since before Natchez. "Yes, but—"

Her eyes shifted. "I've been busy."

"Well, then, this will be a good opportunity for us to catch up. Like old times."

"Yes. Like old times." Leila's breath stuttered as she drew it in. She cast a look over her shoulder. "Where's Angela?"

Angela stood near a couple that he presumed were Marvelle's family. He caught her eye and she gestured for him to approach. Leila followed as they cut their way through the crowd. Angela hovered near a petite older woman of about her own age, beside a younger, taller man. As Leila came into view, the couple exchanged glances.

"Bernice and Randall," Angela said, "I would like to present Leila Brigham—Leila, Bernice Price and Randall Harding, Marvelle's daughter and son."

"Of course. We recognized her immediately." Bernice acknowledged Leila with the same quick and choppy inflection as her mother but not with the same huskiness of voice. "We are so pleased to meet you and to have you join us."

"Yes," Randall concurred, as Leila shook hands with both.

"And this is her guardian, Clarence Myles."

The three exchanged greetings. Bernice then directed her attention to Angela. "Has she seen it yet?"

"Not yet."

"Seen what?" Leila asked.

"Marvelle's last work. André will show you later."

🐟 MYLES OFFERED ANGELA HIS HAND, ASSISTING her from the Mercedes to the curb in front of Marvelle's townhouse.

"I'm not quite ready to go in yet, Clarence," she said. "How about a quick turn around the square?"

"Certainly." He faced Leila, already on the sidewalk. "Will you be alright?"

"Of course I will. I have André." She smiled as the handsome young man came to her side.

André escorted Leila up the steps. She held him with more familiarity than when Myles last saw them together. She appeared to have taken an authentic shine to him.

Angela slipped her arm in his, in her comfortable way.

"What do you make of Leila and André?" he asked as they crossed the narrow street to the shade of the square, which was more oblong and oval, than square.

She chuckled. "He hasn't had her, if that's what you're curious about."

"I wasn't referring to that specifically, but—how do you know?"

"I know André. Hmm … and a woman can tell. I'm surprised you can't."

"I didn't say I couldn't. I simply wanted to know what you make of them. Do you think André has any serious intention regarding her?"

"Well, if he did, it would be a first. And don't worry. I've already given her all due warnings about him. To be honest, I think she's toying with him more than he is with her."

"Like grandmother, like granddaughter?"

"Clarence Myles—what are you implying?"

"Don't be coy, Angela. You know you are every bit the flirt your granddaughter may be, except I believe she is by and large unaware of her own charms. You, on the other hand …."

"I don't know if I should be offended or flattered."

"You're not offended. You know how captivating I find you … though I do wonder about what it is you truly want, Angela. You never did tell me."

"Didn't I?"

"You alluded to love and its *benefits*, but I've had a lot of time to think."

"Perhaps you've decided I'm too complex for you?"

"You could never be too complex, but you do raise curiosities."

Her brow flicked. "About?"

"Please tell me if I'm being too straightforward." He looked her in the face. "I'd like to ask about Garrison."

"I prefer straightforward. And what is it about Garrison you'd like to know?"

"He doesn't actually classify as 'the help,' does he."

"No."

"Who is he to you?"

Her lip twitched with nerves. "Oh my. Sometimes straightforward can be so awkward. I think I should have liked to have a drink for this conversation."

Myles pulled a flask from his pocket. She threw her head back with a laugh as he passed it to her. Without so much as a glance to the right or to the left, she accepted a healthy swig and passed it back. He took a small sip and returned it to his breast pocket.

Her hand remained looped at the crook of his arm. "Hmm... Garrison. You know I grew up with him?"

"Yes."

"Please don't be put off if I offer the abridged version."

"Not at all."

"We were playmates as children. At eighteen, I fell in love with him—call it feeling our oats or whatever you will, but we were in love. One can't hide that. Consequently, Father sent him and his family away, with nothing. Enraged, I got *involved* with Artie—he and Garrison were friends. It was so foolish, what I did ... I'm so ashamed ... a little better than a one-night stand. A great deal of alcohol involved. Poor Artie ... I think he actually thought I loved him." Her fingers brushed her lips as if to hush her words, her regrets. "As soon as I found out I was with child, both Artie and I had no recourse but to flee.

"Garrison's family had people in Delaware, and they had family in Massachusetts. The long and short of it—they took my baby and raised him, though I visited—not as his mother. Simply as benefactor—Miss Angela. To make my way, I modeled in Manhattan. Through Garrison's connections as 'the help,' I became acquainted with Marvelle, who had family in Delaware. She was looking to hire a model. Through her, I met Fran. What little money I made, I invested in art. It provided enough to support myself and help out with Joe.

"Meanwhile, Garrison met a lovely woman in Delaware. They married and had three children. About ten years ago, Multiple Sclerosis took her, but not before bankrupting them. If it hadn't been for Garrison—for his loyalty—I don't know how I would have made it all those years ago. And so, in his time of need, I've taken him in. He's the best-paid butler in the State of Mississippi—he's even putting his children through college."

"You mean, *you're* putting them through college."

"No. He has earned every cent, over the course of a lifetime. He's a good man—a very good man—and his family deserved better. If it weren't for me—for my stupidity —well ... I'm just trying to balance the scale. Not that I ever can ...." She wiped a tear as it formed. "So, when you ask what *I want*? I want to finally feel worthy. To be worthy of being loved, in spite of myself."

Myles squeezed her hand gently. He truly felt for her, but he had one more concern. "After Garrison's wife died—after he became your *butler* ...."

Her pace slowed. "You want to know if I've slept with him?"

"I'd like to know if I'm competing with him."

She sighed and continued to look straight ahead. "We succumbed once, when he first moved back, but we realized *that* wasn't what either of us wanted. He still mourns his wife, and I'm no longer the rebellious child who needs to hurt my father for everything he—" she closed her eyes.

"I hope I haven't been intrusive. I simply don't believe in having secrets if *this* between us is to move forward."

"Well, if *this* is to move forward, I suppose I have a question of my own."

"Please."

"About Leila. Are you willing to be as honest with me about her?"

"You want to know if I have more than paternal feelings for her?"

"What man wouldn't at least entertain the idea?"

"I'd be lying if I said I hadn't considered the notion. I'm not proud of that. I suppose it sprang from my need for unconditional acceptance. For redemption." He paused and looked at her.

"Then you understand the nature of my relationship with Garrison."

On some level, Myles comprehended it. He faced Angela and took her hands in his. He hadn't rehearsed a response to her inevitable wonderings, but he would offer the truth of what he believed. "I can assure you, I do not foster romantic feelings for Leila. It would be utter foolishness on my part and I know that. The fact is, I want more than what she would be able to provide."

"And what is that?"

"Companionship without qualms of conscience. I want a grown woman—an equal—who can love me in spite of myself." He searched her eyes for trust. "As far as Leila is concerned, you have nothing to worry about."

"Except that as long as she harbors romantic feelings for you, *our* relationship can not progress beyond what it is now, without qualms of conscience."

"You do understand."

"Well, I've waited this long, and I would loathe to do anything that would hurt her. I suppose then the bigger, long-term question is, can we each accept the fact that the other has an 'exceptional' friendship that neither intends to give up?"

CHAPTER 30

L EILA WATCHED CLARENCE TAKE HER grandmother's arm and walk away. They actually made a very handsome couple, but she couldn't stand the idea of them together—or being intimate. In her distress, she gripped André's arm tighter. He responded with a smile.

"Wow. It's really warm for the middle of May." Leila unbuttoned her sweater. "I love warm weather."

As she peeled off her cardigan, revealing the sleeveless sweater beneath, he smiled. "I'm glad you're a little perkier."

"Is that what I am?"

"That or perhaps you're taking more of a liking to me." He escorted her through the front door of Marvelle's townhouse, where a white-gloved man offered to relieve them of any accouterments. Leila kept her sweater.

"Figures you would think *that*," she said. "I'm going to quit playing nice at these affairs if you start taking my niceness personally." Leila couldn't help but grin. Conceited or not, he was easy to be around, and he never left her standing alone unless she obviously wanted to be. He did seem to read her moods though she also kept him guessing—he had told her as much.

"So, when do I get to see Marvelle's final work?" she asked.

"Right now, if you'd like."

"You don't have other people to see or connections to make?"

"None as important as you." They began ascending the staircase, alongside each other. He pocketed his hands.

"You do realize how smarmy you sound." Leila hugged her cardigan.

"Yes, and I also know you see right through all that. Which makes you all the more fun."

Leila rolled her eyes. "Is there no possible way to insult you?"

"Of course, but you don't expect me to own up to it."

They rounded the railing, making their way to the third floor. Standing in front of the studio door, André fished a key from his pocket.

"Wow—like a vault," she exclaimed.

"I kid you not. The contents of this room are worth hundreds of thousands of dollars."

"What?"

He shook his head and sighed. "You have so much to learn."

Marvelle's studio brought goosebumps to Leila's torso. The northern-lit exposure of ceiling windows dimmed the room, though it was only early afternoon. Eerie shadows fell around them. Leila draped her sweater over her shoulders. Too numb to cry, she stared at her station, remembering the far-too-few sessions with her mentor.

"Over here," André said. "It's one of her few *chiaroscuro*."

"Her what?"

He shook his head. "*Chiaroscuro*. It's Italian. A lighting effect, contrasting bright light and shadows. You know, you need to study up on your art styles."

"I know, I know ...," she said, moving to his side behind a nearly life-size canvas propped upon Marvelle's easel.

Turning on the work lamp, he positioned it toward the painting. Leila's own eyes stared back in ultramarine oil paint, half of her body lit, and half shaded.

She gazed intently at Marvelle's rendition of her initially recalcitrant student whose smoldering embers she had ignited.

Leila's forefinger pressed her lip. "She used Ian's photo as a study."

"Very likely. There are distinct similarities."

The sight of herself—of who she was, not only weeks, but years ago, through the eyes of her teacher—startled her. Tentative, excited, yearning, as if anticipating each stroke. A portrait completed and signed, yet still underway and so unfinished.

"Her final piece," André said. "Worth tens of thousands no doubt. You should be very flattered."

In tears, Leila turned away from the portrait.

He continued to study it. "What do you think of it?"

Leila wiped her cheeks. "I think she painted me as she wished I were."

"I think it's a perfectly accurate depiction. Passionate, full of life, hopeful—and terrified."

"Is that strictly in the eye of the beholder?"

"It's definitely that. But I believe it's strongly implied."

"Well, she certainly had me pegged right from the start." Leila shook her head, her framework withering. "And sometimes … I just want to climb back into that cage."

André turned her chin to his, lifting it to look at her level-eyed. "But you won't."

"No. I won't."

He studied her face. Was he looking for the spark that Marvelle—that Ian—had so flawlessly conveyed? She evaded his further scrutiny and moved to her own station. The portrait of Karl sat taped to a board. Her work had indeed been under someone's inspection. She sat in front of it and bent to shuffle through several others of her paintings, arranged in a vertical bin beside her easel.

"So, what becomes of my paintings that remain in Marvelle's possession? Are they now part of her estate, or do I get to claim them free and clear?" she asked.

"That all depends. Since there is no signature, can you prove you were the artist?"

She smirked. "And how would I go about that?"

He held up Karl. "Establish them as *your* distinct style. Paint some more like them."

"Or we could just have Karl come and vouch for me," she teased. "But seriously, I can't just pack them up and take them, can I?"

"Seriously? No. Not until her estate releases them."

She stood, still gripping her sweater. "And am I going to need a lawyer for this? Because I happen to know one who has a vested interest in my art."

"Do you?"

She gestured toward Karl. "Harvard graduate."

"That's right." He squinted a grin. "And, no, you won't need a lawyer. There are enough of us who will vouch for you as the artist, but it will be a process, one which is already underway."

"So how does all of this affect the opening of *Chez Goulet*?"

"It definitely affects it. Fortunately, we haven't had the invitations printed up yet. The bad news is, Marvelle's death will postpone the opening for weeks. The good news is—and please understand, I mean this strictly from a business standpoint—we stand to profit greatly from the timing of things. That's the sad truth. We are the exclusive brokers of her art, and, now that she's gone, her remaining works are that much more valuable. Fortunately for us, her family is anxious to get her work out there and make as much as they can from it. Sadly, for Marvelle, neither of her children places any intrinsic value in art, beyond what price tag it might flaunt."

"That's kind of cold."

"You can't really hold it against them. Everyone places a value on something. Some simply don't see it in art."

"I know your father loves art and so does Angela, but what about you? Do you just push the money around and enjoy the glamour of it all, or do you appreciate art for the sake of art?"

"I'm not an art connoisseur of my father's caliber," he admitted, looking carefully at her face, "but I appreciate beauty. In *all* its forms."

"But, the money is your primary motivation."

"Yes. It's what I'm good at. That's an art in itself, and I'm proud of the fact that I'm sought after for *my* art."

Leila stared at him. His eyes shifted and he stepped closer, with a confidential lean. "I shouldn't really tell you this, but you'll be informed soon enough. Do you remember meeting Marvelle's former student, Trudy Winthrop?"

"Yes. We met briefly, a few sessions ago."

"You probably don't realize it but, she is also an accomplished and profitable artist whose work we broker."

Leila shrugged. "I'm not up on all the popular artists."

"You really do need to be, you know."

"Yeah, yeah—so what is it that you really shouldn't tell me?"

"Marvelle set up a trust fund for your further art instruction, under Trudy Winthrop."

Leila's eyes widened and again welled. "She did?"

"Yes."

"When did she do that?"

"As soon as you started your lessons and showed some promise."

"*Why* did she do that?" She wiped a tear.

"Why do you think she did it?"

Leila shrugged in astonishment.

"Sometimes your modesty is annoying, Leila. It won't serve you well in this industry."

"Maybe I'm not cut out for this industry."

"Don't be a fool."

She cast her eyes from his. "I'm not a fool."

"I know you're not." He stepped closer. "But don't let your personal misgivings hold you back. It would be a slap in Marvelle's face to refuse. In fact, it would be a slap in the face to anyone who ever cared about her or her art. You may not want it, but it's a privilege that you have the responsibility to bear."

Leila absorbed the weight of his words. She looked at him with the gratitude that Marvelle deserved. "Then, thank you —for the warning."

"There's something else. At the grand opening—which is being dedicated to the memory of Marvelle Harding—we will be placing special emphasis on her work and the work of her former students, with *you* being her final and promising protégé. Consequently, we would like to display your portrait of Karl. We've all agreed, it's very good and should be included. Additionally, her family wishes to offer her final piece, *Portrait of a Protégé*—as they've named it—in a silent auction."

"You mean, the painting you just showed me?"

"Yes."

"I'm overwhelmed."

"Don't be. This may sound very crass, but having you attend is bound to boost not only *its* worth, but also the desirability of *your* work, and even Ian's."

"But aside from Karl, I have nothing else worth offering."

"Then I suppose you'd better start pouring yourself into more paintings."

"I suppose I will."

"Good then. We'll look forward to you bringing them down for review."

"Perhaps you'd like to take a little jaunt up to the country to see the artist at work in her *milieu*?"

"Now it sounds as if *you're* propositioning *me*."

"I didn't mean it like that."

He folded his arms and chuckled. "You do know what a tease you are."

Leila glanced away. "I don't mean to be."

"Well, you are—and this, from a woman in love." He shook his head. "I don't know what to think of you."

Her eyes dropped and she picked lint from her cashmere.

He tipped his head to draw her gaze. "You haven't told him yet."

She folded her arms tightly, squeezing blood to her face. "No. And I won't."

"I don't get you at all." He recoiled, continuing to shake his head.

She threw her sweater to her chair. "He's *thirty-five* years older than me!"

His eyes shifted—he was calculating. "Not Clarence Myles."

"Yes."

He exhaled a long, loud sigh. "Okay. I see your dilemma."

"I'll bet that let the air right out of your balloon."

"Not exactly. To be honest, I'm encouraged that you like older men."

"This is not funny."

"I know. I'm sorry."

André stepped closer and pulled her limp shoulders to his chest. She allowed it for a moment and then backed off just enough to meet his eyes. She recognized the look of him wanting to kiss her.

"You're not the sort of man who'd take advantage of a grieving woman, are you?"

"Normally … very possibly I *am* that sort. But, no, I will not take advantage of your grief."

"You know, even if I didn't have feelings for someone else, you might as well know right up front that I'm not the sort who would sleep with a man unless I was married to him. And, I sense that you're not the marrying kind."

He backed off a little. "You don't know that I'm *not* the marrying kind. Perhaps the right woman has not yet persuaded me."

"Well, at any rate, I know you're not the *waiting* kind."

"You're probably right about that." He narrowed his view. "But I'm still curious—what *is* it that keeps you so virtuous?"

Leila moved out of his reach. "Quit calling me virtuous. You don't know what I am or the first thing about what makes me who I am."

He didn't close the gap, but something in the genuineness of his expression filled the space. "I imagine that takes quite a bit of time."

How had he put her at ease with a look? She didn't know if she should resent his ability or find comfort in it; the irony of it twisted her lips to a near smile. "Yeah, well, who wants to invest that much time in some insecure, neurotic widow with abandonment issues?"

"Aside from the widow thing, that describes most of the women I've dated."

She rolled her eyes. "Poor you."

CHAPTER 31

New Hampshire

NEITHER CLARENCE NOR LEILA SPOKE MUCH for the first half hour as she wove her way around Boston, through her familiar route and onto northbound Interstate 93. Clarence's head tipped back on the rest, and his eyes closed as though he might be dozing. Over the past months—aside from her last telephone call—she had kept her conversations with him so light that she felt out of practice.

"Oh my gosh—" she blurted, "It was last weekend!"

Clarence rolled his head to face her. He sounded groggy. "What's that?"

"Bonnie's wedding. I completely forgot to ask you about it. I'm so sorry."

"Well, I suppose Marvelle could have picked a more opportune time to die."

"I'm sorry. Here I was all absorbed in myself, again." She picked the middle lane and shifted into overdrive. "How was it?"

He sat more erect. "Best of everything."

"Was your ex there?"

"No. Bonnie and her mother are not on speaking terms yet."

"Then I guess you're the favorite parent, even if you didn't get to walk her down the aisle."

A disparaging breath escaped with his smirk.

"Sorry, that was a lame thing to say."

He sank back into his seat, staring ahead. "I have to hand it to them, though, they made the day as much about Peter as themselves."

"It must have been hard to say goodbye."

"For me, anyway. I think Peter was too overwrought with excitement to have any of it register. Just as well."

"Have you thought any more about moving?" She looked over at him as his eyes closed.

"No." He sighed, more out of fatigue, it seemed, than tedium with the subject. After a minute of silence, he snored softly. He must have been exhausted, and Leila was just as glad to drive in silence. She had so much to think about—her conversation with André provided a good distraction.

The sun flickered through the trees when she pulled into her dooryard. Clarence had been awake since she exited the interstate, but he remained silent.

"Hard to believe we're coming up on another year," she said as she moved to pull her key from the ignition.

Clarence's hand covered hers, sending a rush through her. She looked over at him, meeting his stare. The corner of her mouth twitched but neither smiled.

He squeezed her hand. "What do you say we skip food tonight, and go straight to cognac?"

She wanted to say, *What—no scotch on the rocks?* but didn't. "That sounds about right."

They met out on the deck. He sat on the gliding settee in cargo shorts and his white Oxford shirt—cuffs double-flipped up his forearms. What was it about men's forearms?

As she pulled up a side chair, he patted the cushion beside him. "Sit with me."

Now wearing a loose cotton sundress, she tucked it between her thighs as she drew one leg beneath her and half-faced him. Her stomach tightened as she averted her eyes from his forearms to his chest. *No good*—to his shorts—*Even worse*. And now to his eyes. A stiff swig would distract her. She held out her snifter, trying to maintain her composure. He poured them each two-fingers worth. After a good swallow, he sucked a breath through his teeth and sank into the cushion. His ankle crossed over his knee, and his other foot gently rocked the small couch. Another long draw from the snifter, and the starch left her knees and her insides relaxed. She could now look Clarence in the face, uninhibited. He looked good, and having him at her side felt good. It felt right. She had missed him so much. Several minutes of silence passed before either spoke.

He asked, "So, after all those months of lobbying for your grandmother, what do you now think of her and me?"

Leila took another sip, glancing quickly at him. She didn't want to think about her grandmother or consider the idea of *them*. All she wanted was him, all to herself in this moment. "I don't know."

"Come on now, what do you think?"

"Better question is, what do *you* think?"

He wedged his chin between his thumb and forefinger. "To be honest, I don't know her well enough yet."

She looked away but felt him staring, willing her to look at him. She succumbed. He continued, "I suppose there's still a part of me that thinks if I finally pick someone, the *perfect* woman will be waiting around the corner, and I'll have missed my shot."

"That is such a guy thing."

"What? Women aren't looking for the perfect man?"

Leila's shoulders slacked. "I had the perfect man."

Clarence raised his incisive brow. "Ian wasn't perfect, you know."

"He was perfect for me."

"How will any other man ever live up to your expectations?"

Leila brought her eyes back to his. "I don't know." Though that wasn't entirely true.

"Do you think that perhaps someone who rivals Ian exists? That there is another man you might feel so connected to?"

Now their eyes locked and she would not look away from the glint that beamed from his gaze. She had stared into those blue eyes so many times, under so many circumstances; she knew them better than her own reflection. She could gaze at them for the rest of her life. "Yes. I know he exists."

"You're that sure?"

Her heart pounded and words slipped out, "Oh, Clarence … if you were thirty or twenty or even ten years younger …."

"You think if I were younger, we'd be right for each other?"

She leaned ever so slightly closer to him. "Who could I be more compatible with than someone like you?"

"It's true, we are compatible, but there's more to consider than compatibility."

"I know—there has to be physical attraction." She drew in her bottom lip, her voice low and soft. "Couldn't you ever find someone like me attractive?"

He took her hand the way he had so many times before, and met her lean. "You are a beautiful woman. Of course, I could find you physically attractive, if I were inclined that way. But I'm not."

She moved in closer, keeping her eyes fixed, yet dancing. "But if you allowed yourself, you could be."

"But I'm not."

"You don't know that. You *could.*"

She wanted to read ardor in the way he moved closer still, but his tone, as he said, "If I allowed myself, I could. Yes," remained as flat as his pressure on her hand.

Perhaps she could rouse his passion, make him feel what she felt. Leila leaned closer, bringing her lips to his. For a moment, he did not withdraw; he seemed merely to allow her kiss, but only by way of consolation as he nudged her away.

When pity-mingled compassion beamed from his eyes, she couldn't restrain her tears. "That's a no, isn't it."

"It's no, Leila." His own eyes turned glassy. "You are the dearest person to me, but I don't have those feelings for you. I'm so sorry."

It took a moment for his words to sink in, and then she jolted away from him and covered her face. "Oh, God. I'm so humiliated. I've ruined everything."

Clarence forcibly reclaimed her hand, speaking kindly, "Leila, this is not the end of the world."

She jerked her hand back and stood, gasping. "Is that why you've come back here with me, to drag this out of me?"

His eyes moved all around her and settled on her face.

"I've never been so mortified," she cried. "Why couldn't you just leave me be?"

Clarence sat at the edge of the settee, regaining his composure. "Because we need to deal with this."

Then it dawned on her—"You've known it all along."

"For a while. But you weren't ready to confront it."

"You should have just left me alone. We could have just drifted apart and let the feelings die."

Clarence rose but came no nearer. "And lose what we *do* have along with it. Neither of us wants that." He stroked her arm. "I can't stand the idea of losing you. We'll work through this like we do everything else."

She shrugged away from his touch. "That's easy for you to say. You're not the one who humiliated yourself."

"This isn't easy for me either, Leila."

She began to cry again and blurted, "I don't want to hear it," and retreated into the house and to her room for the rest of the night. She didn't care if he heard her crying herself to sleep.

🐚🦢⌒FOR SEVERAL HOURS AFTER THE LOON'S CALL, Leila ignored the aroma of coffee wafting to her room the next morning. She continued to drift in and out of consciousness. If there were any possible way to send Clarence Myles off without having to see him, she would have done so. She even dreamed that he had called a cab to take him to the airport, but the sounds of him in her kitchen yanked her back to reality. When the back door slammed, she crawled out of bed. Peering sideways out her bedroom window, she saw a sliver of his figure sitting on the partly visible deck. At least she could sneak into the hall and use the bathroom undetected.

Wrapping her cotton robe more tightly, she emerged from the bathroom only to find herself face-to-face with him. Without a word, she returned to her bedroom. She couldn't continue to ignore him, and so she dressed in cutoffs and a tank top. Perhaps he would have the decency to back off from the kitchen for a little while. When she again stepped out of her room, he stood in the open French door. She plodded her way to the coffee pot, poured a cup, and stared out the kitchen window as she sipped.

"You can't just keep ignoring me," he said.

"Yes, I can." She sidled past him, through the open door and onto the deck. He followed. Heading down the stairs, she quickened her step, all the way down to the landing and then to the end of the dock. The sun had not yet broken the treetops, and a cool breeze moved ripples across the water. If only she could dive in and keep swimming.

In several minutes, she heard Clarence's footfall, the way she knew she would. He stood behind her.

"This is the way you want to leave things?" he said.

She continued to stare out over the lake. "I just want to forget that last night ever happened."

He stepped beside her, turning to face her. "What exactly is it that you think happened?"

"You rejected me." She refused to exchange eye contact.

"Is that what I did?"

She'd had all night to think about it, to let her anger stew. "That and you humiliated me, knowing full well how I felt. You even let me kiss you." Her eyes flashed scorn. "That was cruel."

He absorbed her accusation and offered no rebuttal. He kicked a pebble from the dock. It disappeared into the ripples. "Leila, why do you suppose you are wrestling with these feelings?"

She folded her arms. "I'm not talking to you about this anymore."

"Then I'll do the talking."

"I suppose now you're going to offer me some lame 'car and driver' parable."

He sighed. "No, as a matter of fact, I'm not." He nudged his way to the edge of the dock in front of her—just enough to face her. "Leila, you miss your husband. You miss Ian so much—you miss his company—you miss the intimacy, mentally, emotionally ... and sexually." He paused for a moment. "You and I do have an exceptional relationship." He tried to meet her forward gaze, but her eyes remained fixed on nothing. "Do you realize how rare our relationship is?"

She didn't respond.

"No. I don't think you do. I think it's something you can't help but take for granted, because you came across this relatively early in your life. I am fifty-seven years old, and I have never—ever—had a relationship that rivals this, even given the generational disparity. Nor do I know of anyone with a comparable bond.

"You are still hurting and your psyche just wants to make that stop in the most expedient way it can. It's looking to fill a void with the relationship that naturally meets most of the criteria, and it's all too willing to slip in the romantic aspect to make it seem perfect."

He again shifted his stance, seeking her gaze. "You will move through this, just as you would with any other stage of grieving."

"Now you sound like Valerie Jennings."

"Valerie is a smart woman."

"Have you talked to *her* about this?"

"No. But perhaps you should."

Leila closed her eyes. "I don't want to talk about this any more."

He touched her shoulder. "Will you at least concede that this is not the death knell of our *exceptional* friendship?"

"I don't know." She still shook her head. "It's hard for me to even look you in the eye."

"Look at me."

"I can't."

He cupped her jaw, moving her face toward his. Her chin quivered as her eyes filled with tears. When she finally met his gaze, all she saw was a blur. She wasn't simply leaking, she was weeping.

"Why are you crying?"

"I miss Ian. I want him back."

"You want Ian."

"Yes," she sobbed, her hands now entwined with his.

He drew her to his chest. "It's not me you want."

"No."

Philadelphia

🐚 MYLES PUSHED AWAY FROM HIS DINING ROOM table, the subtle banana finish of a South African Pinotage lingered on his taste buds. One more swallow, without savoring it, and he would be ready to call Angela. At least that was his intent. It had taken a full day of reassuring himself, confirming that he had done the right thing with Leila, before he could even consider calling Miss Phillips. He wondered if he should call Leila instead—she likely needed the reassurance more than he did, but he would leave it up to Leila, as always, to set the pace. He blew out another second-guessing exhale. Had he, in fact, let her set the pace by forcing her hand, or had he only coaxed the inevitable? Perhaps he cruelly forced the issue—maybe even to answer a weakness he hadn't wanted to acknowledge. Answer it he did, but at her expense. Either way, he wanted to talk to Angela, needed her consolation and reinforcement.

After he dialed, Angela's first question was, "Did you work things out with Leila?"

"Well, we got things out in the open."

"How did it go?"

Again, the recalculating. "I think we made a little headway but she's hurting."

"Oh, my heart goes out to her. I wish there were something I could do …. Unrequited love can be so painful. Do you think she'll get over it?"

"I do." His voice held the conviction his heart lacked. "It may take some time, but I think she'll come around."

"And what about the grand opening? Will you attend?"

"I don't know. That may be too soon." He knew how he had left her, how tense and silent the drive to the airport had been. But he also knew what she had confessed in the end, fortifying his own stance. But how long would it take Leila to actually accept the reality of it?

He continued, "It will be such a special day for her—I'd hate to add awkwardness to injury."

Angela was quiet on the other end. Myles was about to speak up when she finally interjected, "Well, you certainly know her better than I, but I think not attending would be a mistake. And I'm not just saying that because *I* want you there. It will be a very important day for our Leila, and even if being there has its awkward moments, if you aren't there, both of you will always regret it—a girl never forgets a thing like that. I think you should seriously reconsider."

⚝CHAPTER 32

New Hampshire

R AW FROM CLARENCE'S HEART RENDING, AND still in the Marvellian shakedown of her psyche, Leila began the process of transferring her commotion onto paper. But as she stared at Arches Aquarelle paper, it stared back, mocking her in all its blankness. Perhaps she didn't possess any artistic greatness and had simply fooled herself, like she had with Clarence. She had risked all and still cringed at her own audacity. Were her artistic aspirations equally audacious?

She thumbed through tablet after tablet of the same old teacups and vases—years' worth of trying to portray every detail—of trying to mimic real life. She had sketched and painted her hand so many times that she could follow the progression of a child's overworked attempts on through to the long, slender fingers of a woman. In the end, her work had stagnated in every little detail—nothing left to the imagination.

Perhaps if she brought her art supplies up to the deck and painted *en plein air*, she would find the lake inspiring. Leila yearned for something moving, something about to burst into motion or bursting with desire. Unfortunately, bullfrogs didn't cut it.

She packed up her paints, paper, and Ian's camera, and drove down to the village beach. Children played by the water, some sitting and some wading. She sat at a picnic table. Before starting to sketch, she simply watched them play. What had it been like to be that young? The concept of childhood had no bearing in her reality—she hardly remembered anything earlier than about seven and not with any clarity. When these little humans grew up, would they remember this Memorial Day weekend? Would they recall the little red bucket they scooped sand into? She commenced sketching, happy that even if they forgot, she would capture it on paper.

After sketching and then beginning to paint, she heard a voice from behind.

"I guess I wasn't the only one with this idea."

She glanced up with excitement and smiled. "Jared. Hi."

Approaching in cutoffs and a T-shirt, he rolled his bicycle closer and leaned it against the picnic table.

"Do you mind sharing the bench?" he asked, pulling a sketchpad from his canvas pannier.

"Not at all." She inched aside.

"How about a look?"

She tipped her pad toward him.

He studied it for a moment. "Nice."

Leila thumped his pad. "Your turn."

He flipped back the cover to his first page.

"You're improving," she stated honestly, thumbing the next. "Do you mind?"

"Go ahead."

As she turned the next few pages, he said, "I heard from Ben that Marvelle Harding was tutoring you."

"Yeah. You probably also heard she died."

"Yeah. I'm sorry about that." He sat beside her, straddling the bench. "So, what was it like working with her?"

She swiveled to face him, tucking her ankle beneath her thigh. She thought for a moment. How could she possibly describe her time with Marvelle?

"Hmm ... well ... it was like, after being confined for a long time in a small dark box where you can barely move, and stepping out into a beautiful warm sunny spring day with birds singing and the scent of flowers—and then having someone come up and slap the snot right out of you."

Jared laughed. "Wow."

"Yeah. Pretty jarring—and powerful."

"I can only imagine—and then with the funeral and all."

"It was a very intense weekend." She studied his face, how the concentrated blue of his eyes paled in daylight. "How's Emily?"

"She's good." He blinked. "Did your grandmother and your friend Myles make it to the funeral?"

"Yeah, they did. I haven't seen you with Emily for a while."

"Her mother's spending more time with her. How did it go with Myles?"

"I think you might have been right about not taking all my emotions at face value right now. So, it's good that Sarah is spending more time with Emily, right?"

"Sure. It's good for Emily. So, your feelings for Myles are simmering down a little?"

"Maybe a little. So, things are working out with Sarah?"

"'Working out' is a relative term." He twisted the stud in his earlobe and his eyes shifted. "So, when do I get to see some of the work you did with Marvelle?"

"When her estate releases it. But I should warn you, I think some of it might make you blush."

He grinned. "Doubt it."

She glanced at his strong forearms. "So, you don't embarrass easy?"

"Nope."

"Prove it. Model for me right now."

He laughed. "Are you serious?"

"Yeah. Sit over there on the dam. Let me sketch you."

A pink blotch appeared on his face.

"You're being shy."

"Am not." He stood. "How exactly do you want me?"

"With mostly your back to me. One leg over the edge, the other knee bent skyward with your arm resting on it. And a profile of your face."

"You're a little demanding," he said, as he moved toward the concrete bulwark.

"And lose the shirt."

"What?"

"The shirt has to go."

"I burn easy."

"I won't keep you long."

He positioned himself as she requested—with his back to her—and pulled his T-shirt overhead, tossing it beside him. Though his skin was not tanned, his back was smooth and taut. She saw only a brief smattering of chest hair. Now she wished she had requested a front view.

"Could you move your whole body toward me just a tiny bit?"

As he shifted his weight, his back muscles flexed.

"I didn't take you for the sort to work out," she said.

He glanced over his shoulder. "I don't. I move pianos."

Leila analyzed the light and the contours of his body before putting pencil to paper. The way his eyes sparked when they met hers reminded her of Karl. Seizing the emotion, she let the surge come. Once she had the lines and the first wash down, she took the camera in hand.

"Hey, what's this?" He turned and looked straight at her. "You didn't say anything about photographs."

"Do you want to burn? Now turn back the way you were." He obeyed and she lifted the lens. "This way I can finish you in my studio." She clicked a few times and set the camera aside.

He shrugged back into his T-shirt, fully facing her and tugging the hem as he approached. "Let me see."

"No." She pulled the beginnings of her painting to her chest.

"Come on." He extended his hand. "I showed you mine."

She rolled her eyes and surrendered it. "Fine."

He held the pad away from him, his brow rising. "Where're my clothes?"

LEILA ARRIVED HOME AND, FEELING ELATED with the results of her short sketching spree, she bolted downstairs to Ian's studio.

Leila had no live models to sit for her, but in addition to the photos she took of Jared, she had numerous photographs on file. Many she had shot herself. For several hours, she delved into folder after folder of Ian, leafing through stacks, sorting an array of shots. In some, the light was wrong or the composition felt unbalanced. In others, there was not enough movement. Sidetracked for only a moment here and there, Leila evaluated each based on their interpretability—from photograph to watercolor painting. So many photographs, relying on timing and context, were perfect as snatches of time in a frame. But a painted rendition of that same event or object would likely come across as commonplace and affected. Only a certain few could hold up under translation.

Over the next two weeks, before and after work, Leila immersed herself in paintings of Ian, funneling all the passion and desire she had ever felt for him into each watercolor.

The first in the series was of him sailing on Pleasant Lake, with his boat at a full heel and the sail so full it might have given birth. The second, from a telephoto capture of his bare back, shoulder, and arm breaching the water, scattering droplets in a uniform arc above him. Another—Ian standing pensively on the bluffs of Pemaquid Point, Maine, overlooking the ocean with a fragment of lighthouse implied rather than clearly stated. Then another—shirtless Ian, bent at the waist, exhausted after a local triathlon, with every muscle taut and glistening. And a fifth, Ian, sound asleep beneath a white sheet draped over his hips, and luminous with shafts of early morning sunrays. It was the best work Leila had ever done—better than Karl, in her own estimation. And then there was the rendition of Jared—she shouldn't have allowed such intense desire to shape the body and color the flesh of a married man.

"SIX?" EVEN THROUGH THE PHONE LINE, ANDRÉ sounded shocked. Did his surprise spring from disappointment or pleasure?

"I can probably do a few extra, if it would make it more worth your while to look at them," she said.

"For six paintings? I've traveled a lot farther for less, that is if your off-the-cuff invitation to see the artist in her *milieu* still stands."

"Really? You'd actually come up here?"

"Of course I would. I'm very curious about how and where you live."

"When can you come?"

She heard him flipping pages. "Actually, probably the only time would be Sunday afternoon."

"That's good for me."

"Will you let me take you to dinner?"

"Maybe. We'll just have to see if I grow increasingly comfortable or *un*comfortable with you."

CHAPTER 33

L EILA PINCHED A BULB OF GARLIC AND TOSSED IT into her shopping cart. Even though André had suggested going out for dinner, she didn't know if he might show up around lunchtime, and she should at least have something on hand.

The red bell pepper in hand looked better than the green, and so she selected one of those, too. Perhaps she ought to whip up a batch of her favorite ginger pear scones. She tested the pears for ripeness and passed them over, moving on to the watermelons. Ian had always been better at choosing watermelon—something about the resonance when he thumped it. She gave one a thwack and then thwacked another. They sounded the same. She opted for the smaller. As she laid it in her cart, she glanced down the aisle toward the lettuce. A flash of red hair caught her eye—actually, two flashes.

Strawberry blond curls topped the head of a toddler who clung in the arms of a tall, ruddy-complected man with wild and flaming hair. Leila stared for a moment. The baby sure looked a lot like Emily, but Leila hadn't seen the child in months. And distinguishing one child from another was not her forte. Then, the beautiful brunette Leila had seen Jared with—his wife Sarah—came abreast of them, slipped her arm around the man's waist, and kissed him on the lips. As she took Emily into her arms, the man moved back in for another kiss, and not the sort that could be mistaken for familial affection.

Having lost all interest in shopping further, Leila hurried through the checkout and drove home. Did Jared know? Had he known all along? Leila's stomach twisted and turned. What sort of woman had he attached himself to? He had worse than marital *problems*. If Leila were him, she would want to know, though she hated the thought of telling him what she had seen in the produce aisle.

At home, Leila emptied her shopping bag, glancing at the phone. *Great—what am I going to do with garlic, a pepper, and watermelon?*

When she dialed Jared's number, his answering machine picked up. Aside from the fact that she hated leaving her voice on those recorders, she didn't know what to say. She hung up. She would try again in a few minutes. Meanwhile, she washed and cut up the watermelon. As soon as she wiped her hands and reached for the phone, she heard a knock at her door.

André called out, "Hello?"

"Hi. Come on in." Wiping her hands on her cutoffs, she yanked her tank top neckline up a little higher. She had meant to change and put on a little makeup.

"Hope I'm not too early."

"Well, I did think afternoon meant more like *mid*-afternoon, not twelve-o-five. I didn't tidy up the way I wanted."

He had dressed down in jeans and a polo shirt. "I'm sorry. Traffic wasn't as bad as I expected. I could leave and come back, if you want."

"Don't be silly." She fluffed a pillow and removed a chiffon scarf from the back of her Windsor rocker while kicking her sneakers out of the way. "You'll just get to see how I *really* live."

His eyes moved all around the room. "This is nice. Great atmosphere. Really nice trim work."

"That's all Ian's doing."

Giving the photography on the wall a passing look, he moved to the picture windows overlooking the deck and lake. "Wow, this is beautiful. How long have you lived here now?"

"Going on four-and-a-half years."

Referring to the photos, he said, "We didn't see but a couple of those."

"Yes, well, I was hoping not to overwhelm you in Mississippi."

"May I see more of his work while I'm here, after I see yours?"

"Sure—we'll go down right now, unless you'd like some watermelon. I'm afraid I don't have anything more interesting to offer."

"Then I guess I *will* have to take you out for dinner."

"Perhaps." Leila directed him to the stairwell. Flipping the light switch, she confessed, "I'm a little nervous."

"Seriously?"

"Very seriously." They descended the stairs. "I'm about to show you my artwork—about to bare my soul." She stood with her hand on her studio's doorknob. "I want my paintings to be worthy of your expectations, of what I accomplished with Marvelle—worthy of her expectations."

"And if they're not?"

"I'm afraid I'll be devastated."

"There's that word *afraid*, again."

Leila shrugged.

"Listen," he said, "if I don't like them, I'm going to be honest. But my opinion is by no means the last word. Even if they are not what *Chez* Goulet is interested in, there are many other galleries out there. Your career is not contingent on my opinion or my father's."

"Alright, let's just get this over with." She burst into her room.

The painting of Jared, which she had just finished, lay atop her drawing table. "Wait, don't look." Something less provocative would be a better start. "Okay."

He maintained his distance. "Hold it up for me, in the light."

Leila did so, holding her breath.

"Next."

Leila took another from the table and held it up. She studied his poker face, detecting little reaction.

"Next." That was the way he did with each subsequent painting until she came to her last, Jared, and held it up. Still no reaction.

Finally, he asked, "You have foam board, to sandwich them between, for transportation?"

"Yes. Does that mean you like them?"

André gave her a quizzical look. "Why would I transport them if I didn't like them?"

Leila returned his surprise. "Well, aren't you going to critique them or anything?"

"Leila, I'm not an artist. I'm not an art teacher. I'm not even an art critic. I only know that I like them. I think my father should see them and give his final word."

"That's it? You're not even going to tell me which one you liked best, or what you liked about any of them?"

"You really care what I think?"

"Yes, you moron. Why do you think I brought you down here?"

He laughed. "You realize I don't have the final say. I'm here as an envoy and because I'm curious about *you*."

"Yes. Now don't make me beg like a prima donna."

"Alright. I like the last one most of all, although, the one of the man sleeping—"

"It's Ian—"

"I like the sensuality of that one, although there is implied sensuality to all of your work." He grinned. "Though I would prefer if they were women."

"So, that's all you have to say?"

He approached her. "I think you are a promising young artist with work as good as much of what I've seen move through our gallery. You should feel proud and worthy. Please don't be disappointed with my lack of artistic finesse. Remember—I'm primarily the bean counter."

It fully dawned on her. "You really are here mostly because you want to take me to dinner."

"No. I mean yes, I think I've made that very clear. And I *am* here to collect more samples of your art before our debut. Now, what do you say you show me some of your husband's photography—the stuff that will teach me something about you."

She placed her watercolors in a rigid portfolio, tied it shut and handed it to him.

"This will not be as interesting as you seem to think," she said, leading him into Ian's studio.

Leila turned on the light over his worktable and then carefully selected a short series of pictures that gave some vague impression of her life with Ian. Places they had visited and things they had enjoyed together. Nothing like what she had shown Jared.

"So your life didn't actually start till after you married Ian?"

She detected facetiousness and returned in kind, "Apparently not."

"Well, I'm sure the two of you were very much in love, and pardon me for being so blunt, but none of these—" he fanned her select photos, "—are of defining interest or account for who you are now."

"If you find them uninteresting, perhaps your expectations are too high."

"Rarely are my expectations too high. Tell me about how the two of you met."

Leila squinted reservation.

"So, there *was* something interesting about how the two of you came together."

She folded her arms tightly.

"Oh, come on, I'm very confidential by nature. I have to be, I'm an accountant. I never spill anyone's beans."

"I had a flat. He changed my tire."

"And?"

"I was a student. He was the coach."

"Now that's interesting."

"Yes, and nothing I'm going to expound upon," she said with finality.

"Alright, I won't push … but perhaps you'd fill me in on why Angela refers to Clarence Myles as your 'guardian?'"

She sighed. "You know, I just don't want to get into all that right now …."

"So Myles is still a sore subject."

She clicked her tongue. "I don't exactly know what he is."

"But—" he studied her eyes, "—he's not still in the running?"

"No. And that's all I have to say about that."

"You're making it very difficult to get to know you."

"Knowing me isn't about what I tell you, it's about doing the time." She turned off the light over the table.

"Then how about a swim?" he said.

"You brought your suit?"

He chuckled. "I drove all the way from Boston to a lake in New Hampshire, and I'm going to leave my suit at home?"

She sighed. He had coaxed her grin. "That actually sounds really good. Go ahead and get your stuff. You can change in my room—I mean this one, down here."

Leila made it to the water first and waded out. She swam circles around the cove as André came out the lower back exit onto the little beach.

Wearing a Speedo, he walked to the end of the dock, surveying the surroundings. "How is it?"

"Nice. Come on in." She couldn't deny that he looked good—really good. Although he did ignite a bit of chemistry, he didn't stir the intense desires Ian had, or Clarence—or even Jared. Would spending more time with him change that?

He dove and when he emerged tiny ringlets of hair formed around his face. He turned in the water and swam out a distance. Laggardly following, she swam in his direction. When he reached his farthest point, he then retraced his wake back toward her. She began swimming away. She knew he would try to shorten the distance between them. Rotating to a backstroke, she faced him and continued swimming away.

"A little trouble catching up?" she taunted, stroking toward the shore that came up quicker than she expected.

He closed in on her and grabbed her ankle as she ran aground. She leaned back in knee-deep water. His body moved astride hers.

"Looks like you've been caught."

The chemistry that minutes ago felt latent now flared, and even in the cool water, Leila's body heated. Now, he had opportunity to kiss her, and if he had read her correctly, she might have allowed it. Instead, he only hovered over her, so near that she felt his breath. He pushed himself off her and stood.

"How about an early dinner," he said, offering his hand. His eyes moved all over her as she rose. He did not relinquish his grasp. "Casual or—?"

"—I'm not interested in casual."

"Well, I didn't take you for a *fast* food kind of girl."

"Good, 'cause I'm not. I like a full course."

His coy brow flicked. "Dessert included?"

A dozen flirtatious responses ran through Leila's head, the kind of banter Ian had enjoyed. Her cheeks flamed.

André chuckled. "That's right—you're one of those girls who'd love dessert but won't let yourself."

"I'd eat dessert if I had a sweet-tooth," she pulled back, averting her eyes. "But I don't."

LEILA GATHERED UP THE FLARED SKIRT OF HER chambray dress and smoothed the fitted bodice as she scooted toward the corner of their booth. The dim lights muted periwinkle to a warmer blue.

"Guinness on tap." Leila laid her ID on the table as André perused Peter Christian's wine list.

"Black Russian," he said to the waitress. "Give us a few minutes with the menu."

Their booth provided the illusion of privacy, and André left little space in the corner between them.

"So, tell me about debut night at *Chez* Goulet, Boston. What's it going to be like?" Leila said.

"Black ties, evening gowns, champagne, caviar, string quartet, white-glove catering. Big-money clients. A real gala event."

"I suppose I'll need a special dress."

"Actually, the one you wore to Angela's dinner party would be perfect."

"But it's not a gown."

"Didn't you know that no one really expects the artists to fall in line? You might actually be a trendsetter. And personally, I would love to see you in that again. Perhaps you could even borrow Angela's pearls."

"I'll have you know those pearls are mine—a gift from an admirer."

"Sorry. I should have assumed that."

"Well, your dress preference just saved me a wad of dough and a lot of time doing what I like least—shopping."

The waitress returned to the table.

Leila ordered, "Quiche of the day, please."

"Pork *Osso Bucco*. Thanks." André returned his attention to Leila. "You really don't care about money and all its trappings."

"No."

"Pretty typical for artist types."

"So, what's the actual date?"

"Saturday, July twenty-third, cocktails at five, by invitation only. By the way, each exhibitor receives a complimentary guest invitation, and since you represent two artists, you're allowed two."

"You're assuming I could scrounge up two people."

"I should hope so. But please don't scrounge. This is a very crusty event."

André explained more details and ran down a list of other artists who would be exhibiting. Leila should have known who they were—Ben's censure of her ignorance came back to her—in fact, André had to fill her in on their client's impressive dossiers. She staved off feelings of inadequacy.

She frowned. "I don't have one degree to tack onto my name, let alone an MFA."

"And only one of our artists—besides you—has the distinction of receiving Marvelle Harding's loving tutelage. You have nothing to feel insecure about. Besides, you're very young. Those artists with degrees are considerably older than you."

The waitress returned with their dinner. As Leila poked ham and spinach quiche in her mouth, trying to chew in a ladylike way, she watched André dissect his pork. Several times Leila caught him staring, and several times he caught her.

She had been mulling over her impressions of him. He no longer seemed like the man who was, only months ago, so intent on bedding her. Not that she didn't think it was still his primary objective, but there seemed to be more to him than what she previously assumed; she just didn't know what it was.

"There's something you'd like to ask me?" he said, having caught her scrutinizing stare for the third time.

She smirked at his perceptiveness. "Is money the most important thing in your life or what?"

He sat back and chuckled, wiping his mouth.

She clarified, "I mean, you're always talking about money and how important it is, and everything about you reeks of money, from your Porsche to your Rolex—even your cologne—which I like, by the way. Don't you have any other interests?"

"Leila, money is what I do. I have to drive a certain car and look a certain way to attract people with money. It gives them confidence that I can manage *their* money. It's not who I am."

"So, who are you?"

He looked at her sideways and sipped his drink. "Who do you think I am?"

"I don't know. I'd like to think there's a side to you I haven't seen yet."

"You know, you're not the only one who's complex enough to require time."

When the contemplative look between them became too intense for Leila's comfort, she gazed off, speculating on his hidden side. The waitress came to take away her plate; behind her, another patron came into view. He met Leila's eyes as he passed.

Jared.

It took a second, but he paused with recognition.

"Hi," she said.

Jared glanced at André and back at her. "Hi."

Her heart pounded, recalling what she had seen earlier that day. From Jared's bloodshot and disheveled appearance, she assumed he already knew about Sarah. Leila looked for his diamond stud. His earlobe was as unadorned as her ring finger.

"Jared, this is André—I told you about him. He's connected to the gallery in Boston."

"Right. Good to meet you." Jared nodded and leaned to shake André's hand. "Sorry. Didn't mean to interrupt. You two have a nice evening."

As Jared walked away, Leila's heart trailed with him.

"Would you please excuse me a minute," she said, scooting across the bench and rising from the table. Jared was about to step into the men's room around the corner when she caught up to him. She touched his sleeve.

"Jared."

He turned. His tortured eyes blinked slowly.

"I'm so sorry about Sarah—and Emily," she said, taking his hand.

"You already know?" Both brows arched.

"I saw her with—I guess it was Emily's father—at Cricenti's this morning."

He sighed, looking dazed and on the verge of tears. "You should go back to your date."

"He's not really my date, exactly. Well, he sort of is—a business date."

"Just the same ...."

Leila squeezed his hand. "I'm so sorry."

"Listen," he forced a smile, stepping toward the restroom door, "I really gotta go. *Really*."

She returned to the table, aching for Jared and embarrassed she had abandoned André, if only for a few seconds.

André sipped a fresh drink. "I hope your friend is okay. He didn't look too good."

"I'm sorry. That was really rude of me."

"Did I recognize him from one of your paintings?"

Leila realized how it must have appeared. "Yes. But it's not what it looks like. Jared's a good friend—and he's married." At least she assumed he still was.

"So older men *and* married men, is it?"

"That's not fair. It's not what you think."

"I honestly don't know what to think, Leila. I mean, one minute, I could swear you're ready to jump my bones, and the next ...." He shook his head. "You sure do run hot and cold."

"I'm sorry. I don't mean to." Perhaps Angela was right about the way she was with men, but then who was André to accuse her? "I was under the impression that—"

"That what? I'm impervious to having my feelings injured?"

"Or maybe just your ego. What difference do *I* make to you, beyond business and flirting? I know about your reputation."

"Really? And what's my reputation?"

"That you go through a lot of women. That you're never serious about relationships. Even *you* imply as much."

He nodded, but it seemed more with resignation than agreement. "I see. And that's how you view me?"

"I think you're probably the kind of man who wants what he doesn't have."

"And once I get it?"

"You move on."

"And you think that if I *had* you, I would just move on?"

"Wouldn't you?"

"I suppose that would depend upon what *part* of you I had."

"And what *part* do you want?"

His eyes moved all around the table. He hesitated as if he might divulge his random thoughts, what it was he truly desired, but something Leila had never seen in him wavered behind his expression.

Insecurity.

He took a fifty from his wallet, laid it on the table, and said, "Let's go."

No dessert.

CHAPTER 34

FTER WORK, LEILA PULLED OUT OF THE STORE parking lot, reviewing the directions she had written on a scrap of paper with doodles scrolled around Jared's name. She glanced at the invitations on her dashboard, tossed there after her first look at them. Even now, her self-consciousness piqued at how prominently *The Protégé* was displayed on the front. André had given her no warning of that—in fact, they had both been in such a hurry to end the evening that the envelopes remained unopened until this morning.

She and André hadn't parted on poor terms, but she doubted he had intended for their evening to end the way it had. Nor had she been prepared for the tenderness he stirred in her. She hated that her heart was constantly evaluating each man in her life, trying to make him size up to Ian. She didn't truly think André had a chance, but there was still so much about him to discover. Her heart no longer wished to disqualify him based on her first impression—was this by his design, simply part of the seduction? At least with Jared, she never questioned his motives—he seemed beyond guile, though according to her father, no man was beyond guile.

As she drove, Leila was fairly certain where she was headed. She had passed the old stone barn and milkhouse dozens of times, but she hadn't been on route 103-A in months. Despite his changed circumstances, it was easy to picture Jared in his new setting.

He hadn't sounded so much distraught as resigned when she called him earlier in the day. In fact, she had caught him on his way out with his last packed box.

"She's the one who wants the divorce," Leila had said, indignant for him. "Why do *you* have to move out?"

"Because it doesn't matter to me where I live, and I want what's going to be easiest for Emily."

"Well, would you like some help unpacking?" she had asked. "I wanted to stop by anyway—I have something for you."

He had perked up a little. "Sure—not that there's much to unpack ...."

Spotting the enormous barn and silo first, Leila slowed until the small milkhouse nearer the road came into view. Four white pillars spanned a front overhang forming a shallow concrete porch. She pulled into the dooryard, passing a trunk-like vine crawling up massive stones on the south exposure. A few late wisteria blooms drooped and swayed in the breeze. With invitation in hand, she approached the back, paint-crazed entrance. Before she had a chance to knock, Jared opened the top of the Dutch door.

"Pretty cool place, huh?" he said. His chipper voice sounded forced. He welcomed her into the small kitchen, tiled with tiny white rectangles and octagons. The temperature dropped as she stepped inside the milkhouse.

"This is great in the summer," she said. "Practically like air-conditioning."

"Yeah, but wait till winter," he laughed.

Two boxes lay on the counter to her left, and a few dry cleaner bags of clothes draped over a wrought-iron, spiral staircase to her right.

"Well, this is kind of cute," she said, taking just a couple of steps to stand in the doorway to a larger room, with a front door that overlooked the road. Side and back windows allowed sufficient light to show the irregularities of whitewashed cement and plaster walls. One overstuffed chair and a card table sat in the middle of the room. Antique-framed paintings leaned against chalky, flaking paint.

"Tell me you haven't finished moving all your stuff in."

"No, this is it. Of course, there's loads of stuff upstairs—boxes and boxes. Yeah, that's right—towels and a set of sheets, too. And huge pieces of furniture."

"Up a spiral staircase?"

"I'm a minimalist, what can I say."

Leila was aghast. "You let her keep everything?"

He gestured toward his chair and artwork. "Obviously, not *everything*. And I have a pot and frying pan in the kitchen. *And* I got to keep the phone number."

"Why would you do that?"

"Because changing my number would mess with my livelihood."

"You know what I mean."

His expression turned sincere. "I don't care about the stuff. Stuff comes and goes. The cleaner the break—the less fighting over stuff—all the better for Emily."

"So, how long have you known that Emily isn't yours?"

"Pretty much since she was born. I mean it was obvious, and I knew Sarah's old boyfriend was a redhead."

"She lied."

"I think she believed I would make a better father. Apparently, now she thinks ol' Red will do just fine."

"Oh, Jared. Are you going to try and get joint custody or work out visitations or something?"

"I haven't spoken to my lawyer yet. But what I really need to do is sort out my own motives. Is it going to be easier for Emily in the long run if I just back out gracefully? Is it just selfishness on my part to insist on legal rights, just because I'll miss her? I mean, she's not even two yet. If she were older, I suppose that would make more of a difference to her. I don't know."

"Jared, did you love Sarah when you married her?"

"I suppose I was more in love with a fantasy of being married to her. And I wanted to do the right thing. I believed she was pregnant with my child. No one forced me into the marriage. And Sarah's beautiful. I really thought that if I just tried hard enough, I could make it work."

"Did she ever love you?"

"She said she did, but—well, it's pretty obvious those were just words. I think I wasn't the only one in love with a fantasy."

"I'm so sorry."

"To be honest, if it weren't for Emily, I would just be relieved that it's over. But ... I love that little girl." He choked up but caught himself. "Anyway ... don't you have something for me? I need cheering up."

"Oh, yes." She handed him the envelope. "It's actually kind of a shocker."

He slipped the invitation out, looking at the front, and then read the inside. His brow, as inquisitive as his eyes, returned to Leila. "This is so much like that photo Ian took of you, but more intense."

She laughed. "Well, for several thousand dollars, it could probably be yours."

"If only," he said, looking into her eyes. "I'd be honored to go."

"Think you could manage a tux?"

"I actually own one. Vintage. Thrift store. Mint condition. And I know how to tie a real bow tie—none of those clip-on contraptions for me."

"Perfect." Her feet shuffled as her hand raked through her hair. "Um, it wouldn't actually be a date or anything, in case you're wondering—you know, the two-year rule."

"Well, that's a lame rule."

She smirked. "Besides, technically, your divorce wouldn't be final for a few months anyway, right? And you don't really take me for the sort that would date a married man, do you?"

"No. And I'm not ready for anything—not for a while …."

"Didn't think so."

"But that probably won't keep me from thinking about it."

Neither had moved closer to the other, but suddenly he felt very near as his gaze drew her deepest desires closer to the surface.

She swallowed back an impulse to kiss him and spoke instead. "Just don't let your imagination get the better of you again."

"I'll worry about my own imagination—" his brow twitched, "—you just worry about *yours*."

Her shoulders rose with her chest as she filled her lungs. "I think I'll just go stag for a while."

"So, that guy you were with—is he more than a friend or business associate?"

"To be honest, Jared, I'm not sure what he is."

"And what about Clarence Myles?"

"I'm still trying to figure that out."

Boston

THE CURVES OF A MOORISH-STYLE ARCH ATOP two pillars framed a huge painting, which held Leila's attention for the past ten minutes. She had stepped out of the July heat into the coolness of the Isabella Stewart Gardener

Museum and stalled in the Spanish Cloister—the first exhibit room. She examined the lighting of John Singer Sargent's *El Jaleo*. The sensual Gypsy dancer, with her arms bare and twisted in the foreground, her skirt vibrantly lit from the floor, casting a majestic shadow on the wall behind. The row of musicians sitting against the wall, with light playing upon their faces and guitars. Sargent's style exhibited a certain looseness, while including so much detail. As much as she looked forward to seeing the portrait Sargent had painted of Isabella, up in the third floor Gothic Room, this painting, amidst Spanish architecture of the Middle Ages, enthralled her.

Leila had seen other Singer Sargents at the Boston Museum of Fine Arts with Ian, and she even considered marking this two-year anniversary in familiar surroundings. Instead, she chose the more intimate, uninitiated setting at the museum around the corner. No movie theater, this year. Clarence would be proud.

Across cool, tiled floors, she strolled out to the Courtyard, the museum's centerpiece. From the pillared railing at the front of the enclosed garden, she peered three stories high at the glass roof, at the windows and balconies overlooking the garden's architectural artifacts. Vibrant, spiky blue flowers, small palm trees, and patches of lush grass adorned the Greco-Roman statues. She sighed at its loveliness, wishing she had someone to share it with, but glad for the moments of private introspection it provided. Really, as much as she missed Ian and still longed for Clarence, she didn't need either to find joy in the moment.

Leila ambled around the garden's colonnaded circumference, pausing at each piece of art. While she found the artifacts interesting, her immediate interest lay in the painted works, especially in the upper galleries. She had brought along a notepad to record her favorites and to acquaint herself with the artists. It was time to learn more than simply the technical aspects of her craft. Perhaps she would even take some classes on art history.

Leila's steps wove up the stairway and through one room to another, taking a moment at each window to gaze down onto the courtyard. In the Dutch Room, she admired the intricate detail of Johannes Vermeer's *The Concert*. At the Courtyard overlook, she thought of Clarence.

A month ago, the idea of kissing him made her insides flutter; now, it brought a blush. The utter humiliation had ebbed, but she still felt a wave of embarrassment. How could he have allowed—no, prompted—her follow through on kissing him? She shook her head. He had always been one to utilize object lessons, but this time he had gone too far. Just the same, Leila supposed he was overdue. It had been several years since he had employed such tactics. Object lessons and pushing boundaries—his *modus operandi*.

The fact was, Clarence Myles had been pushing the boundaries of their relationship since the day they first met at her summer job at the mall, back at Sam Goody's in the summer of '77. It was a small thing—him assuming she would locate and obtain obscure musical selections without contact information, for a curmudgeon, no less. She had suffered no consequence except irritation, but it made for an interesting first day at school when she realized he would be her homeroom and then math teacher. He seemed to delight in putting her on the spot. And that was the least of it.

The day he showed up at her apartment as a consequence of her parental no-show at parent-teacher conferences, he had pushed the limits of convention when he promised to keep her unsupervised status to himself. Her customer from hell—turned math teacher, turned accomplice—had invaded her life, putting his own career at risk. She resisted and welcomed him at the same time.

Leila smiled, recalling their conversations, when she purposefully arrived early for homeroom. He even showed up at the movie theater on Christmas, the one-year anniversary of her father's death, and took her to dinner afterward. Another wall breached. But all that paled when compared to the risk he took presenting himself as her counsel at the school-board hearing after she had been accosted in class by her gym instructor, Ian's former lover. She had never felt more cared for than when he petitioned the state for her guardianship—and received it. Clarence Myles had been there for her when she found out about her mother's suicide, and she had been there for him when he learned of his daughter's whereabouts after so many years he had given up hope.

Adversity and stress had solidified their relationship, forming it into their exceptional—rare—friendship. They had survived so much in the past six years, stresses that would have terminated most relationships—but they always came out of it stronger and closer. They had been each other's constant. As risky as it had been for Clarence to push this last perimeter, he did have good reason for confidence that they would come through it, each with their dignity and love for the other intact.

On her way home, Leila dropped another *Chez* Goulet Grand Opening invitation in the mailbox.

CHAPTER 35

Boston

ANGELA LEAFED THROUGH HER MORNING edition of *The Boston Globe*, hoping to have it read before François came down for breakfast. Across the table, André sighed. She looked up from her paper as he downed the rest of his coffee, leaving half-eaten toast on his plate.

"Will you be getting back at a decent hour tonight, dear?" She sipped coffee.

"Probably not till after midnight again."

"Oh, I just thought that with Leila arriving this afternoon...."

"She's coming this afternoon?"

Angela suppressed a smirk. "Didn't you know?"

André tipped his empty cup, bottom up against his lips once more, avoiding Angela's insistent stare. She had a way of demanding a man's focus even if he preferred dodging her.

When their eyes met, his darted away.

"Oh my goodness ...." She fully smirked. "That look can mean only one of two things, and I don't know which is more unlikely, André. Have you fallen for my granddaughter?"

His eyes flashed and his jaw tensed.

Angela folded her paper. "Well, have you told her?"

"I don't have time to indulge the speculations of an old biddy." He rose, thumping his napkin onto the table.

"Old biddy, indeed," she said as he walked away. "Did you learn nothing from Marvelle?"

As soon as the words left her mouth, her own motives tore at her for implying he should confess his feelings. Even if André were in love with Leila, was it simply selfishness to wish Leila would reciprocate? And André of all men? He had broken so many hearts ... but perhaps it was *his* heart in jeopardy now.

A WARM JULY BREEZE PUSHED LEILA'S HAIR from her face as she and Angela walked up Newbury Street, passing boutique after boutique. They paused at a clearance-sale rack, where boxes of designer shoes beckoned a further look. Leila picked up a pair of loafers—perhaps she would expand her foot wardrobe.

"Fifty bucks!" Leila exclaimed with disgust, drawing caustic glares as she dropped the shoe back in the box. "Honestly, Angela, do you really enjoy shopping?"

Her grandmother chuckled as they continued down the sidewalk. "Oh, shopping isn't all that horrid, especially if one isn't looking for anything in particular."

"Then why not just hit the yard sales?"

Angela looked at her with all seriousness. "It's all in the experience, Leila. In seeing what's out there—what's available. One must always be open to any new opportunities."

Leila perceived that Angela was not talking about shopping at all. In her heart, Leila knew there was truth to her grandmother's comment. Just the same, Leila had come to view the woman's admonitions with skepticism. Not that Angela wasn't spot on in her observations. Leila simply liked to find fault with her grandmother for the sake of establishing her own way.

They stayed their course beyond a traffic crossing and Angela sighed. "You know what I miss?"

Leila raised a patronizing brow. "What?"

"Hmm …. Gloves. Lady-like gloves."

"Why gloves?"

"Men. They are so funny. Show them a full *décolletage* but cover your hands, and what do you suppose they can't stand not seeing?"

"Oh please. They couldn't care less about hands."

"It's not about the hands. It's about what's being withheld."

"Men want what they can't have?"

Angela countered with her own patronizing brow.

Leila rebutted, "Aren't women that way too?"

"Sometimes," she said as they approached *Chez* Goulet, ensconced behind white sheeting.

Leila glanced at Angela. Did the woman maneuver conversations to a pre-plotted end? Or had their destination been inadvertent?

They stood at the concrete and brick stairway as if they were mere tourists. "Angela …."

"Yes, dear."

"Are you in love with Clarence?"

Angela inhaled, stressing the buttons of her Evan Picone bolero.

"I care for him …."

"But are you in love?"

"I don't know the best way to answer you."

"Why not be honest?"

Angela studied her manicured hands, stared ahead, and then gave Leila her deliberate focus but said nothing. The reason for Angela's reticence now dawned on Leila.

"Oh my gosh …." Leila's gaze cast aside, sending her head in a spin, her strength fleeing. "He told you—he told you about … our conversation."

Angela hesitated and then confessed, "Leila, it was something he and I needed to talk about."

"Oh my gosh—" her eyes rolled behind closed lids as she turned away. "I can't believe he told you. I am so mortified."

"Leila, there's nothing to be embarrassed about, least of all in front of me. I'm actually in the best position to sympathize—I know how the heart can be. One minute it's convincing you of one thing, and as soon as you obey it, it turns on you, making you feel the fool. It's treacherous."

Leila's vigor returned as she spun back to meet her grandmother. "You don't know the first thing about how I feel. You have no idea what Clarence is to me. You step in, midstream, and think you know what he and I have been through together?" Indignation flamed from her eyes as passersby stared. "How dare you!"

Angela bit her lip but solicited no sympathy from her granddaughter. All Leila wanted was to shred whatever intimacy Angela and Clarence had shared.

Leila's focus bore down on her. "Have you slept with him?"

Angela nudged Leila out of foot traffic and off to the side, near the building. "Leila, that's very personal."

"Don't talk to me about *personal*." She recoiled. "And don't talk to me like I'm a child, Angela. I need to know. I have the right to know. Have you slept with him?"

Angela lowered her voice. "I beg to differ about your right to know, but no, I haven't."

Leila reciprocated. "Why not?"

"Because we felt it best not to become overly emotionally or physically involved until your feelings for him have been resolved."

"You just assume my feelings would resolve themselves —that they'd simply go away?"

"We hope they will work themselves out, though I suppose neither of us take that for granted."

"And what if my feelings never get 'resolved?'"

"Then he and I—then *we* shall both end up very lonely and disappointed."

Leila stared at her a long moment, wagering her deflating anger against what Angela had just divulged. "You'd give him up out of consideration for me—for my feelings?"

"As would he."

The tears that anger had restrained now brimmed from her eyes. "You're in love with him."

"I'm afraid so."

"Is he in love with you?"

"You'd have to ask him."

Something akin to resentment—no, protectiveness—flared.

"Angela, if you ever, *ever* hurt him—I swear to God I will never have another thing to do with you or your life or your friends—" she gestured toward the gallery, "—or any of this. You will never see me or hear from me again. I will hate you until the day I die if you cause my Clarence pain."

NEAR MIDNIGHT, LEILA HEARD ANDRÉ DOWNSTAIRS. Since he had missed supper, they had avoided awkwardness, which had been a relief, but she was disappointed to have not seen him since she arrived.

Footsteps in the hall paused at her door, then three light taps and his quiet voice interrupted the silence. "You awake?"

She didn't hesitate to answer. "Yeah," she said loud enough to detain him as she snatched her robe and cracked the door.

André held an armful of papers. "I hope you weren't sleeping."

"No. I'm like a kid the night before a new school. Too nerved up to sleep."

"I have some paperwork I need you to sign. Would you care to join me for a nightcap?"

She rubbed her eyes. "Sure."

"I need some stuff from my office. I'll meet you in the parlor."

She arrived first and sat in an upholstered chair, waiting only a minute before he joined her. His shirtsleeves were rolled up his forearms. His tie was loose, the top buttons undone.

"You look exhausted," she said.

"It's been a hell of a day." He exhaled, kicking off his loafers. "Let's get these papers out of the way first. I don't want to be held liable for fraud."

"Seriously?"

"Seriously." He rubbed his forehead. "Don't worry, your signature will clear me."

As he handed her several legal-size documents, she asked, "Do I need to read these over before I sign them?"

"That depends." Their eyes met; he did not let go of the papers. "Do you trust me?"

She pondered the gravity of his question. "Yes."

He released the documents and handed her a pen. "These essentially provide you with ownership of your paintings. They also release specific pieces—the ones we discussed—into the custody of *Chez* Goulet. It's all the terms and conditions, like we went over with Ian's work. I'll review them with you, if you like."

"François and Angela already gave me a rundown on all that. Just show me where to sign."

He stood over her, pulling at and stretching the muscles of his neck as she penned her name.

He rubbed his eyes. "Cognac?"

"Why don't you sit?" She didn't give him a chance to respond before she stood. "Let me pour."

"Thanks. Bourbon." He dropped to a low-back

upholstered chair, leaned forward on his elbows, and massaged his temples.

"Headache?" she asked, passing him his tumbler.

"Just tension."

Leila sipped her drink and set it aside.

"Normally, I wouldn't do this," she said, coming up behind him. Grabbing his tie, she pulled it up over his head. "But …."

"But what?"

"But nothing …." She placed her hands on his shoulders and began massaging gently and then with increasing pressure, not the way a woman might if she intended to seduce him but as if she really meant it—as if those kinks in his neck didn't stand a chance. "Just don't—"

"Don't what? Don't go falling in love with you?"

"That's right."

"I'm afraid it's too late for that." He groaned. "Oh, that feels good."

"Don't joke about that, André."

He grabbed her hand and moaned. Maneuvering her back around to face him, he said, "That's one thing I would never joke about."

He pulled her down to his lap and she allowed it. "I overreacted at dinner the other night. I've never been a jealous man. And believe it or not, I don't always get every woman I want, but that's never really mattered to me. I simply move on as you so aptly pointed out."

"André …." Leila's eyes drifted, afraid of what he was about to confess.

"Let me finish." He stroked her hand. "Leila, I haven't been with another woman since I met you. I haven't even been interested in pursuing another woman."

"That's only because you haven't succeeded in seducing me."

"You think I don't know my own heart?"

"How would *I* know, André? I'm still trying to sort out *my* own heart."

"I understand that. I do. But if I don't tell you that I'm in love with you, tonight, I'm afraid you'll slip away. I don't expect you to respond. In fact, I don't want you to respond right now. I just want you to know how I feel. No obligations. No strings. Just think about the possibility of you and me—and I don't mean just a fling. I mean taking the time to really know each other."

"Oh, André …."

"You do feel something for me—of that much, I'm sure …." He pulled her to his lips, kissing her with all the sensuality she had been missing. It felt so good, just to be kissed.

She withdrew. "You do intrigue me, André, and you are a lot of fun. It's true, I do feel something for you—I just don't know if it's more than plain lust."

CHAPTER 36

"COME ON IN," LEILA SAID. IN RESPONSE TO
A tap at the guest bedroom door. Angela.
Despite yesterday's tension, with all that Leila
had vented, her grandmother still treated her cordially, if not
with greater consideration. Although it had been humiliating,
Angela's knowledge of the situation lifted a great burden
from Leila's mind and heart. They had come to an accord.
She hadn't sorted out why that should be the case, but she
felt closer to her grandmother for it—and more settled in her
feelings for Clarence.

As she stood before the full-length mirror, her
grandmother appeared behind her in sapphire crepe and
charmeuse.

"Oh," Angela said, "I thought you were going with the
black cocktail dress, again."

"I was in the mood for peach organza." In all honesty,
Leila's choice had more to do with her independent streak,
given that André had expressed a preference. "It's so much
more summery. Besides, it still has what was apparently your
favorite feature—practically backless. I'm curious. What did
you wear for a bra back then?"

"With breasts like ours, who needed a bra?" She chuckled, giving her own breast a gentle lift. "Of course, all that changes in time. Enjoy it while you can."

Leila turned to face her. Angela adjusted Leila's wide-set shoulders straps and glanced at the plunged V neckline. She ran her hands against tiny tucks of chiffon that skimmed Leila's fitted waist, ending at her hip, where yards and yards of silk organza gathered at the dropped waist.

"No crinoline dear?"

"Too poufy."

"And your hair?"

"Help me put it up, like last time."

"The French twist—so classic. You are stunning."

"Stunned is more like it."

"You're nervous."

"Nauseous, actually."

Their eyes met. "This is such a big day for you."

"Angela—Grandmother …." Leila's eyes misted over. "I must seem terribly ungrateful after what I said to you yesterday. Even before then. I have never properly thanked you for *everything* you've done."

Angela took her hand.

Leila continued, "I know what I said yesterday—and I meant it. I did. But it made me sound unappreciative of *all this*. Of what you provided in Marvelle. Of all that you and François—and André—have done in my behalf. In Ian's behalf." A tear escaped and her grandmother caught it.

"Don't cry, dear. You'll get me misty."

"I just want to say thank you. Thank you so much."

"You are so welcome. You have no idea what joy it has given me." She restrained the full smile that might allow tears. "And I completely understand your independent streak —where do you suppose you got it, after all? I think that you and I shall always butt heads as a reminder that we are our own women, and no one—no man and no woman—will ever take that away from us."

"Perhaps that's why we both love Clarence Myles. He's a man who can love and foster independence in a woman without needing to control her."

"He is a rare man."

"Grandmother—Angela—I want it to work out for the two of you. I do."

Angela studied Leila's face. She kissed her cheek, neither inhibiting their tears. "Thank you, dear."

Leila pulled away. "I sent him an invitation. I haven't heard back. Has he told you whether he'll be coming?"

"He and I have limited our contact. So, no, I'm not certain, though I would not be surprised if he does show up."

🐦A HALF HOUR BEFORE OPENING, LEILA CAME IN through the back entrance of the gallery behind Angela. She fluffed her dress and smoothed her hair up toward her French twist.

"Leave your hair be," Angela said, "or it will all come down in an hour."

Leila fluffed her dress again as they navigated crates and wrappings, then down the narrow passage to the front room, divided off by a tall, marble-topped counter. André stepped into view from the main gallery into the service quarter and greeted them. Angela continued on, into the exhibit area.

André looked Leila up and down. "Well, you're full of surprises. I expected black and slinky."

"Black and slinky didn't suit my mood."

He gestured for her to provide a full-turn view. She cocked her head and shifted from side to side.

"Well still, I like the mood you're in. Quintessentially feminine."

He took her hand the way he had when they first met, but kissed her cheek instead of her fingertips and whispered, "You're beautiful."

She hadn't necessarily hoped to put him off with her divergent wardrobe choice, but she did like to make him squirm. "The bonus is, I don't have to suck in my guts as much."

He chuckled. "You have difficulty accepting a compliment."

"Yes. The wolves that raised me didn't teach me proper manners."

He straightened a stack of cards on the countertop. "Well, for tonight, perhaps you could practice the simple phrase, 'thank you.'"

"Don't worry. I can fake manners. I won't embarrass you."

"I'm not worried." He winked. "Besides, it's pretty near impossible to reel in you artist types. I take it you haven't spent any time around Trudy Winthrop yet."

"No." Leila glanced around the corner to the back of the gallery, separated from the front by a large, nearly floor-to-ceiling partition where an elaborate gold-gilt frame perched upon an equally elaborate brass easel. "Is she here?"

"Oh, you'd know it if she were here." He placed a fountain pen and several larger cards beside the smaller.

"Are any of the other artists coming?"

"A few, but not many attend."

"I didn't know attending was optional."

One of the catering wait staff excused himself from behind, and moved adroitly past them, followed by another.

"Let me rephrase that. Many of our well-established artists don't care to, nor do they feel the need to attend." Now André gave Leila his full attention. "Those who have yet to build a presence often enjoy mingling with potential patrons."

"Trudy will be here, though?"

"Trudy? Absolutely. She never misses a party. She'll gripe about it, but she loves these functions." He swept one palm across the other. "Now, would you like to see it?"

"You mean *The Protégé*?"

He nudged her out from behind. "Of course."

"I suppose."

"A little more enthusiasm, please."

They stood in front of her portrait. She cringed. "So huge. So prominent."

He gestured toward the front of the gallery. "And in full view of the windows."

"Good lighting," she said, moving along to the far end of the floor, where Ian's photography hung beside *Karl*.

François approached with Angela at his side.

"Son, I need you a moment," François said. "Will you please excuse us?"

Both men headed back to the counter, leaving Angela and Leila standing in front of Ian's work.

"I was wondering which ones they finally decided to exhibit," Leila said.

"Not that I have much say, but I voted for these."

"I notice there aren't many portraits—aside from *Karl* and *The Protégé*."

"Portraits don't tend to move as well—usually too subjective for a broader audience, unless it has that something special, a more universal appeal, like some of the figures we have scattered about. Even Marvelle rarely painted non-commissioned portraits, which makes *Protégé* all the more rare and desirable."

Leila folded her arms around her waist. "But portraits are what I'm best at. Seems as though that will put me at a disadvantage."

"Yes, it would seem that way. That's why we have put only *Karl* out. He has that *je ne sais quoi*, which will serve to whet potential patron's artistic appetite for more of your work. Always leave them curious, wanting more. And on the money end, since *Protégé* essentially showcases you, *Karl* will likely be an easy sell, even at this price. The higher the price, the louder the buzz, the bigger the demand for more work—at a commensurate price, of course."

Leila rolled her eyes. "Wow. No pressure there."

"That's why there are agents and brokers, dear, so you can concentrate on what you do best."

"Let's look at some of the others," Leila suggested, slipping around the end of the partition to another display area. The entire lineup of exhibits wound from the front entrance, around the perimeter of the room, and zigzagged between display panels and back toward the front, beyond the counter, and returning to the entrance.

After six o'clock, guests began to arrive. In only a short while, patrons were milling throughout the gallery, weaving between the partitions and comparing the discreet price list to their favorite works. Leila drifted from painting to photograph to sculpture. André came up behind her, his warm hand on her bare back, and whispered, "There are a few people who need to be introduced to you when you get a minute, Leila."

"Now's as good a time as any," she said, wishing to get all her socializing out of the way early so she could focus on Jared when he arrived.

André took her arm in his, and escorted her to an elderly couple, wealthy patrons who had just placed a bid. After them, there was another, and then another, some discreetly comparing her likeness to *The Protégé* and others requesting that she pose beside it. Many placed bids. When the flurry of introductions finally died down, Leila ducked behind the partition to the farthest corner. She stood in front of a sculpture, staring off into space but hoping to look as if she were studying the piece while catching her breath.

CHAPTER 37

C OPLEY STATION ON A SATURDAY EVENING WAS busy as usual when Jared stepped up into diminishing daylight. He loved Boston for giving little regard to what anyone wore. A person could be as inconspicuous in a tuxedo as he could lugging a full camper's backpack.

Giving the wide sidewalk in front of the Boston Public Library a cursory glance, he recalled the last time he had shopped at the Farmer's Market across the street, now all packed up for the day. It had been years. It wasn't as if he had shopped there frequently—he had spent most of his time on the North End and frequenting a half-dozen clubs all over the city, back when he was just out of high school.

He hadn't wanted to arrive at *Chez* Goulet too early; Leila would likely be in a whirl of attention for the first hour or two, but he didn't want to come off as cavalier, as if the invitation meant little to him. It meant a great deal. In fact, the timing couldn't have been better. Without Emily to watch after, he had far more time to himself, and getting back into the singles mode was not something he looked forward to. If it weren't for the prospect of Leila in the wings, the idea of being a single man again—as much as he had enjoyed his bachelor days—had far less appeal than it did several years

ago when he was running with a faster—if not tougher—
crowd. He still cringed at some of the situations he had
gotten himself into—and out of—without injury, that is,
lasting injury, to himself.

Hooking a sharp left up Dartmouth Street, Jared headed
north. One block later, he hung another left onto Newbury,
double-checking the address on the invitation. Within a
block, he stood in front of a massive set of concrete steps
between large bay windows set in red brick. A black sign
with engraved and gold-gilt letters crowned the center above
the door.

Chez Goulet.

Tweaking his bow tie, he ascended the steps and
approached the white-gloved, smileless man who opened the
heavy oak door as Jared flashed his invitation. He scarcely
remembered anything from the evening at Peter Christian's
Tavern—when his wife had used the opportunity of a public
setting to inform him she wanted the divorce—but he did
remember the face of the man with Leila. His was the first to
greet Jared as he stepped inside; had the gentleman seen him
outside and wished to give Jared a *special* welcome?

The curly-haired and coiffed man extended his hand with
a smile. "It's Jared, isn't it?"

"Yes." Jared accepted his hand and gave it a firm shake.
"I'm sorry, please remind me of your name."

Making instant and intense eye contact, he stated, "André
Goulet."

"Nice to see you again." Aware that Jared's large mitts
unintentionally challenged men with more delicate, desk-job
hands, he loosed his grip. André did not. Not only that, he
couldn't help noticing how André's grip tightened ever so
slightly while his stare stayed fixed. Jared knew the tactic
and under other circumstances—or at an earlier time in his
life—he would not have allowed the test to remain unmet.

But Jared had no interest in playing any sort of game or engaging in any contest with André Goulet.

Jared broke eye contact, glancing around for Leila or the portrait.

"Care to have a look at her?" André said, moving toward *The Protégé*. Jared followed. The two stood in front of the tall painting.

Smitten, wishing he had the money, Jared grinned and shook his head. "Oh, if I were a rich man …."

André folded his arms smugly. "So you won't be bidding on her?"

"On the painting?" Jared cocked his clever brow. "No."

They both stared straight ahead. "Your wife couldn't make it?"

"By invitation only—and I received only one invitation." Jared glanced from side to side, hoping to catch sight of Leila. On cue, she came from around the partition but had not yet spotted him. Two older women grabbed her, turning her attention to several nearby pieces of exhibited art.

"Well, if you can't own her, I suppose you'll have to limit yourself to looking." André cocked his own cunning brow. "If you'll excuse me." Appearing quite pleased with himself, André walked away.

Jared came up behind Leila as she chatted with her companions. A few hairs had come loose from her twist. He placed his hand squarely on her back.

"If only I had my paint box," he whispered over her shoulder.

"Jared." She turned and smiled. "I'm so glad to see you."

"Hope I'm only fashionably late."

"You're fine. Perfect timing." She swept a gesture all around, her eyes wide. "Isn't all this just too much?"

The more elegant and attractive of the two women cleared her throat. "Introductions, Leila?"

"Oh yes. Where are my manners? Angela, Trudy, this is Jared Cox, a fellow artist and friend. Jared, my grandmother, Angela Phillips, and my new instructor—one of Marvelle's former students—Trudy Winthrop."

Her grandmother—their familial connection now easily seen in their resemblance—extended her hand.

"It's a pleasure to meet you, Jared." She lifted a brow at Leila. Perceptive woman.

The more artsy of the two ladies—dressed in flamboyant, multi-colored silks, draping from every angle of her body—now took his hand, reluctant to let go. "Perhaps you'd like to model for us in the studio sometime."

Jared grinned, allowing her to keep his hand. "Sorry, I don't model."

Leila's new teacher patted his hand. "If my eye recalls correctly—and I have a photographic memory—you've already modeled for one of Leila's paintings."

Jared now raised both brows at Leila.

She cringed, appearing apologetic. "I didn't know everyone and their *art tutor* was having a behind-the-scenes look at my work."

Ms. Winthrop scowled good-naturedly. "Don't be hyper-sensitive, girl—you can't blame us for wanting a peek under the petticoat."

Jared let out a huff, finally reclaiming his hand, feigning discomfort. "Okay, I think I'm supposed to be the embarrassed one, here."

"I dare say, you're not the least embarrassed." Trudy's gestures flailed with extravagance.

Another perceptive woman. Jared chuckled.

"Leila. Don't lose track of this one. He looks as good in a suit as out." Trudy stroked Jared's lapel. "More champagne —excuse me."

"Dear Trudy." Angela smiled, speaking to Leila. "You're going to love *her*."

Leila shuddered with all of Trudy's ostentation.

Angela turned her attention to Jared. "So, you're also an artist?"

"Leila uses the term loosely. We've taken a couple workshops together, that's all."

"He's good," Leila interrupted, looking at him. "You could be even better if your interests weren't so diverse."

"I'm just in the process of choosing what I want to be when I grow up, that's all."

"He also tunes my piano," Leila added. "And messes with my plumbing, plays psychologist, and plans warm homecomings."

Angela winked. "In addition to modeling."

"That was an accident." Jared glared at Leila.

"Let me show you *Karl* and Ian's work." Leila nudged him to follow and led him away.

Only loud enough so Leila could hear, he said, "Let me just say, that is a great dress."

"Thanks. I have a whole line of vintage *a la* Angela." She passed him a coy smirk. "I think you're supposed to be looking at art."

"I am." He pinched her elbow. "Seriously, I'd love to paint you in that. I can see the exact pose."

"Now you've got me curious."

"Okay." He stood before her, holding his hands at an angle, as if framing her likeness. "Picture this from the artist's viewpoint, sitting on the floor in front of you—the subject. Subject on a low stool. All that fabric between widespread legs. Elbows on knees. Forearms horizontal. Wrists crossed. Shoulders slouched."

Leila cocked her head with a self-deprecating and diminutive smirk.

"… and *that* exact look on your face."

"Oh my gosh, Jared." She let out a quick laugh, tossing her head, "I think you have just captured *me*." Another strand of hair let go.

"So, that's a promise?"

"That's a definite promise."

Their smiles evolved into a more serious exchange as if each was wondering just what had been promised. At the same moment, they turned from each other. Was her heart pounding as hard as his?

"So what do you think of *Karl*?" Leila said, pointing at the painting directly in front of them.

Jared tried not to appear shocked, but his words gave him away. "Wow. That's quite a specimen."

"I don't mean what do you think of his manhood, I want to know what you think of my interpretation."

"It's great. You must know that."

She rubbed her bare arms. "Hmm …. I get excited every time I look at it."

He shot her the risqué version of his arched brow, at which she rolled her eyes.

She stepped back, as if studying it afresh and sighed. "*I* did that. *I* actually painted that. I can't really even remember how, I just remember feeling it—it's hard to describe."

He stared at it alongside her. "You'll do it again."

"I already have—just not quite like Karl. I suppose he was my first. How can you duplicate or even exceed your first, when it sets such a high standard?"

"Just take what you learned and apply it to the next. One day, you may find you've surpassed your first."

"I hope you're right, Jared."

He turned toward her, just enough for her to catch his meaning. "It could happen sooner than you expect."

Leila swallowed and straightened her back, again rubbing her arms.

He couldn't help baiting her. "You have goosebumps—are you chilly?

"No." She looked deep into his eyes. "Just the opposite."

In his peripheral vision, Jared caught sight of André coming up behind Leila. André laid his hand on her back but kept his gaze upon Jared. "I'm stealing her for a moment."

Leila offered an apologetic smile. "Excuse me, Jared."

They moved toward the counter, and Jared moved around to the back of the partition, curious about the other artists' work. Until he turned from the wall, scanning the rest of the back half of the gallery, he hadn't noticed that Leila and André had also rounded the wall. They had found a more secluded corner, far from and opposite him. Leila's back faced Jared as André hovered.

"WHAT!" LEILA HADN'T MEANT to sound curt, but she didn't appreciate the timing of André's interruption.

André grinned, leading her away from guests. "Thought you'd like to know. *Karl* just sold."

Okay—that was worth an interruption. "To who?"

He chuckled, patting his cummerbund. "It's perfect, really —the sixty-something matron, senior partner of the Fleet Street law firm, Kendall, Gordon and Percy—who just took Karl on as an associate."

Leila's eyes widened, taking a moment for the implications to register. "*Oh my*. Perhaps she has *plans* for Karl!"

He stepped closer. "Your first sale—with an impressive price tag for a novice! Not too shabby, eh?"

In a daze, Leila exhaled. "Wow."

"Congratulations." He leaned forward, pulling her close and kissing her full on the lips. Just as quick, he withdrew before she had a chance to react. After one more quick kiss on the cheek, he glanced over her shoulder and said, "I'll let you get back to your married friend."

André walked away as Leila turned, spotting Jared on the opposite side of the room. He was not looking at her, but had he seen the kiss?

Angela came up alongside her. "Shall we freshen up, dear? Your hair is coming down."

She let out a sigh and followed her grandmother into the ladies' room.

Leila's shoulders slumped as she plopped herself onto an upholstered chair. "Oh, Angela, I have a dilemma."

"So I see." Angela peered at Leila via her reflection in the mirror as she dabbed lipstick. "Though it's not really a dilemma at all. It's very easily solved."

"But I hate to hurt André's feelings. I simply hadn't anticipated all this." Leila leaned forward on her knees in the same pose as Jared had just described. She looked up at Angela. "I feel like such a floozy."

Angela turned to her. "You mustn't be too hard on yourself, dear. You can't always anticipate circumstances and especially men's urges."

Leila again threw herself back into the chair. "But, last night, André told me he's in love with me."

"And you have a spark for Jared." Her eyes exuded sympathy.

Leila winced. "It's that obvious?"

"It's not only obvious, but it's obviously mutual."

"But I don't want to break André's heart."

Angela sat in the matching seat and took her granddaughter's hand. "My dear, I have known André since he was a boy. It would do him good to have his heart broken for once—give him a little empathy for all the women whose hearts he's toyed with. Don't get me wrong. I love André better than a son, but he has a manipulative streak that's so ingrained I don't think he's even aware of it. If he is, he simply justifies it as his powers of negotiation. Everything he does is a means to and end—You don't think that kiss out there on the floor was entirely for *your* benefit, do you?"

"Do you think Jared saw?"

"You can count on it."

Leila slumped further into the chair.

"Enough of that now," Angela said. "Your hair is coming down. Stand up so I can fix it."

Leila obeyed. In quick time, they returned to the gallery floor where Angela left her to find Jared. In even quicker time, she moved through the entire exhibit, checking both front and back and in between. She went to the front window, glancing down one end of Newbury to the other, hoping to spot Jared, to no avail. He couldn't have simply vanished—certainly not without saying goodbye.

Leila cringed at the memory of André's lips on hers and the thought of Jared having possibly seen. She couldn't blame him if he left. The possibility seemed more like a probability. *Face it*. She had led Jared on and then stupid André had to go and ruin everything. Let down but trying to muster a brave, social facade, she found herself in front of Ian's photographs. Would he be the only man who would ever have enough patience for her? Who could see through all her convoluted behaviors? God she missed him. She wouldn't allow herself to cry, but she couldn't restrain the softly spoken question, "Why did you have to go and leave me?"

"I only went to the restroom," Jared said.

Turning around, she blushed. "I thought maybe you left."

"Without saying goodnight? Why would I do that?"

"Because—because your wife just left you for some pre-existing relationship," she couldn't keep herself from rambling, "... and maybe you think I'm the kind of person who isn't sure about what I want, and I might be just as fickle and—"

He gave her an incisive look, akin to Clarence's. "Don't you mean, because I saw the way André just kissed you and because you didn't slap him in the face, that maybe I think you want him and not someone like me? That maybe I would just take my toys and go home?"

She folded her arms. "Same thing."

He smiled, gently grazing her arm. "Leila, I don't presume to know what you want, but guys like him don't make me insecure."

"How do you know what kind of guy he is?"

"I only know that he feels a need to stake a claim. I don't need to compete with a guy over a woman as if she's some sort of trophy. He and I are in completely different leagues, and I have confidence you can see that." He allowed a moment before finishing. "And if I've merely deluded *myself* into believing that, then how is that *your* fault? Why should I punish you by stomping off?"

Leila shook her head, again loosening a few wisps of hair. She tucked them behind her ear. "You are just making my choices way too easy."

Jared glanced over at André behind the counter. "Would it help if I let you kiss me passionately, here and now, so you can stake your claim?"

She laughed. "Or I could just give you a great big shove."

"That'll do."

The two strolled to the front of the room so as not to block Ian's work, or *Karl*.

Interrupting them on their way, Trudy sidled up between them.

She snorted, crossing one arm over her middle as her free hand precariously waved a half-empty champagne glass. "It's a bloody violation—this prostituting our craft—bearing our thighs to these art mongers."

Leila and Jared exchanged amused glances as Trudy continued, "And yet, here we stand, waiting for our remuneration, with greedy desire." She winked at Jared. "These affairs always leave me feeling so dirty."

A white-gloved waiter with several available wine glasses came near.

Trudy lifted a glass and passed it to Leila. "Here—have a drink."

Jared helped himself.

"Thanks." Leila sipped a red wine of unknown origin, but it reminded her of Clarence's Gevrey-Chambertin.

Trudy nudged Leila, nearly causing a spill. "I heard *Karl* sold. Not surprising. He's a real doll. Hate to see him out of the modeling gig. You should feel very gratified at the price he brought. But then, they always pay a tidy sum for the virgins. You'll have to come up with some nifty tricks to keep them coming back." Trudy took a breath and continued, "And your late husband's photography. Two pieces out on their own now, abandoning their sibling to some other stranger."

Leila caught a smirk on Jared's face. She hardly knew what to make of Trudy's ramblings. "I heard yours sold, also."

"Yes, well, like a geisha, if you find one wealthy old sponsor, you're set for life. As long as you continue to titillate them."

Leila grinned, on the verge of cringing. "Have you always been so cynical?"

"Absolutely. Which leaves me no excuse, I entered this forum open-eyed. And now it owns me."

Leila looked at her askance and tipped the woman's wrist to view her watch. Nearly nine.

"The suspense must be killing you," Trudy chimed back in. "Knowing that one of these old geezers will win *The Protégé*, hoping he will also win you."

Trudy now turned her gaze to Jared, waving a hand back at Leila. "Look at her. Just like a virgin."

Leila recoiled. Trudy seemed so like Marvelle, in all the best and worst ways. Leaving the two youngsters, the older woman veered off, following another platter of champagne.

"Wow, she's something else," Jared stepped closer. "I like her."

"Yeah," Leila shuddered. "Can't wait to start lessons."

They stood facing the front of the gallery. Leila scoped out André behind the counter, accepting yet another sealed envelope with a silent bid while standing in reconnaissance. He had previously mentioned that he liked to wager on which of their patrons were most likely to purchase, based on their lingering interest in any particular work and their past buying pattern. Probably André had already sized up who would win *The Protégé*. She was curious but not enough to approach him. In fact, his charm had worn thin over the past hours.

"I want to go home," Leila sighed. "You don't have to stick around if you don't want to."

"What? And miss out on the big reveal? Not a chance." He sipped his wine. "Not unless you'd rather I leave."

"No. Please don't leave."

Just then, a tall, exceptionally debonair man stepped inside the gallery. Leila froze and then grabbed Jared's wrist. "He's here."

"Who?"

"My friend, Clarence—Clarence Myles."

"Oh."

Clarence approached the counter and shook hands while exchanging a few words with André. Handsome as he was, Clarence looked different in some way, perhaps his posture seemed not as erect—perhaps he had the gait of a man older than she remembered.

"Shall we go over?" Jared asked, squeezing her hand.

"No. I need a second."

Clarence left his invitation on the counter as Angela came from behind the partition and moved to his side. He smiled and kissed her cheek, genuinely pleased to see her. Side by side, Leila could not deny their congruity of age and countenance. They spoke only briefly before he scanned the room. When he caught sight of Leila he paused, as proud as any father, and came to her without hesitation. Angela strode beside him.

As he stood before Leila, he held both her hands, leaning in to kiss her flushed cheek.

"You came," she whispered, her emotion mounting.

"I wouldn't miss this for the world, sweetheart. You look wonderful. How are you?"

"I'm okay." Her heart sped with nerves. "It's a little overwhelming."

"You're fine." He now looked directly at Jared.

Taking a deep breath, she said, "This is my friend, Jared Cox."

Clarence nodded.

"I told you about him—he tunes my piano."

"Yes, you did mention him." He offered his hand. "Nice to meet you Jared. I'm Clarence Myles."

"Yes. It's good to meet you, sir." Jared gave him a warm shake. "I knew Ian—he spoke highly of you. I'm sorry for your loss."

"Thank you." Clarence studied him, calculating as always. He then turned to Leila. "Speaking of Ian, would you like to show me his work, and your own?"

"Why don't I let Angela show you?"

"You're sure?"

"Yes."

Clarence turned as Angela hooked her arm in his and they walked away.

Jared asked, "You okay?"

"Yeah—" she drew in a long breath. "I was nervous … what if all those feelings came back?"

"Did they?"

"No—not the same ones. Just some of the embarrassment, but not as bad as I thought. Maybe everything *will* work out." She turned back to him. "What did you think of him?"

"He's curious about me, that's for sure."

MYLES WAS FAMILIAR with Ian's pieces, and so they were no surprise, but *Karl*, while not surprising given all Leila's pent-up passions, brought heat beneath his collar. As if trying to mask her own qualms about the blatantly naked man, Angela chatted, filling him in on her recent exchanges with Leila.

"She threatened you, did she?" Myles said.

Angela half chuckled, though her serious tone belied humor. "Let's just say, I've been put on notice. I am forbidden to cause you any pain. Whatsoever."

"That's reassuring as I've been hoping for the unequivocal opposite."

"Why, Clarence Myles. Are you getting fresh with me?"

He intensified his gaze upon her. "Perhaps I am."

Intense pink colored her cheeks as she looked away. "Well, the threats were yesterday. This afternoon—while standing by her threat—she gave her blessing."

Myles found it difficult to fathom. "Did she?"

"Yes, I believe her exact words were 'I want it to work out for the two of you,' but I'm sure you'll want to hear that for yourself."

He nodded, stroking her hand on his sleeve. "So, what do you know of this Jared fellow?"

"Well, this is the first I've seen or heard of him, but it's obvious he's significant."

Myles eyed the young man from across the room as André approached the two youngsters and led Leila away to an older couple. His brow flicked at Angela. "If you'll pardon me, I think I'll take advantage of the moment."

As Myles sauntered toward Jared, André announced the bidding would close in five minutes. Jared met Myles halfway. Each looked the other directly in the eye.

Myles spoke first. "So, you tune Leila's piano?"

"Yes, and we've been in a few watercolor workshops together, and I winterized her house this past February."

"Yes, she is fond of you." Myles did not smile. "She also mentioned you're married."

Jared did not flinch. "I'm in the process of divorce."

Myles squinted, hoping clearly to convey his concern.

Without hesitation, Jared replied, "It has absolutely nothing to do with Leila."

Myles drew in a long, dramatic breath and slowly exhaled with gravity. "I'm sorry. Divorce is a difficult thing to go through, no matter the reason. Are there children?"

"Yes. Unfortunately, she's not mine."

"Then you're in for quite a ride. As someone who's been down that road myself—well, you may want to consider giving yourself *plenty* of time."

Jared nodded. "I've heard two years is minimum, though I suppose that varies with circumstances." He held his ground. "Just the same, I can't guarantee that I'll have that sort of restraint with Leila."

Myles' jaw tensed. "Perhaps you don't realize how vulnerable she still is."

Jared met his concern with eyes exuding empathy. "Sir, I understand what a disadvantage you're at, having just met me. Let me assure you that I am in no hurry with Leila. I appreciate your insights on her, and I will certainly take them into consideration. I hope you will have the opportunity to get to know me better and feel more at ease with me."

Jared's unapologetic straightforwardness reminded Myles so much of Ian—of Ian's lack of guile or selfish motive.

Myles was genuinely curious. "And why should you care how I feel about you?"

"Because you are the most important person in Leila's life, and your feelings matter to her, so they matter to me."

Myles continued to study him. He was hard pressed to find anything amiss with him, or unlikable. Even from their brief exchange, he perceived why Leila was so smitten with him.

Just then, Leila came and stood between Myles and Jared. She grabbed Myles' arm and whispered, "André's about to announce the winning bid."

Myles took another deep breath and clutched Leila's hand. "Nervous?"

"Terribly."

"Don't be."

Angela joined the three.

Metal clinking against crystal broke the din as François commanded the group's attention.

"Your appreciation of Marvelle Harding—as a peerless and timeless artist, whose life work, love, and spirit cannot possibly be summed up in any one artistic endeavor—has here, tonight, found testimony in the enthusiastic and unreserved reception of her final work, *Portrait of a Protégé*. I would like to thank each of you for your attendance and support of this event. You have made it a true celebration of the life and work of Marvelle." He looked down at the winning bid and held it up. With a deep inhalation, he announced, "For sixty-seven thousand, three hundred dollars … *Portrait of a Protégé* goes to … Mr. Clarence Myles …. Thank you all for coming."

Leila gasped, her eyes flashing at Myles. "Are you nuts?"

Angela sighed with surprise, "Why, *Clarence Myles* …."

Myles chuckled. "You didn't expect me to let my Protégé fall into other hands, did you?"

Leila threw her head back. "I always knew you were loaded."

Myles glared and then chuckled at her impertinence, pinching her chin. "Your hair is coming down."

She stood on her toes to kiss his cheek.

Glad that her former ease with him had returned, he said, "Now, if you'll excuse me, I should like to go settle up."

LEILA AND JARED STOOD ALONE for a moment, as Clarence maneuvered his way to the counter with Angela, interrupted repeatedly by hand shakers and congratulations. Then the flux of congratulatory attention rolled her way. She simply repeated "Thank you," with all the politeness of a well-groomed socialite, though she couldn't for the life of her understand why she deserved any accolades. She hadn't even posed for the painting. All she had done was show up for lessons she hadn't deserved.

And then to think of what Clarence had done—what he had *spent*! Still, there could not have been a more perfect recipient. Since before she turned eighteen, she had been his protégé, the beneficiary of his loving guardianship, through tribulations that most friendships would never know, let alone survive. Like no one else, he had been, and remained, her true constant.

When the crowd dwindled to less than a dozen, quietly socializing and trickling out the entrance, Jared finally said, "Well, I should probably head out."

Leila hated to see him leave. "I could walk you to your car."

"I'm parked in Cambridge," he chuckled. "I took the T. But you could walk me outside if you want."

She tugged at his arm. "Is that just so André will see?"

"No, actually, that way André won't see, and maybe you won't feel so inhibited."

As they walked to the front door, Leila resisted the urge to check André's attention from behind the counter.

Jared held the door open and followed Leila outside into the considerably warmer evening air. She took his hand as they walked down the steps onto the sidewalk.

"I saw Clarence talking with you," she said with sympathy. "Was he giving you a thorough cross-examination?"

He spread his fingers, plucking imaginary rubber at his wrist. "Need I say latex gloves?"

She heaved a sigh. "Sorry."

"No, I really didn't mind," he let out a quick, nervous laugh. "I mean, okay, it was a little uncomfortable, but I respect the position he's in."

All seriousness beamed from Leila's face. "He's better than a father to me."

He matched her tone. "I know. That's why I don't mind. I hope I'm allowed to get to know him."

"He takes time. But he'll like you. I can tell he already does."

"Really?"

"Well, I can tell you that he won't even bother giving André the shakedown." A breeze lifted her loose strands from her shoulder. "So did he have any words of wisdom?"

He nodded, keeping his eyes on hers. "He advised we take our time."

"That's going to be hard."

Jared tucked wayward hair behind her ear and took her other hand. "I know. But I think it's a good idea."

"I agree. That said, would I be sending you horribly mixed signals if I were to kiss you right now?"

"No. Nope. Not one bit. Not at all." The humor that sparked in his eye turned to something like apprehension and then anticipation.

Leila took the initiative, stepping in close and pulling him to her.

"You are very forward," he said, the tendons of his neck tightening along with his hands now holding her waist, nearly joining from thumb to finger.

"I just want to stake my claim before all the other single women in Sunapee find out you're available. A man like you won't last long on the singles scene."

"I think you have an inflated idea of my desirability." He did not move in closer but she did.

"I don't think so." She stood on her toes. "Kiss me."

He stared at her a moment as if he couldn't catch his breath. Now he moved in without hesitation, his lips grazing hers, but after only a moment he withdrew. The sigh that escaped sounded pained, and when she looked into his eyes they were glassy.

"Should I have not done that?" she said.

"No. It's okay. I just. I wasn't expecting our first kiss to feel quite like that."

"Like what?"

"I'm sorry." He swallowed. "I can't say it so soon."

Leila searched his eyes.

He whispered, "All I know is that I've never felt *this* before."

With all her heart, she replied, "I have."

His jaw squared as something like a smile pulled at his lips. He drew her in and simply held her. When he stepped back, his expression relaxed. "Thank you for inviting me tonight. It's been a memorable evening."

"Good night, Jared. Be careful out there on the T," she said as he began walking away, letting go of his hand.

"Oh, I can handle myself." He walked backward, breaking the tension in his offhand way as he chuckled, "Did I mention I boxed for a few years?"

"Did not."

"I did." In a boxer's stance, he gripped his bicep and grinned, still moving away. "No one's gonna mess with these bad boys."

"Good night." He walked across Newbury Street toward Copley Square until he again turned and smiled, then disappeared around a corner.

Leila shivered in the heat and then walked back in, wrapping herself in her arms. André moved away from the front window but his eyes landed on her as she stepped inside. It was his own fault if he had spied upon something he didn't like.

"You certainly are a mystery," he said, his brow fixed with cynicism. "I didn't take you for the mistress type."

"What?"

"Your *friend* Jared, he is married, isn't he?"

"Not that it's any of your business, but he's in the process of divorce—and *no*, it has nothing to do with *me*." She met his snide remark with irritation. "And honestly, André, that's about the most idiotic, insensitive thing I've ever heard you say."

He closed his eyes, remorse coloring his face. "I'm sorry. That was so uncalled for." He shook his head. "I just—I …."

She softened. "André …."

"I'm truly sorry. You don't need to explain. I was caught off guard—and a bit let down …," his words faltered. "It's been pretty obvious all evening where your heart is wrapped up. Lust can't compete with love."

Leila sighed.

He moved back behind the counter. "After all, you did give me fair warning."

Leila rested her arms on the cool marble, fidgeting with business cards. "You and I are not right for each other, André. We haven't a thing in common beside superficial stuff."

"Perhaps once you've gotten to know me better, I'll grow on you."

"Perhaps. But I only have room for one difficult-to-know man, and that slot will be filled for the rest of his life." She sighed, catching his undivided attention. "After everything I've been through, I shouldn't have to work that hard at a love relationship. I need it to feel natural and spontaneous and more fulfilling than lust."

"Fair enough." He nodded, regaining his composure. "Shall we join the others?"

"Alright."

They came up alongside Clarence, François, and Angela. Leila slipped her hand through Clarence's arm in her comfortable way. He glanced at her with affection.

"I can't believe you bought that painting?" she beamed. "Where will you hang it?"

"I don't know. Perhaps over a fireplace."

"Your fireplace is all bumpy fieldstone. That won't work."

"Perhaps I'll hang it over some other fireplace," he said, casting a clever look at Angela.

Her grandmother responded with a wink. "I happen to know of an ideal setting."

"Will you excuse us?" Clarence said. Securing Leila's hand on his, he led her to a more private corner.

Leila looked up, meeting his gaze. "I don't know what I could possibly say to you at this moment that would come near to expressing what I feel and what you mean to me."

"This moment isn't about the words, Leila."

Tears filled her eyes. "How many different nuances can the word love have? I think we've exceeded the limitations of the English language."

"We have, indeed."

"Thank you, Clarence."

"What you have never seemed to understand about our

relationship, Leila, is that I am forever in *your* debt. Not the other way around."

"Everything is going to be okay between us, isn't it?"

"It was never *not* okay. It was only evolving, as it always will."

TO BE CONTINUED...

MEET THE CAST

of *Girl Running* & *Protégé*
(A READER'S GUIDE OF SORTS)

Leila paces the group's perimeter and then sits. The circle of chairs begins to fill. I draw in a nervous breath.

Ian walks in with Jared. Both of them eye the seats on either side of Leila. One is reserved, and Jared acquiesces the other to Ian who sits beside her, arms folded. I smile apologetically.

So far, Miss Angela Phillips, François and André Goulet, have seated themselves, Angela beside the reserved seat. Little Peter snuggles between Bonnie and Dr. Louis Flanders.

I clear my throat. Joe Phillips and Garrison assist Artie Sparks onto a chair beside Buddy. They chat quietly as Kyle and Micah enter the room, the aroma of marijuana drifting with them. Maryanne follows but chooses not to sit. Ms. Thorpe fills in an empty seat beside Andrea Michaels, Leila's former art teacher, who is chatting quietly with Trudy Winthrop. Several seats remain empty.

"Could we just get this over with," Ian says as Dr. Valerie Jennings steps in and sits quietly.

"Um ...," Leila glances at the seat beside her, "we should really wait."

"Seriously?" Maryanne cuts in. "This is ridiculous! I'm out of here!" She turns on heel, brushing past Clarence

Myles as he steps into the room with Marvelle clinging to his arm.

"I apologize," he says, "We were enjoying a tot and lost track of time."

"Oh what fun!" Marvelle clutches her chest. "I do so love a bit of drama, da'ling."

Leila shakes her head good-naturedly. Myles escorts Marvelle to the chair beside Trudy and without hesitation claims his reserved seat beside Leila. His arm rests comfortably on the back of her chair.

Leila gestures to the remaining empty seat. "Is Karen Weiss coming?"

Thorpe chimes in, "I'm afraid she shares Maryanne's sentiment, with a few expletives."

Leila rolls her eyes and shrugs.

Thorpe adds, "Also, the school board and Judge Moore send their regrets."

Micah pipes up. "So, like, why are we here, man?"

I take a deep breath. "Apparently some of you have issues with how you fit into the plot. I just thought this would be a good way to air some of your gripes or share your feelings about how you were handled."

"I got no gripes," Micah says, his head bobbing. "I mean, sure Leila didn't really go for me, but at least I got to kiss her. That was cool. Besides that, I'm an ace guitar player! It's all good."

Kyle smirks at him, "Yeah, well, in the first draft, Leila and I were a whole lot more than just friends. We spent a lot of time together doing more than just running. We even went to the prom, did some serious making out, and some other stuff I won't mention since this is G rated." His brow furrows. "Jeez JB, she and I were a solid couple. You cut so much stuff. I feel seriously marginalized. What's that about?"

I nod sympathetically. "I know, I'm sorry, but it was a matter of word count and I wanted to highlight the teacher-

J. B. CHICOINE

student relationships and make the story less high-schooly. Besides, either way, the two of you didn't end up together when all was said and done, and after the revisions, I did leave you with more of your dignity intact."

"That's it?"

Leila blushes. "Sorry I broke your heart. I was screwed up." At least *she* gets it.

Kyle slouches back and rolls his eyes. "Fine, but I still feel used."

André huffs. "I'm with Kyle. I mean, I feel like such a plot device or something."

Micah snickers, "I think the term is *tool*."

"Hey, I might have come across like a tool in the beginning, but I have some real depth that Leila never explored. I wasn't given a fair shot."

"Whatever, man."

Jared chuckles. Ian remains stolid.

"Now boys," Angela speaks up, "Leila can hardly help it if she possesses that *je ne sais quoi*. Just remember, you all provided her with some difficult choices, contributed to great dialogue, and heightened the tension. You are wonderful and unique characters. I believe she loved each of you for who you are and how you contributed in a noteworthy way to the overall plot. You should feel good about that."

Myles beams approvingly at Angela. I nod in agreement.

Jared catches my attention. "You have something to add, Jared?"

"Well, first of all, let me just say how pleased I am that Leila and I were really hitting it off at the end. I think there's some real potential there. That said, I have the utmost respect for Ian." Jared looks at him. "I hope there's no hard feelings."

Ian pulls at his neck muscles and sighs. "No, we're good —not your fault."

Jared turns to me and raises a single brow, "Just curious here—but why exactly is there a disproportionate number of men in these two novels? I'm not finding fault, it's just a curiosity."

I spike my own brow. "You were intuitive from the start, Jared. I'd be curious to hear what you think about that."

"Well, at first glance, it might appear that Leila craves male attention, but ... I'm thinking it has more to do with her being raised by a bunch of men—her overall comfort with the male gender. She knows men and is more comfortable interacting with them. Simple as that."

Dr. Valarie Jennings nods. "I think it's more complex than that, probably a combination of both issues. What do you think, Dr. Flanders?"

Louis Flanders rakes fingers through his curly blond mop. "I concur. Yet I was glad to see her grow as a character—I mean, she did branch out to embrace her alpha females in Marvelle and Angela." He strokes his chin. "But what I find particularly interesting is that Marcus Billings, Leila's father is not present."

"Yes," Valarie concurs, "would you care to share your feelings on that, JB?"

"Well, he was only in a brief flashback scene and mentioned only in narrative. Besides, Joe is Leila's real father and he's here."

Joe coughs. "And since I am here, I'd just like to say that I kind of resent being cast into the stereotypical drug-abusing blues musician."

"But I think I did it sympathetically," I respond. "I provided you with enough backstory to make it believable and even if you have weaknesses, you're a likable character. I mean, I even had you show up for Artie's funeral. Be thankful for that."

"What?" Artie turns to me. "I died?"

"Sorry Artie, I thought you understood that's why your role ended so abruptly."

"Wait, I'm confused," Artie scratches his peppered chin.

I sigh.

"I'll explain it to you later," Garrison says.

"Is there anything else you'd like to say, Garrison?"

He shakes his head slowly, "I guess I just like being in the background ... I like knowing a whole lot more than I say."

The door creaks open and a head peeks in. "Ooops—Sorry—wrong cast—"

"*Uncharted* meets after *Spilled Coffee*, Samuel," I say. "Why don't you hang out with Benjamin for a bit—he's two doors down."

Samuel nods and closes the door.

"Where were we?" I clear my throat and direct my attention to Ms. Thorpe. "Have you anything you'd like to say?"

"Not really. I'm a strong female character, I stood by my principles. No regrets."

"And the other staff member, Miss Michaels?"

"I didn't really play a big role, but I'm glad to see Leila stuck with her painting and grew as an artist. And let me just say how thrilled I am to be included alongside Marvelle Harding, and you too, Trudy."

Marvelle flails her unlit cigarette wand. "You wouldn't believe the walls I had to break down, da'ling."

Miss Michaels grasps Marvelle's hand. "Can I just say you were one of my favorite characters! So dynamic. Oh! and the shenanigans you pulled in her lessons."

"Shenanigans indeed! I rent her soul! I've never seen such pent passion!"

Leila winces. "Okay, lets not get into all that. I'm still blushing from that scene."

"Which scene is that, da'ling?"

"You know—"

"Cagey girl—can't even say it!"

In Leila's behalf, I cut in, "François! A word or two?"

He grins wide. "It's been a hoot! I'm just curious, though, did Angela and I actually have a romantic relationship at some point in the past?"

"Yes, you were the married man she fell in love with who divorced but decided your true preference was—"

"Ahem—yes. Enough said."

Valarie Jennings speaks up. "We haven't heard from Clarence Myles yet."

Leila smiles at him and grabs his hand.

"Yes, speaking of whom, I sort of wanted the two of you to get together—sorry that didn't work out."

Myles' brow flicks at Valarie.

Valarie returns with a smile. "That's kind of you JB, though I will concede that he and Angela are well suited."

"Indeed," Myles says.

Leila blushes. "As much as I love him, I'm glad he and I didn't end up together, I mean, I know sometimes relationships like that work, but it would have been kind of weird—"

"Psychologically speaking, not as weird as you might think," Dr. Flanders says.

Bonnie sputters, "Speak for yourself. Leila has serious daddy issues and her attraction to my father was sick!"

"You know what Bonnie," Leila comes alive. "I've about had it with you. You exist only because JB gave you a role. Who are you to call into question what she does or how I feel? Sometimes you make me so mad I just what to—"

"What? Convince JB to cut my character? Doubt it. I played an intrinsic role."

"Careful Bonnie," Ian looks directly at me, "she is capable of killing."

Leila steams, "JB can't kill her off now. The story is finished. Final edits are complete."

Valarie chimes in. "Ian, this must all be very awkward for you."

"Awkward?" He huffs, scanning the group and then lands his sights on Leila. "I *loved* you. I loved you with everything I had." He now looks at me. "And I was a good character, I mean, not just as a character, but I'm a good person. Sure I have my weakness, but even you portrayed me as a great guy after you married Leila and me. She gave me her virginity...." He chokes up. "How could you kill me off? How could you just do away with me and let her move on?"

Leila's eyes well as she struggles with composure. "I loved you too. But I was messed up!"

They both look at me. I sigh. "I'm sorry—"

"Sorry?" Ian cuts in. "You drowned me—do you have any idea what a slow and agonizing death that is?"

"I knocked you unconscious first—"

"That's beside the point."

This is more uncomfortable than I bargained for. I exhale a tight breath. Gosh, if my cast is this irritated with me, I can only imagine what my readers must think.

"What can I say?" I shrug sheepishly. "A writer has to do what a writer has to do to move the plot forward!"

"NOVELS BY J.B. CHICOINE

All Books Available as Paperback, Hardcover, and eBook

PORTRAITS SERIES
BOOK I
PORTRAIT *of a* GIRL RUNNING

ALL LEILA WANTS IS TO GET through her senior year at her new high school without drawing undue attention. Not that she has any big secret to protect, but her unconventional upbringing has made her very private. At seventeen, she realizes just how odd it was that two men raised her—one black, one white—and no mother. Not to mention they were blues musicians, always on the move. When her father died, he left her with a fear of foster care and a plan that would help her fall between the cracks of the system. Three teachers make that impossible—the handsome track coach, her math teacher from hell, and a jealous gym instructor. Compromising situations, accusations of misconduct, and judicial hearings put Leila's autonomy and even her dignity at risk, unless she learns to trust an unlikely ally.

PORTRAITS SERIES
BOOK II
PORTRAIT of a PROTÉGÉ

FOUR YEARS AFTER THE CLOSE of *Portrait of a Girl Running*, Leila is twenty-two and living on a pretty, little lake in New Hampshire. A new set of circumstances throws her into a repeating cycle of grief that twists and morphs into unexpected and powerful emotions. Leila must finally confront her fears and learn to let go while navigating the field of cutting-edge psychology, protecting herself from the capricious winds of Southern hospitality, playing in the backyard of big-money art, and taming her unruly heart. Even her 'guardian' has a thing or two he must learn about love and letting go.

PORTRAITS SERIES
BOOK III
PORTRAIT *of a* GIRL ADRIFT

JUST WHEN LEILA THINKS she has everything under control, her deepest insecurities resurface when she must confront her unresolved issues surrounding the mother who abandoned her as a baby, and the men who raised her. Not even Clarence Myles can show her the way, and so Leila embarks on a journey of self-discovery that sends her drifting from place to place in search of answers.

In the process of zigzagging her way between North and South, Leila encounters a series of intense psychological twists and turns that send her reeling, grappling with more questions about her identity. Embarking on a final quest for what it means to be 'whole,' Leila risks everything she knows about maintaining control; on a calculated whim, she boards a boat with a young woman who is everything Leila is not. While navigating her own heart, nothing could prepare Leila for the biggest truth she's about to learn.

PORTRAITS SERIES
BOOK IV
PORTRAIT *of a* SOUJOURNER

IN THE AFTERMATH OF relocation, Leila is still adrift in her own life on Grand Cayman, chasing an idealistic identity as an artist in search of a true counterpart, someone with the 'artistic temperament.' She remains within the safe orbit of found family and the man she once pushed away, while coming to terms with patterns that shaped her.

After a catastrophic loss, she navigates the murkiest waters of recovery at the quiet sanctuary of Grand Oaks, in Natchez, where she discovers how art and music can be both a refuge and a reckoning, and that healing can come from unexpected sources.

Tender, unflinching, and deeply human, *Portrait of a Sojourner* is a meditation on claiming identity beyond trauma and grief. It's about resilience, and the slow, deliberate act of becoming whole, choosing family, and the courage it takes to stop drifting and claim a life—on purpose.

SPILLED COFFEE

BENJAMIN HUGHES IS ON A mission. He has just bought back the New Hampshire lake cottage his family lost eighteen summers ago, in 1969, just before he turned fourteen—just before his life blew apart.

Still reeling from a broken engagement, Ben has committed himself to reliving that momentous summer for the next twenty-four hours.

Every summer as a boy, Ben has gawked at the pretty redhead Amelia, granddaughter to the richest man on the lake, Doc Burns—owner of a Cessna floatplane and the Whispering Narrows estate. During the summer of '69, Ben not only sneaks around with Amelia, but he also learns how to fly with Doc and meets an eclectic cast of characters that will change him forever. The best summer of Ben's life turns out to be the worst as the Burns' family dysfunction collides with his own family's skeletons.

BLIND STITCHES

NIKOLAI SOLVAY HAS BEEN dreading his sister's wedding, but when his father dies unexpectedly two weeks beforehand, his return to New Hampshire promises to rake up his worst nightmares.

Meanwhile, talented young seamstress Juliet Glitch has been putting the finishing touches on the wedding dress. Mother of the bride — former prima ballerina and Russian expatriate—asks Juliet if she 'would hem her blind son Nikolai's trousers for the funeral' ... and the wedding.

When Juliet meets Nikolai, he draws her into the whirlwind of his unraveling family that makes her own quirky domestic situation seem normal. Confronted with the Solvay's delusions and narcissism, Juliet must decide if her developing relationship with Nikolai is worth the turmoil as she deals with her own unreconciled past.

Either way, Nikolai cannot stave off the repressed memories surrounding his mother's defection from the Soviet Union twenty years earlier. Against the backdrop of autumn 1989, during the Glasnost era, Nikolai's family secrets crash alongside the crumbling Berlin Wall.k

Uncharted:

Story for a Shipwright

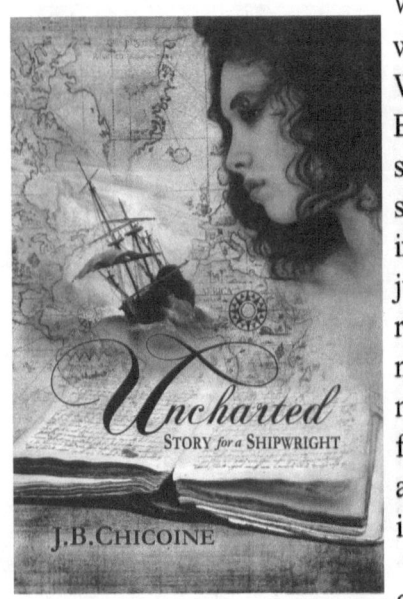

When a peculiar young woman shows up at the Wesley House Bed and Breakfast with a battered suitcase and stories to tell, shipwright Sam Wesley isn't sure if she's incredibly imaginative or just plain delusional. He soon realizes that Marlena is like no other woman he has ever met. Her strange behavior and far-fetched tales of shipwrecks and survival are a fresh breeze in Sam's stagnant life.

Sam isn't the only one enchanted by Marlena. With his best friend putting the moves on her and a man from her past coming back into her life, the competition for Marlena's heart is fierce. In the midst of it all, a misunderstanding sends Marlena running, and by the time Sam learns what his heart really wants, it may be too late to win her back.

About the Author

J. B. Chicoine was born on Long Island, New York, and grew up in Amityville during the 1960s and '70s. Since then, she has lived in New Hampshire, Kansas City, and Michigan. New England is her favorite setting for her stories, though she does love to explore new places.

When she's not writing or painting, she enjoys volunteer work, traveling, knitting, and working on various projects with her husband.

She can be contacted via her J.B. Chicoine author page on Facebook or via strawhillpublishing@gmail.com.